About the Author

Romantic Book of the Year author, Kendall Talbot, writes action-packed romantic suspense loaded with sizzling heat and intriguing mysteries set in exotic locations. She hates cheating, loves a good happily ever after, and thrives on exciting adventures with kick-ass heroines and heroes with rippling abs and broken hearts.

Kendall has sought thrills in all 44 countries she's visited. She's rappelled down freezing waterfalls, catapulted out of a white-water raft, jumped off a mountain with a man who spoke little English, and got way too close to a sixteen-foot shark.

She lives in Brisbane, Australia with her very own hero and a fluffy little dog who specializes in hijacking her writing time. When she isn't writing or reading, she's enjoying wine and cheese with her crazy friends and planning her next international escape.

She loves to hear from her readers!

Find her books and chat with her via any of the contacts below:

www.kendalltalbot.com
Email: kendall@universe.com.au

Or you can find her on any of the following channels:

Amazon
Bookbub
Goodreads

Books by Kendall Talbot

Lost in Kakadu (Winner: Romantic Book of the year 2014)

Jagged Edge

Double Take

If you sign up to my newsletter you can help with fun things like naming characters and giving characters quirky traits and interesting jobs. You'll also receive my book, Treasured Kisses which is exclusive to my newsletter followers only, for free.

Here's my newsletter signup link if you're interested:

http://www.kendalltalbot.com.au/newsletter.html

Zero Escape

A MAXIMUM EXPOSURE NOVEL

KENDALL TALBOT

Published 2020 Kendall Talbot

Zero Escape

Book three in the Maximum Exposure Series

© 2020 by Kendall Talbot

ISBN: 9798637906017

This is a work of fiction. Names, characters, places, and incidents are either the product of the author's imagination or are used fictitiously, and any resemblance to actual persons, living or dead, business establishments, events, or locales is entirely coincidental.

V.2023.1

❀ Created with Vellum

Chapter One

Sorrow coiled in Charlene's heart as she inched toward her father's body on the metal slab. The pungent air crackled with the stillness about her, and her bones sagged with an emptiness deep in her soul.

Her father didn't look peaceful.

She should've expected that, given the way he'd died. The stubble in his beard was longer than usual, and she was surprised at how many gray whiskers he had. Lips that had always been quick to smile were tinged the color of acid-washed denim.

His almond-colored eyes were closed, destined to remain that way forever.

With trembling hands, she curled her fingers beneath the seam of the white sheet concealing his body and eased it down from his neck. Fighting the quiver in her chin, she stared at the jagged knife wound in his chest. It was surprisingly small considering the amount of blood that'd gushed from it.

Charlene squeezed her eyes shut, trying to force the brutal attack from her mind. But it was there to stay. Every precise second was permanently etched into her memory.

The woman who'd stabbed him was a stunning brunette with olive skin and fierce brown eyes.

She'd looked petrified.

Clearly her father and the woman had known each other, but Charlene had never seen her before. They'd argued in Spanish. Charlene didn't speak any other languages, and she'd had no idea her father did either.

When the woman had grabbed her father's steak knife, Charlene had seen the look in his eyes. It wasn't fear. It was resignation. Like he'd always expected that moment to one day come.

Shaking the recollections free, she opened her eyes and touched his forearm, just as she'd done a thousand times over, except this time she had to resist recoiling at the cold beneath his flesh. As a single tear trickled down her cheek, she wondered if their past had finally caught up to them.

Twenty-two years it'd taken.

Twenty-two years since her father had whisked her away in the middle of the night.

Twenty-two years since she'd last seen her mother.

They'd moved to twice as many cities in that time. Just the two of them.

Charlene inhaled the tangy disinfectant and the emptiness around her. "What am I going to do?" Even her voice sounded hollow, lacking in emotion.

Life as drifters had meant she had no friends.

Her time with her mother was nothing but a whispered dream. Her father never did tell her what happened when she was six years old. And after a while, she'd stopped asking. In fact, she'd often wondered if it was just a silly childhood nightmare.

Now she was all alone.

The enormity of it had hit her yesterday when the police started asking questions.

Her father had no identification. No driver's license. No credit cards. Not even a Social Security card. Just a small amount of cash and the key to their rented apartment. It hadn't surprised her.

The police, however, had implied that it was abnormal. Deceitful even. Charlene had explained away all their questions, yet Detective Chapel had looked at her like she was hiding something.

She'd learned to live with inquisitive gazes; she'd been the new student at twenty or so schools. Being the stranger in a crowd was completely normal.

The door cracked open, and the sound ricocheted about the room like a bullet. She jolted at the interruption and turned. Detective Chapel had a look of sorrow that for some reason seemed forced . . . too practiced. She flicked the tears from her cheeks and stepped back from her father's lifeless form.

"Ms. Bailey, are you okay?"

Charlene swallowed the lump burning in her throat and shook her head. *Okay?* His question was ludicrous. *Nothing will ever be okay again. Ever.* She turned back to her father's body and through her murky tears scanned his face. Finally, she nodded. "Yes."

When she turned to look into Chapel's eyes, she had a strange feeling he didn't believe her account of what happened. She blinked and tried but failed to cast the unfounded feeling aside. "What happens now?"

"If you're up to it, we'd like to ask you a few more questions."

She glanced at her father one last time, hardly able to believe what she was seeing. He'd always been full of life . . . the first to try out a dish he couldn't pronounce at a restaurant or jump off the bus to explore a new vista.

He taught her to appreciate the sunrise and the glow of the moon over the ocean. His days were long and his nights short in his attempts to squeeze the life out of every second.

All that had been stolen with the slice of a blade.

She bit her lip in an attempt to halt her quivering chin, and before she succumbed to the burgeoning tears again, she allowed Chapel to lead her from the morgue.

Charlene wasn't sure if the odors inside the police interview room were any better than the sterile atmosphere of the morgue.

Detective Chapel attempted to placate her with offers of coffee and sandwiches, but the idea of eating was repulsive. The last food she'd had were the spicy buffalo wings she'd shared with her father. It was impossible to believe that would be their last meal together.

"Charlene." Detective Chapel pinched the skin on the back of his hand. "We're sorry to do this so soon after your father's death, but the quicker we have answers, the more likely we are to catch his killer."

She nodded and moved her tongue around her mouth, trying to produce moisture. "I understand."

He flipped open a notebook and rolled a page to the back of the spiral. "So, you said you'd only arrived in New Orleans three weeks ago, is that correct?"

"Yes."

"Where'd you come from?"

"Chicago."

"And why did you move?"

She shrugged. "For work." It was the same reason they'd moved nearly every six months or so for as long as she could remember.

"What work did Peter do?"

"Whatever was available, really."

"What job did he have here?"

"He was working as a gardener at Paradise Spring Hotel on Magazine Street."

Chapel jotted the details on his notepad. "We'll have a chat with them. Do you know any reason why someone would want to kill him?"

She'd been asking herself the same question every waking moment since the woman had fled with the knife in her hand. "No. He was gentle and kind. Everyone loved him." She sniffed back a sob.

"Have you thought about the woman who murdered him? Can you tell us anything else?"

She'd done nothing but think of that woman. It horrified her how little she could recall. "It happened so quickly. Isn't there any video footage?"

"Oh, we wish. But no, there's no footage." He cocked his head, and his left eye narrowed, looking at her even harder.

Charlene's chest squeezed at his intense gaze. When his eyes darkened even further, her gut churned. It suddenly occurred to her that she might be a suspect. "What about the waiter, and the other people in the restaurant, and that bus stop outside? Someone must've seen something."

"We're interviewing everyone at the moment."

Her thoughts again turned to the woman who'd stabbed her father . . . her brunette hair, pulled into a high pony tail that flung from side to side as she snapped her eyes from Charlene to her father.

The fire in her eyes that blazed both fear and bravado.

Her white knuckles as she'd clutched the steak knife.

The visible throb of pulse in her slender neck.

The pause. That moment when she'd stopped for a split second, frozen with apparent indecision, the blade aimed at her father.

Yet Charlene couldn't remember anything else. Not what the attacker had been wearing. If she'd had jewelry or tattoos. She couldn't even remember the woman approaching their table.

One minute, Charlene and her father were deciding whose turn it was to stock up the fridge; the next second, the brunette was screaming at her father in a foreign language.

"Do you have anyone you can stay with?" Chapel interrupted her tumbling thoughts.

"What?"

"Is there anyone you can stay with?"

She lowered her eyes. "No."

"Family?"

"I don't have anyone."

His brows bounced together, his eyes narrowed, and again she had the impression he thought she was lying. He tapped his pen on the table, sounding out a metallic heartbeat. "What about your mother?"

Her brain screamed at her to run. But she fought the panic as her mind flitted from one possible response to the next. The vice that was clamped around her chest squeezed tighter.

Insecurity crept in like a thorny vine.

Her pause had his unfounded guilty glare darkening, and it was a couple of thumping heartbeats before she decided the truth was the best response.

She raised her eyes to Chapel and met his gaze. "I haven't seen my mother since I was six."

"Hmm." His pen tapping stopped. His eyebrows nudged upward. "What about friends? Do you know anyone here?"

"No."

"Is there anyone who can stay with you?"

"No. I don't know anyone."

His brows drilled together this time, and when his pen tapping got faster, she felt the need to clarify. "We moved around a lot."

"A lot . . . how often is a lot?" The pen stopped, and somehow the silence was worse.

"Usually every six months or so."

"Hmm. It would help us to piece things together if you retraced the last few years. Start with what you did in Chicago."

* * *

As Charlene listed her and her father's recent moves, Chapel jotted notes on his notepad. The scratching of his pen was as harsh as a nail being scraped down a board.

But the silence when he stopped was worse.

So she continued, blurting out one detail after another. Her mind danced to a game she and her father always played while on a road trip. It was a memory game. She'd say something like: we were eating ice cream on a pier, and a child flew a red kite into the railing right beside us. Where were we? Her father would have to answer.

He'd then ask her a question about somewhere they'd been. They could do it for hours. Recalling where they'd been or something unique they'd seen.

She'd never play that game again.

"Wow, you do travel around." Chapel yanked her back from that horrific thought as he flipped the page. "Do you know if Peter retained his bank statements?"

She blinked at him, suddenly nervous about her response. But once again, the longer she paused, the guiltier she felt. "We don't have bank accounts."

He sucked air through his teeth and leaned back on his chair. "That's highly unusual, Charlene."

"Dad didn't trust the banks with his money. So we only ever used cash."

"You never had a bank account either? Credit card?"

"No. And I never needed one either."

"What about wages?"

"Cash."

He pinched the back of his hand again. "Rent?"

She huffed. "Everybody loves cash."

"Well, that's interesting."

"Interesting how?" She had no idea what he was implying, but the look on his face confirmed he was suggesting something. And it wasn't good.

"Most people who don't use bank accounts stash their money somewhere. Under a mattress. In the wardrobe."

Charlene huffed out a laugh. "You're implying that we have surplus cash. We earned enough to pay the rent, buy food, and occasionally have a treat. That's it."

"Maybe Peter's killer thought he did?"

The grin fell from Charlene's face. "I can assure you we didn't have extra cash."

"Did you know Peter didn't have a driver's license?"

"Yes. He never had a need for one."

"What about his Social Security number? Do you know it?"

Her father didn't have a Social Security number. Neither did she. "No! Why would I?" It wasn't a complete lie.

Her heart leapt to her throat at Chapel's glare. Her father had ranted many a time about remaining untethered to any government programs.

He was stubborn like that.

But after hours of implications from Chapel, she couldn't help but wonder if he'd had an ulterior motive.

Was he keeping us off the grid for a different reason?

Chapter Two

An odd feeling gripped Charlene as her mind stewed over that disturbing thought. Was Peter keeping her off the grid? Or were they just living a carefree life?

But it wasn't just carefree; it was more than that.

Peter went to great extremes to avoid any form of documentation. The windowless interview room grew suddenly both hot and cold. A venomous snake curled in her gut, and the urge to throw up was so strong she clenched her jaw and swallowed.

Detective Chapel leaned forward. "Are you okay?"

"No." She cleared her throat. "I'd like to go home, please."

"Of course. I'll have one of my men drive you."

"No. It's okay. I'll catch the streetcar." She stood, flipped her handbag strap over her shoulder, and clutched it.

"Miss Bailey, we'd like to have a look through Peter's property . . . see if we can find anything that'd help with the investigation."

Her mind whizzed through her father's measly belongings, and she couldn't fathom what would be of any interest to the police. "Okay. When?"

"How about tomorrow morning—say, nine o'clock?"

"Sure. That'd be fine." She turned for the door.

"Oh, and Miss Bailey."

She spun to him, nervous about his impending comment. "Yes."

"Don't leave town."

She captured the detectives gaze with hers. "Where would I go?"

During the trip home, she contemplated how easy it would be to up and leave. She'd done it dozens of times. She and her father had moved so many times, they could pack up and go in the space of two hours.

Their entire belongings could fit into three suitcases. That's the way her father liked it. Freedom. That's what he called it.

Freedom.

She didn't feel free now. She felt trapped.

Sometimes she hadn't wanted to move. Like in Seattle, when she'd met Charlie at the bar she'd worked at. Charlene and Charlie . . . they'd joked about their names sounding like a couple of b-grade movie bank robbers.

He'd been nice. So nice, in fact, she'd given her virginity to Charlie, and for the first time since she'd hit her twenties, she'd felt like a sensual woman.

It was one of the few times she'd fought with her father. In the end, she'd left Seattle and Charlie without even a good-bye. She'd never even gotten his phone number.

Not that it mattered; once they'd left Seattle, she knew she'd never see him again. Just like every other person she'd met. She didn't have a single person she called a friend. Not that it bothered her.

It was the way they operated. They owned no assets, set down no roots, and tied themselves to nothing and nobody. Ultimate freedom.

It was easy. Move to a new town, pay cash upfront for one month's rent. Find a job, any job that paid cash. And her father had made every new town, new house, and new school seem like an adventure. After school finished, every new city brought a new job to look forward to.

Most of the time Charlene loved it.

Now, though, with nobody to turn to, she wondered how she'd arrived at age twenty-eight without anyone she could call a friend.

The urge to leave New Orleans was huge.

She could head back to Chicago. She'd had a good job there in a café overlooking Lake Michigan. Her boss would give her old job back to her in a heartbeat, of that she was certain.

But she wouldn't go. Not when her father's killer was still out there. Charlene needed answers.

She made herself a toasted sandwich, their meal of choice when time and funds were short. Her father often said the toasted sandwich was under-appreciated, and they'd have competitions trying to outdo each other with their own personal spins on it.

Charlene had become the master chef when it came to making dessert toasties. Raisin bread with sliced bananas and Nutella was one of her favorites. It cost less than a buck and took all of three minutes to make.

With a toasted bacon, onion, barbecue sauce, and cheese sandwich in hand, she headed into her father's room and sat on his bed. The springs twanged in protest. As she nibbled on the crusty corner of her sandwich, she scanned the room. Her father's entire assets were in that room.

The wardrobe was only half full, and the bulk of the clothes were over ten years old. The only time he'd bought something new was when he needed it.

Her father's only splurge item was his pillow. Each new rented apartment qualified for a new pillow. He'd said it was his kind of pure luxury and insisted that she have a new pillow too.

His most expensive item was a pair of leather shoes. The only time he wore them was for job interviews. That same pair were about twelve years old, yet they appeared as if they'd been worn only a couple dozen times at the most. He looked after his things.

After finishing her sandwich and washing up the plate, she went through his drawers. She was snooping, and acid burned in her gut with every handle she pulled forward.

But she had to know.

She had to confirm that Detective Chapel wasn't going to find anything about her father that Charlene didn't already know.

Within half an hour she had her answer . . . there was nothing.

Chapter Three

A fortnight after her father's murder, Chapel arrived at her front door unannounced. She was surprised to see him so late at night, and even more surprised when he accepted her offer of a cup of tea.

While he settled into the living room, she boiled the kettle and stewed over what could've brought him over at this hour.

When she sat opposite him on the weathered sofa, the look in the detective's eyes convinced her he had something to share.

And whatever it was, it wasn't good.

When they'd gone through Peter's belongings a couple of weeks ago, they'd found exactly what she had . . . nothing. But as Charlene sat rigid on the chair opposite Chapel, the intensity in his eyes scared the hell out of her.

She'd been scared before. Like the time she and her father had slept in the bus shelter because they'd missed the coach. They'd spent the whole night guarding their life's belongings. She'd been about twelve at that time.

After that night, Peter made her learn self-defense. Each new town brought a new technique. Karate. Taekwondo. Kickboxing. Even sprinting. Fight or flight had been their mantra.

Charlene could drop a man to his knees and break his finger if the situation warranted. Yet the one and only time she'd needed her self-defense techniques, she'd frozen. She'd allowed that woman to plunge the knife.

The knife had penetrated her father's flesh with such ease, she hadn't believed it'd happened. It was only when the blade was yanked out and blood had splattered across the white tablecloth that she'd comprehended what the attacker had done.

He'd died because Charlene had failed.

She'll never forgive herself for that, and her only chance at some kind of resolution was to get answers. But the look on Chapel's face had her fearing that the answers would be as shocking as the murder itself.

After waiting long enough for Chapel to initiate the conversation, she opened her palms. "I assume you have news for me?"

His shoulders rose with a deep breath. It was almost like he was steadying himself for a funeral speech, and his heavy pause only instilled greater dread. He let a breath out in a big huff. "Yes. But you're not going to like this, so . . . so just hear me out."

The hairs on her neck prickled. For the hundredth time since her father's death, she couldn't believe this was happening.

They'd always been careful. They never went to neighborhoods that were notorious for trouble. Always checked a room upon entering. Never mixed with the wrong crowds.

Whatever Chapel was about to tell her had to be wrong. Her father was a good guy, of that she was certain. Charlene rubbed her clammy hands together and wedged them between her knees. "Okay."

Chapel pushed the end of his pen onto his notepad. The click that hid the nib was like a whip crack in the windowless room. "We've gone through every record we can get our hands on—Social Security, tax returns, employee records, birth records, housing, traffic violations—and, well, there's no record of Peter Harrison Bailey."

He looked at her as though she'd understand the implication of his statement. She didn't. "And?"

"And." He lowered his eyes, and then after an exaggerated blink, he met her gaze. "We don't think that's his real name."

"What? What's his real name?"

"We don't know. But, Charlene, there's something else."

The finality in his voice had her heart exploding. "What?"

"You know how we took your blood sample?"

"Yes."

"Charlene . . . Peter isn't your father."

"Are you crazy? Of course he's my father."

"DNA doesn't lie, Charlene. I know this is hard to comprehend, but you're not related to Peter. Or whoever he is." He looked like he'd swallowed his tongue.

"What?" she snapped.

"There's more."

Charlene swallowed the tang of bile in her throat. "What?"

"There are no birth records for you either, Charlene. We don't think Charlene Bailey is your real name either."

"What? How can that be?"

"Well . . . we do have a theory." A line of sweat trickled down his temple.

He paused.

She waited.

"We think you're a kidnap victim."

His words pulled the pin on a memory grenade, and shocking images from twenty-two years ago exploded across her mind.

Peter squeezing her to his chest while he ran through the jungle.

Clutching his neck as shouts and explosions boomed behind them.

Hiding in a rusty old car until daybreak.

It was like it'd happened yesterday.

She clamped her jaw, refusing to voice the memories she'd been repressing for decades. Chapel's eyes drilled into her, and the longer she paused, the more severe his gaze grew.

"That's impossible." She finally found her voice. "He loved me. I loved him. He was the best father anyone could ask for."

"We're going through our records, and there are several abductions that fit the time frame for your age. Provided you are twenty-eight, that is."

"What?"

"Well, if he's lied about *who* you are, then there's every likelihood your date of birth is not correct either."

Charlene stood and strode to the other side of the room. "You've lost your mind. My father never laid a finger on me. He loved me." Her voice quivered.

Chapel rubbed his hands on his pants. "We understand that, but things aren't adding up. Charlene, please, just sit and hear me out."

It was a long moment before she convinced her feet to move. But when she did, every step toward him was like walking through wet cement. She eased onto the sunken sofa and wedged her hands beneath her knees, willing them to stop shaking.

"We're going to need to document everything you remember, try to slot the pieces into place."

She stared at the blue dolphins painted on her favorite coffee mug. They'd bought that on the Santa Monica Pier, about ten years ago. A very public place. I

f she was a kidnap victim, why was she allowed to be out in the community?

Surely, he'd have kept her in hiding. Charlene had been allowed to come and go as she pleased.

Charlene straightened her shoulders, glared at Chapel, and shook her head. "You're wrong."

He nodded as if he'd been expecting this response. "I hope I am, but at this point in time, it's the only theory we have to go on."

Chapter Four

Noah Montgomery stood and twirled the chunky gold ring around what was left of his little finger. The simple habit, something he'd been doing for over twenty years, reminded him of just how powerful he was.

He scanned the faces in the courtroom. Every single pair of eyes was looking at him. The front of the courtroom was his stage. He owned that stage.

He lowered his eyes to the defendant and waited until he turned to him. It took a few heartbeats, but when the diminutive fool finally met his gaze, it was obvious he knew he'd already lost.

The air in the room bristled with anticipation, and Montgomery absorbed the rush of adrenaline as he buttoned his designer suit jacket and strolled toward the jury.

He smiled at the middle-aged woman in the front row with poorly applied makeup. "Ladies and gentlemen. The defendant, Mr. Robert Dobenheimer, is guilty of many things. And *proving* it is what we are here for. I promise you that, by the end of this trial, I will prove, with every ounce of certainty, that Mr. Dobenheimer is guilty of the charges laid against him."

It was all an act. An act he'd been perfecting for thirty years. He was good at it too. So good, in fact, that it had become a double-edged sword. In the hundred and fifty-two cases he'd tried, the jury had failed to reach a verdict in his favor in just two cases.

He didn't consider them as failures as both of those defendants had committed suicide during the trial. In his mind, that proved they were guilty. But his impeccable record meant that he rarely went to court anymore. His cases were finalized with a stack of carefully worded documents and the flick of a gold pen.

Once he was hired as the plaintiff lawyer, most defense attorneys used his impeccable record to convince their clients to settle out of court. It wasn't even a fraction as exciting as seeing the look in a defendant's eyes when they knew they'd lost.

By midmorning, he'd presented enough evidence to have the defense attorney looking grayer by the minute. By the end of the day, Montgomery expected to have a settlement offer on his table overnight.

When the judge's gavel thumped the sounding block for the last time that day, Montgomery turned to his client, and her doe-like eyes looked up at him. Mrs. Dobenheimer was both a lucrative client and a beautiful woman, representing his usual clientele perfectly.

He'd seen that look on many of his elite Hollywood clients before. She idolized him. In Mrs. Dobenheimer's eyes, Montgomery was a god —a god who'd saved her from the ongoing torture that was her marriage. And he'd make her a bucket load of money in the process.

He had no doubt she'd be thanking him with more than just his obscenely expensive retainer very soon.

She placed her hand on his arm and ran her tongue over her plumped lips. "What happens now?"

He offered her his most becoming smile. "You go to your hotel and indulge yourself with a spa treatment and champagne, because I expect we'll be receiving an offer from your husband before morning."

"Oh." Her long black lashes fluttered. "So soon."

"You look disappointed."

"Oh, no, it's just, I've booked my suite for a week."

"Well, darling, with the amount of money I expect you'll be offered, you can buy your own suite at the Four Seasons."

Her lip twitched like he'd said the magic words. "Would you like to come over and share a drink with me?"

"I do believe I would. Eight o'clock?"

She tugged her lip into her mouth, and her eyes glimmered. "Lovely."

He indicated for her to walk in front of him, and as she squeezed past him and he placed his hand on the curve of her hip, her breath whispered from her lips. Montgomery knew the reaction well.

They strode from the courtroom and into the throng of hungry paparazzi. He eased his client in front of him, positioning her to stage the perfect photographs for tomorrow's papers.

After the customary wait for the reporters to settle, he pointed at the pretty blonde in the middle of the crowd. "Ms. Chantilly."

Her eyes lit up, and she spoke into her microphone. "Mr. Montgomery, do you think you're going to win?"

"I always win, Ms. Chantilly. You know that." The reporter blushed at his comment.

"Mrs. Dobenheimer, did you know about all the affairs?"

"Mr. Clarkson," Montgomery answered for his client, "we shall be saving our response to that question for a more appropriate time."

After answering a series of redundant questions, he led Mrs. Dobenheimer through the crowd, making a point of eyeballing some of the regular reporters. It was important to keep them on his side.

Once the trial was over, Montgomery would assist Mrs. Dobenheimer in securing a lucrative six-figure sum to sell her exclusive story about her life as the wife of a philandering A-list movie star.

Montgomery had the senior editors of all the major magazines and talk show hosts on speed dial.

However, these days, they usually called him.

He paused at the limousine, and as Mrs. Dobenheimer eased into the car, Montgomery turned to scan the crowd behind the barrier. Four of his women were there. He spotted them easily. They were beyond stunning. Their pleading eyes proved they were hungry for him.

He liked to think they were hungry for more than just his money. But in reality, he didn't care. They provided a service his wife couldn't, so he needed them as much as they needed him. He nodded at Felicia, and the blonde showed a mixture of both joy and relief.

The remaining three looked physically deflated at the rejection. But when he didn't turn away, the threesome straightened, and their long lashes fluttered with eagerness.

He made them wait a full half minute before he inclined his head at Rochelle. Her lips broadened into a beaming smile, and he could already picture what those gorgeous lips would be doing very soon.

With the decision made, he stepped into the limousine and turned his attention back to his client. She didn't hesitate to rest her hand on his thigh . . . a sure sign she'd be a wild cat in the bedroom.

Once he'd delivered Mrs. Dobenheimer to her hotel and made promises to return in three hours, he eased back in his seat and rode the rest of the way to his office in silence. This was the part of the ritual he hated the most.

Once the adrenaline that'd fueled him in the courtroom ebbed away, his mind was left to wander. And it wasn't a safe place to be. A niggling feeling that his entire world, one in which he was currently riding at the pinnacle of his legal career, would come crashing down, plagued his every thought.

But he'd been careful, and that stupid night some twenty-two years ago was barely a long-forgotten memory. They had no proof, he reminded himself as he twisted the gold ring around the stub of his little finger.

His finger began to throb, not the part that was left, but the missing part that'd been bitten off twenty-two years ago. It was a weird sensation to feel pain from a body part that was no longer there. But he did. It was like the bitch was haunting him.

The limousine pulled up outside the Solow Building on West 57th Street, jolting him back from his troubling thoughts. Mansour jumped from the driver's seat and raced around to open Montgomery's door.

"Shall I wait for you, Mr. Montgomery?"

Montgomery handed his trusted driver a hundred-dollar note. "Give me forty minutes."

"Yes, sir."

Montgomery strode from the limousine and into the office towers that'd been home to Montgomery and Pearce for nearly a decade. When he'd first rented the space, he'd had just one floor. Now, though, his firm owned and occupied four floors. His office took up one-third of the fiftieth floor, the top floor.

He entered his office, and the hint of sweet perfume confirmed that his girls had arrived before him. As he loosened his tie, he crossed the plush carpet to his private quarters.

Both Rochelle and Felicia were naked, and as they'd been trained to do, they'd started without him. His erection bounced to life as the striking blonde looked up from Rochelle's abundant breast and ran her tongue over her lips.

He paused a few feet from them and the two beauties curled off his oak desk and sashayed toward him holding hands.

The murky waters that'd threatened to tip him into a pitiful depression just ten minutes ago abated the second Felicia lowered to her knees in front of him.

Chapter Five

Three weeks of interrogation by Detective Chapel had them no closer to finding Charlene's father's killer. All it had done was fill the giant cork-board in Incident Room Four with cards detailing snippets of Charlene's transient life.

Chapel was a very patient man, and other than the occasional flicking with his pen, he remained relatively silent.

Charlene had already spent hours spewing random memories of her father, or Peter, or whoever he was. Yet despite Chapel's accusatory gazes, she was adamant that her life had been perfectly normal.

Normal . . . it was such an ambiguous word.

What was a normal family anyway?

Was it the couple with the two young children in which the wife knew her husband was having an affair with his boss?

Was it the newlyweds who'd raced off to have an abortion after discovering they were pregnant?

Was it the family of six who had both sets of grandparents living in trailers in their front yard?

Was it the middle-aged American man who'd ordered his young Thai wife over the Internet, then produced a set of triplets?

Was it the lonely wife who spent every night nursing her baby while praying her husband would return from Iraq in one piece?

Charlene had met every one of these supposed normal families. What she and Peter had was a loving, supportive, nurturing father-daughter relationship.

So what if nearly every six months of her life they'd moved hundreds or even thousands of miles to settle in a new town?

So what if their total assets could fit into three suitcases, two of them being hers?

So what if Charlene never finished school?

None of that mattered.

What mattered was that they loved each other. Peter taught her respect and love.

He taught her how to cook the best pancakes in the world and how to avoid a brain freeze when eating ice cream.

He was there when she needed advice about the boy in the school band with the plump raspberry lips.

He was the responsible parent who took her into Macy's to buy her first trainer bra when she was thirteen.

No topic was ever off limits, and he was the best father Charlene could have asked for.

She refused to believe Detective Chapel's ludicrous claims.

Charlene stood and strolled to the board. They'd pinned the cards in a time line, with her most recent memories on the far right, and each day Chapel and his fellow officers had coaxed her back further.

With each story she told, they added another card to the time line. Each afternoon, while she returned to her empty apartment and wondered what the hell she was going to do next, Chapel's team would search for evidence to corroborate her stories.

A witness. A document. A record of some sort. Friends, coworkers, iconic places, bus companies, rental properties. Even names of restaurants they'd frequented and what she'd recalled either of them eating.

Some of the cards had pictures attached to them, like the elderly woman who'd shown her how to feed the rescued cats when she volunteered at the animal shelter in Boulder City, Nevada.

Thankfully Mrs. Pierce had remembered her too.

As did the young woman in Hot Springs, who'd been the same age as Charlene, who spent every night trying to stop her baby from suffering from colic. In the photo, the poor woman still had bags under her eyes that made her look middle-aged.

Some of the cards, however, had a big red question mark, indicating that more evidence was required. After a couple of weeks listening to Charlene rattle off certain unique details about each town, Detective Chapel expressed his surprise at her level of recall.

"It's a game we play. We *did* play." A pang of sorrow twisted in her heart.

Chapel cocked his head and frowned.

"Dad and I played a memory game. He'd say something that we'd done, like the time my flip-flop fell into the water when we sat on the pier over the ocean, and I'd have to guess the town where that happened. Then it'd be my turn to try to stump him. It was a fun way to remember all the things we did together."

The twisted look on Chapel's face confirmed his turmoil. Everything Charlene said indicated she'd lived a wonderful life, yet the stoic detective was still adamant she was a kidnap victim.

It ate away at him. It ate away at her.

And as the days rolled on and he was no closer to proving his theory, she grew more tired of the accusations.

Her eyes scanned the years written in a thick black Sharpie at the top of the board. It was like one of those charts she'd seen in a classroom somewhere that documented the evolution of man.

This time line documented the evolution of Charlene.

She'd been dreading the day they arrived at her early childhood. Today was that day.

As she perused the cards, inching along the wall as she went, Chapel silently waited with the everlasting patience she'd learned to appreciate.

The oldest memory on the board at the moment was her eighth birthday. Her father had taken her to the Museum of Pop Culture in Seattle. They'd formed a fake band called Restless Natives and had dressed up to pose for a photo.

She'd giggled herself stupid at the wild wig and silver-studded leather jacket her father had worn.

Sighing, she wondered where that photo had gone. If she knew, the card for her eighth birthday wouldn't have a big red question mark.

Charlene choked back the knot in her throat and turned to Detective Chapel. He leaned against the table, his hands in his pockets, and the kindness in his eyes nearly reduced her to tears.

When their gazes met, her chin dimpled. They'd arrived at the moment she'd been dreading for weeks. It wasn't that she didn't remember further back. Quite the opposite actually. But every slice of that memory betrayed the perfect life she'd been describing for weeks.

"Charlene." The way Chapel said her name, with a pleading, knowing intonation, confirmed he knew she was hiding something.

She let out a shaky breath. "May I have a moment, please?"

"Of course, I'll grab us some of that crappy coffee." Chapel slinked out the door, leaving her to her documented life.

She squeezed her eyes shut, covered her face with her hands, and tried to make sense of the images that'd been playing across her mind for over two decades. I

t was always the same nameless faces. Always the same emotions. Always the same meaningless details.

Ever since she was six, she'd been denying they were real. Just the figment of a child's overactive memory, she'd reasoned. Simply confusion between reality and fiction, maybe from a movie or conversation she'd overheard.

They weren't, though. Every blink of that night was true. She knew it.

But the implications were devastating.

She was still of two minds over whether or not to reveal those images when Chapel returned with the steaming mugs.

"Here you go. Take a seat."

He sat opposite her and wrapped his hands around his mug. "Take your time."

She nodded and lowered her eyes, not wanting to see the optimism in his gaze. It was obvious Detective Chapel believed he'd reached the precipice between speculation and confirmation. He just had to tip her over that edge.

His certainty only increased the guilty tendrils inching up her spine.

She sipped the bitter coffee, and the sting on her tongue perfectly represented the dread prickling her thoughts. Plonking the mug on the table, she let her breath out in a big huff. "I've always believed it was a dream."

He nodded but remained silent. She liked that about him. Chapel had immense patience. Maybe it was the perfect interrogation technique, as it was difficult not to fill the empty void with words. Words that would eventually reveal details. Details that would put Chapel on the path to answers.

Her only hope was that the answers were not proof of his shocking accusations.

She prolonged the silence, trying to work out the chronological order of that night. In her mind's eye, it'd always been a jumble of mixed-up images. Like a broken film on an old movie projector. Half a picture. A word or a shout. Night. Day. Silence. Screaming. Stillness. Bedlam.

"What were you wearing?"

His words surprised her, and she blinked at him.

"Do you remember?"

Charlene stared at her fingers, picking at a flap of loose skin near her thumbnail as she went back to that night. She'd never thought about her outfit before, yet she remembered it perfectly. "It was a yellow dress. Pale yellow, like whipped butter. It had four little white daises that'd been sewn onto a panel here." She indicated across her chest. "I loved that dress because I could put my hands in the pockets on my hips."

Chapel smiled, and she did too. It was a nice memory, one that she hadn't recalled until now. But her mind wandered to what he'd do with that information. They probably had a database of kidnap victims and what they were wearing when they were last seen. The instant she left today, he'd be punching her description into his computer.

Had she already said too much?

It was too late now.

I am not a kidnap victim.

With that conviction rolling around her brain, she met his gaze. "I'm certain I was six years old. Don't ask me how I know. I just do."

He inclined his head. This was the moment he'd been waiting for, and his wide eyes indicated that his mind was open for every bit of information to leave her lips.

"My mom and I were in the back of a car. I remember thinking how weird the car was, as it had no roof, and I giggled a lot because my hair whipped up in the breeze. It was only years later that I learned the car model was a type of jeep. It was olive green, like the ones you see in those army movies." She tried to smile, yet she was certain it'd look more like a grimace.

"Two men were in the front, and the drive seemed to go on forever. They drove us through town after town, with miles of nothing between each one."

"Nothing?"

"Yeah, trees, open paddocks. Not farms as such, just . . . nothing."

"Hmm. Who was driving?"

She shrugged. "No idea. Two men were in the front, and they never spoke to my mom. In fact, I can't recall her saying a word to them for the whole trip either."

"Tell me about her."

"Oh." He caught her off guard again. So far, Chapel had remained silent whenever she told her stories. "Mom was beautiful. She was always hugging me and telling me stories, and she tucked me into bed every night. Sometimes we slept in the same bed."

"Hmm." Frown lines dented his forehead.

"Hmm what?"

"Where do you think your father was when you slept in her bed?"

Charlene blinked at him, searching her brain for an answer. In the end, there wasn't one. "I don't know." She snapped. She hadn't meant to yell, and the venom behind it had surprised her as much as it appeared to shock Chapel.

"It's okay, Charlene. You're doing great."

Her shoulders slumped. "It's just random memories. I can't put them in order."

"That's okay. Tell me about this trip. Was it day or night? What sights do you remember? Did you stop anywhere along the way?"

Uncurling her fists, she stood and strode to the board. With her back to him, she said, "I'll just tell you the bits I remember."

"Okay, take your time."

She huffed out a sigh. "Once the sun set, it got cold, and I climbed onto my mother's lap. I was straddling her legs, facing her so I could snuggle into her chest. She wrapped her arms around me, and I can remember hearing her heart beat. Between that and the bumpy road, I must've fallen asleep, because the next thing I remember was waking up after we'd stopped."

Charlene returned to her chair, but she was no longer seeing Chapel; she was seeing that night like she'd just lived through it. "I was pulled from the car, and Mom was screaming at the men. They had guns, big long rifles that were slung over their shoulders. Some of them aimed their weapons as us, but most were just standing around, smoking and laughing."

"Do you remember what your Mom was saying?"

She blinked at him, suddenly recalling that her mother had been speaking in Spanish. She'd never realized it until now.

"What?" Chapel must've seen her confusion.

"She spoke in Spanish."

"Spanish? Like the woman who stabbed Peter?"

"Yes. I didn't remember that until now."

"Hmm. So, what happened after you were out of the jeep?"

"I . . . I just stood there as they pulled Mom out of the car and tied her to a pole near this shed."

His brows shot up, and the muscles in his jaw bulged. "Can you describe the shed? What else do you see?"

"It was dark. Trees everywhere. There were about five or six men. All in green uniforms. All carrying guns. I clutched my arms around her waist, and a few of the men just laughed at me. At us. There was this really loud noise, and the men started shouting. Some ran into the bushes. Two hid behind the jeeps. But this one man just stood there in the jeep's headlights. His feet were apart, and the gun was aimed at something. We couldn't see past the shed."

As Charlene twisted her fingers, bolts of memories flashed across her eyes, and she blurted out the snippets like she was tripping in a drug-induced high. "A brilliant light lit up the area. It grew brighter by the second. A huge gush of wind peppered us with rocks and bits of trees. Years later, when I saw a movie, I realized that it'd been a plane that'd landed near us. I remember screaming at how loud it was. Mom's hands were tied behind her so she couldn't hug me, and when I looked up at her I saw the whites in her eyes. But she smiled down at me like she'd done thousands of times, and I knew that everything was going to be okay."

She sipped her coffee, but the now cold brew stung her taste buds, and she put it back down. "But it wasn't okay."

He shook his head as if knowing exactly what Charlene was talking about.

"When the noise stopped, the shouts started. Mom was trembling. Then they started shooting. I don't know who or what they were shooting at. A man fell over right near us, clutching his neck. Mom told me to close my eyes. But I didn't. I just clung to her and watched the man roll about with blood gushing through his fingers."

Chapel's lips drew to a thin line, turning them pale. "What happened next?"

"There was more shouting and more guns going off. But the shouts got more distant. I think the men were all running into the trees. It was almost silent for a bit. But then I felt Mom stiffen, and she looked down at me. This time she told me to run. But I shook my head. She screamed at me to run. I didn't want to let go of her."

A memory came to her like a bolt of lightning. She'd never had it before.

"What?" Chapel's eyes bulged.

"It's Peter."

"What's Peter? Tell me what you remember."

"Mom kept screaming at me to run. But when I didn't, Peter grabbed me. He was dressed in that uniform. He had a gun too."

"What'd he do?"

"He dragged me from her and scooped me up. As I screamed for my mother, he took me into the bushes. His gun dug into my thighs, and I remember having a bruise there for days."

It's funny what she'd blocked out. She'd always pictured that bruise and had recalled it many times over the decades, but she'd had zero recollection of how she'd gotten it.

Had she deliberately blocked out that it was Peter's gun?

Had she forced the image away, not wanting to believe it was true?

But it was true. And the implications were brutal. Peter had been one of those soldiers. Or whatever they were.

"That was the last time I ever saw my mother."

"So you ran into the bushes. What happened then?"

Charlene searched for the answer. But it wasn't there. It was as though a black cloud had smothered every recollection.

After a few thumping heartbeats, her shoulders sagged, and she shook her head. "I . . . I don't know. One minute, we were hiding in a rusted-out old car in the middle of the woods, with guns booming and lights flashing in the distance. The next memory I have is sitting in the sunshine on a beach, sharing an ice cream with Peter. It's like I've lived two different lives."

Chapel moaned as he reached forward and placed his hand on hers. "Charlene, I think you have."

Chapter Six

C harlene was completely drained by the time Chapel drove her home. After saying good-bye and making promises to return to the station in the morning, she entered her apartment and locked the door behind her.

Her mind was in a fog as she went through the motions of showering and dressing in her pajamas. After that, she was torn between curling up in a ball on her bed and pacing the length of the tiny kitchen. She did the latter.

The apartment consisted of a combined kitchen and living room area, a bathroom and two bedrooms. None of the furniture belonged to them. Not a single knife or fork. Not the bedding. Not even the decorations.

It'd never bothered her before. But after weeks of defending her lifestyle with Detective Chapel, she'd begun to second-guess her upbringing.

Scanning the meaningless objects in the room—the flower print on the wall, the plain white lamp with the yellowing edges, even the hardcover books on the shelves—she had never felt so foreign in her own home.

Peter's absence added to her alienation. All the energy had been sucked from her life. She felt empty. Devoid of emotion. Devoid of care. Devoid of love.

She was hollow.

Nothing but an empty soul.

She stomped across the tiny space, and before she knew what she was doing, she plucked her beloved coffee mug off the sink and hurled it at the wall, smashing it to pieces.

Her chest heaved, and staring at the shards, she slid down the wall and hugged her knees to her chest.

A sob burst from her throat, and tears flowed. Great heaving pain spilled from her body. She'd cried more in the last month than she had in her entire life, yet the tears that gripped her now tore a hole through her heart.

Retelling that shocking night to Chapel had opened this wound.

Charlene had thought she'd remembered all the important aspects of that night. But she hadn't. It surprised her how many memories she'd repressed.

Her mind had rewound and played that night over and over many times in the last two decades, but she couldn't understand why she'd never recalled Peter in that uniform nor the gun that he'd slung over his shoulder.

Until today.

She couldn't help but wonder if she'd played into Chapel's hands. Had she just given him what he wanted to hear?

No!

She refused to believe that. Yet when she squeezed her eyes shut, she could picture with perfect clarity the moment Peter had snatched her from her mother's arms.

His uniform matched those of the other men.

The gun he'd carried had given her the bruise on her inner thigh.

Her mother had screamed something at him, yet he hadn't even looked back as he'd carried Charlene into the bushes.

She never saw her mother again.

Charlene collected one of the broken pieces from the floor. It was the handle, still attached to a chunk of the mug. She pushed it onto her finger and absently spun it around.

Chapel's allegations burned in her soul. He had a one-track mind, and he had so many reasons to believe he was right. But the worst thing was that he'd tapped into her own doubts. She was no longer one hundred percent certain of Peter's innocence.

Did Peter kidnap me?

The absurd notion began seeping into her brain like black ink, redesigning her memories, giving Peter new motives. Wicked sinister motives. Suddenly her past took on a whole new light. A dark fragmented light.

She heard her own breaths, short and sharp. And her pulse thumping in her ears. With each harrowing thought, dread stacked on another layer, threatening to engulf her in a giant quivering mess.

Was her whole life a lie?

Their constant moving and lack of records would've made it impossible for anyone to find them. She sat bolt upright as a new thought blazed across her brain. All this time, she'd been so fixated on what had happened to her that she'd never stopped to think about what had happened to her mother.

Did she try to find me?

As the plain white clock on the kitchen wall ticked away, thoughts rolled around her mind. *Tick. Kidnap victim. Tick. Move every six months. Tick. No identity.*

Tick. Is my mother still alive?

With that critical question burning in her brain, she tossed the broken crockery on the linoleum floor, pushed to her feet, and strode into Peter's bedroom.

No matter what the outcome, she had to know what had happened to her mother.

And Peter was the only link she had to her.

The police had already been through Peter's measly possessions, as had she, but they'd found nothing. But they didn't know him like she did, and now she was more focused.

She yanked out the painted wooden drawers and examined every item of his clothing more thoroughly. His familiar scent lingered. As she tugged out each item, her neck hairs bristled at the notion that this was all some kind of sick joke. She half expected Peter to step into the room at any moment.

Casting the creepy feeling aside, she moved from the drawers to the closet.

After checking the pockets on his four pairs of trousers, she'd only found one cash receipt that Chapel and his team must've missed. She contemplated giving it to Chapel for his proof wall. But that was the last thing she wanted to do. Chapel didn't need any more ammunition. She did.

She went through his jacket pockets and his hanging shirts. She checked the bottom of the closet and the top. And just like the drawers, the closet offered nothing.

His battered old suitcase gave her a momentary hope, and she tugged it out, flopped the flimsy case onto the bed, and zipped it open.

Nothing.

She checked under the bed, tugged off the bedding, examined the pillow, and even flipped the mattress. Still zero. In the bathroom, she found nothing either.

Once she'd exhausted every possible hiding spot, she sat on the bare mattress. Her shoulders sagged with the overwhelming feeling that she'd missed something. A single tear tickled her cheek, and she flicked it away.

A sense of failure gripped her. The mountain of pressure made her feel like she might implode, and she gripped the edge of the mattress, digging her fingernails into the foam until they hurt. With each tick of the kitchen clock, she sank deeper and deeper into despair.

A broken sob reached her throat, but she fought it. She'd had enough of crying. That time was over. Now was the time for fighting.

Fighting back the tears.

Fighting for answers.

What would Peter do?

She pictured him standing in the doorway, hands on hips, that shrewd look of confidence on his face. They'd been in many situations that'd had her in a mild panic. But he was eternally calm and had an answer for everything. His favorite saying was "A wise old owl always knows."

Peter's walking cane caught her eye.

She sat bolt upright. *The cane!*

The cane had always been in plain sight, and she'd walked past it nearly every day of her life. Yet it didn't fit into their transient lifestyle puzzle.

Her mind bristled as she walked to it. Peter didn't need a walking cane, and she'd never seen him use it, yet it was the one thing that'd accompanied them all around the country. Convinced she was onto something, Charlene carried it to the kitchen and placed it on the table.

The length of the cane was a dark wood . . . oak or something. At the base was a rubber stopper that had barely any marks because he'd never used it. Each time they packed up their things, Peter would pile his clothing and toiletries into his ancient suitcase, and his other hand would carry this cane.

She couldn't believe she'd never pushed Peter about his attachment to it before. Every time she'd asked, he'd simply skirted her question with one of his own.

He was good at that. Answering a question with a question. It was the perfect way to give no answer at all. It was also another angle of deceit that she'd never recognized before.

At the top of the cane was a silver owl. *A wise old owl always knows.*

"What does the owl know, Dad?"

She ran her fingers over the figurine. It was intricately carved, the bird's head and wing feathers completed in incredible detail. The owl's eyes were two red stones, and for a fleeting moment, she contemplated that they might be rubies.

But she quickly cast aside that thought.

Another one of Peter's mantras was that jewels were a waste of precious money. As far as she knew, he'd never owned any jewelry.

She herself had only a simple pair of silver hoop earrings and a small silver cross on a chain. Her one ring was a gold filigree pattern of a parade of four dolphins. She'd begged Peter to buy it for her twenty-first birthday.

She can still remember the look on his face when he'd given it to her. Despite all his vocal distaste for the wasted money, he'd been as excited by her reaction to the jewelry as she had been.

The ring hadn't left her finger since that day.

A wise old owl always knows.

"What were you trying to tell me, Dad?"

The owl's taloned feet clutched a branch that formed the connection to the wooden part of the cane. Charlene ran her fingernail beneath the seam connecting the two and felt a little latch. She raised it to her eyes, examining it in the light. A prickle of excitement teased her thoughts.

The owl's eyes glistened. Taunting her with suggestion.

Sitting upright, she positioned both her thumbs on the owl's ruby eyes and pressed. The owl jolted apart, its body separating from its legs. Charlene gasped as she eased the bird back on a tiny hinge that'd been concealed by the silver tree limb.

Her breath stopped as she peered into a secret compartment.

Inside was just one thing . . . a key.

Chapter Seven

Charlene sat back with the brass key nestled on her palm. This was no ordinary key. It was a fancy skeleton key detailed with a miniature crown at the top. It was about the size of her little finger.

But it had no markings to indicate what it opened.

Not even numbers or letters.

It was obviously important, though. It was not for a desk drawer or gym locker. This key locked something that was made for keeps. Like a safe-deposit box.

The fact that Peter hated banks no longer seemed relevant. She already had proof he was a liar.

After staring at the key for five minutes, she set it down and made a cup of tea. As the kettle boiled, she searched her memory for anything Peter had said that might hint at what the key was for. But it was futile. He'd done a damned good job of keeping it a secret.

She'd always thought they'd had no secrets between them.

A chill raced up her spine as she questioned how many other secrets he'd kept.

Peter went to great lengths to conceal the key, so its purpose was important. And that made it important to her. She contemplated telling Chapel, but the instant she considered it, she put a full stop to that thought. This was her secret now, and she was determined to unravel its mystery without Chapel's help.

Jiggling the bag of peppermint tea in the boiling water, she returned to the table with the mug. As she stared at the pretty key, she realized she had another problem.

Would a bank let her access the locked box?

She had no idea. On top of that, she didn't even know if the key would open something in New Orleans? If it didn't, then she had no hope of figuring out where to start.

Casting the troubling thoughts aside, she decided that first thing tomorrow morning, she'd start with the banks around town.

* * *

Charlene was up, showered, had eaten breakfast, and had done one more search of the apartment—all before the sun had even split the horizon. Once she was certain that she hadn't missed anything, she went to plan B.

She headed out the door with the precious key wrapped in a tissue in her bag. The banks were the most obvious place to start. Yet even as she walked toward the center of town, she was uncertain how to make her inquiries. After all, she had no proof of her identity.

Then again, neither had Peter . . . at least none that she was aware of.

She walked to the closest telephone booth first and contacted Chapel. He answered on the first ring, and feigning a migraine, she told him she wouldn't be in today.

He was so sympathetic that she felt horrible for lying. He even made an offer to drop by later to ensure she was okay. After she declined, they promised to touch base again in the morning.

Charlene's next call was to her job. Her attendance had been sporadic since Peter was killed. In light of everything that'd happened, she didn't think she'd be back, and she did something she'd never done before: she resigned via a phone call.

She'd handed in her notice dozens of times in her life, but always in person. Doing it over the phone just didn't seem right. Yet the tone in her boss's voice gave her the impression he was glad she'd quit. He deserved to be, with all the time off she'd been having, she was probably the most unreliable employee he'd ever had.

With the calls made, Charlene walked to her first stop, Liberty Bank. It was barely a fifteen-minute stroll from her home, but she made it in seven and then had to wait for the doors to open.

She could probably count on her fingers the number of times she'd entered a bank.

One of the joys of dealing only in cash meant she was in control of her own money, which was exactly how she liked it, although she'd never had a significant amount that would warrant opening a bank account anyway.

If her memory served her, the most money she'd ever had at any one time was when she was saving for a pair of Vans shoes that she just had to have. They were new, and Peter had tried to convince her to wait until they were out of season, but she didn't. It'd taken her five weeks of overtime to save enough extra money to buy the shoes. But once she had them, she'd worn them nearly every day for over two years.

Armed with Peter's death certificate and with forced tears brimming her eyes, she approached the first available counter. The man behind the dark mahogany desk had a bushy mustache that he'd probably worn for three decades. His hair, combed over his head in greasy clumps, added to his disheveled appearance.

As she neared him, she simultaneously read his name badge and forced back the anticipation bristling her thoughts.

"Hello, can I help you?"

"Hi. Do you have safe-deposit boxes?"

"Yes, ma'am."

Charlene fished into her bag, unzipped the secret pocket, and plucked out her precious asset. "Do you recognize this key?"

The man leaned forward to examine it, and a frown rippled his forehead. "No, ma'am, it's not one of ours. You could try Capital One across the street."

Charlene flicked a tear from her cheek. "Okay, thanks."

Hour after hour, she repeated the process. Tears produced. Key displayed. Thanked the bank official and moved on. She had no idea how many banks there were in New Orleans, but Charlene managed the challenge like she did with every difficult situation . . . by breaking it down into manageable portions.

After purchasing a map of New Orleans and a highlighter, she set about walking the streets and marking off each one as she went. Common sense told her that Peter would have chosen a bank within walking distance, so she started with the streets nearest her apartment.

It would be easier to narrow down the banks if she had a way of searching the Internet, but she didn't. She hadn't touched a computer since she'd finished school, and she'd never owned a phone, let alone one that connected to the Internet.

It was all legwork, and it was a very long day.

By the time the sun set, she was both exhausted and no closer to answers.

As much as she wanted to spend every day solving the key puzzle, she was also aware that Chapel would soon be chasing her for more information, so she decided to split her days between time with him and hours trolling the streets of NOLA.

In the end, it took nine days to visit every street on the map and all the banks, building societies, and credit unions.

She lost count at fifty.

She was at the first bank before the staff even arrived, and at the last of the day, they were shuttling her out the door at closing time. Yet every person she spoke to was more than helpful. She ate on the run, and she walked in blazing sun and pouring rain. Each night she went home, disappointed yet optimistic that she'd have an answer the next day.

Until she ran out of banks.

In the end, all she had were sore feet and a love for the people of New Orleans.

It was another week before she had a stroke of luck. It turns out that private safe-deposit box companies were a thing.

Some people didn't trust banks, Peter being one of them. She'd never seen him go into one. And she especially couldn't imagine him placing anything precious in their control. So it only made sense that he'd sought out an alternative.

Charlene couldn't believe she hadn't considered this possibility sooner.

Even so, if she hadn't seen a company advertising safe-deposit boxes on television, she would never have thought of it.

For the first time in days, she went to bed with a flicker of hope easing her into sleep.

Charlene had a skip in her step as she headed toward the center of town. Revelers from the previous night still peppered the streets, and some were passed out cold on the pavement.

Despite her and Peter's limited funds and transient lifestyle, there were only a handful of times Charlene hadn't had a solid roof over her head at night. But even on those occasions, she'd still felt safe.

She caught a streetcar to the Garden District and didn't even stop for coffee as she headed toward the building housing the company called The Vault. The building stood alone, the walls washed in blue paint and iron bars covered the windows.

She arrived at 8:20 and was surprised to see a security guard already standing outside the entrance, his feet shoulder width apart, his hands fisted at his sides, and a scowl on his face that was certain to create some serious wrinkles later in life.

Being a drifter meant Charlene was always meeting new people. She liked to think she'd mastered the art of the first greeting. Charlene could be bold or shy. Friendly or serious. Curious or aloof. She'd learned how to read people. And she could read body language.

Peter taught her about assessing situations before she entered a doorway, like where the exits were, and looking for mirrors. She was an expert at judging how many people were in a room. And her many self-defense lessons taught her how to handle herself. In class, she'd thrown many unsuspecting men over her shoulder.

The guard was at least six foot six and built like a fridge, and he sported a flattop haircut that would make any soldier proud. His no-nonsense scowl didn't falter as she approached, and she simply gave him a curt nod and pushed through the gold-trimmed doors.

A middle-aged woman with flawless ebony skin was positioned behind the counter. Her hair was braided into an intricate pattern that threaded into angular rows and culminated in a large bun on the top of her head, giving the illusion that she was a good four inches taller than she was.

When she looked up and smiled, her lovely straight teeth were as white as chalk, and she looked like she wouldn't hesitate to wrap anyone up in a big bear hug.

"How can I help you, sugar?"

Charlene slid the key over the counter. "Can you tell me if this is one of your keys?"

She'd been faking tears for days, but the second the woman nodded, confirming she did indeed recognize the key, tears of relief stung her eyes.

"Oh, come now, honey; it can't be that bad." The woman handed over a tissue.

Charlene's shoulders sagged, and she sucked in a shaky breath. "My father passed away a few weeks ago. He was, he was . . . umm . . . murdered actually. Perhaps you heard of it. He was stabbed by a woman in Café Degas."

Her eyes bulged. "Oh my, yes. I saw that on the television, and I said to my kids that I knew him. I'd met him just before it happened. Oh, you poor dear. Come now, take a seat over here." The woman came out from behind the counter, and Charlene followed her to a table at the side of the marble-lined room.

"I'm sorry." She tabbed a tissue to her cheeks.

"No need to say sorry. Let me get you some water." Her polished mules tracked her escape across the marble tiles.

Charlene removed an envelope from her bag. It contained Peter's death certificate. She'd read it when Chapel had first handed it to her. The cause of death was exsanguination.

She had to ask Chapel what it meant. Loss of blood. She'd tried desperately to stop that blood flow. Pressing her palm to the wound. Feeling the warmth ooze through her fingers. Pulling the tablecloth off and holding it to his chest. Blood seeping through the white linen.

All the while, she was screaming for help.

It seemed like a wretched dream.

Now it was reduced to one clinical word: exsanguination.

"There you go, sugar."

The woman's voice was as smooth as warm honey, gently luring Charlene back from the nightmare. "I'm sorry."

She flicked her hand. "Don't be. You've been through such a trauma. Now tell me how Louisa-Ann can help."

Charlene had noticed how the locals here sometimes spoke of themselves in the third person. That was another thing she was good at . . . recognizing idiosyncrasies unique to certain locations. She offered a lopsided smirk. "I'm hoping you can help me. I was going through my father's belongings, and I found this key. Would it be possible for me to access the contents of the box?"

"Of course, sugar."

Charlene did a double take.

"What?" Louisa-Ann frowned.

"Well, I didn't think it would be so easy."

"That's what we do here at The Vault. Make it easy."

"So, you don't need to see his death certificate or identification."

"Oh, hell no." She flicked her hand, and Charlene noticed the rows of gold rings lining her fingers.

"But how can that be safe?"

"Ahh, that's the simplicity of it. We keep the contents very secure behind our thirty-eight-ton, multiple-combination, keyed-steel door. What our customers do with their key is their business. All they need to do is pay their bills, and we'll look after their precious items forever."

Charlene forced back the burning question of how much the box had cost.

"So, all you need is a key and the locker number."

Charlene's heart lurched. "What if I don't have the number?"

Louisa-Anne chuckled. "Then I hope you aren't in a hurry." She directed Charlene to stand. "Come on. I'll show you."

She led Charlene through two sets of cast-iron gates to a giant steel door and indicated to the left-hand side of the small entry area. "Can you wait there, please?"

As Charlene shuffled aside, Louisa-Anne stepped up to a large steel door and punched a series of numbers into a concealed keypad. She turned the large wheel, and after the bolts thudded into place, she stepped back and tugged on the door. A loud sucking noise announced its release, and the door gradually yawned open.

"Here we go, sugar. Seven hundred and twelve safe-deposit boxes. Take your pick."

Charlene's jaw dropped as she scanned the room. "Can't you look up the records? Tell me which one?"

She giggled, and the sound echoed about the space. "Now that would be a breach of confidentiality."

The boxes lined all four walls of the room. Smaller boxes were at the top, and they became progressively larger toward the bottom. "I should've packed lunch," Charlene said.

Louisa-Ann's laughter had her enormous breasts wobbling. "I'm sure you'll find it in no time."

Charlene didn't share the same optimism as she approached a random box with her key. Number 441. The key only went in a quarter of the way.

"Okay, I'll leave you to it."

Charlene watched her leave and then turned back to the wall. A methodical approach was the only way to do this. So, she stepped up to number 1 and inserted her key.

Lock after lock, she pushed in her key, and the hours drifted past slowly. The time for lunch slipped by. The only breaks she took were to use the bathroom. Louisa-Ann checked in on her every hour or so with offers of water and tea.

Her back was aching, as were her fingers, when all of a sudden, the key fully entered a lock. She gasped. She'd been at it for so long, robotically moving from one to the next, that she'd begun to think it would never happen.

Holding her breath, she turned the key, and the door popped open.

She reached in and tugged out a metal container, similar in size to a shoebox. It wasn't heavy, and with her hands on the cold metal, she carried it to the table. Using the same key, she unlocked the box. Her heart thumped in her neck as she peeled open the lid.

Charlene froze.

She'd imagined there'd be letters or photos, but never in a million years could she have guessed this.

Chapter Eight

I t was days like today that had Marshall Crow hating his new career choice. Not that it was really a choice. If he did have a choice, he'd be back as a special warfare combatant, executing risky missions in treacherous environments. Working with his brothers.

Life sucked like that. One minute, he was king shit, running his own game, getting respect from everyone around him. Next minute, his body packed in and told him to shove off.

He could've handled being discharged because of injuries sustained during battle. Hell, he could've handled losing a few body parts in the process too. But to be forced to leave on account of his eyes—well, that was fucked up.

The navy had done the right thing and offered him an office job. But that was no kind of life for him. Four walls and an oak desk. No, thank you! He was born to be on the ocean. Battling the wind and currents. Sea air had filled his lungs for as long as he could remember.

That's why he'd moved a few thousand miles south, bought his own boat, and started his charter fishing business.

It wasn't the same, though. There was no respect out here. His clients figured their cash meant they were in charge. Tourists, high on life and usually high on something else, were the worst customers.

But that's what he got for choosing Key West as his home . . . tourists.

His navy pension, however, was barely enough to buy diesel. So as much as he detested the tourists, he needed them. And they seemed to be getting younger and younger. He was beginning to feel like an old man. Which was also fucked up, given he was only in his late thirties.

He tried to ignore one of his customers barfing over the side as he showed his other customer how to put the pilchards on the hook for the third time. After helping the turkey to cast his line, Marshall went to the aid of the other guy.

Thankfully turkey number two was no longer hurling chunks, but he was still leaning unsteadily over the railing and spitting into the wind. Marshall clapped him on the shoulder. "You alright there?"

"Nope."

Based on the green tinge to the man's lips, Marshall believed him. "Stay there. I'll get some water." Marshall didn't feel sorry for him. He'd warned them both not to do the third round of tequila shots. But they were young. And stupid. So why would they listen to an old sea dog like him.

Marshall slid down the seven steps to the lower deck, and just like every time he entered this space, he felt like he was home. *Miss B Hayve* was the love of his life.

He'd bought the forty-six-foot cabin cruiser three years ago from a guy who had zero respect for her. She was in dire need of some TLC. Marshall had nursed her back to her former glory with his bare hands. In turn, she'd helped nurse him back to the real world.

He'd been in murky waters before he got his shit together.

Things were good now. Well . . . most of the time.

He returned upstairs and handed the plastic cup to turkey number two. "Here you go. Just sip it."

"Oh, shit! I think I've got one."

Marshall spun to the other guy. His rod was flat-lining. He did indeed have one. Marshall strode across the bow. "Okay, this is it. Reel that sucker in." He'd thought today was going to come up dry. But if the bend in that rod was anything to go by, then they were about to score big-time. Providing the stupid turkey could land it, that is. "Nice and easy. Just like I showed you."

"Jeez, it's hard." The man's knuckles were bone white as he spun the handle.

"Steady, mate." Marshall tapped his shoulder. "You've got to coax it in or you'll lose him."

Marshall reached over and showed the guy how to use the rod to its advantage.

"That's it. Ease back on the rod, wind him in."

He was a fast learner, tipping the odds away from the fish.

Turkey number two joined their side. "Must be a big one." His lips were no longer green.

"I reckon it is." Marshall agreed.

Their grins showed how much they were enjoying the battle, and it was moments like this that made the vomiting and bitching all worth it. It'd taken Marshall five disastrous years to get over the blow life had dealt him.

Five years of wallowing in alcohol-infused self-pity.

But he'd dug himself out of that sewer pit, bought a shack on the beach and *Miss B Hayve*, and turned his life around. He tried to appreciate the good days. Sometimes those days weren't even full days. They were just moments.

When the blackfin tuna shot through the surface and the two turkeys screamed with joy, it was one of those moments.

"Holy shit! Do you see the size of that thing?" The guy with the rod was grinning like he'd scored a touchdown.

"Sure did. Don't lose him. Keep your calm."

Minute after minute, pull after pull, the guy managed to fight the fish toward them. Marshall leaned over the side with the gaff, ready to ram the hook. "Nice and easy. Don't blow it now."

The second the fish surfaced below him, Marshall hooked the tuna through the shoulder and hauled it onto the boat.

"Holy shit!" His customers whooped. "How big is it?"

"About a thirty-pounder." Marshall was impressed.

The guys clapped each other on their backs, their seasickness and hours of impatient bitching long forgotten.

"Pick it up, fellas," Marshall said. "I'll take a few photos."

The men manhandled the fish into their arms, and Marshall took about a dozen shots. This last half hour of exhilaration made the first four hours of the charter worth it.

"Alright, shall we head into shore?" he suggested.

"Shit, yeah, I need a beer." Turkey number two was obviously over his sea sickness.

Marshall left them to take more photos and climbed up to the flybridge. They were forty-five miles off shore, and he guessed they'd pull into the harbor at about four o'clock, just in time to beat the rush at Pirate Cove. Not that there was ever a rush. If there were more than two dozen people in there, he'd walk right back out again.

The turkeys were much happier on the journey home than they'd been on the journey out, and despite himself, Marshall enjoyed chatting with them about their travels.

He was surprised to learn that the thirty-one-year-olds had taken off after Hurricane Katrina had robbed them of their jobs at a theme park in New Orleans. But the pair had bounced back by wandering the world for over a decade, stopping at whatever town offered work or adventure. Or both.

Marshall fought a pang of jealousy as they rattled off some of the things they'd done.

By the time Marshall was their age, he'd already served fifteen years in the navy and was working his way up to become a navy seal. *He'd* seen a fair whack of the world too. But not like they had. Some of the rat-infested hovels he'd been to would be better served being wiped from the face of the earth.

His mind flashed to the horrors he was forced to work through after the Indian Ocean tsunami. He'd rather have been in a war zone than lived through some of that shit.

The kids were the worst. Fragile, innocent children who'd lost every single thing they knew. Their homes. Their families. Their friends. Even the clothes on their back. And the navy was supposed to help. It'd been impossible to know where to start.

He cast the horrid memories aside and concentrated on his customers retelling of their trek through Peru. Yep . . . he was jealous.

After arriving at the marina, he saw the two guys off with their prize catch filleted and bagged into meal-sized portions. Then he set about cleaning his baby. He hosed the deck, eradicating all traces of blood and sea water, paying particular attention to the side the fool had puked over.

Marshall washed the dishes and filleting gear, and sorted the fishing tackle. Then he packed up his day bag and locked up the cabin.

The sun was still blazing high on the western horizon when he jumped onto the wharf and aimed for his favorite drinking hole. Pirate Cove had seen better days. The décor was tired, and it smelled of stale ale and Cuban cigars.

But that's exactly why he liked it. You didn't pay for posh glasses, and there wasn't one fancy money-grabbing cocktail on the menu. Not that he'd order one anyway. Marshall came for the homemade lemonade and the relaxing atmosphere.

"Look who the cat dragged in." The barman greeted him with a grin and a sturdy handshake.

"Hey, Red, how's the day?"

"Same as every other day."

Marshall placed a zip lock bag on the counter. "All yours."

"Hey, thanks, man. What've we got?"

"Blackfin tuna. Ready for tonight's sushi." The turkeys wouldn't miss the small portion Marshall had carved off for Red and his missus. Besides, they had enough to feed themselves for a week or more.

"Nice. Shona's going to love you." Red was referring to his wife of thirty-one years.

"She already loves me." Marshall shot Red a cheeky grin.

"Ain't that the truth. When you gonna come around for dinner?" Red and his wife were as homey as the Waltons and notorious for feeding random people like they were stray cats. Red asked him to dinner nearly every time he graced the bar.

"Next time. I promise."

"Yeah. Yeah."

Truth was, Marshall was beyond embarrassed by what Shona had seen of him. He'd made a mess of himself a few too many times and woken to find that Shona had cleaned him up. Shona wasn't judgmental. Neither was Red.

But he couldn't forgive himself for what he'd put them through, and the damage was done. Every time he saw her, he was reminded of those dark times and the people he'd hurt. It was better that Red told her how good he was doing now.

And he was doing good. Three years, six months, and eighteen days sober. And it was getting easier each day.

Red didn't ask for Marshall's order. He already knew . . . lemonade and the best darn smoky barbecue ribs in America. And Marshall would know; he'd sampled the American staple in more places than he could count.

Marshall eased onto his favorite bar stool and huffed out a big sigh. *This was living.*

The music was subtle enough that he could hear the conversations from the dozen or so patrons dotted around the tavern. One of his pet hates was places that insisted on drowning out conversation with thumping music. If you asked him, the art of conversation was being outweighed by too many distractions. Music needn't be one of them.

His lemonade arrived, along with Red's genuine smile. "How many victims did you have today?"

Marshall huffed. "Two young guys. Had no idea what they were doing. One guy spent most of his time *feeding* the fish."

Red rolled his eyes. "Know that feeling."

Marshall had never experienced seasickness himself. But he'd seen it enough in his life to know that it was a type of hell. He'd love nothing more than to take Red out on his baby and show him a good day fishing. But it wasn't to be. They'd have to settle for good old conversation over the bar. Which was fine with him too.

Red shifted away to serve a couple of young blondes who'd entered the bar.

The occasional tourist managed to find their way into Pirate Cove. Marshall didn't blame them. The bar probably had the best view in all of Key West. But it wasn't your typical tourist destination, so they rarely stayed long.

He'd never seen these women before, so he pegged them as tourists, which meant they'd probably be leaving right after this first drink. Pity . . . they were nice to look at.

Marshall didn't get up close and personal with many women these days. He'd been in love once, but that was a whole other life time ago. But he still saw Leyna and her folks each time he went to Cuba, and it was nice to know Leyna had moved on from their failed engagement.

The blondes took their glasses of wine and sat at one of the bar tables at the full-length windows overlooking the ocean. In the distance, a fleet of trawlers was making its way out to sea, no doubt hopeful for a lucrative evening haul.

From his vantage point, Marshall could take in the lovely tourists, the ocean, and the front door, and via the mirror behind the bar, he could see just about every other aspect of the tavern. Exactly how he liked it.

His smoky barbecue ribs arrived, and Marshall didn't miss the glances from all the other patrons. The smell alone was enough to have people lining up to order their own serving.

Once, when Red had drunk too many Havana rums, he'd told Marshall his secret. Both sweet and smoked paprika, and good old Basil Hayden's Kentucky whiskey. But the final key to his best ribs was in the cooking. Eight hours in Red's homemade smoker and basting every half hour with his thick hickory sauce was the trick.

It was a labor of love for Red. Yet it paid off. He usually sold out each night, and the locals always came back for more.

Marshall's current nemesis, Warren McVie, stood up from the corner of the room, and when he licked his fingers and slicked his greasy hair over his ears, Marshall groaned. He knew what was coming . . . trouble. Trouble had a way of following Marshall. And it seemed the more he tried to avoid it, the more it snaked its way toward him.

Warren's exaggerated saunter confirmed he'd started his drinking early today. Marshall had already had a few run-ins with Warren, given that the two of them were competing for the same clientele. But Warren was a cowboy, and his shifty eyes and greedy palms were his downfall. Tourists, no matter how naïve, usually saw through his scheming techniques.

Marshall gnawed the meat from a bone, licked his fingers, and reluctantly wiped the rest of the tasty sauce on his napkin. As much as he was enjoying the feast, he had no doubt he'd be needing his hands pretty soon.

Warren eased up to the two women and must've missed the cringes on their faces, because his dumb grin remained. "Hey, ladies, how're you enjoying our view?"

"Well, it *was* good, until this second." They giggled.

Clearly Warren didn't get the hint, because he placed his arm around the back of one woman as he leaned on her chair and tilted toward them. "I could show you lovelies around town if you like."

"No, thanks." The taller blonde's answer was swift.

"Oh, come on, it'll be fun." Warren did some weird hip-thrusting thing that had both the girls easing back.

Marshall couldn't hold back a moment longer. "Leave 'em alone, Warren."

Warren glared at him. "Stay out of it, Crow."

"The ladies said no."

The blondes were looking at him now, and Marshall couldn't tell if they were nervous or pleased with his assistance. But he was involved now, so if Warren didn't back off, Marshall would have to make him. It wouldn't be the first time.

Warren turned back to the women. "Can I at least buy you a drink?"

"No, thanks. We're fine."

"It's just a drink."

For fifteen-odd years, Marshall had been assessing situations for possible danger or harm to others. He never thought his skills would come in handy once he was dismissed from the navy.

But they did, more often than he'd ever thought possible.

When trouble followed him, it usually ended in blood.

And not normally his, though that didn't worry him either. "Warren. Fuck off and leave 'em alone." Marshall stood, showing Warren he meant business.

Warren had never learned when to back down. And when he turned and squared off, Marshall sighed. He tried to portray annoyance at Warren's decision, but in reality, he didn't mind getting his hands dirty when the reason was right.

Out the corner of his eye, Marshall saw two things. One was Red moving closer to the situation, although Marshall assumed it was only so he had a better vantage point, not because he was worried.

The other thing he saw were Ernie and Buck standing up from their booth at the back of the bar. Warren's twin brothers were just as stupid as he was.

Marshall pointed at the beauty-challenged siblings. "Stay out of it, you two."

"Why don't you stay out of it, Crow?" Ernie barked across the room.

"'Cause the ladies don't want Warren's attention."

"Well, let 'em tell him themselves."

Marshall resisted a chuckle at his stupidity. "They already did, dipshit."

Ernie clenched his fists and took another two steps forward. Marshall shook his head. Three on one would normally be a lopsided fight. But Marshall was six foot six, weighed two hundred and twenty pounds and had made a career of getting people to stand down.

The closest these three had ever come to hand-to-hand combat was probably arm wrestling over who would pay for the last beer. Add to the mix that they were scrawny and undernourished and no doubt had a belly full of grog. The best decision for them would be to walk away.

But they wouldn't.

Buck still had a gap in his mouth from where Marshall had knocked his tooth out a few months ago. It probably explained why he was easing in behind his twin.

"Hey, guys, we just want a quiet drink, and then we'll go. Okay?" The blonde closest to the door stood and eased back from the table with her drink in hand. Her friend, however, remained seated. When she lifted her glass and sipped her wine, she seemed quite comfortable with the trouble brewing around them.

Marshall wanted to ask the women to leave, but not only was it not his place to do so, he actually thought they might be enjoying the attention. Drink and a show . . . by the look of the three brothers they were about to get it. "See, Warren?" Marshall said. "They don't need you hanging around."

"Well, I was fine until you got involved." Warren made two mistakes. One was taking a step closer to Marshall; the second was shifting his eyes to his brothers, indicating he needed their help.

If he planned on doing what Marshall assumed he was about to do, then he absolutely did need their help.

Marshall had a sip of his lemonade, which was extra sweet today, and as he did, he assessed where everyone else in the room was. The last thing he needed was collateral damage. He'd never made that mistake before and intended to maintain his record.

Warren made the stupid move of stepping closer while he thought Marshall was distracted. But he wasn't. Marshall's eyes might be color blind, but his peripheral vision was excellent.

Marshall turned to face Warren and saw the very second the dipshit tipped over the edge of hesitation. His twitchy lip gave away his intentions as though he'd fired a warning shot. Warren dove across the distance.

Marshall planted his feet and was ready to plough his fist into the dipshit's solar plexus the second it'd make maximum impact. Warren's momentum and Marshall's driven fist robbed Warren of his ability to breathe.

Marshall then stole the stunned look from Warren's face with a quick jab to the bridge of his nose.

Warren fell to his knees and flopped face-first onto the weathered wooden floor.

Ernie announced his charge with a wild scream, and all Marshall had to do was dodge his flaccid body and use Ernie's impetus to shove him into the solid oak bar. He too fell in a silent heap onto the floor.

Marshall turned to the third brother. Buck's bottom lip quivered, and Marshall shook his head. "Don't do it, Buck!"

Buck's wild eyes shot from one brother to the next, then up to Marshall. Without a word, he strode to his table, chugged his beer, and then raced out the front door.

Marshall inclined his head at the tourists, who blinked at him with wide eyes and dropped jaws. "Enjoy your quiet drink, ladies."

He turned from them, stepped over Warren's legs, and prepared to tuck back into the best smoky barbecue ribs in the world.

Chapter Nine

C harlene's heart thumped out an erratic beat as she stared at the contents of the safe-deposit box. With clammy hands, she lifted out the videocassette and placed it aside. But it was the rolls of cash beneath it that had her mind screaming.

Her heart pounded . . . in her chest, in her neck, coursing blood too quickly through her veins. Her head swooned, and as she gripped the table, the room swam around her. Dizziness threatened to engulf her. To close her eyes would be so simple. Block it all out. Pretend it wasn't happening. The temptation was strong. Too strong.

But she clenched her jaw and fought the easy escape.

Forcing herself to focus, she picked up the videocassette and examined it. It contained no labels to indicate what was on it, and her mind whizzed as she considered that it might have all her answers. Although she didn't have a video player, somehow she'd figure out how to watch it before the night was out. That was the easy part.

What to do with the money was another problem.

Chapel's comments came tumbling into her brain. *People who don't use bank accounts always stash their money somewhere. Under a mattress. In the wardrobe.*

As far as she knew, they'd never had surplus cash. Peter had taught her how to be frugal. They budgeted every cent.

She hated that her mind skipped to Peter being involved in criminal activities. He wasn't like that. Yet the doubts were there. The floodgates had been opened. There was no stopping the thoughts now. All the certainties she had about Peter were cracking like solid ice in tepid water. He kept secrets. He told lies. He was an armed soldier. He stashed cash.

From this day forward, Peter would be two separate people in her mind. The one she loved and the one she didn't know at all. Once again, she wondered if her whole life was a lie.

She was of two minds over what to do with the rolls of cash. She herself had about seventy dollars to her name until she found another job. She didn't stash cash. It was either in her purse or she didn't have it.

The seventy bucks should last her about three weeks max. The rent was paid for another month, and there was already enough food in the fridge to feed her for two weeks at least. She didn't have a car or a phone. And she didn't need medicine or clothes. Public transport would be the largest expense.

One thing she was confident in was finding work. The longest she'd ever been without an income was four days. She wasn't fussy. As long as she was busy and the work was regular, she was happy. She'd never even worried much about the hourly wage. That might change now that she was on her own.

But before she even considered getting back to her normal routine, she needed answers.

She picked up a roll of cash and flicked the rubber band.

The questions were piling up like sand in an hourglass, and time was ticking away with it. To get answers, she needed time. Going back to work would erode precious time. To have time, she needed cash. Without any further hesitation, she stashed the rolls into her handbag. She would need to carry the videocassette.

She put the safe-deposit box back in compartment 669, locked it, and then, with her bag tucked under her elbow and the video in her hand, she walked out through the vault's thirty-eight-inch steel door.

Louisa-Ann turned to her with a welcoming grin. "Oh, hey, sugar, how did you do? Find what you wanted?"

Charlene didn't know how to answer. There were so many things she'd hoped to find, but she'd found exactly the opposite.

"I'm always fascinated by what people put in these boxes." Louisa-Ann must have seen Charlene's confusion. "When people stop paying for them, and all hope is lost, we have to drill them open. If we're lucky, there's something valuable that we can auction off to recoup our costs. But most of the time, it's just random stuff like photos and letters. The occasional will. You know, one time . . ." She flicked her hand. "Oh, listen to me rambling on. Looks like you found a video. Maybe some cute home movies on there?"

Charlene's eyes stung with tears. Home videos would be a nice relief. "I don't know. We don't have a player, though, so I'll have to get one first."

Louisa-Ann's eyes bounced from the cassette to Charlene and back again. "Say, how about you come over to my place for dinner? I'm cooking up my famous shrimp gumbo."

Charlene blinked at her, hardly able to believe this stranger's generosity. "Oh, no, I couldn't."

"Hell yes you can. Who you got to go home to anyway?"

She had a point there. "Are you sure?"

"Of course, sugar. You can eat your fill, then I'll set you up to watch the video in private."

One thing Charlene had learned in her travels was that most people were incredibly generous. It was part of the fun of being a drifter: she never knew where she might end up or who she'd spend time with. "Thank you so much. It's very kind of you."

Louisa-Ann flicked her hand. "It's the least I can do considering all you've been through. Now here's my address." She reached to a notepad. "Come around any time after six."

"Thank you." Charlene reached for the note, then passed the fancy skeleton key across the counter. "I've finished with this."

Louisa-Ann's perfectly trimmed eyebrows bounced up. "You won't be needing it anymore?"

She shook her head. Charlene had no plans of ever returning.

"But you're paid up for five months."

"Oh." Five months? That was a specific term. She wondered if there was a reason for that.

"Maybe I can talk to the boss about giving you a refund. Given the circumstances. You've only had it for six weeks."

"Oh, that's very kind of you. Thank you."

"No promises, sugar."

"I know. I'm just grateful that you'd ask."

They said their good-byes, with Charlene promising to see her again in a few hours. She went straight home and dumped the contents of her bag on the kitchen table. The cash rolls spilled out, some rolling to the floor.

She glanced at the clock and noted she had two hours before she'd have to leave for Louisa-Ann's, and she had no intention of shirking that invitation. With a hot cup of tea at her side, she started counting the cash. As she released each rubber band, the cash curled back up, making her wonder how long Peter had been storing the rolls.

When she finished, she sat back, sipping her cold tea and staring at the curled-up notes. Five thousand, six hundred and thirty dollars. There had been no system to the rolls; each one had a different value and combination of notes.

For some reason, this pleased her.

In her mind, she convinced herself that if Peter was involved in anything sinister, then the notes would be in large denominations.

It was a stupid rationalization really.

Then again, to still be considering Peter as innocent was stupid.

She stacked the cash again, keeping all like notes together this time. Then, without any better idea, she wrapped them in tinfoil and had a nervous giggle as she put them in the freezer. If Chapel did a surprise search now, she'd be in deep trouble.

As she showered, her mind played ping-pong with all the events since Peter's murder. It was impossible to block it all out. With her mind and body on autopilot, she managed to change her clothes and get back out the door on time.

Louisa-Ann's home was in the French Quarter, and it was typical of the homes in that area. The Creole-style town house had whitewashed walls tinted pale pink and an elaborately decorated ironwork balcony.

Charlene passed beneath a grand wrought-iron arched gateway that led through to a central courtyard. Centered among the rough paving stones was a disused well that was topped with a metal grill and potted plants.

She knocked on a turquoise door marked with a large copper 7, and Louisa-Ann opened it moments later with a huge NOLA greeting. "There you are, sugar, come on in. Don't mind my crazy family; they're not shy."

Charlene was led up the stairs to a room filled with knickknacks, photos, and pages decorated with crayon drawings. Two kids were kneeling on the floor, coloring at the coffee table.

Pangs of sorrow skipped across her heart at the sight.

She and Peter had spent many hours drawing when she was a child, even though her skills barely went beyond being able to create a stick man. Peter, on the other hand, had been very talented.

Delicious aromas filled the room with a comforting homely feel and had her stomach growling, reminding her she hadn't eaten for twelve hours. Louisa-Ann introduced her two daughters and her husband, and they all welcomed her as if she was family.

As dinner was served and she sat with the boisterous family, she allowed herself to forget all her recent horrors for a while. The kids were loud and funny, and for the first time in weeks, she found herself laughing.

Louisa-Ann's gumbo was the most delicious meal she had eaten in a very long time—rich, creamy, packed with chunky ingredients, and full of flavor. "This is delicious. I've never tasted anything like it."

"People line up for my missus's gumbo." Louisa-Ann's husband spoke with pride.

"I bet they do."

Louisa-Ann feigned surprise and waved their comments away. "Alright, you lot, us women have got some things to do."

Charlene allowed Louisa-Ann to guide her from the table and into a room at the back of the house. Kids' toys were strewn everywhere, and the room was a kaleidoscope of color and creativity. Charlene couldn't remember a time in her life when she'd had a room this interesting.

Louisa-Ann indicated for her to sit; then she popped the videocassette into the player and made sure it was working. She paused it and handed over the remote. "There you go, sugar. Take your time." Louisa-

Ann placed her hand on Charlene's shoulder for a brief second before she left the room and closed the door.

Charlene inhaled a deep, calming breath and let it out slow and steady. Then she eased forward on the chair and pressed PLAY. The footage didn't have any lead-up. It opened on a woman with a large microphone at her lips, halfway through a song. Around her, a dozen or so women danced about wearing colorful, flowing dresses.

The camera moved from one dancer to the next and back to the singer. It didn't seem to focus on any one person. Although she'd heard the song somewhere before, she didn't know it well. The singer finished to thundering applause, and when the thick velvet curtain was closed to conceal the entertainers, a man walked onto the stage.

Charlene's heart lurched. The man on the stage was Peter, and he spoke to the crowd in Spanish. After a brief introduction, he began singing. His voice was extraordinary, and Charlene stared at the screen, hardly able to believe what she was seeing and hearing. Never had she heard Peter sing. Not once. Not even in the shower.

What the hell?

His voice was magnificent, and when he finished, the crowd gave him a standing ovation. The video jolted to another singer, but this time whoever was behind the camera was focusing on one of the dancers, rather than the singer.

The woman taking all the camera's attention was young—in her early twenties, Charlene guessed. She was beautiful, with flawless olive skin, silky auburn hair, and gorgeous dark eyes rimmed with long lashes.

The camera zoomed in, and Charlene's breath caught in her throat.

She paused the video and studied the woman on the screen.

It could be the woman who'd plunged the knife into Peter's chest.

She was much younger, though, and she was smiling and happy— the complete opposite of the woman she'd met. But Charlene's heart raced all the same. It'd all happened so quickly, she couldn't be sure. The picture wasn't perfect either.

She pressed PLAY again and watched the video to the end. It was about twenty minutes long, and once it went to fuzzy gray static, she rewound to the beginning and watched again, looking for the woman.

The video was the first clue she had to the killer. Yet she was still no closer to working out who she was.

The door cracked open, jolting Charlene from the footage. She fumbled with the remote, trying to stop it.

"Oh, that looks wonderful. Is it your parents?"

The screen had stopped on a couple doing a duet. Peter was the man, but she didn't know who the woman was. Charlene cleared her throat. "Yes." She lied. It was easier than saying it was the man who'd kidnapped her and not a relative at all. Charlene nearly chuckled at the absurdity of it. If what she was going through was in a book or movie, it would be regarded as fanciful fiction.

"How nice that you found this. Now . . . would you like some tea?"

"Oh, no, thank you." Charlene stood. "I've taken enough of your time."

It took some convincing to get Louisa-Ann to allow her to leave, but Charlene eventually made it downstairs into the courtyard again. But now she was also carrying a take-away container filled to the brim with Louisa-Ann's famous shrimp gumbo.

Instead of going home, she headed toward Bourbon Street. It was the street that never slept. Glitzy lights flashed and twinkled, trying to lure people into overflowing bars and crowded fast-food joints. Everyone around her seemed to be in a state of alcohol-induced euphoria. It was wonderful to see, yet instilled in her a deep sense of jealousy.

These were the types of experiences that she and Peter had lived for. Every town had something unique to offer, often surprising both of them.

Like the time they'd arrived at Chincoteague Island. It was the day before the annual pony swim. Neither of them had had any idea of the festivity until their landlady at the time had mentioned it.

She'd been looking forward to coming to New Orleans. Most of the towns they'd lived in were tiny in comparison. Many didn't even have a movie theater. Their destinations were always chosen out of a necessity for work. But as she thought about it, she realized that might not have been Peter's major motivation to move. Not when they both found work so easily.

Peter moved because he wanted to. Not because he needed to.

The more she thought about it, the more she considered that he was running from someone. And each time that video had come with them.

She couldn't understand why he'd hidden the videocassette. It didn't show anything incriminating. Not that she noticed, anyway. And he couldn't have been embarrassed by it; his singing was excellent. She contemplated showing it to Chapel. It would be the smart thing to do. But she quickly dismissed that thought.

There was obviously something on the video Peter didn't want her to see.

She just had to figure out what.

Halfway along Bourbon Street, she turned into a side street, nodded at the security guard standing at the front of the brightly lit shop, and then entered Second Treats, a pawn shop she'd walked past when she was handing out her résumé.

After a quick glance around, confirming that she was alone, she strode to the counter barricaded behind glass, and waited for the man to stop watching a television set up high on his desk. She was certain he was ignoring her, yet she gave him a moment to redeem himself. It was at least a minute before he looked her way.

"Oh, sorry. You must have snuck in." When he smiled at her, her initial opinion of him changed in a heartbeat, and she was annoyed with herself. She normally gave people the benefit of the doubt. Finding out about Peter's deceit and lies was changing her, and she didn't like it one bit.

She grinned at the man as she waited for him to hobble up to the other side of the glass. "Hello. Do you sell video players?"

"You bet ya. Got a dozen or so over there. They all work. I've checked 'em out myself." He moved back, and assuming he was coming out from behind the barricaded gate, she held up her hand.

"Please, stay there. I only need the cheapest one." She strolled to the shelving he'd pointed at, and the price was the only thing she needed to look at. Twenty dollars was the winner. Ignoring the dust, she carried it the counter. "That was easy."

He glanced at the machine and then pulled out the drawer at his side. "I have the remote here. Just hang on a sec." He flicked through a series of yellow envelopes; Charlene was impressed with how organized he was.

She pushed the twenty dollars through the gap in the glass, and he, in turn, handed her the remote. "If it don't work, just bring it on back."

"Okay. I will. Thank you."

It was nearing eleven o'clock when she arrived home, but she had no intention of going to sleep. She put the kettle on the stove, then carried the video player to the television. Most houses they'd lived in already had their electrical equipment set up.

But if anything was required, it was usually Peter who did it.

Yet within a few minutes, she had the machine lights registering that it was working, and she was impressed with how easy it was.

With a cup of tea on the coffee table, she hit PLAY on the video again.

Each time she watched it, she concentrated on different aspects. Peter. The other singers. The dancers.

That woman.

The fourth time she watched the footage, she concentrated more on the background rather than on the stars of the show. Behind the stage was a large screen, and it showing a series of photos.

The more she watched, the more she realized the photos were a visual journey of each of the singers' lives, showing their progress from young teenagers to their current status.

Her effort to scrutinize Peter's life journey was hampered by the grainy footage. But from what she could tell, there was nothing important in those background stills.

She had nothing.

She couldn't even work out the country where the video was filmed.

By the time Charlene crawled into bed, she was both exhausted and no closer to answers.

Chapter Ten

Noah hated going home. Actually, that was a lie. It wasn't his home that he hated. Lord, no! The sprawling three-story apartment overlooking Central Park was one of the most pristine residences in New York City.

What he hated was the people who lived there. His wife and his two children. Porsha had been beautiful when they'd first married. Some would probably say she still was. But Noah knew beauty, and Porsha was well past her used-by date.

But as much as he hated to admit it, he needed her.

Porsha was the only child of Winston Harold Bollinger III, the *New York Times* executive editor-in-chief and arguably one of the most influential people in New York. That also made him one of the most important, yet the most dangerous, men in Noah's life.

It was because of him that Noah had received his first lucky break in the early nineties. Winston had put Noah in the limelight. And that front-page article had skyrocketed him up the law-firm totem pole. Winston had been instrumental in many of Noah's major career-making cases too and had ensured he made front-page news on a regular basis.

Winston had threatened him once. Just once. But that was enough. It'd been over a few glasses of expensive brandy in Winston's plaque-lined office, and he'd delivered it with the needle-sharp precision, insidious calm, and unblinking eyes that'd made him one of the most revered yet feared authorities in the country.

Noah had been so rocked by the threat he'd suffered a nosebleed later that night.

The editor-in-chief's threat had been simple. If Noah ever embarrassed, shamed, or divorced Porsha, Winston would make front-page news out of Noah for a whole different story. He'd then stated that Noah's past might be gone, but it certainly was not forgotten.

Noah had no idea what Winston knew. And given what he'd done over two decades ago, he didn't want to find out.

Instead, he sucked back the antipathy that being with his wife produced and pretended they were a happy family. He was an actor, after all.

It wasn't a complete loss. His clientele seemed to trust him once they learned of his thirty-year marriage. Not that it stopped them from jumping his bones when the opportunity arose.

If Porsha knew of the affairs, she'd never said. Even if she did, she wouldn't have the guts to leave him. She needed him too. His profession and income allowed her to live the life she'd become accustomed to.

She was the poster child for "lifestyles of the rich and famous." Exclusive custom-made jewelry. A multimillion-dollar art collection. Invites to fancy parties, a personal fashion designer, a private jet. She also had her personal hairdresser and beauty therapist. Not that it helped. Not when the palette was beyond help already.

Ironically, she'd actually helped in securing a decent portion of Noah's business. Being a woman, Porsha reached inner circles that Noah could never penetrate, and consequently, she was one of the first to know when a marriage was on the rocks. Exactly the scenarios he lived for.

"May I get you something, sir?" Richard, his butler, greeted him at the elevator to take his coat.

"A brandy, please. In my office."

"Yes, sir. Right away."

Noah strode to the entrance to the living room, pushing through the double doors that opened to a space the size of two basketball courts that was furnished in all things white. A groan caught in his throat at the sight of his daughter and wife standing near the freestanding fireplace. One look was enough to know they were fighting.

He shouldn't have been surprised. Barely a day went by without some major disaster in Crystal's life. Some days he wished his daughter was like his son . . . so high on dope that he could barely utter a word, let alone an aggressive one.

But that made him dangerous too. I

f the paparazzi got hold of that, it'd be an editor's wet dream. And that was why Noah made his son's drug supply easy to come by and his bedroom a young man's paradise.

"Daddy." Crystal turned toward him, her eyes burning with fury.

Noah cringed at the reference. He still didn't consider himself a father.

The children had been Porsha's idea.

Crystal blazed her icy blue eyes up at him. "I was invited to the Brooklyn Museum Gala first. Me! Not her." She aimed her manicured red fingernail at her mother.

He had no idea what the implications of this apparently disastrous clash meant, so he waited. Noah liked to think that he'd instilled some of his infinite debating skills in his daughter over the years, but she'd practically been born with them.

She'd been a master manipulator since she'd spat out her pacifier at twelve months, and he was simultaneously proud and frustrated whenever she managed to outwit him.

"We can't both go." She waggled her head as if that impacted on her argument.

He waited. She was yet to elaborate on her reasoning.

"I've been championing the Brooklyn fund-raising committee since February. I'm their spokeswoman, and I've been invited to make a speech on stage. It's my charity, not hers. She has no right to be there."

"Surely anyone has a right to be there. It's a charity ball." He tilted his head in a signature move that'd been known to make women quiver. His daughter didn't fall for his charms, though. "And you still haven't explained why."

"Daddy!" Her eyes blazed. "This isn't the time for one of your stupid lessons."

Again, he waited.

She huffed and fisted her hands on her hips. "I'm representing the Montgomery family at the annual gala dinner. Me. It shouldn't look like I'm being chaperoned by my mother."

He turned his gaze to Porsha.

She rolled her eyes. "I've been to the gala ball every year since the charity foundation started."

Sighing, he leaned in to his daughter's ear. "You will not win this fight. The best you can do is outshine your mother." He slipped his wallet from his back pocket and, avoiding Porsha's view, handed over his credit card. "You know it's what you do best."

Crystal's shoulders slumped, yet the devious look in her eyes gave him a feeling she'd expected this result. She released an exaggerated growl and stomped toward the stairs, no doubt to lock herself in her oversized bedroom.

"What did you say to her?"

"I told her you had the upper hand."

A dimple punctuated the folds of Porsha's left cheek as she smiled. "Good. You'd think at twenty-six, she'd have learned that."

"I think she has learned it, dear. That's the problem. She doesn't feel the need to just do as she's told."

"Well, if she doesn't like it, she can move out."

It was his turn to huff. They both knew that wasn't going to happen anytime soon. Not when Crystal's bedroom was a luxurious haven overlooking Manhattan that her parents paid for.

Noah doubted his children would ever move out.

Porsha strolled toward him, and the silky fabric of her nightgown failed miserably at hiding the lumps and bumps that existed beneath it. Reaching up on her toes, she pecked his lips. "Thank you."

"Just doing my job."

"Not really." His gut churned when he looked down at her. Porsha had that look in her eyes. Lust. He should consider himself lucky to have a wife who still had such a healthy libido. But he didn't. Porsha didn't arouse him one bit. Not when he had women at his disposal that were stunning in looks, physique, and sexual abilities.

But he wouldn't deny her. The last thing he wanted to do was give her any idea that he wasn't interested. He allowed her to push her hand into his.

"I hoped you'd come to bed with me tonight." She put on the hideous voice that he assumed she thought was sexy.

Swallowing back the disgust, he gave her the seductive eyes that apparently had attracted her to him in the first place. "Really? What do you have in mind?" It was a little game they played that had his stomach heaving. But he reminded himself that he was an actor at the top of his game. *Faking it* was what he was good at. And he'd been faking it with Porsha for years.

"You'll have to come and find out." She swung her silky belt and turned her abundant hip to him.

"Okay, babe. Give me a minute to clean up. I'll see you up there."

She waddled away, and he reflected on his business partner who complained nonstop about his wife's desolate sex drive. It was the only time Noah envied Pearce.

It was impossible to comprehend how a woman of Porsha's size, with such blatant lack of physical fitness, could have such strong sexual urges. He was the first to admit it'd been what'd attracted her to him in the first place. She'd been a wild woman in the bedroom. Some would consider that she still was. It was her body that obliterated his attraction to her.

But he had to do it.

He took a long shower, hoping she'd have gone to asleep by the time he made it to the bedroom. With the towel wrapped around his hips, he padded across the plush carpet and eased open the door.

But his wish wasn't granted.

Porsha was naked except for a see-through negligee that failed to hide anything. If he'd had an erection it'd would've been rendered flaccid at the sight.

"What do we have here?" he feigned sexual allure.

"Your little honey cup."

He forced the distaste from his mind at her reference to the nickname he'd given her back when she was worthy. It was times like this when his acting skills came fully into play.

Noah was an expert at sex. He'd done it thousands of times with probably hundreds of women. But there was only ever one woman who'd truly satisfied his needs. That need for ultimate power. She'd been no match for his strength, but she'd fought like a demon when he'd held her down and raped her. The hatred in her eyes had made him the hardest he'd ever been in his life.

As Porsha rode on top of him, her flesh wobbling in hideous waves as she achieved her own climax, he reached up and clutched his hands around her neck.

Usually she pulled his fingers away. But this time she didn't. It'd be so easy to squeeze. Just like he'd done twenty-two years ago. His erection throbbed at the memory. The power was like nothing in the world. It placed him in a unique class. A powerful, untouchable class. It was just a shame he could never tell anyone. That secret would go with him to the grave.

His fingers gripped tighter, and Porsha's eyes snapped open.

Her hands went to his. "Hey."

He tightened his grip, and his manhood grew greater, thicker, harder, throbbing to a powerful beat.

"Stop it." Porsha bent his finger stub back, snapping him from his ecstasy.

She slapped him across the face, and when she tried to roll off, he grabbed her and rolled her over. There was no malice in her fight. In fact, she giggled as he eased up to her rump and slapped her abundant derrière.

He closed his eyes, blocking out his reality, and as he took his wife from behind, he imagined it was the Cuban woman. Silky olive skin. Supple flesh. Young muscular physique. Killer glare. Jaw clenched and hatred burning in her eyes. It was the only way he'd reach a climax, but as much as it wasn't amazing for him, judging by the groans from his wife, it was for her.

When it was over, Porsha nuzzled into the crook of his arm and trailed her fingers up and down his torso. She was completely oblivious to how easy it would've been for him to strangle her. Like crushing an empty beer can.

When she began snoring, Noah wished he had.

Chapter Eleven

W hen Chapel advised Charlene that the coroner had finished with Peter's body, she'd initially had no idea of the implications of that statement. She'd never discussed her father's wishes with him.

Death wasn't a topic they'd ever spoken about.

The closest she'd come to it was when they were in Cumberland, Wisconsin. One of their neighbors had taken a tumble with his horse, and the stallion had to be put down. Charlene had cried for a week, while their neighbor hadn't even shed a tear. Yet she knew he'd loved that horse.

Her father had sat her down and explained that every living thing would one day die. It was how they lived that mattered. That horse had lived a wonderful life with an owner who'd loved him. To put the horse down when he was in pain was the most loving thing their neighbor could have done. The horse was cremated in the biggest bonfire Charlene had ever seen, and she'd seen her share of bonfires.

Her father never owned anything of value, so she was of two minds as to whether she should give him a parting asset in the form a tombstone. On the other hand, he probably would've hated the wasted money.

Charlene trekked from one funeral parlor to the next and was both shocked at the cost involved to send someone off and grateful that she'd found the money in Peter's secret box.

New Orleans was built on a swamp, which meant people couldn't actually be buried. Well, they could, but they would eventually float to the surface. That had happened to many of the ancient caskets in the wake of Hurricane Katrina.

As a consequence, the deceased were "buried" aboveground in stone crypts or mausoleums. Charlene was given a tour of New Orleans's most famous cemetery, St. Louise Cemetery, which was also a major tourist attraction.

At first, she couldn't understand why anyone would want to tour such a morbid place, but it wasn't long before she was captivated by its history and elaborate structures.

What had shocked her was the cost.

To bury someone there, they had to first decompose in an aboveground "oven" for a year. Only then would their remains be transferred to a crypt. It cost nearly eight thousand dollars for the burial, and then just as much to maintain the crypt each year.

She thanked the woman for the tour and quickly hightailed it out of there. In the end, she decided on having her father cremated in a cardboard box. It sounded terrible, but the saleswoman "sold" her on the eco-friendly aspects of the cardboard cremation capsule and the price.

When the day of the service arrived, angst and sorrow filled the same space in her heart. Images of the man she knew before the attack and the man she had come to learn about afterward flipped across her mind like cards in a tarot deck. Each image was a polar opposite to the other.

When she was allowed a moment alone with the body, the undertaker offered a smile that looked like all the muscles in his face were failing, then slunk behind the velvet curtain that separated her from the crowd gathering for the next service.

Peter didn't have a crowd to send him off. No family. No friends. No former coworkers or bosses. Not even the detectives who thought they knew him better than she did.

It was shocking to reduce a life down to a single cardboard box. That was Peter's legacy. Ultimate freedom. *Apparently.*

Charlene felt far from free. She was trapped.

Trapped in a weird dimension that thrived on unanswered questions.

Thrived on twisting what she thought was the truth and giving it a whole new, sinister angle.

Thrived on subjecting her to sleepless nights and troubled daydreams.

Alone with her cold thoughts, she began to cry. She had assumed she'd exhausted all her tears. But evidently not. She let them flow unabated down her cheeks and forced her brain to think of all the good times.

Her mind drifted to the two of them bathing in the mineral springs that lined the main street of Sulphur, Oklahoma. She'd giggled nonstop as Peter had pretended to know every person in town and invented whacky, made-up names and even more hilarious career choices for everyone who walked by.

They might not have had any assets to their names, but they were rich in fun and adventure. Staring at the cardboard box containing the body of the man she'd known as her father, she realized he'd probably be happy with her choice of burial for him. He'd had nothing for as long as she'd known him. He would go out with nothing too.

She leaned over, kissed the varnished cardboard box, and fingering the tears from her cheeks, she waked away.

Feeling a headache throbbing behind her eyes, she walked to the nearest phone booth and called Detective Chapel. She hadn't spoken to him in over a week.

Why would she?

The last three conversations she'd had with him were the same. They had nothing further to report. No new evidence. The murder investigation had gone stale. He was still working on her kidnap theory, though, and had sought help from international sources.

She hadn't shown him the videocassette. As Louisa-Ann had said, it was just a home video, and although she'd viewed it about two dozen times, she hadn't seen anything to help with either her past or Peter's. The only additional detail she had was that Peter had been an excellent singer.

Each time she'd watched the woman in the video, she became more doubtful that she was Peter's killer. Even though, based on Peter's age in the footage, the recording had been taken about thirty years ago, there was something about the woman that wasn't quite right. The angle of her jaw. The shape of her nose. It was something, but she couldn't figure out what.

The last thing she wanted to give Chapel was a false lead.

She arrived home and succumbed to the gnawing in her stomach by making a ham-and-cheese toasted sandwich for lunch. With a cup of tea and the steaming sandwich, she sat in front of the television.

Resisting the urge to watch the video yet again, she grabbed the remote and began flicking through the channels. Music blared from the speakers, and her heart slammed into her ribs at the scene on the television.

It was the same club that was on her video.

Ramping up the volume, she nudged forward and stared at the screen. She had no way to record it, so she forced her brain to block out what she'd done all morning and focus on the now. A male singer was on a microphone, strutting up and down a central stage that divided the crowd in two. Behind him, young women danced in colorful dresses.

It was almost identical to the footage she had of Peter. Even the song was the same. The notion that she was dreaming skipped across her brain, until the show broke for a commercial.

Charlene used the break to grab a notepad and pen, ready to jot down anything that would help her recall. The show returned with a logo in the corner announcing it as a National Geographic program. Scripting along the bottom detailed that the footage was of *Legendarios del Guajirito*, a traditional singing and dancing show in Havana, Cuba.

She scribbled down the name and underlined Cuba three times.

Cuba! Adrenalin coursed through her veins. Her fingers tingled. *This was it. Finally, a clue.* Her mind dashed to Peter. It was hard to believe the coincidence that on the day he was buried she received a significant clue.

A wise old owl always knows.

Shoving the timely saying aside, she focused on the television. The footage shifted to a man with a microphone; the scripting announced him as Mr. Carter Logan, National Geographic photographer.

"The Buena Vista Social Club is perfect for tourists looking for the musical nirvana made famous in Havana in the 1950s. Every night it's like they're playing their very first concert. It's vibrant and fresh. Natural. They feed off the audience, giving the energized crowd a feel for the Cuba of old.

"Most of the legends are over sixty and, wait for it, the star of the show is eighty-one-years old. Eighty-one! And still bringing the house down."

As the footage shifted from Mr. Logan to a drummer doing an energetic drum solo, Charlene knew she had to get herself down to Cuba.

The credits begin to scroll up the screen, and she jotted down anything that seemed relevant.

Once it was over, she sat back, staring at her notes.

This is it. She finally had a solid clue to follow. She just had to figure out how to get to Cuba.

* * *

The next morning, Charlene was the first customer to enter the Serenity Travel Agency on Henley Street.

The lady behind the counter went through the usual niceties before she got down to business. "So where would you like to go?"

"Cuba."

"Great choice." The woman stood and turned to the wall behind her, plastered floor to ceiling in travel brochures. "We have some great tours; seven days is the most—"

"I don't need a tour."

The woman turned; her face washed with confusion.

"I just need to get there."

"Oh, well, why didn't you say so? I can book you a flight today. All we need is your passport."

Charlene's empty stomach twinged. "What if I don't have a passport?"

"Honey, you can't travel abroad without a passport."

The little band of hope she'd been clinging to snapped. Peter often said that every day was an opportunity to learn something new. Today Charlene learned how naïve she was.

77

She wished there was someone else she could talk to. Someone smarter, stronger, more courageous. Someone who could tell her what to do now. But there wasn't. She was all alone.

After a few awkward minutes in which the travel agent explained travel 101 to her, she left the agency with a Cuba brochure under her arm and her thoughts in turmoil. She took the long way home, taking in the southern uniqueness that was New Orleans. It'd been a good idea because, little by little, creative ideas had crept into her mind.

When she finally walked through her front door, she had a new plan.

It was time to go off the grid again.

Chapter Twelve

Marshall had been looking forward to today's clients, and they didn't fail to live up to his expectations. When they'd made the booking three weeks ago, they'd asked the right questions about rigging, bait, and their potential catch species. When they'd arrived at his dock at six o'clock this morning, they were dressed for a day of fishing in the sun.

These were his ideal clients. And they didn't fail to deliver.

During the day, they'd succeeded in landing one of the biggest sailfish Marshall had ever seen. According to his customers, the catch had made Marshall's charter the most enjoyable one they'd ever taken. And given that they'd spent their retirement years chasing the illusive big one, Marshall was mighty happy with that title.

At the end of the charter, Marshall did something he'd never done before . . . he offered to buy the men a drink at Pirate Cove, and they accepted immediately. In return, they helped him fillet all the fish and clean *Miss B Hayve*, which put them way ahead of every other client he'd ever had.

"Right this way, boys." Marshall led them through the door of his favorite haunt and up to the well-worn leather stools at the bar.

"Marshall?" Red cocked his head at Marshall's guests, which was justified as he'd never brought anyone into the bar with him before.

Red offered his hand to each of the men. "How y'all doin'?"

"We're great. Just had a magical day fishing with Marshall here."

"They landed a hundred-and-twenty-pound sailfish." Marshall grinned, and it felt damn good to do it too.

Red whistled. Not that he'd have any idea. The guy had never been fishing in his life. He tapped his hands on the bar, slapping out three beats of a tune. "Sounds like you need to celebrate then. What'll it be?"

The men ordered a beer each, and Marshall ordered his standard lemonade. He was impressed that they didn't question his choice of beverage, but he wouldn't have been embarrassed to tell them if they had.

He'd found out the hard way that sharing his daily count on the wagon had been instrumental in keeping him motivated. It'd taken way too damn long to get to that stage, and he had no intention of turning back.

Warren and his brothers occupied their usual booth at the back of the bar, and Marshall couldn't decide if their glares were because of the last time they'd met or because he'd taken their clients yet again. He didn't care, as long as they stayed right where they were.

As his two customers bounced off each other with random details about their day fishing, Marshall sighed with contentment. If all his days were like today, he'd never dwell on what could've been. Red delivered the drinks, and Marshall raised his glass. "Congratulations on a good catch."

"It's all because of you, captain."

Marshall grinned at that. *Respect.* It was a dying trait.

They shared a few more laughs and a double serving of Red's second-best dish—spicy buffalo wings with blue cheese dressing. Then, despite Marshall's best efforts to talk them into another beer, the men announced that they had to get back to their wives or they'd be castrated before dinner.

The men shook his hand prior to leaving, with promises to return.

He hoped so too.

Just as the men walked out, a woman walked in. She had a movie star look about her—not the glamorous, don't-touch-me kind of look, more like an action star. Her bare arms were well toned, and he guessed it wasn't from fanaticism at the gym but rather years of manual labor as opposed to pencil pushing.

She glanced around the room with the awareness of a cat on the prowl, and her eyes fell on him for the briefest of moments. After a cursory glance, she broke eye contact and strolled to the other end of the bar.

Red plastered her with his well-practiced southern greeting, and she placed an order for a soda and lime. While she waited for her drink, her eyes played about the room with the attentiveness of a sharpshooter.

Something radiated from within her. The expression on her face was a curious mix of nerves and confidence. If he had to guess, he'd say she was here out of necessity, not for the view. The more he watched her in the mirror, the more he convinced himself she was no ordinary tourist. She was after something.

When she received her drink and carried it to the booth where Warren and his dopey brothers were sitting, Marshall knew she was trouble.

Or in trouble.

No woman in her right mind would approach those three. Especially not a beautiful woman like her. She needed something. Why she figured they'd have it was beyond him.

He'd seen that move a few times in Key West. Dumb tourists came looking for Cuban cigars and rum. But they never looked like she did. They were usually young guys out for a wild night . . . or three.

The second she strolled toward Warren and the twins, they sat up and smiled their goofy grins. Why she didn't run the other way was a mystery. The threesome looked as devious as unskilled pickpockets. Either she was confident she could handle them, or she was off her rocker.

It was baffling enough that he continued watching the exchange, and although they kept their voices low, with each word he did hear, dread crept up his spine.

Overnight. Fast. Havana. Secret.

It didn't take much brain power to figure it out. This woman needed to get to Cuba in a hurry. What in God's name for, was another question. Nobody *needed* to get to Cuba. It was usually Cubans begging to come back the other way.

She had come to the right bar, though, so obviously she'd done her homework. Although pretty much anyone with a boat in Key West could get her there, it was Marshall and Warren who had the reputation for it.

Of course, she could fly there. But the fact that she was here, and that she wanted her trip to be a secret, meant she was making an illegal crossing. She either didn't have a passport or didn't want the authorities to know where she was going.

And that put her at the top of his "most interesting people" list. The fact that she was a woman on the high side of stunning made it even better.

She eased back from their booth, and as she set her still-full glass on the bar and adjusted her bag on her shoulder, the three brothers squeezed out from behind the table.

A loose grin crept through Warren's stubble, boasting that he'd just scored something big. Warren would be a shitty poker player.

Marshall waited until the four of them were on the move before he swiveled his stool to face them.

"What's going on, Warren?"

Warren's eyes blazed with hostility. "None of your fucking business."

Marshall turned to the woman, and their eyes met. The fact that she didn't look away impressed him. "Are you sure you know what you're doing? These three losers aren't the best choice."

"I can handle myself." Her clamped jaw said that she thought she was in control of the situation.

"Yeah! Fuck off." Ernie's vocabulary was limited.

"Three against one." Marshall tilted his head at her. "That's not exactly—"

"As I said, I can handle myself." Her lips drew to a thin line.

Marshall showed his palms in a peace gesture. "I'm sure you can. It's these three knuckleheads I'm worried about. They're not the most reliable of—"

"I said fuck off, Marshall." Warren clenched his stubbled jaw.

"I heard you." Marshall eased off his stool. "But I can't do that. I'm invested now."

"Oh, yeah. How? The woman's with us." Ernie took a step forward, yet still retained his distance.

"Maybe now. But once she sees your boat . . ." He trailed off, letting her fill in the blanks.

"There ain't nothin' wrong with my boat." Warren sounded like a snotty-nosed kid defending a Tonka toy.

"Yeah? You fixed the toilet yet?" Marshall went straight for the jugular. With the women, it was always about the facilities.

"Shut the fuck up. We fixed that last week." Warren's lip twitched, alerting Marshall to his lie. Shithouse poker face front and center. Warren squared off at Marshall, just like he'd done a week ago. The dumb shit didn't learn.

"Don't do it, Warren."

"What?"

"You know what. Didn't you learn your lesson last week?"

Marshall didn't miss the woman's resolve melting. He felt sorry for her. She'd made a tough call, got through the negotiations, and committed. Now he was throwing a wrench in and making her look like an amateur.

But when she adjusted her stance, embodying that of a nimble warrior—light on her feet, but ready to strike—his opinion of her changed. She wasn't here on a whim. She was determined to go through with her harebrained idea. And that made him even more involved.

If he didn't take her across the water to Cuba, then she'd find somebody else. Of that, he was certain. He just had to change her mind about the brothers.

He'd planned on letting his verbal communication skills win the debate, but when Warren and his stupid siblings formed an arc in front of his bar stool, he got a better idea.

Unconscious men can't captain boats.

"Don't be fools. Haven't we done this enough already?" Despite his words, Marshall was grateful they'd started it. And something unprecedented also shot across his brain . . . he was actually looking forward to showing this woman his skills.

83

It was a strange realization.

There was something about her that took him back to his long-forgotten youth, reminding him that he was a virile, young man . . . still well and truly in his prime.

In that frozen moment, when the threesome shifted their gazes from him to each other, Marshall assessed his surroundings, calculating distances and possible weapons with clarity and commitment.

Good opponents would ensure their faces were unreadable. Not these guys. Their intentions were written on their expressions like they were advertising blimps. None of them wanted to fight, but they were stupid enough to go through with it anyway. And each of them was waiting for the other to go first. Marshall didn't blame them.

"When you men finish beating your chests," the woman's clipped voice cut through the tension like a machine gun, "I'll be waiting outside."

Marshall was utterly bemused by her actions. Bar fights were like watching a train wreck; while you know there's going to be injuries and blood, you can't help but watch. Not her, though. Maybe she'd already seen her share of fights. Or blood.

He tucked that observation away, wondering how soon it would be before he'd need it again.

"Well, you heard the lady," Marshall egged them on after her departure. "Either walk away or get this over with. Your choice." His words were final, yet he knew nothing would change their minds.

These guys were dumb, dumber, and damn stupid.

Warren balled his fists, announcing his impending attack to Marshall and potentially to his brothers; he was ready. Marshall was ready too, though he resisted showing it. He was even tempted to sip his lemonade just to prove how undaunted he was.

The growl that tumbled from Warren's throat triggered his charge, as did his size-twelve boots pounding across the floorboards. Warren lowered his shoulder, going for a linebacker charge, and Marshall braced for it side on, giving him less of a target. At the last second, he dodged aside, wrapped his arm around Warren's neck, trapped him in a headlock, and squeezed.

Sure, Warren's arms flailed, attempting blows that failed to land, but without the blood flow to his brain, his attention quickly turned to Marshall's bicep. Warren's fingers clawed at Marshall's upper arm, and he made a mental note to put antiseptic on the scratches later.

Marshall eyeballed the ugly twins, even grinned at them as their brother slipped into unconsciousness.

Why the three hadn't charged simultaneously was beyond Marshall. If they had, it'd be a much fairer fight. But it was like they were waiting to see the success, or failure, of their sibling before they launched their own attack.

Ernie was next to step up. He had a temper like dynamite; once it was lit, it was near impossible to snuff it. Ernie chose the same attack plan as his older brother. Shoulder low, full-blown run, fury-driven growl.

"Really?" Marshall even had time to drop Warren's lifeless body and shake his head before Dipshit reached him. This time, though, Marshall repeated the move he'd made the other day and simply stepped aside and timed his shove perfectly to torpedo Ernie into the bar. He too fell to the floor in a puddle of useless flesh and bone.

"Now, Buck." Marshall spoke in a fatherly tone, which given their upbringing, the three brothers had probably never heard in their life. "Do you really want to lose another tooth?"

His head bobbled, and his tongue pushed through the gap in his teeth.

"Good decision. Now, I'm going to walk out this door, and you're going to buy your brothers a few beers when they wake up. Come dinner time, you'll be laughing at this." Marshall tugged out his wallet and tossed a Benjamin onto the bodies. Buck's eyes followed the hundred's flutter downward, and Marshall wondered if he'd even tell his brothers about the cash.

"Buck." Marshall commanded his attention. "Do we have an agreement?"

Buck dragged his eyes from the money long enough to give a nod.

"Okay then." Marshall stepped over Dumb and Dumber and strode back to the bar. Red was shaking his head with a look that said he'd enjoyed the show more than he wanted to admit. "Hey, Red, buy these guys a side of ribs, will ya? Actually, make it two." He slid a fifty over the counter.

Red slipped the note into his top pocket. "Sure thing. Hey, I hope she's worth it."

Marshall glanced over his shoulder to see the woman watching through the glass. When she saw him looking, she spun away, showing him her back.

"You know what. I think she just might be."

The dazzle in Red's eyes had Marshall laughing as he strode away from the bar.

She greeted him with hands on hips and a crease in her brow. A silver cross, nestled in the dip of her throat, glinted red from Pirate Cove's tacky neon sign. "Is that the way you settle all your disputes?"

"Only with those three. They don't listen to reasoning."

"Reasoning." She huffed. "Is that what you call it?'

He narrowed his gaze at her. "What would you call it?"

"Railroading."

"Well . . ." Her forthrightness was a refreshing change, yet it still caught him unawares. "I was actually doing you a favor."

"Really?" It was sarcasm rather that a question.

"When you see their boat, you'll be thanking me."

"And what will I do when I see your boat, Mr.—"

"Crow. Marshall Crow." He held his hand forward. "And you are?"

She hesitated for a little too long, and he couldn't decide if she was nervous about giving her name or touching his hand. But when her eyes met his and he saw both the gold flecks in her caramel irises and the determination in her glare, he decided it was neither.

There was something else going on behind the scenes.

Which was blatantly obvious given that she wanted to do a covert run to Cuba.

"Charlene Bailey." Her grip was firm enough to show that she wasn't a pushover.

"So, Charlene, I understand you need to get to Cuba."

She nodded. "Fast."

"I can do fast. But I have to know why didn't you approach me in the first place, rather than those three goons?"

She hesitated, seemingly stewing on her answer. "You looked too intelligent."

He did a double take, and his brows shot up. "And that's a bad thing?"

She glanced about, and her wavy brown hair fell around her bare shoulders. "It is . . . if you plan on asking too many questions."

Nicely played. In one sentence she'd both flattered him and told him to keep his nose out of her business.

"Alright then. Meet me at the marina entrance over there at nine tonight," he pointed toward the arched metal gateway over the main wharf. "And I'll have you in Havana before the sun comes up." He didn't wait for her response. Instead, he turned on his heel and pictured her blazing eyes throwing daggers in his back as he strode away.

He didn't usually go for dramatic exits. But he liked this one. There was something about her that riled him, and it wasn't until he'd nearly reached his shack on the beach that he realized what it was. For the first time in years, he felt the need to protect someone.

Lucky for him, she was a feisty beauty who promised to make the next day or so very interesting.

The midnight run had never looked so enticing.

Chapter Thirteen

Charlene had to walk several streets before the anxiety snaking through her brain subsided. She'd seen men fight before, but they'd been drunken bouts of wild fist throwing after an ugly exchange of insults and profanity.

Usually it was over a woman.

What Marshall and the three brothers did, though, seemed almost practiced. Choreographed. From the limited verbal exchange to the physical one, it was obvious it wasn't their first brawl.

She half expected to see Marshall around every corner she rounded. Or the three brothers, but so far, so good. She did feel a bit of a fool for choosing them.

Her desperation had made her reckless.

Her choice had been based purely on their half-witted behavior. They seemed a long way from intelligent, which would've played into her plans for utilizing her feminine touch to get them to do anything. Including not asking too many questions.

But if it hadn't been for Marshall, she would've climbed aboard a boat with three men with the intention of making an illegal trip across a hundred miles of ocean. Three!

She could handle one man, possibly two, given that they were so scrawny. But three at once, was highly unlikely.

Shaking her head, she bristled at her stupidity.

Her brain snapped to a mental image of her body being washed up on a beach. With no ID and nobody to report her missing, she'd be labeled a Jane Doe and live out the rest of eternity in a nameless metal tube. As much as she hated that her brain went there, she needed that reality check.

The fact that nobody knew where she was going was a double-edged sword.

On one hand, it gave her the freedom to make the illegal move unhindered.

On the other, she could vanish forever and nobody would know. Not one person.

She could've told Detective Chapel, she supposed. But she didn't want him questioning her motives. When she'd found the Cuba connection, it'd taken a few days of debating before she'd decided to leave without communicating her intentions to Chapel.

It might take a few days of zero communication from her before he went around to her apartment. It might take him another day or two before he convinced the landlord to open the door.

Once he did, though, he'd find the place empty.

By now, all her father's clothing would've been farmed out to worthy recipients via the Daughters of Charity donation service. A share of her clothing had made the charity bin too, reducing her total assets down to just one suitcase and a bundle of money that was now in a tin she'd found at a secondhand shop.

She'd kept the cane too. For some reason, she couldn't part with it. The wise owl was her last connection to the life she'd lived until three months ago.

The aromas drifting from a burger bar overlooking the ocean smelled so good that she decided to pause for dinner. She hadn't eaten since the pie she'd wolfed down at the bus stop at seven o'clock that morning.

After ordering the special—cheeseburger, curly fries, and onion rings—she chose a seat at the far edge of the eating area, where she could see both the diner and a 180-degree, uninterrupted view of the Atlantic Ocean.

According to the brochure from the travel agent, Cuba was approximately a hundred miles across that stretch of blue. It was hard to believe that'd be her next destination. It'd taken just one day to find someone willing to take her to Cuba, and that was either pure luck or because she'd asked the right people the right questions to direct her into that bar.

One thing she hadn't thought to ask any of those men, though, was how long the journey was expected to take. *Could it be days?*

The longest train trip she'd ever taken was from Chicago to Portland, approximately twenty-two hundred miles. And that had taken two days. It wasn't really a comparison, but surely crossing a hundred miles of ocean would take only a couple of hours, not days. It'd be one of the first questions she'd ask when she met Marshall again.

Marshall hadn't discussed his fee either, and she mentally debated whether that was because he assumed she had a lot of money or because he could tell she was desperate enough to pay anything.

Or maybe it'd slipped his mind.

She was convincing herself of the latter when her meal arrived courtesy of a young woman in denim shorts and a T-shirt that would've been better suited to playing Frisbee on the beach.

It was a rare occasion when the burger that arrived on her plate matched the burger displayed on the menu board. But this one did. It smelled divine too. Wrapping both hands around the squishy bun, she bit into the burger and groaned at the delicious combination in her mouth.

It'd been way too long since she'd ordered a decent meal. Wracking her brain, she realized that the last restaurant meal she'd eaten was the entree she'd shared with her father. Peter.

With the information she now had, confirming that he'd lied on many occasions, she was fairly certain Peter wasn't his real name. And as much as she didn't want to admit it, he was also not her father.

It suddenly occurred to her that she'd put zero thought into who her real father was. She'd been so fixated on finding out more about Peter that following up on her own lineage had slipped her mind.

With a bit of luck, she'd have all her answers within a couple of days. If Marshall came through.

Once she finished her burger, she turned her attention to the fries and onion rings. As she stared out over the ocean, she wondered what the crossing to Cuba would be like. And, in particular, what it'd be like sharing that limited space with a complete stranger . . . Marshall.

She'd met enough armed forces personnel to know one when she saw one. Yet there was something about Marshall that set him apart from the others. First, he had tried to talk those silly guys out of fighting.

Every other military man she'd met would've been itching for a fight.

Then, the way he'd handled himself afterward, talking the third brother down and paying for their drinks and food. Now, that was new to her.

And she'd worked in more than enough bars to know that Marshall wasn't drunk, and not just based on the pale soda he was drinking. He was in control of all his faculties, and he didn't smell of alcohol. That was strange too, given where they'd met.

But that wasn't all. Marshall had an unusual demeanor about him, simultaneously awkward and confident. Like he knew what he had to do but was embarrassed by it. He'd also said he had no choice but to help her.

Whatever that meant. She just hoped he had that same feeling come nine o'clock tonight.

When she'd made the decision to cross to Cuba illegally, she hadn't actually thought it through enough to realize it'd be done under cover of darkness. It made sense now.

But it also hit home just how risky her plan was.

Worst-case scenario, she'd vanish from the face of the earth.

Best-case scenario, she'd find out who her parents were. She decided she'd be happy with anything but her body being washed up on shore. Besides, Charlene had absolutely nothing to lose. The money maybe, but then she'd been penniless many, many times before.

The one big thing that was about to change was that for the first time in her life, she was about to break the law. Big-time.

Charlene didn't even jaywalk.

That aspect of her plan hit her with such brutality it felt like a hive of bees had exploded in her stomach, and she couldn't swallow the onion ring already in her mouth. Pain nipped at her insides—once, twice, a thousand times—as she contemplated that winding up in jail would be worse than her lifeless body floating up onto a deserted beach.

She'd always had freedom.

Freedom to do whatever she wanted.

Being caged up would kill her.

She wanted her old life back. To be curled up with her feet on the sofa, watching reruns of *Friends* with her father. Back when running out of popcorn was a major catastrophe. Back when the worst day of her life was a figment of her childhood imagination.

But it wasn't a young child's fabrication. Every single bit of it seemed to be true.

She was ripped from her mother's arms. By Peter. The man who claimed to be her father.

Charlene swallowed the onion ring and shoved the plate aside. She needed answers.

No matter what happened in the next couple of days, she would never be the same. Then again, she hadn't been the same since that woman had plunged the knife into Peter's chest. Now Charlene literally had nothing to lose.

Quite the contrary—she had everything to gain.

Crossing to Cuba illegally was a dangerous risk, but not only was it imperative, it was also her last card. If she still had no answers after Cuba, she had nowhere else to go. She'd still be lost.

With her belly full and the sun kissing the horizon, she left the café and forced her feet to maintain a stroll along the road that skirted the beach. It would've been more natural to run.

She was good at it too.

The only times she'd ever stood out in a crowd was when she'd won the track event at school, which happened several times in her child-hood. Running was her therapy. All she had to think about was placing one foot in front of the other and concentrating on her breathing.

She needed to conserve her energy. She had no idea how tonight would play out, but she intended to be awake through every second of it. So far, everything she'd planned before she'd left New Orleans had come to fruition. Getting rid of her excess things. Making her way down to Key West. Finding someone who'd take her across to Cuba.

It was the next step in Havana that threw all the questions in the air.

But it was a waste of energy to even think about it. *One step at a time.*

The setting sun was busy transforming the sky into shades of citrus when she returned to the transit station. Another busload of people was disembarking, and mingling in with the crowd, she made her way to the lockers and removed her suitcase and Peter's cane.

After a couple of minutes in the bathroom, she'd changed into jeans and a T-shirt, and put sneakers on her feet. With her teeth brushed, she was ready to get moving again.

The only practical way to carry the cane was to hold the silver owl. So, with her satchel handbag secured diagonally across her torso and her suitcase trailing behind her, she used the cane like it was her own walking stick and sauntered out of the bus station.

The trek back toward the marina was now familiar; however, the setting sun had transformed the streets into intimidating gauntlets. During the day, they hadn't felt so uninviting. Drunkards spilled out of dim doorways and showed her enough unwanted attention that the hairs on her neck bristled. She'd run if she needed to. She'd fight if she had to.

Her decision to keep the cane shifted from being just a sentimental choice to a brilliant one, as it elevated the sturdy wood from being a link to her past to an efficient weapon. Should the need arise.

With her grip intensified on the owl, she picked up her pace and had the wheels of her suitcase sounding like rolling thunder on the uneven pavement.

She arrived safely at the marina at 8:30 that evening with a cool sweat and a dominating thirst. Ignoring both, she slinked into the shadows, eager to spot Marshall's arrival. From her vantage point, she could watch the entire marina complex and the entrance to the main wharf.

There were a few people about, mostly couples and small groups who, based on their laughter and wobbly legs, appeared to have been drinking for hours.

Several boats were lit up like Christmas trees, displaying both their owners' opulent wealth and their blatant disregard for precious energy. Some of the yachts were so enormous they were as big as mansions.

The one closest to her was called *Slave to the Ocean*. The giant ship had sleek lines and polished chrome railings, and although she didn't have much experience with marine vessels, she guessed it would be worth millions.

The one beside it was just as big, as were all the other ones she could see from her position. It had her pondering if her crossing to Cuba was going to be surrounded by sheer luxury. It'd be a nice change.

Nine o'clock came and went, and with every passing minute, her hopes sank lower. She hadn't even considered that Marshall would renege on his commitment. He didn't strike her as that kind of guy. Then again, she'd been wrong before. Peter was a perfect example.

It was another twenty minutes before she conceded she'd been duped. With her cane in one hand and the handle of her case in the other, she left her concealed spot and headed away.

"You're late." The first words she heard from Marshall were not friendly ones.

She spun to the voice and saw him striding up the central wharf, toward the main entrance. Halting her stride, she unclamped her jaw. "No, I wasn't. You are. Nine o'clock you said, and it's half past."

He pointed at the wrought-iron arch. "I told you to wait there. So, I've been looking for you *there*."

"What? I haven't seen you."

"Of course, you haven't. You were hiding in the shadows. Why?"

Even if she had a good answer, she didn't want to tell him anyway. "I thought our agreement was that you wouldn't ask questions."

"Lady, I don't know what agreement you're referring to, but it ain't with me. We haven't even agreed on a price." His eyes were enigmatic and his face utterly masculine, especially when he clamped his jaw.

She strangled the silver owl in her grip and angled her chin up to him. "Okay, Mr. Crow, what *is* your price?"

Something flitted across his gaze before his shoulders softened and his eyes drifted skyward, as if he was searching for the answer. She found herself admiring his strong jawline and snapped her eyes away before he returned his attention to her. "How about I show you my boat first?"

"No, thank you. I don't need to see it. I just need your assurance that you can get me there fast and at a fair price."

The edge of his mouth curled, bordering on a smile, yet his eyes showed surprise. Maybe Mr. Crow wasn't accustomed to dealing with a woman who spoke her mind? If that was the case, then they were in for an interesting trip.

He collected himself by placing his feet shoulder width apart. "You want fast, right?"

"Correct."

"In that case it's going to cost four hundred."

"Done."

His eyebrows launched upward. "That's not how this is supposed to work, you know."

"What's supposed to work?"

"Haggling. I say a price, you undercut me. Eventually we meet in the middle."

Nerves and confidence became one in her brain, and she didn't want either to show her naïveté. "I assumed you were a man I could trust."

His expression washed with confusion. "You're correct."

"In that case, I trust you to charge me the going rate."

"Hmm. That price is one way. I assume you want a return trip?"

Strangling the silver owl in her fist, she broke eye contact. Charlene hadn't thought that far ahead. But the answer was obvious. "Of course, I want a return trip."

"Okay then. When?"

"When?"

"Yes, when exactly did you want to return?"

His question had her nerves fraying, and she glanced away, silently debating a suitable response. A crescendo of raucous laughter sounded behind her, and she spun to watch a group of three young couples stagger onto the main wharf.

Grateful for the interruption, she stepped aside for them to pass and systematically contemplated a suitable answer to his question. She wouldn't leave Cuba until she had her answers. But she didn't want to stay even a day longer than she needed to.

Once the noisy group had faded into the shadows, she finally met

Marshall's gaze, and his expression signaled he'd been waiting her response.

But she was taken off guard by his emerald-green eyes. They were flecked with copper that shimmered in the surrounding yachts' twinkling lights. But it was something else she saw in them that had her breath catching in her throat.

Honesty. Integrity. Loyalty.

But, most of all, security.

She hadn't felt safe in months, yet within a couple of minutes in Marshall's company, she already felt like he'd protect her with his own life. It was an overpowering sensation.

He lowered his gaze first. "Look." He rubbed his hands together, emitting a rough sandpaper sound. "Let's get going, and you can fill me in on the finer details once we're underway." He grabbed her case without asking, turned on his heel, and strode down the wharf, with the suitcase wheels making enough noise to wake anyone lucky enough to be sleeping in the opulent yachts around them.

After a moment of bewilderment, she dashed after him.

The marina was much bigger than she'd initially thought, and the boats gradually became smaller with each berth they passed. It was several minutes before he stepped onto a side wharf.

He finally stopped at a boat that for some reason seemed to perfectly suit him. It wasn't ostentatious like many of the boats they'd passed. Its shiny chrome proved that he looked after it, and it seemed efficient and practical, much like her first impressions of Marshall.

She glanced at the name. "Miss B Hayve?"

He cocked his head at her. "Yeah. You have a problem with that?"

His tart response had her wondering if she'd hit a nerve. "Not at all."

"Good. Follow me." He stepped onboard with her bag in hand and headed down a set of steps.

Charlene followed him down the polished wooden steps, holding the railing as she went. The room below was bigger than she'd thought it would be and was decorated in honey-colored wood, stainless steel, and navy-blue fabric.

His military training could well be the driver behind the immaculate condition everything was in. He carried her case to the far end and plonked it on a bed that must've been custom-made to fit the triangular space.

He turned to her and seemed to be much taller in the enclosed space. Broader too. "What do you know about boats?"

After a second's pondering, she decided to give him one of her father's favorite sayings. "I don't know what I don't know."

The muscles along his jawline bulged. "Right then. Come and give me a hand."

"Yes, boss."

He shuffled past her to climb the steps. "Captain. Not boss."

"Yes, sir." She giggled, plonked her handbag onto her suitcase, and then followed him up the stairs.

She stood at a central position on the lower back deck, while he pulled in the gangplank and nestled it alongside the rail. "What do you want me to do?"

"Can you unhook the bowline?" He didn't elaborate by pointing out what he meant, and she assumed this was a test. Aware that he was watching, Charlene climbed a set of three stairs and edged along the narrow ledge toward the front of the cabin cruiser. She knelt down at a rope dangling over the side and tugged on it to edge the boat closer and provide some slack.

At the perfect moment, she flicked it from the T-shaped cleat on the wharf, and when the loop holding the boat in position released, she flipped it up to catch it and then looped the length of rope into position.

When she stood and turned to where she'd last seen Marshall, his gaze perfectly depicted a man impressed. Her intentions were complete. "What next?"

"Come on back, and we'll get underway."

She retraced her steps and met him on the small lower deck. Behind him, she spied a smaller boat elevated in a secure position at the back. It was wrapped in white canvas that showed zero signs of aging. Just like the rest of the cruiser.

"Ladies first." He indicated the set of steep stairs that led to the upper flybridge.

As she climbed up, she tried not to picture him looking at her butt.

Men were like that, though. Her years of waitressing had taught her to ignore the ogling. Most of the time.

When it became too creepy, she was known to spill the odd drink or two on the culprit.

Twice she'd had men that didn't get the hint, and both times she'd applied enough pressure to the nerve below their collarbones to have them on their knees long before the security guards caught onto the situation.

She'd always thought Peter's insistence that she learn martial arts was because of the nature of the "cheap-labor" jobs she'd held. But maybe he'd had a grander plan. Maybe he always knew that his secrets would eventually be revealed. And maybe, all along, he was preparing her for this mission.

That was a lot of maybes. Too many.

She turned her attention back to her current situation.

The flybridge at the top of the stairs was fully contained, giving them an elevated view while protecting them from the elements.

"Take a seat." Marshall's gruff voice showed his no-nonsense attitude, and she instantly scrubbed the potential for small talk from her unwritten agenda.

On the front console, the steering wheel was positioned in the center, so she sat on the right-hand side of the white leather seat, allowing plenty of room for Marshall. He plonked himself at her side and flicked a couple of switches, triggering the engines.

Within a few minutes, they left the berth and were navigating their way out of the marina. Marshall remained silent, so she did too. Over the years, she'd learned that some people were just wired that way, and if Marshall didn't want to talk, that was fine with her.

In the distance, the ocean was as black as the sky, and the only lights were the red and green markers highlighting the shipping channel.

As they passed the last set of berths, Marshall pointed toward the last boat tied up alongside the wharf. In the dimmed marina lights, it appeared to be a dirty mustard color, and the canopy over the bulkhead was tilted at a precarious angle. "That's Warren's boat."

She assumed he was seeking recognition for saving her, so she turned to him and met his gaze. "Thank you." She contemplated elaborating, but decided that he didn't seem to need nor want that.

"You're welcome." He pushed the throttle forward, and the boat quickly gained speed.

He waited until the marina lights were barely a few dots behind them on the horizon before he cleared his throat. "You can head downstairs and sleep if you want."

"Oh no, no. I'm not tired, thanks."

"Hmm." Silence again.

It was a further ten or so minutes before he adjusted in his seat. "You don't talk much, do you?"

"Neither do you. I figured you weren't the conversational type."

"You told me not to ask questions."

"Not true." She gave in to a smug smile. "I asked you not to ask *too* many questions."

"Right."

"Aren't you going to ask for your money?"

"You'll pay me." He said it with a confident smirk.

She half giggled, half huffed. "Oh, I will, will I?"

"Yep. Or else you'll be living on Cuban soil for a very long time."

He had her there. She had no intention of staying any longer than she needed to. Not that she had anything to come home to. She didn't even have a home. Charlene should be used to that. There'd been many times in her life when she didn't have a home. But now—now that she was homeless *and* alone—it seemed so much sadder.

"So, you know what we're doing is illegal, right?" As his cast-iron glare captured her eyes, she decided that he must've held a high rank in the military.

"Yes. I'm aware of that."

"Are you going to tell me why you have to get to Cuba in a hurry?"

She angled her head up at him and decided to reply using one of her father's tricks. "Army, navy, or air force?"

"Hmm, that'd be a no then." He shifted his eyes back out to the blackness surrounding them. "Navy. How'd you guess?"

"I've seen my share of military personnel."

"Yeah, how so?"

"I spent a bit of time in Charleston, South Carolina."

"Huh. What'd you do there?"

She shrugged her shoulder. "Waitressing."

"Is that where you learned your boating skills?"

Although she'd barely shown him anything yet, she liked that he was impressed enough to call them skills. "No, we spent a bit of time on a houseboat in Austin, Texas."

"Texas. You get around a bit, huh?"

"You could say that." After her experience with Detective Chapel, she had no intention of trying to explain her nomadic life to anyone ever again.

"Right then." He rolled his eyes at her. "Change subject."

"Why did you leave the navy?" She decided to take charge of the conversation.

"I didn't leave."

As much as she wanted to bite, she remained silent instead. *Miss B Hayve* carved through a wave that Charlene hadn't spotted, and as she clutched at a chrome rail to stop from hurling forward, water washed up over the windshield.

"I was medically discharged."

He showed no concern over the height of the wave that'd just engulfed them, so Charlene tried to quell the anguish welling up inside her. "I'm sorry to hear that."

"Color blindness."

She huffed. "That's very unfortunate. How long were you enlisted?"

"Fifteen years."

"Wow, you must've joined up young."

"Thank you. Yes, sixteen."

For the first time since they'd met, he smiled, and the transformation was stunning. It changed him from a man who seemed to be going through the motions of life to a young man, eager to please. She liked what she saw. It showed another layer to Marshall that she hoped to see more of. "That's so young. I had no idea what I wanted to do when I was sixteen."

"So, what did you do?"

She huffed. "Everything. And nothing."

"Cryptic."

"Waitressing. Bar work. Whatever paid the bills." Before he could ask another question, she added, "So are you married, have kids?"

"Nope. I was engaged once. To a Cuban woman. No kids."

"Really? How did you meet her?"

"I was stationed at Guantánamo Bay for a while. I thought it was love, she thought it was her ticket out of Cuba. Not that I blame her. It was pretty rough for a woman back then. Still is, I guess. I still see her from time to time."

Charlene's ears pricked up as she realized Marshall's knowledge of Cuba might be able to help her with more than just a trip across the ocean. "So, you cross over to Cuba often?"

He cocked his head at her, his lips drawn into a wry grin. "I'll answer that when you tell me why you're going to Cuba." Then he leaned forward and flicked a switch, plummeting them into absolute darkness.

Chapter Fourteen

The instrument panel offered enough light for Marshall to see Charlene's wide eyes and clenched jaw, yet he was impressed that she didn't completely wig out.

Her grip on the chrome rail made her knuckles white, and she glared up at him, her eyes ablaze with fury. "What the hell are you doing?"

"Hiding from the Coast Guard." He pushed the throttle to maximum speed, and his baby responded with a deeper rumble and an elevated bow.

Her eyes skipped from him to the blackness ahead and back again. "What if we hit something?"

"If we hit something, we're in deep shit."

"Well, that's comforting."

"Just telling the truth. Now hang on, while I get us through this." The quicker they crossed into international waters, the better.

Miss B Hayve charged through wave after wave, skimming over the liquid black ocean like a dream. Lack of moonlight made it impossible to see the waves. Their first knowledge of when they'd hit one was with the boom of the water breaking the bow, followed by the water over the windshield.

He tried not to look at Charlene's eyes or her white knuckles clutching the railing. His focus needed to be on the water. If he did see something, he'd likely be right on top of it, with little time to react. He just prayed it wasn't a shipping container.

Or worse . . . a boatload of refugees.

The only good thing about the lack of moonlight was that a Coast Guard patrol would stand out like a dog's balls, and conversely, they'd have little hope of spotting *Miss B Hayve*.

To chance even one spotlight would put their freedom in jeopardy. And although he'd taken this very risk several times before, for some reason, having Charlene in the firing line had his brain rubber-banding from "We can get through this" to "We're fucking stupid."

He'd been on many lifesaving missions. He'd also completed thirty-one missions that'd put his men front and center in life-threatening territory. But they were trained for it. Some even begged for it. Him included.

The thrill of being in jeopardy became as necessary as oxygen. They also knew the ultimate cost. There was not a chance in hell Charlene knew the consequences of what they were doing. And it was going to be even more dangerous once they hit the other side.

Even once *Miss B Hayve* crossed that imaginary line that put them in international waters without a hitch, hope and trepidation still filled his mind. He cut the speed back a fraction to give him a couple more seconds of reaction time.

Charlene's ability to remain silent was both a refreshing change and annoying, to the point where he was beginning to feel stupid for not asking more questions. But rather than shoot the herd of elephants in the room, he decided on a different approach. "You hungry?"

"Umm, just a bit."

"Good. Me too. Down in the galley you'll find ham-and-cheese sandwiches already made up in the fridge. I hope you're not one of those vegan, gluten-free types?"

She giggled and backed that up with a smile that was stunning. "No, I eat anything."

"Great, me too. We're going to get along just fine. There's a sandwich toaster down there if you want to heat it up."

A sudden look of sorrow engulfed her, making him wonder if she was about to burst into tears. But before he had time to question it, she slipped off the chair and disappeared down the steps. Her floral scent lingered, though, and he admonished himself for liking it so much.

Other than Red, Marshall hadn't had decent company in a long time. The closest thing he had to a companion was the stray dog who'd taken to sleeping on his front porch. He hadn't had the heart to shoo the three-legged mutt away, so he'd named him Hoppa and started tossing him his dinner scraps. Despite himself, Marshall liked having the scrawny mongrel for company.

And that there made him a sad sack of shit.

The instant his mind went to considering Charlene as nice company, he clenched his jaw, eased forward on his chair, and attempted to concentrate on the blackness around him.

But the empty void ahead had his thoughts bouncing right back. Charlene was young and beautiful and didn't need a has-been like him ruining her future. Nope. The second she was done with his unique skills, she'd be off like a rocket. And he wouldn't blame her one bit.

The intercom button on his panel buzzed, triggering a smirk as he pressed it. "Yes."

"Would the captain like a drink?" Her voice sounded cheeky, and he imagined that beautiful smile he'd seen brightening her face.

"A Coke, please."

"Coming right up."

He couldn't recall anyone else thinking to use the intercom to talk to him on the flybridge. Every other person who'd wanted his attention called from the bottom of the stairs. Her resourcefulness put her way ahead of most of the people he'd had on *Miss B Hayve*.

It also showed confidence and initiative. Charlene was already on his most-interesting-person list, but the more he learned about her, the more he wanted to know. Getting her to open up was the challenge.

Her footsteps announced her approach, and he had to resist glancing around to watch her arrival. "There you go." She placed a can of Coke and a plated sandwich on the ledge beside him.

"Thanks. You not having any?"

"Yes. I took you up on your offer to toast it. I'll be back up in a sec."

She left to return downstairs, and he decided to wait for her before he started eating. A couple of minutes and a few huge waves later, she returned with her meal and a bottle of water and slipped into her seat.

"Smells good," he nodded at the sandwich.

"Oh, do you want me to toast yours?"

"Nah, it's all good."

"It's no trouble, only takes a minute."

"No. I'm good. Love a good toasted sandwich, though, don't you?"

She spun to him, a frown wobbling across her forehead.

"What?"

"It's just . . . my father and I, well, we made toasted sandwiches into an art form. We'd compete over the title of best sandwich maker."

"Ha, that's right up my alley. Your father still around?"

She snapped her eyes away. "No, he, umm, passed away a few months ago."

"Sorry to hear that. Sounds like you were close." Despite the limited light, he didn't miss the turmoil on her face.

"Yeah, we were."

"What about your mother?"

"I haven't seen her since I was six." She nibbled on the corner of her sandwich.

"Oh, sorry about that."

She shrugged. "No need to be."

He lifted his Coke, and as he sipped, he stewed over how to get her talking. It was an unusual conundrum. Most women he'd met didn't shut up.

His thoughts bounced to some of his darker days in the navy. The times when he'd stepped very close to the edge in order to get a man talking. He'd heard some pretty horrible stories over the years, and more often than not, he wasn't surprised about who the story implicated. It took a certain type of man to do certain kinds of torture.

One particular man, Captain Ithica Randsome, had dark, soulless eyes that'd scare the crap out of most sane men. If Marshall had ever been on the wrong side of Randsome's radar, he would've been tempted to jump overboard.

Marshall reflected that the kind of techniques that Randsome used to make people talk probably wouldn't work on Charlene anyway. He'd already pegged her as a woman who had nothing to lose.

Then again, that was blatantly obvious given her radical plans.

So he couldn't go with the what-has-she-got-to-lose angle. He decided to try "what did she have to gain." The answer was easy . . . knowledge.

He waited until she'd finished most of her meal before he spoke. "I've made this trip seventeen times in three years. Most of those times, my customer was on Cuban soil for a duration of approximately two, maximum three hours." He huffed. "Though I did have four dipshits who got themselves so doped up they missed the scheduled departure time and spent an extra day shitting their pants in a Havana gutter."

Her eyes were on him, her mouth curled into a curious smile, and she seemed to be listening to every word like he was teaching her CPR or something. When she didn't speak, he continued. "The reason why they had such short times on Cuban soil were threefold. One was because I helped them get what they wanted. Two was because I have no intention of hovering around with the Cuban coast guard up my ass. And three was I never leave a man behind. Or woman."

He watched her process this information and waited for her response. Her eyes flicked from the instruments on the panel to the blackness ahead of them. With each passing second, it grew clearer that she was in more trouble than she was letting on.

Her refusal to open up was beginning to piss him off. "Look, I'm risking a hell of a lot doing this. Don't suppose you'd like to tell me what mess you've gotten yourself into?"

Her jaw dropped. "Mess? Why do you think it's a mess?"

He waggled his head. "Beautiful young woman with her life ahead of her wants to risk it all by doing something that could ruin her life forever. I'm guessing it's not by choice."

Her blinking eyes confirmed her battle with a response. "Well, you're guessing wrong. This is my choice."

"Really, huh. This's your first time to Cuba, right?"

Her momentary debate had him fuming over her secrecy. Most of his midnight-run customers were young guys wanting to add a stupid notch to their ego. Usually they were chasing rum, cigars, or women.

Occasionally, it'd be a gun or drugs, but he mostly stayed away from those. Unless money was so tight that he had no choice.

Charlene, though, ticked none of those boxes, and that had all his curiosity sensors bristling. She was in over her head; that was a given. But what she was drowning in was the question.

"Yes, it is." She finally answered.

"What's your plan when we hit land?"

Her eyes looked up at him, yet she seemed to be looking through him. She appeared conflicted. Like telling him was breaking some kind of sacred vow. She wiped her hand across the back of her mouth, collecting the tiny crumb that he'd wanted to thumb away himself. Placing her drink down, she turned to him. "Do you know *Legendarios del Guajirito*?"

As much as her question was progress, it was also a step backward. "The dance show? In Havana?"

"Yes, do you know it?"

"Uh huh." He showed her the skepticism her question deserved.

"I want to go there."

"You're doing an illegal trip to Cuba to see a stupid dance show."

She nodded.

"Okay then." He huffed at the absurdity. She was either nuts or making shit up. Either way, she was a grown woman, so if this was the game she wanted to play, then who was he to stop her? "Right then. What's your plan to get around Havana? Do you even speak Spanish?"

When her shoulders deflated, he figured he'd hit a home run. Which made him certain that by the time they set foot on Cuban soil, she'd be asking for his help. It was time for him to shut up and wait for her to arrive at the same conclusion.

She adjusted her seating, and just as he thought she was loosening up, a glimmer of light on the horizon caught his eye. And then it was gone.

Two seconds later, it was back.

As they drove through one wave after the next, he maintained his visual on the light. Within two minutes, his worst nightmare was realized. "Shit!"

"What?"

"We got company."

"Where?" Her breath hitched.

"Dead ahead. Wait a sec and you'll see it."

Her eyes snapped to the invisible horizon. "That light. What is it?"

"That's probably the US Coast Guard, and I'm guessing they know we're here."

"Can't we outrun them?"

He shot her a you've-got-to-be-fucking-kidding glare. "We've got about twenty minutes before they board us."

Her brows shot upward, yet she seemed to look through him. "What do we do?"

"We'll shut down the engines and pretend we're fishing." He cut the speed right back and rode the boat's slump into the water.

"That works?"

"If all goes well, they'll check our IDs and give us a rap on the knuckles."

"What if I don't have ID?" Her voice elevated a notch.

He glared at her, momentarily lost for words. "What? Nothing?"

"No." She spat the word at him.

Despite how weird that was, he believed her. It also meant she was in way more trouble than she was letting on. And now they both were.

"In that case, we've got trouble."

"What's your plan B?"

He cocked his head. "What makes you think I have one?"

"Every good soldier has a plan B. And you strike me as a damn good soldier."

There she goes again, simultaneously flattering him and applying pressure. "You're right. But you're not going to like it."

She lifted her chin. "If it stops me from rotting in a six-foot cell, then I'll like it just fine."

"Okay then. I hope you can swim."

Her eyes bulged. "What! You've got to be—"

Ignoring her outburst, he killed the engines and jumped up from his seat. "Come with me."

Using the chrome railing, he glided down the stairs without using his feet, then spun to his left and repeated the move to the lower deck.

He strode to the bow section and pulled out a panel beneath the bed. He'd built it with concealment in mind, and it had passed detection many times already.

Tucked inside, to the left of the secret hold, was the harness that he'd had to use only twice before. Each time, it was with a man. Each time, they'd thought it was part of the thrill ride.

He doubted Miss. Bailey would share those sentiments.

Marshall yanked the harness free, then turned to the rapid breathing behind him. Her eyes showed her fear, but otherwise she hid it well. "In that cupboard you'll find three wet suits. They'll all be too big for you, but it's all I got."

"I'm really getting in the water?" Her voice quivered, yet she didn't look as terrified as the situation warranted.

And that told him she'd been through hell before. "Yep. No choice."

Time was against them, moving in some kind of a weird warp. One second it was going a million miles an hour; the next second it was slow, allowing him to see every movement in perfect clarity—her trembling fingers as she pulled open the cupboard, the muscles in her toned arms flexing as she tugged a wet suit free, the blank expression on her face as she took the suit to the bathroom and disappeared behind the door.

She seemed numb, robotic. Horrified, yet committed to what had to be done. He had to know what shit she was into. So if they got through this, he was going to belt it out of her.

If they got through it.

Fifteen minutes.

He turned his attention back to adjusting the straps on the harness. The last guy he'd had in it had been just a fraction smaller than him. He just hoped the damn thing would hold her in. Otherwise, they had a whole new set of problems.

She stepped out from the toilet. Despite the oversized wet suit hiding all her curves, with her flushed cheeks and her hair up in a high ponytail, she looked like she was ready for a photo shoot for the cover of *Sports Illustrated*. He'd never been in the company of a woman who was so beautiful, period.

He'd thought his young Cuban fiancée would be the most stunning woman he'd ever meet. Boy, was he wrong. A wave broadsided *Miss B Hayve*, snapping him to attention.

Focus, Crow!

"What's in the case?" He pointed at her suitcase, which was still on the bed.

"Just clothes." A new wave of fear rippled her features.

"*Just* clothes? So if I toss it overboard, you won't mind."

"Of course, I'll fucking mind. It's everything I own." The fire in her response was the emotion he'd been looking for.

"If it's just clothes, it can be replaced."

Her eyes shifted.

"I'm fucking serious. I'm tossing that case overboard with you."

She strode to the bed, unzipped the case, and reached beneath her neatly folded clothing. "This can't get wet." She gripped a tin box that was plain except for a couple of twirls engraved in the lid.

His gut clenched. This was the last thing he'd expected. Yet given her cagey responses, he should've guessed. He met her gaze. "If it's drugs, I'm throwing it overboard."

"It's not drugs."

"I mean it, Charlene. They'll bring sniffer dogs on board. So if you got drugs in there, I need to know. Now!"

She undid the clips and peeled open the lid. "It's not drugs."

Blinking at the rolls of money, he felt like he was on the set of *Miami Vice*. But this was real. And the way that money looked, banded together in neat rolls, convinced him it wasn't something an innocent woman would possess. *Trouble. She was trouble.*

"My father left it to me. It's all I've got." She sucked on her bottom lip, and her demeanor shifted from despondent to defiant, yet her eyes pooled. The last thing he needed was tears.

"Give it to me." He snatched it from her hand.

"What're you going to do?"

"I've learned that if you put stuff in plain sight, they barely give it a glance. Hide it, and they sniff it out every time. And not just the dogs." He leaned over the bed. At the top, next to the pillows, he'd built small nooks, ideal for a novel or a bottle of Bud. The tin didn't quite fit and jutted out over the mattress, but it was a perfect spot. He pointed at her handbag. "Anything you need to take out of that?"

She shook her head and he shoved it into her suitcase and zipped it back up.

Charlene looked like a person who'd given up. He'd seen it before on soldiers who had been caught with their pants down . . . when all hope was lost. "It's not over yet." He opened the harness. "Step into this."

She had no choice but to hold on to his shoulder as she stepped into the device, which he'd stitched together himself. Just the touch of her hands gave him all sorts of signals that even he found creepy. Blocking the uninvited reflexes, he yanked the buckle into place, pinching her in at the waist. If it hurt, she gave no indication.

Eleven minutes.

He lived for this kind of shit, and his nerves were buzzing. But having a woman in the crosshairs was fucking up his focus.

He met her gaze. "You ready?"

"No."

"You don't have to do anything but keep your mouth shut. Even if something brushes against your legs."

That had her eyeballs popping.

"Trust me. It's better the shark in the water than the sharks about to come on board."

"Oh, that's just great. Why'd you have to tell me that?"

"Because you're gonna start thinking it anyway."

She did an eye roll that confirmed he was right.

"Let's move."

He clutched her suitcase, launched up the stairs, and scanned the horizon. It took two seconds to see it. The light was closer and brighter, and if his brain was working well, they had about nine minutes. Behind him he heard both the clang of the harness buckles and Charlene's panicked breathing. It wasn't good. Not if they were going to avoid the dogs.

As a tornado of anxiety twisted his gut, he grabbed the string attached to the rope he'd secured beneath the rim of the bow for this exact purpose. By the time he'd hauled its short length aboard, Charlene was at his side.

He squared her shoulders so she faced him.

Her lip quivered. Her wide eyes begged for another solution. But there wasn't one. This was it.

"I've done this twice before. Each time with success. The only thing stopping us from cell time is your silence. Understand?"

She nodded, but the expression on her face didn't match it.

"Good."

"How long will I be down there?" She bit on her bottom lip, but it didn't stop her chin from quivering.

"Longest so far was twenty-two minutes. It's going to feel like hours. Have you done meditation?"

"What?" Her face twisted with confusion.

He glanced at the growing light. *Seven minutes.* "Meditation takes you to your happy place. Find it. Go there. Got it!"

"I've been trying to find it for months." A tear spilled down her cheek.

The urge to thumb it away, to pull her to his chest and tell her everything was okay, was huge. But not a damn thing was okay. Not when a young woman's life was on a slippery slope to deeper trouble.

Six minutes.

A lot can happen in six minutes.

He clutched the brace at her waist. "Sorry." Then he picked her up and tossed her overboard. Her scream was cut off when she hit the water, feet first and with a huge splash. The second she surfaced, he yelled down at her. "Charlene."

Five minutes.

"Charlene!"

"What?" She screamed up at him, while simultaneously treading water and wiping hair from her face.

"Look up. See that hook. To your right. Charlene!" He yelled and hoped her clenched jaw was a sign of both determination and fury. That's what she'd need to get through this. Along with a good dose of luck.

And he didn't usually believe in luck.

"There's a loop on the rope. Get it over that hook. Do it!"

Her panic seemed to abate in a flash, replaced with a sense of urgency, impressing him once again. She hooked herself up quicker than the two men had done, and he now had to lean right over the railing to see her. That's what made that hook the perfect position. Unless the Coast Guard approached him from that side, she should go undetected.

"Good work." He hooked a rope onto her suitcase and lowered it down. "Grab hold."

She did. No fuss. Efficiency plus. She'd make a great marine.

Four minutes.

"Hook it on, but keep it in tight to the hull." Again, she followed orders efficiently.

"Okay, Charlene. This is it. I'll get you up as soon as I can. And no matter what, keep silent."

Marshall pushed off from the railing and dashed back down the stairs. His training kicked into place as he yanked the telescope from the compartment beneath the oven, shut the door, and raced back up the stairs. At the stern deck, he plucked open the three legs of the tripod and pushed the plugs into the precision-aligned holes he'd drilled in the decking a year or two ago.

Three minutes.

With the telescope in position, he yanked open the door concealed beneath the stairs leading to the flybridge and hauled out the frozen blackfin tuna that had been in place for a few weeks. He tried to ignore the sensation of centipedes crawling in his gut as he drove the hook through the tuna's lip, raced to the rear, and tossed it overboard.

The other end of the line was threaded to his trusty Calstar rod, which he'd set up before they'd left the marina. He unhooked the rod from the base of the stairs and rammed it into the port-side holder at the stern. The line was zipping out with the weight of the frozen fish, and he adjusted the gear to slow it a fraction.

Satisfied with that ruse, he returned downstairs, cracked open a Bud, tipped out a good slosh, washed it down the sink, and climbed the stairs again. Just before he edged into the swivel chair next to his rod, he flicked the switch to turn on the back spotlight.

The brilliant beacon lit up a good hundred and fifty yard of ocean behind them. Hopefully, it'd lure the Coast Guard into that position.

He swigged his beer, fought the bitterness on his tongue, sucked in a few calming breaths, and prepared himself for the best acting of his life.

A foghorn split the silence, and he jumped up and spun toward the noise, playing the part of the surprised fisherman to perfection. If his thumping heart was any gauge, he'd win an Oscar. He waved his hand and lifted his beer in an alcoholic salute to the blazing lights.

At fifty-seven feet, the patrol boat wasn't much bigger than *Miss B Hayve*, yet when it drew up alongside, Marshall felt dwarfed by its presence.

"Fuck, Crow, what the hell're you doing out here?" The booming voice bellowed over their diesel engines.

Marshall squinted against the glare, desperate to see the face that matched the voice he'd heard a thousand times before. Kirt Kilpatrick. Friend and foe rolled into one.

"Killer Kirt, is that you?" It was a stroke of luck he hadn't expected.

"Permission to come on board." Kirt's gravelly voice sounded much older than Marshall recalled. Which shouldn't be surprising; it'd been a good ten years since they'd seen each other.

"Of course. I've got beer and cigars for all of you."

The two of them started out as strangers sharing sleeping quarters and grew closer as the years went on. But when Marshall got the jump in rank over Kilpatrick, things didn't sit so well. Nothing had ever been said, but Marshall felt the hostility.

It was a shame. Years of comradeship, ruined over a set of stripes.

Last he'd heard Kilpatrick was still in the navy. Some serious shit must've gone down for him to be doing a job like this. Not that Marshall would ask. At least, not this night.

Kilpatrick stepped aboard, and Marshall's first thought was how chubby the guy had gotten. Years back, Kirt had been a champion boxer and would have been disgusted by someone in the shape he was in now. Marshall offered his hand, prepared to let Kilpatrick dominate the squeeze.

"You know you're outside American waters, Crow." Kilpatrick strangled Marshall's fingers in his oversized paw.

"I am?" He edged toward the Calstar that was still feeding out the line.

"Caught you on the radar about twelve miles out."

"Sorry about that. I've got a big one here, lost track."

"Want to tell me why you have your lights off?"

Two patrol officers climbed on board, along with a big, black German shepherd. Marshall nodded at the two men, who'd halted at Kirt's side, clearly awaiting instruction.

Marshall pointed at the telescope. "I've been doing a bit of star gazing. Works best out here. No lights and all. Check it out."

Kilpatrick's dubious expression said it all, yet he didn't shift his stance.

Marshall held his hand toward to the officer without the dog first. "Hi, Marshall Crow. Nice to meet you fellas."

He took Marshall's hand without the pretentious grip Kilpatrick seemed to need to showcase. "Max Tucker."

The other guard shifted his hold on the dog's lead as Marshall held his hand toward him. "Tony Livingston."

"Nice to meet you too." Marshall strode to his seat, picked up the rod, and began winding in the frozen fish with all the showmanship he could create. "So," he shot a glance at the men, "how you coping with Killer Kilpatrick here?"

Kirt shot him a glance, and Marshall knew what he was thinking. Kilpatrick might've been a killer in the boxing ring, but he got his nickname because of his bodily functions. When you shared sleeping quarters with seven other guys, and one of them could clear the bunks with his rumbling farts, it was not something that you tended to forget.

The two guards looked from him to Kilpatrick.

"Oh." Marshall continued to pretend he was fighting against a feisty fish. "Hasn't he told you he was the boxing champion for two years running?"

Kilpatrick's gaze was as sharp as ice picks. Marshall had just lied, and Kilpatrick was probably wondering what the motivation behind it was.

When Kilpatrick leaned back on his heels and met Marshall's gaze with a distrustful glare, Marshall's nerves twanged. He detested the feeling.

"We're gonna search your boat, Crow." Kilpatrick raised an eyebrow.

Marshall shrugged. "Sure. Help yourself to a Bud while you're down there." He raised his beer bottle and took a swig.

"We gonna find anything we shouldn't? Drugs?" The curl on Kilpatrick's lip confirmed he'd enjoy such a find.

"Nope. Mind if I stay here?" He indicated toward the rod. The line was about half a mile out, and if he wasn't careful, something bigger would come along and take a chunk out of his fish. Marshall eased into the chair, and while he played the part of the excited fisherman hauling in an immense catch, Kilpatrick, the men, and the dog disappeared downstairs.

His mind shot to Charlene with half her body dangling in the water beneath the curve of the bow, possibly straining to hear what was going on.

She'd be cold. Even with the wet suit.

He'd always hated the cold. But he hated it even more now that he had a slice of shrapnel still wedged in his collarbone. The damn thing was barely bigger than a maggot, but it stung like a bitch when he got cold.

Charlene wouldn't have much light down there either, not wedged in under the bow like that.

Cold and dark she could probably handle. But it would be her fear-loaded thoughts that would become the wild card. Her mind would play cruel tricks. He'd seen battle-hardened soldiers crumble under delusional thoughts. It wasn't pretty. Charlene played a tough game, but this was different. Her life depended on her complete silence. Not an easy ask when you pictured sharks lurking below your dangling bare feet.

How long could she last?

Now he had a new clock ticking in his brain. He guessed she'd been down there about seven minutes. Seven minutes too long.

He cursed himself. What he should've done was talk her out of this nonsense before they'd left the marina. But even as the thought blazed across his mind, he knew it would've been pointless. She was determined enough to go through with it. Or stupid enough. The jury was still out on which one it was.

Kilpatrick appeared at his side. For a big man, he was light on his feet.

"How'd you go? Find any stowaways?" Marshall offered what he hoped was a cheeky grin.

"What you got on the end of the line?" The question was loaded with suspicion, and Marshall's gut burned with the ramifications of it.

"Don't know till I land it, but I'm guessing a tuna."

"Right. Let's see it then."

Shit! Marshall hadn't even considered this scenario. He was in trouble. First up, he had so much line out there, it'd take a good ten minutes to wind it in. Time that Charlene shouldn't have to spend in the water. And he'd have to make a show of it, like he was fighting the fish. But that was the least of his problems.

Fishermen don't catch dead fish.

The second he got the fish to the surface; they were going to know something was up. And third, if he got it on board and the damn thing was still frozen, they'd be likely to attach electrodes to his balls and question him till sunrise.

They probably wouldn't, but it pissed him off that his mind went there.

He started winding in the tuna. Fast. But with each spin of the handle, his mind spun through all the possible scenarios. One of the first things he needed to do was create a distraction. "Hey, fellas, down in the cupboard above the sink, you'll find a box of the best Cuban cigars. Help yourself to a couple."

The two guards looked to Kilpatrick with hope in their eyes.

"Sure. Why not?" Kirt indicated with his head, and the officer without the dog disappeared down the stairs.

Nine minutes.

"What's the dog's name?" Marshall shot a glance at the German shepherd; although it was sitting, its ears were forward, on alert, and he knew from experience that one simple command from the handler would have those canine teeth around his wrist in a heartbeat.

"Pepper. She's four, still a bit feisty, but she knows her stuff."

"She looks healthy. I've taken in a stray, and I'm working on putting some meat on him. Poor thing looked to be on his last legs when I first found him."

"This them?" Max returned with a polished wooden box that he held up like the Olympic torch.

"Sure is. Check them out. Light one up if you want. Trust me, they're the best."

The three men reached into the box, plucking out a few cigars each. Marshall didn't care how many they took, as long as they were distracted.

Twelve minutes. He tried to think how long it would take for hyperthermia to set in. The water wouldn't be that cold, but Charlene didn't have an ounce of fat on her, not like the last two guys he'd had dangling over the side. She'd be shivering by now. Her gorgeous lips would probably be blue.

That thought had him winding faster and forcing his brain to make a plan.

"Hey, Holland, send us over a lighter." Kilpatrick called up to a guy leaning on the railing of the law-enforcement vessel.

During the time it took for the fourth man to board *Miss B Hayve*, Marshall knocked a plan together. It wasn't the best plan. It was hardly a plan at all. But it was all he had.

The additional man didn't bother introducing himself, and while the four of them got busy squirreling away his cigars and lighting them, Marshall simultaneously wound in the frozen fish and rehearsed his intended actions in his mind.

He was about to execute one of the greatest performances of his life.

The fish reached the surface. It was time.

Sixteen minutes.

Usually when either he or his customers successfully lured a fish to the surface, it would be met with much celebration. Not this time. The last thing he wanted was any of the men watching his next move.

He put the brake on the line, eased out of his chair, and plucked the gaff from its spot beneath the siding. Marshall leaned over the side, reached for the line, and tugged the fish closer. He contemplated letting the whole lot go, gaff and all, but that'd only make Kilpatrick more suspicious.

Laughter from the men both confirmed their distraction and raised his hopes he'd get away with this.

Normally, he'd drive the hook into the tuna's shoulder to haul it on board. Generally, that would still have the fish flopping about once it hit the deck.

Dead fish don't flop. Especially frozen dead fish.

He needed to look like his gaff had killed it. It'd make him look like an amateur, but that was a label he was willing to risk. Once he'd done that, his only hope was that the tuna had had ample time in the water to defrost enough that it didn't bounce like a giant hockey puck once it hit the deck.

Another burst of laughter was the trigger he needed.

Taking into consideration the potential for the tuna to still be frozen, Marshall rammed the hook though the fish's eye and hauled the twenty-pounder out of the water. Rather that his usual flourish, he lowered it to the deck gently. "There you go, boys. Who wants sushi?"

Chapter Fifteen

Charlene's jaw ached. Her fingers throbbed. And her eyes stung so much, she wouldn't be surprised if they were bleeding. Yet she held on, hanging there like she'd been committed to some form of evil punishment.

The water hadn't been cold at first, but as it leeched into her wet suit and settled at the pit of her back, icy serpents began slithering up her spine. They crawled up her neck and entered her brain as tiny, painful daggers. And the paralyzing spread of cold inched through her veins, settling in her extremities like frozen cement.

Each time she unclenched her jaw, her teeth started chattering.

It wasn't long before holding on became as difficult as believing the situation she'd gotten herself into. But she had gotten herself into this situation. Even if she'd had a year to plan this, she would never have considered this scenario. Sure, she knew what she was doing was illegal. But the ramifications of it had escaped her attention. She was stupid.

Freezing. Scared. And stupid.

Her fingers throbbed out a painful beat, matching the thumping heartbeat in her ears. She took turns peeling her fingers off the rope and repositioning them, like an octopus readjusting its tentacles.

When she couldn't hang on a moment more, she let one hand go. Her free hand remained in the cramped position, and she had to truly focus to stretch her fingers out. When they did, it was with stiff, jolting movements that shot pain through her knuckles.

A wave came out of nowhere. The force of the water ripped her hand from the rope, and she slammed, nose first, into the hull. Pain shot behind her eyes, stinging her forehead. Her suitcase was yanked from her grip between her legs, and it too banged against the side. She clawed her hair from her eyes, desperate to see again.

But it was pitch-black. Even if she could've seen through the stinging and her tears, the complete blackness made it impossible anyway. The stars were tiny pinpricks, tempting with their pretty twinkle but useless for anything else.

Marshall's brace held her in position, but hanging loose subjected her to the mercy of the water. Waves tossed her around like she was in a washing machine, and her knees, elbows, chin—hell, all of her body— slammed into the boat without warning.

And that wasn't good.

For either her body or the sound it might have made.

Pushing through the pain, she gripped the rope again and turned her back to the hull; clutching the handle, she guided the case back between her legs.

But it wasn't just her knuckles that ached now. Her eyes stung so much she had to squeeze them shut. Salty water flooded her mouth nonstop, making her tongue a dry slab, useless at producing moisture. And spasms wracked her back from both cold and dread.

Her bare feet hurt too. She wished she'd thought to put on shoes. Or even socks would have helped. Anything to stop the mental image of creatures lurking in the blackness below, eying her toes as their next meal.

She couldn't say she was scared of sharks. The truth was that she didn't know much about them. The closest she'd ever been to one was the glass tunnel at the aquarium in San Francisco. But she'd had six inches of glass separating her from row after row of razor-sharp teeth. Now there was nothing. And the murky blackout around her didn't help.

Time ticked on.

Waves tumbled in.

And her brain bounced from one awful thought to the next. Sharks. Jail cell. Missing toes. Blindness. None of the thoughts were good. Not one.

A big wave barreled into her, slamming the back of her head into the hull, and it took all her might not to cry out. With stiff fingers, she shoved her hair from her eyes and wiped the salt off her lips with the back of her hand.

The blackness seemed to be getting blacker, and she blinked back the sting in her eyes, fighting the new panic rising within. The bow of the hull made it impossible to look straight up, but when she looked out, the stars were no longer there. A dense layer of clouds were rolling in, covering the minuscule light the stars provided.

As she watched the relentless creep of clouds across the sky, a new sense of foreboding gripped her, and she knew she couldn't do this for much longer. All of a sudden, the idea of a ten-foot cell became appealing.

The silence too was disturbing. Other than the foghorn that'd had her heart exploding in her chest, the only sounds she'd heard were her own erratic breathing and the tumbling waves.

She had no idea what was going on, but the longer it took, the worse the images her mind produced. Fear gripped her like a murderer strangling a victim, squeezing her life away.

She tried to think of good times, like when she and her father had shared a picnic on the southern rim of the Grand Canyon. Or horse riding through the lush countryside in Wyoming, or even simple things like being the first to create a trail along a snowy, tree-lined path.

But as the minutes ticked on, the good times failed to come to her, replaced with memories of bad times that leeched into her brain like the freezing water. Sheer exhaustion had her mind and body failing. She couldn't go on. Not like this.

A burst of laughter jolted her out of her misery.

It had to be a good sign.

The dark clouds gradually shifted, and the stars in their wake were glistening again. Closing her eyes, she forced herself to count the waves pelting into her. At twenty-seven, she'd run out of patience, and she fought the urge to scream.

The roar of an engine broke her despair. Loud at first, it quickly abated, and she glanced up, scouring the boat's overhang, desperate to see a friendly face. It was several thumping heartbeats before she heard footsteps. The sound was the glimmer of hope she needed.

And there he was. Marshall. Tears pooled in her stinging eyes, and a sob burst from her throat.

"Charlene, are you okay?"

"No." Tears streamed down her face, and her nails dug into her palms as she strangled the rope.

"Okay. Okay. I'm coming to get you. We just have to wait a few more minutes to ensure they've gone. You've done so well. It's over, Charlene. You did it."

He continued talking, but she no longer heard. Absolute exhaustion took over. All sense of purpose was gone. The ticking clock persisted. The relentless waves continued their beating. And her tears flowed unabated.

She barely registered the huge splash to her left, and she realized Marshall was in the water only when his hand touched her cheek. "Hey, Charlene, you can let go now."

She tried to unravel her fingers, but they refused to release. "I can't." Her voice was a desperate croak.

Marshall peeled her fingers free, wrapped his arm around her waist, and lifted her up to release the hook and lower her into the water. Her breath caught as the water covered her shoulders, but that was her only response. Marshall wrapped his arm over her chest and guided her to the back of the boat.

"Can you climb the ladder?" He put her hands on the railing.

Her legs were jello, but with Marshall's help, she climbed aboard. At the top, she hunched over and gripped the rail, and within a heartbeat, he was at her side. He wrapped his arms around her, pulled her body to his, enveloping her in his warmth. "They're gone, Charlene. You were amazing."

The comfort of his embrace was overwhelming, yet it also somehow made her feel complete. Her heart danced to a wonderful beat as she allowed his hug to feed life back into her body.

He eased back, and his emerald-green eyes were laced with tenderness. When he cupped her face in his hands, something about the familiarity of his touch squeezed her heart, and it took all her mental power to remind herself that she barely knew him.

"Come on, let's get you warmed up." He helped her down the stairs. "Can you take your wet suit off?"

Her arms were like lead weights, and she tried but gave up on reaching the zipper behind her neck.

"Here, let me help."

The zipper glided down her back, and the comprehension that he was undressing her jolted her out of her imbalance. "I'm okay. I'm okay. Can you give me a minute?"

"Sure." He touched her arm. "I'll be at the top of those stairs. Just yell if you need me."

She nodded. "Thank you."

"No, Charlene. Thank *you*. What you did was incredible. You saved us both." His voice was as warm as chocolate pudding, and the look in his eyes was just as comforting. His words confirmed that she'd surprised him, and she liked that, because she'd surprised herself too. Peter had always said that every day was an opportunity to learn. Today she learned she had a mental toughness that she hadn't known she possessed.

"May I shower?"

"Of course." He plucked a towel from a cabinet over the bed and handed it to her. "Take your time." Marshall retreated up the stairs, and Charlene pushed her weary body through the process of showering. Her wrinkled fingers felt foreign as she washed the salt from her water-logged flesh, and it seemed an eternity before the cold embedded in her skin abated.

The engines were rumbling again as she studied her reflection in the mirror. She looked exactly how she felt . . . terrible. Bloodshot eyes stared back at her, with puffy bags beneath, and her lips were red and raw, and still felt crusty.

It was only when she stepped from the tiny bathroom that she realized she had no dry clothes. She was tempted to wrap the towel around herself but opted for one of Marshall's shirts instead. It was so big, she tied a knot in the bottom hem; then she tugged on a pair of his shorts with a drawstring that she pulled in to keep them in position.

By the time she climbed up the stairs to the flybridge, she was almost feeling herself again. Almost.

"Oh, hey." His eyes bulged at her clothing.

"Sorry, I had nothing else to wear."

"Oh," he scanned up her body again, then shifted his gaze to the ocean. "It's fine. I should've thought of that."

She slipped into the seat at his side. "So, what happened?"

As she sipped on a water that tasted absolutely heavenly, Marshall shifted his gaze from her to the ocean ahead of them and relayed what'd happened with the Coast Guard.

They laughed together when he told her his thoughts about the frozen fish skipping across the deck like a hockey puck. She was truly impressed with his forward planning and knew now that she was with the right captain to take her to Cuba. God knows what would've happened should she have continued her irrational decision to go with Warren and his brothers.

"In the end, we got lucky," Marshall said. "They got a call about a suspicious boat that was spotted by a cruise ship about fifty nautical miles that way." He pointed starboard. "So I've been instructed to head back to Key West."

Her jaw dropped. Her mind raced. "We're still going to Cuba, right?"

He spun to her. "Fuck no! I've turned around."

His statement punched the air from her lungs. "What? I hired you to take me to Cuba."

"Yeah, that was before we nearly got ourselves arrested." His jaw clenched, and he looked at her like she had an ice pick in her eye.

It was a couple of heartbeats before she found her voice. And her fortitude. "Fine! I'll pay Warren to finish the job."

Marshall rammed the throttle back so quickly she was thrown forward on her seat. "Fucking hell," he roared. "Are you serious?"

She nodded. "One hundred percent."

His lips pinched together. His eyes bulged. His face reddened. If he was a volcano, he'd be set to erupt. "You need to tell me what the fuck's going on."

She clenched her fists so hard her nails dug into her palms.

He shifted in his seat to glare at her with his arms folded across his chest.

Charlene was at his mercy, and she didn't like it one bit. Nobody but Detective Chapel knew her story. And even he, a seasoned detective who'd probably seen and heard almost everything, couldn't fathom it.

The more she'd explained her way of life, their way of life, the more she'd felt like an alien on her own planet. *And* the more he'd been skeptical. He'd taken her life story and twisted it in a way that changed her history forever.

She'd thought she'd never have to explain it all again.

She'd thought she'd never see an accusatory glare again, implying she was guilty.

She'd thought wrong.

She was looking at it now. But Charlene was in a unique position. She'd already lost everything that'd ever meant anything to her. She had nothing to lose.

So she flicked her wet hair off her shoulder, cleared her throat, and met his gaze. "Three months ago, a woman, who was a complete stranger to me, stabbed my father to death right in front of me."

She detailed how he'd died in her arms, despite her trying to stem the gushing blood.

She described the onlookers who stood around, equally horrified and fascinated by what they were seeing.

She explained about the ambulance arriving, only to tell her what she already knew.

The more she told, the easier it became. It was almost like describing scenes in a movie; yet although she'd seen it, and lived through it, it was still unreal.

And once she'd started, she couldn't stop. It was cathartic, and she settled into a pattern, laying down the foundation, layering it with all the events, and then waiting for Marshall's response to each shocking revelation.

He was a good listener. His eyes showed his sorrow, his surprise, and his confusion as her details of the last three months slithered back and forward like a serpent. At some point, his arms had unfolded, and the animosity she'd felt from him when she'd started gradually, yet convincingly, shifted. She sensed amazement and shock, but most of all belief.

Marshall's reaction was light-years apart from Chapel's. While Chapel showed skepticism, Marshall showed acceptance. Chapel questioned nearly every comment, whereas Marshall nodded, apparently believing every word she spoke.

The urge to have his muscular arms embracing her felt as necessary as the air she breathed. But she didn't move. When she'd reached the end, the point where she'd walked into Pirate Cove, she rubbed her hands on her thighs, met his gaze, and shrugged. "So, that's it. Now I just need someone to take me to Cuba. Is that going to be you?"

He leaned over, kissed her cheek, and spun to face forward. "You might want to hang on." He triggered the engine, and when he rammed the throttle and ripped the boat around in a quick 180-degree spin, she squealed and clutched onto the railing.

Seconds later, she burst out laughing.

He turned and grinned at her. "What?"

"I'll take that as a yes then?"

He nodded. "But it's not gonna be smooth sailing."

"Thank you."

"Thank me when have your feet in Havana."

"I mean thank you for believing me."

His eyebrows bounced up. "Why wouldn't I? Your story is so unbelievable it has to be true. Nobody could make that shit up."

As a giant wave exploded over the windshield, she contemplated how to answer that.

"I see truth in your eyes, Charlene." Marshall cut through her thoughts, and she blinked up at him.

"Military training, huh?"

He waggled his head. "You could say that."

As *Miss B Hayve* skipped over the ocean again, they settled into a comfortable silence. It was a bizarre experience to be sitting next to a complete stranger, yet to be feeling absolute faith in his abilities. But that was exactly how Charlene felt.

She could hardly believe she was twenty-eight years old and the only person she trusted was a complete stranger. Having only one trusted person in her life was always going to end in profound loss.

Except she hadn't realized that until it was too late.

Maybe Chapel had been right. The relationship she'd had with Peter was abnormal. Charlene decided, there and then, that after this was over, she was going to choose a place to live and stay long enough to make real friends.

The rest of their crossing into Cuban waters was uneventful, and they arrived under the cover of darkness at three in the morning. Marshall let go of *Miss B Hayve*'s anchor and then set about unhooking the smaller boat off the back.

He attached a Cuban flag to a pole off the back of *Miss B Hayve*, then leaned over to cover her name with a banner that read *Bailarina del Océano*, which, he explained to Charlene, was Spanish for "Ocean Dancer."

Once that was done, he asked her to help him below deck, where they emptied the contents of the fridge, freezer, pantry, and medicine cupboard into three bags that he removed from beneath the mattress.

He didn't elaborate on what they needed the supplies for, and she didn't ask. She'd already worked out that he was difficult to talk to when he was focused. No, difficult wasn't the right word; *impossible* described his demeanor better.

Once they loaded the supplies onto the smaller boat, along with her suitcase, money, cane, and his night bag, they climbed aboard themselves.

Charlene was in awe of his planning, so she went along with his instructions without question. Within ten minutes of releasing the anchor, they were motoring toward the set of twinkling lights she assumed was Havana with a pile of groceries, all her worldly possessions, and a man sporting a don't-mess-with-me expression.

The trip wasn't anywhere near as smooth as the ride in *Miss B Hayve*, and Charlene soon found herself wincing at every bone-jarring swell they bounced over. Marshall didn't seem to notice. Instead, his gaze flitted between the surrounding horizon and the flickering lights in the distance.

Although they traveled under the cover of darkness, Charlene wanted to point out that the roar of their motor could probably be heard from about a hundred miles away. But talking to Marshall was impossible over the din. The closer they got to shore, the more desperately she wanted to ask him how their arrival could go unnoticed with such an ear-piercing racket.

Marshall had got them this far, though, so she stared ahead, clutched onto the railing, and prayed a bright spotlight didn't suddenly appear out of nowhere.

The sun still wasn't even a glow on the horizon when Marshall eased back on the engine and shifted back on his seat. The change in his stance had her thinking that they'd made it past some pivotal point, although she couldn't work out what it was.

Lights dotting the distant shore grew closer and brighter, and soon she could make out shapes of buildings and other boats and, more importantly, land.

He'd done it. Charlene was about to step foot on Cuban soil.

Now what?

The question came out of nowhere. She hadn't even thought through her next step.

She figured she'd somehow make her way to the *Legendarios del Guajirito* show. But that was the easy part. What was she going to do when she got there? She didn't have a photo of Peter to hand around. She doubted it was even his real name. And the likelihood of someone remembering him after twenty or so years was narrow.

On top of all that, she didn't speak Spanish.

Her eyes shifted from the approaching shore to Marshall's bulging muscles as he worked the tiller. He'd already done enough. Just getting her here had been a huge risk. But she'd need his help some more.

A lopsided sign, its bottom right corner touching the water, announced that they were heading toward Marina Hemingway. She turned to Marshall, grinning at the prospect that they were nearly there.

But he must've read her thoughts and offered a shake of his head.

So she went right back to stewing over the day ahead and watching their approach to the shore.

The marina materialized as a city of ship masts and pretty lights, but

Marshall veered away from it, heading toward a bay that she hadn't noticed. Rather than go down the middle, Marshall hugged the boat to the shore. They passed rickety jetties and a few newer ones.

Marshall turned on a torch and lowered the engine a fraction. And as the whine in her ears abated, she contemplated how she'd ask Marshall for more help. He struck her as a man motived by two things: honor, a trait born out of his lengthy navy career, and money, a thing of necessity.

She was prepared to use both.

The bay gradually narrowed to a river, and that, in turn, became a small creek that *Miss B Hayve* wouldn't have fit through. They passed a few more jetties with small, practical boats tied up alongside.

This area was old, and if Charlene had to guess, she'd say it was also verging on underprivileged. Her mind flashed to her tin of money, nestled amongst her handbag and wet clothing in the suitcase, and she wondered if she'd been foolish for letting go of the prepaid, locked safe-deposit box in New Orleans.

Finally, Marshall angled the boat into a jetty that was leaning at such an angle, it was a wonder it was still standing. He looped a rope around the closest pylon to the shore and turned off the engine. The silence screamed in her ears as if the motor was still going. It made her think of her earlier question.

"So that wasn't exactly a discrete entrance." She wriggled her right ear for emphasis.

He shrugged. "Exactly. If we were trying to be discrete, we'd attract attention as someone trying to sneak in. This way we looked like every other boat heading into shore after a fishing trip."

Charlene offered him an approving grin. Marshall seemed to have thought of everything. "So, what now?"

"Grab as much as you can. Anything you leave behind will be gone when we get back."

"Oh." The first thing she grabbed was her case—not for the sodden clothing, but for the money stashed inside. The second was the cane. Marshall smirked at her choices.

When she'd told him about the cane and, in particular, what she'd found inside, he'd seemed to be fascinated by it. He'd asked a few questions, mainly clarifying why she hadn't thought to ask Peter about it. And she'd responded that she wished that she had asked.

Without a word, Marshall dashed into the bushes with his flashlight, and she stood, hands on hips, wondering what the hell he was doing. A repetitive screeching sound announced his return through the bushes, and when she spied him again, he was pushing a rusted-out wheelbarrow that no longer had rubber on the tire.

Between the barrow and her, they managed to carry everything from the boat. Lugging her suitcase over the gravelly track, and carrying one of the bags they'd filled with pantry items, she followed Marshall into the bush and wondered if she'd ever see American soil again.

Chapter Sixteen

The two most important things in Marshall's life right now were both in jeopardy. One was his boat. Despite the Cuban flag and changing her name to a boat registered in Cuba, she was still exposed.

If the Cuban coast guard found *Miss B Hayve* without any crew aboard, they'd seize her for sure, and he'd never see her again. Of that he was certain. And while he had her insured, an insurance payout would be a pipe dream. Not when he'd left her to ride the swell in Cuban waters.

The other most important thing in his life right now was Charlene.

Despite knowing her for less than twelve hours, she'd sure made an impact. She had gone from being a complete stranger to a woman he was totally infatuated with. And that was no mean feat; it'd been a decade or so since a woman had captured his interest.

And it wasn't just her beauty. It was everything. Her innocence. Her bravery.

Charlene was no ordinary woman.

She was tough too, with nobody to turn to, and no assets, other than those mysterious bundles of money. Not too many people could handle that.

Several years ago, he'd woken from his alcoholic stupor long enough to realize that he had nothing.

No money. No home. No friends. No life.

Ending his life had never been an option.

He wasn't a quitter, and he wasn't about to start then. The only things he had going for himself were his navy pension and his love of the ocean. Fortunately for him, he'd made it work. He went cold turkey from the drink and set himself up in a rusty shed that rattled like a beast in a storm.

But he considered himself lucky.

The shed belonged to a little old lady who exchanged her measly accommodation for his handyman skills. And that allowed him to save nearly every cent of his pension. *Miss B Hayve* came first, and he lived on her until he had enough to buy his own little shack. It'd taken him three years to recover from his destitution.

As he listened to Charlene's footsteps behind him, he wondered how long she'd take to recover from the grenade life had thrown at her.

She was quite literally a damsel in distress. And while he'd never considered himself as any kind of knight in shining armor, he was good at a few things. Saving people was one of them.

He'd lost a few civilians in his time—six, to be exact. Every one of their faces was permanently etched into his brain. Every one of them deserved to live.

It was a shocking thing to have an unwitting hand in someone's death. But that was the nature of war. And not just war. Some of the people he'd tried to save were the product of their society. No clean water. No medication. No food. He'd seen enough desperate situations to know that most people didn't know how lucky they were.

That was how Aleyna's family was before he'd met them. Dirt poor. His ex-fiancée, her five brothers, and her parents all lived in a tiny shack that leaked in the rain and had a dirt floor. They ate once a day, and that was usually day-old bread and whatever else they could scrape together.

Things had changed significantly for them since the day Aleyna had reluctantly taken him to her home to meet her family.

Ironically, that meeting had been the demise of their relationship. Not because he was put off by her upbringing. Hell no, it was the opposite. It made him realize that she wasn't in love with him at all. She was in love with what he offered. Stability. Money. Freedom.

When he'd broken up with her, he'd promised to help. Yet he was pretty certain Aleyna hadn't believed him at the time. She was wrong. He just hoped Aleyna and her family were willing to return some of that favor now.

Without his flashlight and the trodden-dirt track weaving through the underbrush, he'd get lost for sure. He'd trekked this exact trail seventeen times, twice that if you included both ways, and each time was more grueling than the last.

The damn vegetation grew thicker and more robust each time. Dangling vines threatened to strangle them around every bend, if they didn't claw the shit out of them first. Based on the occasional wince from Charlene, he expected her to have her share of scrapes and scratches by the time they reached their destination.

Not that she was complaining. He liked that about her.

Her willingness to go along with him, a virtual stranger, without a million questions showed her determination. Or stupidity. He hoped it wasn't the latter. He didn't do stupidity.

He reached the small clearing and moved to the left so Charlene could step in beside him. When she did, he maintained the flashlight's angle at the ground, yet there was enough light to see her face. They'd been on the go for seven hours, and he had no idea when she'd last slept.

Add to that the ordeal she'd had in the water and she should be close to passing out. Her eyes were bloodshot, her breathing labored. Though she looked shattered, what stood out the most was her willpower.

"Where are we?" she whispered.

"My ex-fiancée's house." There was no real point in elaborating. "Let's go."

"Oh." She stepped in beside him, and together they climbed the small rise to the ramshackle house he knew was at the top. As they approached, he noted they'd put on a back patio since he'd last visited. It wasn't a masterpiece, but he could already tell their home was improving.

He rolled the wheelbarrow in under the cover and went to the back door. It would be unlocked. There was no point locking doors around here. If someone wanted to get in, they'd smash their way in. Besides, there was nothing of value inside anyway.

"Hey, Yelena, ¿qué tal algunos de tus famosos cafés?" Marshall called from the cramped, yet tidy kitchen.

"What're you doing?" Charlene shot him a glare.

"Waking them up. You might want to stand back for this."

He snapped on the yellowed bare light bulb dangling from the ceiling, and three seconds later, Aleyna's mother came waddling into the room with her arms open and her expression joyous. "Hola, Marshall, qué bueno verte."

Yelena got smaller every time he saw her, but her strength didn't falter. She cupped his face and pulled him down so she could kiss both his cheeks. "Es mucho tiempo desde que te vemos. Creí que nos habías dejado."

Yelena was complaining that the times between his visits were too long. She said that every time. He glanced at Charlene to see her slink back against the wall in time to miss the barrage of family members who poured into the room. There were only three bedrooms in this home, yet ten people lived under the roof. Nearly all of them were now crammed in the kitchen, hugging and kissing Marshall.

Marshall watched Yelena's eyes widen when she spied Charlene, then she wriggled through the crowd and repeated her greeting for Charlene too.

The old woman turned to Marshall with an enormous, yet mostly toothless grin lighting up her face. "Has traído a tu esposa?"

Marshall chuckled at Charlene. "She thinks you're my wife."

Charlene's eyes brightened, and she shook her head. "No, no, we're just friends."

"She doesn't speak English. Hardly any of them do."

"Oh." Charlene frowned. Her confusion must be running at maximum capacity about now.

The room was chaos, but once Marshall told them that he had indeed brought supplies, the bedlam shifted from the kitchen to the patio outside. "No la maleta."

"I just told them not to touch your suitcase, but you may want to grab it just in case."

Charlene raced outside. "Sorry. Excuse me, I'll just take that—" With her suitcase in hand, she edged back from the frenzy, and Marshall stepped in beside her.

"I try to bring them as much as I can. Some supplies are very scarce here."

Rusian, Yelena's husband, held up a fishing tackle. It wasn't a new one, but Marshall knew it would be Rusian's prized possession for a very long time. "*Ahh, sí, sí, gracias, gracias.*"

Yelena plucked out the medicines, soap, shampoo, creams, toothbrushes, sugar, coffee, and jars of spices and scooped them to one side.

"I know it looks chaotic, but don't worry." Marshall winked at Charlene, who was staring wide-eyed at the mêlée. "They'll have a look through it all, and some of the boys will beg Yelena to keep some things, but it'll be pointless. She runs the house, so who gets what is totally up to her. Even Rusian's claim to the fishing tackle will be up for debate."

"It's really nice that you do this."

He shrugged. "It's the least I can do. They lost the best son-in-law in the world when I separated from Aleyna."

Charlene chuckled and playfully slapped him on the arm. "So she doesn't live here?"

"Yeah, she does, actually. She and her husband and their daughter, Mariana."

"Oh."

"Hi, Marshall." He turned to the voice. "Speak of the devil." He leaned down to kiss his ex-fiancée's cheeks. "Hi, Aleyna. You look well."

"*Gracias.* So do you."

"Thanks. I'd like you to meet Charlene." He couldn't quite read the expression on Aleyna's face, but it was probably a mixture of suspicion and jealousy. Aleyna didn't like it when someone challenged her in the beauty department. And even though Charlene had battled through a rough couple of hours, her natural beauty still shone through.

The noise from the action on the patio grew explosive when they found the chocolates and coffee at the bottom of one of the bags. Seven adults fighting over three packets of Reese's Peanut Butter Cups was not pretty. Charlene covered her ears, and her mouth dropped, but it was clear she was enjoying the spectacle.

"How about a coffee, Aleyna?"

"*Sí*, come on. They crazy." Aleyna rolled her eyes and turned.

He indicted to Charlene to follow his ex-fiancée back into the kitchen. Marshall didn't have much time, and the ticking clock on the wall wasn't any help. It was already 4:30. In two hours, the sun would begin to glow on the horizon. He was cutting it close.

Aleyna busied herself with filling the kettle on the stove, while Marshall gestured for Charlene to sit.

When Aleyna turned back to him and wriggled her eyebrows, he got straight down to business. "We need your help."

Aleyna crossed her arms and eased back so her butt was against the hundred-year-old stove. "I'm listening." Even after all these years, she still glared with animosity toward him.

None of the donations he made each visit seemed to make up for the freedom she thought their so-called marriage would have brought. They'd been engaged for a total of nine months when he'd called it off. He'd have done it sooner if he'd had the guts.

But it wasn't just Aleyna he was letting down. It was her whole family.

Their only daughter had been offered the opportunity for them all to escape their sheltered life.

He'd ruined that opportunity.

He met Aleyna's fiery gaze. "I need you to take Charlene to *Legendarios del Guajirito* tonight."

"What?" Charlene blurted. "What about you?"

"I've gotta get back to *Miss B Hayve*."

"You're leaving me." Charlene's eyes just about popped out of her head.

"I have to move her into international waters or she'll be seized."

"Yes, but . . . you're leaving me?"

"I got you here. That's what you wanted, right?"

Her jaw dropped, her eyes blinked, but that was the total extent of her reaction. "But what will I do?"

He liked that she seemed disappointed about him leaving but then realized how desperate that made him seem and smacked that thought away. "Do whatever it is you came here to do."

"But—"

Her eyes pleaded with him, and he dragged his gaze away to look at the clock. "Aleyna will look after you. Right, Aleyna?"

Aleyna's arms were crossed, and her glare intense. Her spunk had been one of the things that had drawn him to her in the first place. But she'd probably never forgive him. Even with a husband who looked after her better than he probably could have, especially when he'd been deployed for over ten months of every year of his enlistment. "Aleyna?"

She rolled her eyes and huffed. "Yeah, sure."

"Good. She'll need some sleep. Her clothes need washing too."

"What am I?" Aleyna blurted. "Her fucking mother?"

Marshall plucked out a hundred-dollar note from his pocket. "No, Aleyna, you're looking after a paying guest." He placed it on the bench.

"Marshall, I can—"

He waved his hand to cut Charlene off. "Get a bit of shut-eye. Then do what you need to do." Marshall stood. "I'll be back for you at midnight tonight. Don't be late."

Charlene stood too, and the pause between them was agony. His gut told him he should stay. And he wasn't happy with that—he usually listened to his gut. But his brain told him to get the fuck back to his boat. Charlene would be fine. Come this time tomorrow, she'd be safely back onboard *Miss B Hayve*, and the two of them would be scooting back across international waters.

"You look after her, Aleyna."

Aleyna huffed. "I will."

It took all his effort to stride away. He went to Aleyna's family to say good-bye, and Yelena robbed a couple of minutes of precious time as she tried to talk him into breakfast.

With the tick of the clock resonating in his ears and his flashlight showing the way, he began to run.

Chapter Seventeen

Charlene watched openmouthed as Marshall sprinted down the hill and disappeared into the underbrush. It was like watching a plane crash on the news. Even though she knew it was going to happen, she still couldn't believe it when it did.

But this was exactly what she'd asked for. To be taken to Cuba.

She felt like a complete fool.

Charlene turned to Aleyna, whose steely gaze and folded arms radiated animosity. She cleared her throat. "I'm sorry to put you out like this."

"Is he your boyfriend?"

Charlene nearly choked on her tongue. "No. Not at all. We only met last night. I barely know him."

She huffed and turned to the kettle. "Didn't look like that to me."

"Well, I can assure you it's true."

Aleyna stepped up to the sink, and when she looked at Charlene over her shoulder, she braced for the next question. "We were lovers, you know."

"Yes, he told me."

Aleyna poured the hot water into a cup and offered it to Charlene. "What else did he say?"

When Aleyna placed her hands on her hips, drawing attention to her womanly curves, Charlene decided that the Aleyna wanted to hear praise. She thrived on attention and commanded it too. And because Aleyna had just been declared Charlene's new best friend, she decided she'd better lay it on thick.

"He said you were the most beautiful woman he'd ever met."

"Really?"

"Oh, yes. He's never found another woman like you. That's why he never married."

"Ahh, yes. I know." A smile curled at the edges of her plump lips, but a heartbeat later, her eyes shifted, and her dark irises seemed to grow darker. "He left me. Did he tell you that?"

She nodded and lowered her eyes to the black brew. "He did."

"*Bastardo.*" She didn't say it with malice. It was more of a matter-of-fact comment.

Charlene didn't need a translation of Aleyna's comment, yet she had no idea how to respond. She didn't know either Marshall or Aleyna and had no right to choose sides or offer opinions. Her best option was to change the subject. "So, Marshall said you would know *Legendarios del Guajirito.*"

"*Sí,* everybody in Havana knows of it. If you have job there, you very lucky."

"When can you take me there?"

"Tonight."

"Oh. We can't go during the day?"

"No. Show start eight-thirty tonight."

Charlene groaned. She had hoped they'd have a matinee show.

"You have ticket? It always booked up."

"No."

Aleyna shook her head. "Well, then, it not possible—"

"I can pay." Charlene interrupted Aleyna. "I will pay double for a ticket. I have to go tonight."

"Double? Maybe I can get you ticket."

"Thank you."

"Why you want to see so bad?"

Charlene contemplated lying, but a plausible lie was impossible. In the end, the truth was the perfect answer. If nothing else, it might draw some sympathy. "My father passed away a few months ago. When I was cleaning out his things, I found a videocassette of him singing in the *Legendarios del Guajirito* show. I want to see the show for myself."

Aleyna's shoulders softened, and she brought her mug to her lips and blew on it. "I will take you. You want sleep? You can have Tajo's bed. Top bunk."

"Oh, I don't want to put anyone out."

"I have orders." She picked up the hundred-dollar note Marshall had placed on the table and slotted it down her top. "Wait here."

Aleyna strode away, leaving Charlene to glance around the kitchen. It was very tiny. But she'd had tiny before and knew that as long as everything had a place, then tiny was irrelevant. Practical was more important. And when funds and supplies were limited, you tended to get very good at practical.

She returned her attention to outside. Other than Yelena, all the residents of the house were men. They were all similar in height and build; the only one who looked completely different from the others was the father, and it was only because of his gray hair. They seemed to be still arguing over the chocolates. She'd never had siblings to fight with.

That thought produced another thought that'd never occurred to her before. Was she an only child?

"Come." Aleyna appeared in the doorway.

Charlene pushed off the stool, grabbed her rolling case and Peter's cane, and followed Aleyna down a dark hallway.

"My husband," she waved her hand in a flourish. "He still sleeping. He even sleep through big storms. My daughter too."

Charlene smiled at that. Peter had been the same way. There were many mornings when she'd complained about thunder keeping her up all night, but Peter had slept through the whole thing.

Aleyna stepped into a room with two sets of bunk beds, and Charlene's eyes darted about the room. "I can't sleep here."

"Why not?" Aleyna snapped.

"Your . . . your brothers sleep here."

"I will keep them out while you sleeping."

Charlene flicked her hand. "It's okay. I'm not tired anyway."

Aleyna shrugged. "Okay then." She strode from the doorway.

Charlene took another glance around the room. The four beds all looked like the person had just jumped out of them, which was mostly likely true given that Marshall had woken them up well before sunrise. She'd slept in many rough beds in her lifetime. But at least they'd always appeared to have clean linen. The idea of crawling into those sweat-stained sheets gave her the creepy crawlies.

She lugged her suitcase back up the hallway. Behind the counter, Yelena was busy slotting Marshall's donations into the cupboards. Aleyna was outside with her brothers now, and they looked to be fighting over a razor. Charlene returned to her coffee and nodded at Yelena. "*Hola.*" The extent of her Spanish was dismal. But then, she'd never had a need for it before.

"*Sí, hola. ¿Tienes hambre?*" The old woman smiled, showing off her one solitary tooth.

Charlene shrugged. "Sorry, I don't understand." She made a hand gesture that she hoped portrayed what she was trying to say.

The old woman must've understood, because she demonstrated "eating" with her hands.

Charlene shook her head. "Oh. No, thanks. *Gracias.*" She patted her belly and puffed out her cheeks like she was full. The truth was she wasn't full at all; in fact, she was very hungry. But the thought of taking food from these people didn't seem right.

The old lady smiled again and then went back to shoving her goodies away. A piercing light caught Charlene's eye, and it took her a moment to realize it was the sun cutting through the trees.

The first rays of sunshine had the family members filing in from outside and disappearing into various rooms of the house.

Charlene sipped her rocket-fueled coffee and watched the family morph from bickering siblings to a united team. Each seemed to have a job, and neither parent felt the need to dictate who did what.

As the sun made its way over the treetops, two brothers, wearing just shorts and flip-flops, disappeared into the bushes carrying an assortment of gardening tools. One of the brothers collected a few buckets and headed for the gap in the trees that Marshall had vanished into. The last two brothers stayed near the house and flitted from one job to another.

Aleyna appeared at her side. "I wash your clothes."

"Oh, no, no, it's okay. Show me where the washing machine is, and I'll do it."

Aleyna cocked her head in a way that implied Charlene was joking. Charlene slipped off the chair, wrapped her fingers around the handle of her suitcase, and nodded. "Lead the way."

After a shrug of her shoulders, Aleyna led the way through the house and out the back door. To the left of the yard was another small building. The door was open, and half a dozen chickens were pecking the ground in front of it.

Aleyna shooed the chickens away and then fully opened the door with a grin at Charlene that implied she was enjoying this. When Charlene stepped into the dank space, she knew why. There was no washing machine and no dryer. Nothing that required electricity. Not even a light bulb.

She wanted to slap herself for her naïveté.

"Washing machine there." Aleyna pointed at a square concrete sink with a green tinge lining the sides. A cake of yellow soap rested on the edge, along with a scrub brush that looked like porcupine roadkill.

"Dryer out there." Through the cracked window, she pointed at a clothesline. "I did offer." Aleyna laughed all the way back into the house.

Alone with her dirty laundry and troubling thoughts, Charlene's resolve began to unravel. The urge to cry had her covering her eyes with her hands, and a sob caught in her throat.

She'd never felt so alone in her life. Even her heartbeat sounded hollow in her ears.

But she couldn't give up.

Not now. Not after risking everything to come this far. She had to get answers, if not to clear Peter's name, then certainly to put clarity and sanity back into her life. She already knew her life would never be the same, but until she got answers, she was destined to live in a spiral of hostile thoughts and impossible questions.

She sucked in a shaky breath, wiped her eyes, unzipped her suitcase and placed the tin of money and her sodden handbag aside.

By the time she finished rinsing the saltwater from her clothes, her back was killing her, her hunger pangs were getting angry, and the sun was a blazing fireball in the sky. The heat coming off it, and the steady breeze drifting up from the creek below, would ensure her clothes would be dry in an hour.

Deciding to leave her suitcase there, she reached for the tin containing the rolls of money and shoved as much cash as she could into her handbag. All the remaining rolls stayed in the tin. With her handbag slung over her shoulder and the tin in one hand and the cane in the other, she headed back into the house.

Her first couple of steps through the door were met with silence. The bedlam from this morning was replaced with domestic calm. Yelena was sewing a patch on a pair of jeans. Aleyna was scrubbing dirt off a mountain of potatoes, and Rusian was weaving a few loose threads into a fishing net.

"How did you do?" Aleyna's grin confirmed she was enjoying Charlene's welcome to Cuba.

"All done."

"Good." Aleyna returned her attention to the potatoes, and Charlene wondered what she should do now.

"Is there anyone who can take me into town?"

"No." Her answer was abrupt.

"Is it far to walk?"

Aleyna burst out laughing. "*Esta mujer tonta quiere caminar a la ciudad.*"

When both Aleyna's mother and father started laughing too, Charlene assumed her question had been a stupid one.

Charlene felt like a fool as she waited for their laughter to die down. "Would you like some help with those?" Charlene hoped her offer would alleviate the negative vibes coming off Aleyna.

"No, thanks."

Apparently not. Charlene had met her share of unfriendly people, Aleyna was up there as one of the most blatantly obvious ones. She slipped onto a stool at the kitchen bench and shared her gaze between the potato scrubbing and handcrafts.

Soon utter exhaustion took hold, and her eyes began to droop. When she glanced at the clock, she did a mental calculation to confirm that she hadn't slept in twenty-seven hours. And even that had been a disjointed sleep while sitting up on the bus that had transported her from her relative safety in New Orleans to the vast unknown in Key West.

Once her head bounced a few times, she knew she couldn't fight the fatigue a moment more. Much to her surprise, the sweat-stained sheets were actually appealing.

"Sorry, Aleyna, but I need to sleep. Is it still possible to use one of the bunk beds?"

"Yeah, sure." Without taking her hands from the dirty water, Aleyna pointed down the hall with her chin. "No need to lock the door; the lock doesn't work anyway."

Charlene's body seemed to crumble beneath her as she inched toward the bedroom. Once inside, she shut the door and turned to the beds. They were all made now, but the smell in the room was that of a male locker room after a football game.

She'd know too; she once had the job of cleaning the locker room for the Jaguars college football team in southern Alabama. It had taken days to get that stench out of her nostrils, and by then, she'd be due to go back in again anyway. So if she survived that, she told herself, this would be a breeze in comparison.

She took a top bunk, figuring it would be the safest. Crawling up there was a challenge, though; her arms were still like jelly, and the clothes washing hadn't helped her recover. The mattress was rock hard and so narrow she had no idea how any of those men slept on it.

Deciding to remain on top of the covers, she shoved her precious tin and handbag under the pillow and pulled her cane in behind her. She'd never been more proud of her decision to keep the cane than she was now. And she wouldn't hesitate to whack it across someone's head, if required.

The extent of her loneliness ached in her chest, and sorrow hung in her belly like a wet, knotted towel. Trying to ignore her growling hunger pains was like trying to ignore a snake in a bathtub. She rolled to her side, curled her hand around the silver owl, and squeezed her eyes closed.

The wise old owl always knows.

Charlene woke with a jolt, and it was a couple of thumping heart-beats before she realized where she was. Pins and needles in her fingers confirmed she'd barely moved, which wasn't surprising given how exhausted she'd been. The room was a strange sepia color, and when she glanced out the window between the bunks, her heart leapt to her throat. The sun was setting.

She bolted upright and slammed her head into the ceiling. Wincing, she rubbed her head, and her next thought went to her money. She rammed her hand beneath the pillow.

It was there.

Ignoring the new throb above her eye, she climbed down, put her handbag across her chest, and clutched her tin and her cane as she headed toward the lively music coming from the other end of the house.

It seemed the entire family was on the back patio, creating their own music. Aleyna and one of her brothers were dancing to the steady beat provided by a variety of instruments played by the rest of the family. A young girl who Charlene assumed was Aleyna's daughter was singing.

Music was the key that connected the family, and their obvious joy in sharing it was another nail in Charlene's loneliness coffin. It seemed that every day she was shown another example of how unusual her upbringing had been. And it only served to increase the anger brewing inside her.

When Aleyna spied Charlene, she separated from her brother, but he continued to dance, and the music continued to play as she skipped over to Charlene. "I was beginning to think you'd never wake up."

"Why didn't you wake me?" Charlene hissed through clenched teeth.

Aleyna waggled her head. "Do I look like your mother?"

Charlene was seconds from letting her fury rip when she caught herself. Like it or not, she needed Aleyna. "We need to get going."

"Yes. But we're not leaving till you get changed." Aleyna ran her eyes up Charlene's body. She was still wearing Marshall's shirt and shorts. Charlene wanted to kick herself as she realized that her dress choice might have been the reason for some of Aleyna's spite.

"Hurry up." Aleyna pointed at Charlene's suitcase, which was on the floor by the table. The lid was up, and all her clothes had been folded back inside.

Charlene palmed her chest in surprise. This was the last thing she'd expected. "Thank you."

"Not me. It was *Mamá*."

"Please, thank her for me."

Aleyna turned to the jovial crowd. "*Ella dice gracias, Mamá.*"

Yelena held a battered tambourine above her head and banged it with her palm.

"We go in three minutes," Aleyna said. "Oh, and dress pretty." The Cuban woman skipped back to her brother, and they fell straight into a dance like the move had been professionally choreographed.

Charlene tossed her tin of money into her case and ran with it back to the bunk-filled room. She desperately wanted a shower. She'd even be happy for a quick wash. But there was no time.

A mental summary of her clothes confirmed that she didn't have anything pretty. Pretty wasn't Charlene's thing. If Aleyna's fancy flowing dress with layers of frills was anything to go by, then Charlene had no hope of meeting Aleyna's expectations of pretty. She was more of a practical girl.

The one and only dress she did own was a simple red frock that came in at her waist and flared out into a flowing skirt that fell to her knees. The stretchy polyester traveled well and never needed ironing, and its simple design made it easy to dress up or down. She changed into it, dabbed on deodorant, pulled her hair up into a high ponytail, and put on flat sandals.

That was the extent of her pretty.

When she zipped up her case, she realized she had a new problem. What to do with her assets: the cane, the cash, and the case. She couldn't take all of them with her. Leaving them here wasn't an ideal option, but it was all she had. With a bit of luck, they'd still be here when she returned.

She put a wad of cash into her bra, then took several bundles out of her handbag, placed them with the remaining rolls in her suitcase along with the tin, and zipped it back up. Then, with nothing else to do, she slipped her handbag over her neck so that it sat diagonally across her body, grabbed her cane, and strode out the door.

Aleyna was waiting for her in the kitchen, and when she cast her eyes over Charlene's outfit, a look of disgust twitched at her lip. Charlene ignored it. "Ready."

The Cuban woman huffed, then spun on her heel and strode away. Charlene followed her outside to a car that looked like it belonged on the set of a classic movie. It was a long red convertible with shiny chrome trim and white leather seats. She'd only ever seen cars like this on the big screen.

The man behind the car wore a big white cowboy hat, and his western-themed pink shirt was complete with fancy embroidery over the lapels. He tipped his hat when he saw the ladies approach and smiled a very broad smile.

"Oh, wow, this car is lovely," Charlene said as the driver opened the passenger door and tilted the seat forward for her to climb into the back.

"It's a 1960 Buick." Aleyna answered for him. "This my husband, José."

Charlene held her hand forward. "Nice to meet you, José."

"*Hola*, welcome to Havana." His Cuban accent was strong yet easy to understand.

"Thank you." Charlene slipped into the back seat, and after José pushed the seat back, Aleyna moved into the front passenger seat.

José took his place behind the wheel, put the car into gear, and they drove off. Despite its age, the car was in immaculate condition. The leather seats showed little sign of wear, and the dashboard too looked to be in original condition. "Is this your car, José?"

"No. We not so lucky." Aleyna spoke for him. "It his boss's car. José is driver, and he takes tourists around Havana."

The road shifted from gravel to potholed asphalt, and the landscape quickly changed from the occasional shack nestled among dense foliage to rows and rows of houses. Some were dilapidated homes verging on collapse, while some were mansions. Some of those mansions were pristine; some, however, were in dire need of attention. The disparity between the conditions of the homes was incredible.

Soon the streets shifted from houses to more diverse architecture.

Peter had taught her to appreciate architecture, and it had been nothing for them to spend a whole day in a new city spotting gargoyles and admiring elaborate wrought-iron decorations.

Cuba, it seemed, was a mixture of all the architectural classics. She recognized Spanish influences, and Italian, Roman, and Greek styles. Some of the buildings, however, were derelict and had plants growing out of the windows and creeping down from the rooftops. Many had collapsed altogether, leaving elaborate marble staircases to mark their existence.

People were everywhere. Spilling into the streets were young lovers strolling hand in hand, families that looked to consist of several generations, couples with children.

The thing that struck Charlene the most was that despite the abundant rundown buildings, indicating poverty, everybody seemed happy.

Dancing and music were everywhere. Every street corner had small groups putting on what seemed to be an impromptu show that had tourists filming and locals clapping along. It was easy to get swept up in the fun. But Charlene wasn't here for fun; she was here for answers. So if Aleyna wasn't going to be helpful, she decided to try José.

She leaned forward, easing between the two front seats. "José, what can you tell me about *Legendarios del Guajirito*?"

"*Ahh, sí.*" He shot a glance at her that showed off his crooked white teeth. "*Legendarios del Guajirito* is most famous of all dance show in Havana. They do beautiful dancing and singing. Here all the tourists go."

"Yes, I know. Can you tell me about the singers?"

He wobbled his head. "Only little. They are legends in all of Cuba. Everybody dance."

Charlene attempted a few more pointed questions, but it quickly became apparent that the extent of his knowledge of the show was that it was a major tourist draw and that he could get tickets at a special price.

About forty minutes after they left Aleyna's place, José pulled the car alongside a small park centered among four roads. All the other cars in the street were as old and as impressive as José's Buick. It was like stepping back in time.

José came around and opened the door for Aleyna and Charlene. Aleyna kissed José on his cheek and said something in Spanish that had his eyes darting to Charlene. "We here." She turned her back to Charlene and crossed the road toward a grand building plastered with posters of the dance show.

Charlene nodded at José. "Thank you." Then she clutched the strap of her handbag, gripped the cane, and raced after Aleyna. A large crowd was lining up along the side of the building, but Aleyna avoided the line and went inside to climb the internal stairs. The crowd's excited din bounced off the narrow, marble-lined stairway. At the top of the stairs, she said something to a man blocking the door and then turned to Charlene.

"You need to pay him."

"Oh, umm, how much?"

"One hundred."

Charlene hoped she meant American dollars, because that's all she had. She adjusted her positioning so neither Aleyna nor the man could see her pluck the money from the inside pocket of her bag. She closed the zipper before she handed the cash to the man. He frowned at the note for a nanosecond before his eyes lit up. With a grin lighting his face, he slotted the note into his pants pocket and then shoved the door open.

His confusing reaction had Charlene making a mental note to check with Aleyna once they were settled. They entered into a saloon-type bar with dark wood and circular bar tables dotted about. People were everywhere, and the noise of the crowd was triple that of the stairway.

Aleyna pushed through, leading Charlene to another passage. Along the way, Aleyna paused briefly to chat with several barmaids who were dressed in low-cut, white cowgirl uniforms and matching cowboy hats. She didn't bother translating anything, and Charlene began to wonder if anyone spoke English.

Through another doorway, Charlene was led into a room that echoed the sets of a bad 1970s western film. Giant wagon wheels hung from the ceiling, with bare light bulbs dangling below them, and the mustard-colored walls were dotted with horseshoes and cow horns.

The tables were set up in long rows leading from the back of the room to the front stage. Directly in front of the stage was a bar, with several young women already busy making colorful cocktails. The stage was T-shaped; a large extension extended down the dining room, separating the tables.

Aleyna led Charlene to the front of the room, to the seat wedged in the very corner between both the front stage and the central stage. It was probably the best seat in the house. She indicated to a simple wooden chair at the very front.

Charlene adjusted her bag to her hip, nestled her cane against the stage, then sat down and pulled her chair aside for Aleyna to sit too.

"Okay, I wait for you out front at end of show."

Charlene blinked up at her. "You're not staying."

"No." She waggled her head like Charlene was nuts.

"Does anyone speak English?"

She rolled her eyes. "I don't know."

Charlene's glimmer of hope was yanked out from beneath her. Her eyes darted from the empty stage to the young waitresses running around with trays full of drinks and wondered how any of this was going to give her answers.

A heavy cloak of hopelessness smothered her.

"They look after you." Aleyna flicked her hand toward the waitresses, then without so much as a good-bye, she was gone. Charlene followed her stride through the crowd spilling into the showroom, and then Aleyna disappeared altogether.

Once again, Charlene was all alone.

"You want drink?" Charlene jumped at the voice. A waitress appeared at Charlene's side.

"Oh, you do speak English."

"Yes. You want drink? Here is drink list. There is food list. I make order." The waitress pointed at a laminated menu on the table that had all four of its corners curling up.

Charlene's dark cloud of despair petered out at both the waitress's ability to speak English and at the mention of food. She hadn't eaten anything since the toasted sandwich with Marshall. As the pretty waitress loudly chewed gum, Charlene ordered a water and her preferences from the three courses on the menu.

Alone again, she scanned her surroundings. It was vaguely familiar, and it should be, given that she'd watched video footage of this stage about twenty times. It looked like it hadn't been renovated in those twenty or so years. Or if it had, they'd kept its original appearance.

Both her drink and entrée arrived before any of the people who were sharing her table were seated. She devoured the cold starter within minutes and was sipping her water when guests began filling up the chairs around her. They made polite conversation, and she did the same, relieved to be speaking English.

Her main meal of spicy chicken stew and something called moors and Christians arrived; she was relieved to discover that the moors were black beans and the Christians simply brown rice. A few bites later, the music ramped up, the curtain lifted, and a woman who had to be in her late sixties belted out a tune and strutted her stuff better than many women half her age could have done.

In the background, a dozen men and women in colorful outfits danced to the beat. Charlene shared her gaze between the elderly singer and the slideshow of the singer's life at the back of the stage. She had no idea what she was looking for, but whatever it was, she was desperate not to miss it.

The woman left the stage and was promptly replaced with a man of equivalent age. He too was impressive, both in his vocal range and his dance routine. His song was in Spanish, and Charlene couldn't understand a single word.

As she watched him strut his stuff up and down the stage, she wondered if the man ever knew her father. At the same time, she wondered how on earth she would ask him. She had no picture of Peter, and their language barrier was going to make any such communication impossible.

Song after song, dancer after dancer, the show went on. Each one was spectacular in its own right, and as the night wore on, the singers became progressively older.

The crowd went wild when a man with a walking cane appeared on the stage; the screen behind him listed his age as eighty-two. *Will I be as spritely at that age? If I live to be that old.* Given her latest life-threatening experiences, she might not.

Charlene hadn't been willing to leave the spectacle for fear of missing something, but she couldn't ignore her bursting bladder a moment more.

When there was a gap in the music, she excused herself from the table, grabbed her cane, and wove between the tables to the back of the room. She exited through a side door into the bar area and followed signs to the bathroom.

After washing her hands, she turned to dry them, and a gasp tumbled from her lips. Right in front of her was a photo of Peter. Tears stung her eyes as she snatched the frame from the wall. Her heart launched to her throat. "Oh my God."

"Are you alright, dear?" A woman waiting in line blinked at her.

"Yes. Yes. This is my father. I've been . . ." Blood coursed through her veins. Her fingers trembled; her legs threatened to buckle. Tears spilled down her cheeks, and before she knew what she was doing, Charlene tucked the frame under her arm and went in search of an English-speaking waitress.

Several people were milling about, many waiting in line for one of the six pretty waitresses to serve them. The staff, all in white cowgirl outfits with matching hats, were dotted behind the long bar. Charlene didn't wait for her turn. She stormed to the front, placed the photo frame on top of the bar, and leaned toward the young waitress who was busy pouring a beer. "Hello, do you speak English?"

"*Sí*, a little."

"Can you tell me who this is?"

The woman's eyes widened. "Did you take that off the wall?"

"I'll put it back. Please, can you tell me who this is?"

"He must be one of our singers. But I—" She turned to the woman beside her and spoke to her in Spanish. When she shook her head, the barmaid turned to another waitress who was much older. They spoke briefly before the woman came over.

She pointed her chipped fingernail at the photo. "He Pueblo García, but he not here anymore."

"Pueblo García? Are you sure?"

"Yes, he was big star. But one day he gone."

Charlene's heart slammed into her chest as she leaned forward, desperate to hear the woman over the restless crowd. "Did you know him?"

She wobbled her head. "Yes, some. He was nice man."

Charlene's mind blazed over a dozen questions, trying to prioritize the right ones to ask. "What happened to him?"

The waitress made a face that was loaded with confusion. "Hmm, it was big story. Lots of guesses. He had girlfriend; she was dancer here, and she vanish too."

"Oh my God." Her heart slammed against her ribs. "Do you know her name?"

She shook her head frowning. "Hmm, I no remember, but her brother . . . he big businessman in Cuba."

"He is? What's his name?"

"Diego Álvarez."

Charlene's mind raced. Her heart skipped a beat. Finally, she had a direct clue. "Please, can you take me to him? Now."

The woman glanced around the bar, frowning, and shook her head. "I working."

"I'll pay you. Please. Please, help me, this is urgent." Charlene reached into her bag, ready to pluck out an entire roll of cash if she needed to.

"I can take you after—"

"I can't wait till then. Please. I'll pay you three hundred."

Her eyes bulged, then she leaned in. "Three hundred!"

"Yes. Three hundred. If we go now."

The woman spun to another waitress at her side and spoke to her in Spanish. She turned back to Charlene. "Wait here." She dashed along the bar, behind all the bartenders, and disappeared through a door.

Charlene's eyes fell to the photo. The man in the picture was definitely the man who'd claimed to be her father. He was much younger, but there was no mistaking it was him. Charlene glanced toward the doorway where the woman had exited, and with trembling fingers and a silent prayer that no one saw her, she flipped the frame over, unhooked the clips, and removed the photo. She folded the photo, slipped it into her bag, and then put the frame on a bar stool.

Her heart was still thumping when the woman returned with a handbag over her shoulder and a look of urgency on her face.

"Quick, we must go before my boss come."

"Okay. Yes. Thank you so much. What's your name?"

"Kamila."

"Thank you, Kamila. You don't know how much this means to me."

Kamila led Charlene toward the front of the stage, where the bar was; then they skirted to the left, down a staff-only access corridor. At the end of the corridor, they went down a steep set of steps. Halfway down, she stopped to look up at Charlene. "You have my money."

"Oh, yes, of course." Charlene propped her cane against the wall to reach into her bag. It was impossible to see in the dim light, and in the end, she had to remove a whole roll of cash to separate out the right notes for Kamila.

Kamila sucked the air in through her teeth as she eyed the notes, and Charlene wanted to slap herself for her stupidity. This was not like her. Safety had always been paramount for her, and her haste to get answers was making her do foolish things.

Risky, dangerous things that'd get her into trouble.

The moment she had time to herself, she'd sort the cash properly. She handed over three hundred-dollar notes, and Kamila accepted with a huge smile before shoving the cash into her bra.

Kamila continued down the stairs, and at the bottom, they stepped out into the night air. Charlene recognized two of the singers leaning against the walls, a man and a woman; both looked to be in their seventies, and both were smoking thick Cuban cigars. Kamila spoke briefly to them before they strode up the narrow lane.

The buildings lining the lane were a potpourri of peeling and faded paint and crumbling façades. Wrought-iron balconies served as clothing hangers, and sheets were draped from one side to the next.

Ahead of them, where the lane met another road, Charlene saw a throng of people all seemingly enjoying Cuba's party atmosphere. Music was everywhere, and all of it was coming from live musicians. Radios, it seemed, hadn't reached Havana yet.

Kamila turned to Charlene. "We take taxi."

"Oh, okay."

She led Charlene to a side street where four old cars were angle-parked at the curb. The TAXI signs on their roofs were the only indication that they were cabs. Each one was different in color, make, and model. The only thing they had in common, besides the sign, was their age—all the vehicles had to be at least fifty years old.

Kamila approached the first cab, a faded, ruby-red Chrysler, with polished chrome trim and vinyl seats. She leaned into the driver's window, and they shared a conversation Charlene couldn't follow.

After a pause, she pulled back to glance at Charlene. "You pay, *sí*."

"Yes. Yes, of course. How much?"

The driver and Kamila fired off a rapid exchange before she turned back to Charlene. "He says one hundred, but I said it too much, so we agree on ninety. Good, *sí*?"

Charlene knew it was too much. But at this point she'd pay triple that if it meant finding answers. She made a show of thanking Kamila before she plucked the right change from her bag. Once that was settled, Kamila opened the back door and climbed in. Charlene slipped in beside her.

The driver kicked the car into gear with a gritty crunch, and they backed out. Charlene had thought the party atmosphere was impressive earlier, but it was even more so now. The dancing and singing in the streets were now accompanied with pretty paper lanterns and old-fashioned street lamps.

A very large Georgian-style building lined one side of the street. This one was in pristine condition and seemed to mark the center of town. "Where are we going?" Charlene asked.

"He take you to Airshee factory."

"Airshee?" Charlene frowned.

"Yes, you know." Kamila brought her fingers to her mouth like she was eating. "Airshee, chocolate."

Charlene's frowned deepened. "I thought you were taking me to Diego Álvarez."

"Yes, *sí*, he at Airshee factory."

"Oh, okay, good. How far?"

She rolled her eyes and gave a big wave with her hand. "Oh, it *long* way." The great emphasis she put on the word *long* had Charlene's brain swimming with the consequences. If it was too far, she wouldn't be back in time to meet Aleyna. Her solution to that would be asking the taxi driver to take her to Aleyna's home. But then a truly terrifying thought hit her. She had no idea where Aleyna lived.

What she was doing was going against everything she'd ever learned about safety. Yet she wouldn't stop. Couldn't stop. She had to get answers. The paralyzing hurt of not knowing everything about her past was more important than anything. She couldn't move forward until she'd solved it. And if that meant taking risks, then she was going to do it.

One thing she'd learned in her nomadic lifestyle was that the vast majority of people were honest. It was a rare and unfortunate thing to meet someone who was deliberately out to deceive or inflict harm. Charlene was relying on those odds now. If that failed, she had her martial arts training and Peter's cane.

With her grip tightening on her make-do weapon, she turned to Kamila. "Can you tell me about Peter, please? I mean Pueblo? What do you remember about him?"

"Oh, he nice man. Always smiling. Happy. He good singer, you know."

"Yes, I know. You said he vanished, and there were rumors about what happened. Can you tell me, please?"

She nibbled on her fingernail. "They say many things. He kill her and then go hiding. They both dead. They even say he went to America."

Charlene's mind flicked back to the uniform he'd been wearing and the gun strapped to his shoulder. "Do you know if he had another job? Like in the army?"

"Army?" She shook her head. "I don't know."

"What else? Tell me about his girlfriend."

"I didn't know her. She was dancer at social club. She very quiet. Just do her job, then go home, you know." She flicked her hand and turned her attention outside.

Charlene eased back on the seat and glanced out the window. Her brain told her she should try to memorize where she was going, but as the mansions and shanties flicked by, she couldn't focus on anything but the possibility that she was about to meet the brother of Peter's ex-girlfriend.

What was she going to say? Would he even remember Peter—or Pueblo, as Kamila had called him? It was over twenty years ago. And if he did remember Pueblo, would he blame him for the disappearance of his sister?

The questions tumbled through her mind like rocks in a gold mine. Except the chunks weren't precious nuggets; they were lumps of coal . . . dark and sinister.

Although it was the middle of the night, it was still very humid, and the only air-conditioning was the open window. They cruised along a section of road that had hotels on one side, except they were deserted and looked more like a scene from an apocalypse movie.

On the other side was a long esplanade that skirted the ocean, and hundreds of people were enjoying the broad expanse. Some were eating ice cream. Some were fishing, some playing cards; many were dancing and making music. None were on cell phones. It was vastly different from any city she'd visited in America.

"What's this place?" Charlene pointed out her side of the window.

"It's the Malecón. It beautiful, *sí*?"

"Yes, it's beautiful."

"Lovers meet there. It where I met my husband."

"Oh, that's wonderful."

"Yeah, it long time ago now."

The giant sea wall continued for about four miles, then the driver turned inland from the ocean. The houses lining the streets were a mixture of opulence and poverty, but the farther they went, the less opulence there was. As the miles rumbled beneath the bone-rattling car, sweat dribbled down Charlene's back.

She had no way to judge time. The clock on the dashboard hadn't moved since she'd stepped into the car, and neither Kamila nor the driver wore a watch. It seemed that time wasn't a driving force in Cuba, unlike in her home country.

Her home country. That was an interesting thought. Was it possible that Cuba was actually her home country? The thought came out of nowhere. If it was, then where did that leave her? Was she an undocumented immigrant? As much as she didn't have a home to go back to, America was the country she wanted to return to.

That thought had her thinking about Marshall. If she missed his deadline, she had no idea what she'd do. And, in turn, she had no idea what Marshall would do. They had no way to contact each other.

The car slowed and pulled into the curb, dragging Charlene from her tumbling thoughts. "Oh, are we there?"

"No." Kamila chuckled. "This my home. Eduardo take you to Airshee."

"What? I thought you were coming."

Again, she chuckled. "No. Too far. But no worry. Eduardo know where you go. He look after you."

Charlene's heart set to explode as Kamila opened her door.

"Wait! Please."

When Kamila slammed her door shut, fear ripped through Charlene like icy tentacles. Kamila ignored Charlene's pleas by stepping around to the driver's door and when she spoke to him, the only words Charlene recognized were *Airshee* and *gracias*. But before Charlene could do anything, the driver took off again.

She was trapped.

With her fingers clutching the cane, she contemplated jumping from the moving car. But the images that came with that idea forced her to rethink. The driver seemed harmless. Besides, he was just doing the job he'd been asked to do.

As the darkened streets whizzed by, she played out what would happen if she did jump from the taxi. If she survived the tumble. She had no idea where she was. No idea where she was going. She couldn't speak the language, and she had no way to contact anyone. On top of all that, she had nobody to contact anyway.

The image that she'd had yesterday of her unidentified body washing up on the beach morphed to her being bound and gagged and locked in the trunk of the taxi. She slapped that vision from her mind and forced herself to focus on what she did know. If Kamila had been right, then Peter was actually Pueblo García. And if that was true, she was on her way to meet someone who knew him.

That was the best opportunity she'd had in weeks.

Despite the horrifying images feeding her thoughts, she had to go through with it.

She pushed forward on her chair. "Hello, do you speak English?"

He smiled a crooked smile over his shoulder but shook his head. "*Lo siento, señora. No hablo inglés.*"

That'd be a no. But the move hadn't been a total loss. She saw enough of the driver to be certain she'd be able to overcome him should he attempt anything. With his pudgy belly and double chin, he'd have no hope of catching her, and if he did, within three seconds his testicles would be wishing he hadn't.

With that knowledge comforting her a little, she eased back on the seat, and as she watched the scenery whiz by, she tried to picture how the meeting with Diego would play out. She pulled the photo from her bag. This would be her first tactic. With a bit of luck, the big businessman would speak English.

The journey seemed to go on forever, and soon there was nothing but paddocks of nothing. Her mind flashed to one of her interviews with Detective Chapel. She'd described traveling through fields of nothing on the night that'd changed her life forever.

She sat up and scanned the landscape, looking for something, anything that would trigger a memory to prove she'd been along this road before. They seemed to be following a pair of long, straight tracks. Train tracks. Only these tracks were covered in weeds, and she hadn't seen one train station. These train tracks hadn't been used in some time.

The minutes ticked by, as did the miles, and it seemed to be an eternity before the driver changed gear. Her heart skipped a beat when he pulled to a stop in front of an enormous brick fence. He pointed out his window. "Airshee factory."

Charlene glanced ahead and stared unblinking at the sign dangling from a rusted archway over the entrance. "Hershey? Hershey chocolates?"

"*Sí, sí.*"

Charlene sat in stunned silence for a couple of heartbeats before she comprehended that the driver was waiting for her to get out. It was only now that she realized she should have asked Kamila to instruct the driver to wait for her. She reached into her bag and held another hundred-dollar note toward him. "Can you wait for me?"

He took the cash from her. "*Sí, sí gracias.*" His enormous grin showed off two missing teeth.

"Good. Okay then. Wait for me here. I come back here."

He nodded. She nodded.

Then, clutching her cane and bag, she opened the door and climbed out. Her back groaned as she stood upright, and her neck cracked as she rolled it from side to side. The taxi's headlights showed the condition of the building.

A couple of steps closer revealed that the building wasn't just in need of a fresh can of a paint—it was derelict. The windows were either smashed or missing glass altogether. Some of the upper levels had collapsed upon themselves.

She took another step, and the sound of the taxi's engine revving had her spinning to the noise. Next second, the car drove off. Charlene dropped her cane and raced after him. "Stop. Wait!" Her sandals were no match for the rocky road, and each step jarred her heels. She pumped her arms and legs, desperate to catch him. She waved her arms, trying to catch his attention.

But he didn't stop.

Gasping for breath, she picked up a rock and threw it at the departing taillights. "Asshole!"

Soon he was gone altogether, and Charlene was alone on a road that was barely visible beneath her feet. Above her, the stars were a million twinkling lights, and she was reminded of her stint beneath the bow of Marshall's boat. Somehow, that seemed easy compared to what she was facing now.

She turned and tracked her way back to her cane.

On the way out here, she'd relied on a flicker of hope. Now though, as she looked through the rusted gates of the derelict Hershey factory, all hope was lost. She stepped through the threshold and eased to the side so that her back was against the fence wall.

Charlene slid down the wall, clutched her knees to her chest, and cried.

Chapter Eighteen

Marshall kept one eye on the digital clock on *Miss B Hayve's* console and one eye on the Cuban navy men who were busy hauling a bunch of refugees off a boat that looked as big as and as seaworthy as a Cadillac.

When he'd first spotted the Cuban cutter flying toward him, Marshall had almost shit his pants as he'd thought they'd somehow seen him, even with his lights off.

That'd been forty minutes ago. It'd been his lucky night. Not so lucky for the people in the other boat, though. Marshall had cut the engines, and he rode the swell as he watched the action through his binoculars.

They were taking their time too.

Time he didn't have.

He promised Charlene he'd be back at midnight. That was twenty minutes away. He was going to be late.

He didn't do late.

The failure of the refugees' escape, although it was shit luck for them, was actually good news for Marshall. It meant the Cuban navy would be occupied for the next couple of hours. And given that he was running late, he was going to need that distraction.

It was ten past midnight when the patrol boat fired its engines again and headed off. Marshall had been ready for this moment. The second he decided it was safe, he pulled the rip cord on his runabout and aimed full-tilt for the shore.

The whole time he bounced over the waves, his thoughts were on Charlene. She'd probably be thinking he'd abandoned her. God knows what she'd do with that thought. He didn't dial back the speed as he neared the marina. Instead, he shot straight into the cove and continued full power right up to Rusian's dinky jetty.

He tied up the boat, jumped ashore, and, using his flashlight, raced up the path to the house. The second he burst through the clearing, he knew something wasn't right. All the lanterns were lit, and it seemed the entire family was in the kitchen.

He raced into the house, and everyone turned to him with alarm flaring across their faces.

"She's gone." Aleyna's first words sliced him like a machete.

"What?" He strode through the crowd to the kitchen bench.

"She's disappeared. I took her to *Legendarios del Guajirito* like you asked. But she no come out. I look for her but she gone."

"How could she disappear?"

"I don't know." Panic flashed in Aleyna's eyes.

"Jesus Christ." Marshall threw his hands up. "Did you ask around?"

"Yes. Nobody see her. She just vanish."

"Fuck." Marshall's training was based on a lifetime of choices involving risk assessment, often done at breakneck speed. But that was in war zones and involved good guys and bad guys. He had no idea what Charlene had gotten herself into. But his gut told him he was about to meet a whole new round of bad guys.

In a split second, he made a decision that would be forever categorized as fucking stupid. "Where's José?"

"He still in Havana. He looking for her."

Marshall turned to the oldest of the brothers. "*Maceo, todavía tienes tu moto?*"

"*Sí*, come, come." Maceo raced out the back door, heading toward the only mode of transport the family had. Marshall was right on his heels.

Maceo led him to his motorcycle, which was wedged between the chicken pen and the outhouse. The vintage Russian Ural motorcycle and sidecar was built in 1943, still had most of its original parts; based on what Marshall had seen the last time Maceo had ridden it, the damn thing was still fast as hell. Marshall had ridden in the sidecar once and just about lost his teeth on the bone-rattling ride.

Marshall sacrificed courtesy for speed, and without asking for permission, he jumped onto the bike, kicked the stand up, and rammed his foot down on the ratcheting lever. The bike coughed and died.

He gripped the handle, straightened the wheel, and stomped the pedal again. When the bike roared to life, Marshall turned to Maceo and told him he'd look after it. Maceo's eyes bulged with an uncommunicated statement that told Marshall he had better. This bike was the only thing keeping the family in contact with urgently needed supplies.

Marshall turned the throttle and shot up the nonexistent drive like he'd been released from a catapult. The bike was originally built to aid fighting the Germans in World War Two, and that's exactly how Marshall felt now—like he was heading off to war. At least that's what his gut told him. He refused to believe Charlene would just wander off by herself. Nobody would be that stupid.

The Ural was made for traveling rough terrain, but its original shock absorbers had long ago been obliterated, and Marshall felt every single bump.

Top that with the sidecar clamped onto the Ural's body, and he had to wrestle the handlebars to stop the bike from veering into the ditches lining the road. And the damn racket made his old landlady's rusty secondhand mower sound like a lullaby.

With each mile he hurtled over, his brain fought with his decision to go after Charlene. He was risking everything . . . his boat, his freedom, his reputation.

The second he'd laid eyes on her, he'd known she was trouble. He would never have guessed this much trouble, though. He thought she'd told him everything, and it pissed him off that she'd held back.

If she was stupid enough to get herself lost in Cuba, then he should let her go. But he wasn't built like that. Never before had he left a man behind, neither alive nor dead, and he had no intention of starting now. He just hoped it wasn't a body he'd be bringing home.

Marshall knew his way around Havana. Thanks to his seventeen midnight runs, he could get his customers to the finest Cuban cigars or the best rum in the space of thirty minutes. But he didn't need those contrabands now. What he needed was someone from the Buena Vista Social Club.

He just had to find them.

The average income in Cuba was just twenty bucks a month, so most people needed two jobs to survive. Despite the continual upheaval between the United States and Cuba, the number of tourists from other countries was increasing each year.

Smart Cubans were capitalizing on that, and what the tourists loved was the music. So Marshall had no doubt that some of the entertainers from *Legendarios del Guajirito* would be continuing their night shift with more gigs in old-town Havana.

He headed straight for Plaza Vieja. It was the oldest neighborhood in town and the most popular. The narrow cobblestone streets were a bitch to navigate, and the muscles in his arms were already burning.

Despite the early hours of the morning, the party atmosphere was still rocking, and Marshall had to dodge tourists and locals, stray dogs, horses, and people selling their wares on rickety old carts.

At a strip of restaurants overlooking La Fuerza fortress, he left the motor running and ran into La Bodeguita del Medio. The place was famous for both its mojitos and its music.

Marshall squeezed between the tables, overflowing with people in various stages of dinner, and raced up to the four-piece band. He didn't even wait for a pause in the song as he leaned into the ear of the guy playing the kettledrums. "*Hola, ¿alguno de ustedes trabajó en Legendarios del Guajirito?*"

"*No señor, no esta noche.*" He shook his head.

"*Gracias.*"

Marshall turned and raced back out. The next three bars offered similar opportunities, but all came up empty. Marshall cruised up and down the streets, asking both the street buskers and the full band ensembles in the fancier hotels.

In one street, he found four men who had to be closer to a hundred than fifty, each with an instrument that was as old as they were. They puffed Cuban cigars and belted out tunes with intensity.

When Marshall asked the question, he again came up empty, but he dropped fifty Cuban pesos into their tip hat all the same. The money would feed the foursome for about a month.

Somewhere in the back of his brain, an incessant clock was pounding out the seconds. Time was against him. Against both of them. He'd gone into plenty of military situations where he'd had limited intel. Tonight he had nothing but a niggling feeling that Charlene was in trouble and the sooner he got to her, the better.

A few blocks from El Capitolio, he stopped at La Floridita. The two-hundred-year-old bar, made famous by Hemingway's penchant for daiquiris with no sugar and double the rum, was packed with people stupid enough to pay twelve bucks for a drink.

Fortunately for Marshall, the six-piece band was right at the front door. Over the ruckus of the crowd and the music, he shouted his question to the closest guitarist.

"*Sí, señor, Daylin, trabajó detrás del bar.*" The man pointed at the lead singer.

Marshall's pulse quickened as he eyeballed the woman. She had thick black hair that fell in waves down her back, lips that required zero fillers, and a little blue dress that hid none of her voluptuous curves. The woman knew how to use those curves too, and the crowd seemed to be loving every minute of it. Marshall, however, tapped out the tune with his foot, waiting with dwindling patience for the song to end.

The second the crowd burst into applause, he made his move.

"*Hola, Daylin, puedes ayudarme por favor. ¿Trabajaste en Legendarios del Guajirito?*"

She nodded and flicked a wad of hair over her shoulder. "*Sí. Trabajé en el bar.*"

Daylin had worked the bar at the social club, and after a few fruitless questions about Charlene, about whom she claimed to have no knowledge, he changed tack and asked if anything unusual had happened. He'd hit pay dirt. Apparently, a young American woman had stolen one of the pictures off the wall. Despite Daylin's obvious disapproval of the American's actions, the incident was music to his ears.

169

Five minutes later, he'd learned that the bar supervisor had left with the woman. But even with that knowledge, he still had nothing other than the supervisor's name.

Daylin had no idea where the supervisor lived nor how Marshall could contact her.

Chapter Nineteen

The first sign of daybreak came with a series of shouts that had Charlene jumping to her feet and searching the derelict building around her. The remains of the Hershey factory looked even worse in the mushrooming daylight.

She'd spent the night dozing in and out while huddled between the front brick fence and a pile of rubble. She stepped around the loose bricks and walked into a large central courtyard that'd once been laid with rust-colored pavers.

The large expanse was dotted with overgrown weeds, both alive and dead, and bits of the crumbling building. The courtyard was surrounded by dilapidated buildings that jutted up from the ground like broken molars.

On the right-hand side stood the remains of a building that stretched the length of the area. The brick walls had crumbled away, and what was left was just a rusted skeleton of broken girders and fallen beams. Barely a third of the original construction was still standing.

To her left was an equally large building. This one at least had a front façade; however, it had no roof, and the windows were either shattered or missing altogether.

The sign over the door said: WELCOME TO HERSHEY TOWN,

THE SWEETEST PLACE ON EARTH. Above that, EST. 1916, was carved into the brick. *Over a hundred years old.*

She glanced through the gap where the doors had once been, and based on what she saw—broken glass-topped counters and empty shelving—she imagined it was once a shop selling everything Hershey.

Shouting cut through the silence, and crouching down, she searched for the source of the voices. She stared in amazement when lights came on in the distant building.

They weren't direct lights, but more a dim glow emanating from somewhere inside. It was impossible to believe people lived in there. She'd spent the entire night grappling with a serious bout of failure. Sometime during the early hours, she'd decided that Kamila had deceived her. Just like the taxi driver.

But now, as she watched a few more lights flicker on, she became hopeful that Kamila did actually have good intentions.

Charlene dusted off her backside, straightened her dress, clutched her bag and her cane and stepped across the broken pavers toward the building. The only sound was her feet crunching on dead weeds and a blackbird that made a noise like it was crying.

Her brain fought simultaneous urges to run away and keep moving forward. Each step came with a forced affirmation.

Step . . . *I have to do this.*

Step . . . *nobody will do it for me.*

Step . . . *if I don't do this, I'll be forever wondering who Peter was.*

Step . . . *if I don't get answers, I may never find out who I am.*

The bird's mournful tune sent shivers up her spine, and she gripped the cane tighter. A glint of light shimmering off a broken upper window confirmed that the sun had pierced the horizon.

The building at the end of the central courtyard had once been a grand Georgian construction, with giant pillars marking the entrance. Its front façade had survived the decades, but a long-dead vine was the only thing holding the peeling paint in place.

Crumbling plaster humped in chalky piles at the base of the front wall, and the only remains of the windows were dangling frames. The far right of the building had a huge chunk missing, as though a giant monster had taken a bite out of it. The lights, however, were at the opposite end, and they appeared to be in the back.

A yellowed sign on a building signaled the entrance to the Hershey museum and restaurant. It didn't seem possible that someone lived in the building; yet the lights indicated otherwise.

Two huge doors marked the entrance. Both were bare of paint, and the original wood was splintered and cracked. What was left of the handles were just four holes in each door. Charlene stepped through the gap and paused at what was obviously once the foyer of a very grand building.

A large, two-story, open-air void marked the entrance. Remarkably, this building still had its roof. The marble floor was covered in all manner of debris, and two grand sets of marble stairs curled up either side to what was once another level.

But that level had crumbled to the floor below, so the stairs went nowhere. A small amount of graffiti dotted the walls, including a couple of very accomplished line drawings of a man with shaggy hair, a thin mustache, and a beret with a star in the middle.

Between the two sets of stairs was a burnt-out car with no tires. The hairs on Charlene's neck bristled as she contemplated its existence. A tangle of vines had taken over the far wall, smothering it in a field of green and brown. Among the foliage, a flock of birds flitted back and forth.

A man's shout had the birds taking flight and Charlene racing for cover behind the charred wreck. The noise was gone before she ducked behind the rusted trunk. She remained there for an eternity.

Waiting for her pounding heart to settle.

Waiting for another sign of human existence.

Waiting for courage to return to her limbs.

Water dripped somewhere, and the echoing sound created a creepy heartbeat for the soulless surroundings.

With each passing minute, the darkness that'd draped the walls in a morbid tapestry faded, allowing Charlene to see more of her surroundings. Peter had taught her to look for idiosyncrasies when she walked into a room. What or who was the odd man out?

She eased up from behind the rusted carcass and examined the foyer.

At first, she saw nothing, but soon tiny aspects began to stand out. A faint path that wove through the debris on the floor. Cigarette butts dotted about on that debris. Candy wrappers and Coke cans.

And then she saw the bullet holes in the mottled plaster walls.

Charlene didn't think. She just clutched her bag across her chest, gripped her cane, and bolted toward the front doors. Her pretty sandals slipped out from under her, and she fell full force onto her backside. She hadn't meant to scream; it'd been involuntary. But it was too late. Her scream was matched with shouts coming from somewhere inside the building.

She launched to her feet, and her heart was in her throat as she aimed for the door. The more she ran, the more the shouts increased, and she imagined crosshairs aiming at her back. Her sandals were no match for the jagged pavers, slowing down her usual sprinting pace.

"¡Detente!"

"¡Detente!"

The voices behind her were loud and angry, but she didn't stop. More shouts joined the first, and she pictured twenty men chasing after her. The loudest sound she'd ever heard boomed from behind her, and when a hole punched into the brick fence ahead of her, she fell to her knees. Her heart invaded her throat, and she shot her hands up, still gripping the cane. "Don't shoot. Don't shoot."

She squeezed her eyes shut, praying this wasn't the end.

Feet pounded behind her.

A shove to her back sent her tumbling face-first to the pavement. A brick carved a slice out of her cheek, and her only weapon was torn from her grip. "*Por favor*, don't hurt me. *Por favor*."

She stayed on the ground, her face downward, and the men kept their distance. They spoke over each other, and there didn't seem to be a clear leader among them. For some reason, that gave her hope, as did the fact that they hadn't shot her already.

None of them spoke English, yet their tone indicated confusion rather than anger. After a couple of thumping heartbeats in which they didn't shoot her, she turned her head to the side. Her breath caught at the sight of the first man. He was dressed exactly as the men in her childhood nightmares. Khaki-green uniform, shin-high boots, and a long weapon. If that wasn't enough, the gun was pointed directly at her.

"*Por favor.* Help me, please. *Por favor.*"

There was a moment's silence in which the crying bird was the only sound. Charlene was dragged to her feet. The adrenaline that'd coursed through her body just moments ago evaporated. Her legs had become jello.

Her captors' grip on her biceps was the only thing keeping her upright as they dragged her back into the dilapidated Hershey museum.

Charlene had seen many soldiers in her time. If these guys were soldiers, then they were light on both training and health. They were gaunt and disorganized. They had missing teeth, dirty hands, and bad body odor.

Gaffer tape was wrapped around the weapon held by the man to her left, and the man on her right was missing an eye. Besides the two holding her, she counted another five. But that was just the ones in front of her; she had no idea how many were behind.

"*Por favor*, do you speak English? I need help."

None of them spoke. Instead she was manhandled through the foyer, over a threshold, and into a long corridor dotted with doors that'd seen better days.

The corridor offered little light, but they were heading toward a glow at the end. Her heart pounded out a frightful beat with each yard of debris she was carried over.

They had trouble working out how to get her through the final door and opted to shove her forward. She fell to her hands and knees at the boots of a man who was standing with his feet planted shoulder width apart.

Charlene pushed back to look up at him and knew instantly she was looking at their leader. With his chiseled jaw, crooked nose, and black eyes that glared with hate, he commanded attention. Where the other men looked to be starving, this guy looked like he always took his share first.

Charlene snapped her hands over her head. "*Por favor*, don't hurt me."

"Who are you?"

"Oh, you speak English, thank God."

"Who are you?"

"My name is Charlene Bailey. Are you Diego?"

The muscles along his jaw line clenched, but he didn't reply.

"I need to talk to Diego about my father, Peter, I mean Pueblo García. Here, I have a picture." She reached for her bag, and the men shouted and lunged with their weapons.

She gasped and snapped her arms up. "Don't shoot. Don't shoot. I have a photo. *Por favor.*" Sweat trickled down her back.

The leader did a little head shuffle, and the men backed off.

Charlene plucked the photo from her bag and unfolded it. "Here. This is Pueblo García. Do you know him?"

A flicker of recognition crossed his eyes. He snatched the photo, stared at it for three seconds, then burst out laughing. The remaining men laughed too, and when he said something to them in Spanish, their laughter increased a notch.

Charlene had played this moment in her head a dozen times, but not once had she considered this reaction.

"This man your father?" He pointed at the photo.

"Yes. Do you know him?"

"*Sí. Sí.* Come, we will talk." He offered her his hand to help her up, but declining his grasp, she climbed to her feet and dusted off her hands.

"I apologize for my men. They are, how do you say . . . eager."

She scanned the faces of the seven other men around her. They didn't look eager; they looked more exhausted than anything. "It's okay. It was my fault. I was trespassing."

He eyes flared. "*Sí.* You were." He burst out laughing again, and Charlene had no idea why. She used the moment to dust off her dress and scan the room.

It looked like some kind of headquarters—in the crudest form. Maps and spreadsheets scrawled with numbers were pinned to one of the walls. Another wall was pockmarked with bullet holes, which Charlene decided was damn stupid considering the fragile state of the building. Along another wall, a couple of decrepit sofas with stained purple jacquard fabric faced each other; a coffee table loaded with empty beer bottles was nestled between them.

In each of the corners, wooden crates were stacked to the ceiling, and in the middle of the room was a large metal table surrounded by ten chairs. Half-eaten bowls of food topped the table. This wasn't the kitchen, though, so she wondered if there were more people in the building.

"Please, sit. Are you hungry?"

"No, thank you." She lied. She was starving, but she didn't want to waste any more time. Her mind flashed to Marshall. She was already well past her scheduled meeting time. He'd told her about two men who'd missed their rendezvous and how he'd returned to get them the following night. Her only hope was that he'd do the same for her. "May I have my cane back, please?" She nodded at her only weapon.

"*Sí.*" He turned to one of the men, barking an order at him, and he stepped forward to give it to her.

"Please, sit." The leader tugged a chair at the head of the table, angling it away from the table.

Charlene accepted the offer, and the instant she did, her body seemed to melt. Exhaustion crept in, liquefying her limbs, but she had to fight it. This was far from over.

Although the leader was being friendly, the remaining men peered at her like she was an armed alien, and not one of them had let go of his weapon. The man pulled out a chair, sat opposite her, and her stomach churned at the slow, creepy grin curling his lips. "Are you Diego?"

His hand went to his chest. "My apology. *Sí*, I am Diego Álvarez. You have heard of me, yes?" His dark eyes seemed to twinkle.

"No. I'm sorry, I umm . . ." Charlene was about to say that she had only arrived in Cuba last night but quickly snapped that admission from her tongue. "Can you tell me how you know Pueblo?"

"No, you first. How do you know Pueblo?" He plucked a tiny stick off the table and used it to rub his front tooth.

"Oh, well, he was my father."

"Was?" Diego cocked his head.

"Yes, he, umm, he died a couple of months ago."

He turned to his men and rattled off a series of sentences that had them all laughing. Her insides curled with disgust as she watched them cackle. "What's so funny?" she demanded.

"Peter was with us." He glared at her, obviously keen for her reaction.

She swallowed, unsure how to answer. After seeing these men, their uniforms, their weapons, she had no doubt that Peter had once worked for him. But acknowledging that would make her look like a fool who'd deliberately walked into the enemy's lair. She didn't mind them thinking she was a fool, as it might come in handy later, but she decided it would be better to look naïve. "No. I didn't know that. He never told me."

"Do you know your mother?"

A gasp left her throat. "No, do you?"

His creepy smile strengthened. "Her name was Benita Álvarez. She my sister."

Charlene's jaw dropped. "How do you know she's my mother?"

"You look exactly like her. When you walked in door, I thought I seeing ghost."

"Oh my God. Really? Are you certain?"

He shoved back on his chair, scraping the metal legs over the concrete. "Come, I show you something."

"Oh my God. I can't believe this. I've been dreaming of this day for years."

"Me too." He smiled at her, but his smile didn't reflect the same elation she was feeling. His smirk had tendrils of dread inching up her spine, and she had no idea why. He'd just declared himself as her uncle. As far as she knew, he was the only family she had. Charlene should be over the moon. But there was something about Diego and his men that wasn't right.

The other men were all weedy little rats, simply following their leader. She knew she could outfight them. Outrun them too. But Diego was the problem. His sinister intelligence bristled just below his skin.

He paused at the door and indicated for her to go ahead. "You first."

Clutching the cane, she stepped ahead of him and walked along the hall. The corridor wasn't the same one she'd traveled earlier, yet it had a similar feel, with dilapidated doors and a dim glow at the end. The urge to run toward that glow was powerful, but not as powerful as the desire to know exactly what was going on.

"In here," Diego announced behind her, and she stopped to turn around.

He opened a door and stepped through. She followed him, and the second she did, he gripped her arm. "Hey! Let go."

He drew her closer; his bloodshot eyes were wild, and she heaved at his rotten breath. "You should not have come back, Claudia."

Diego dragged her toward a large hole in the floor. She planted her feet and whipped the cane around fast and hard. It hit him square in the nose. His head snapped back, and blood burst onto his lips and chin. But his grip remained. She clawed at his face and put all her energy into reversing his direction.

But it was pointless.

Charlene screamed as he tossed her into the hole.

Chapter Twenty

N oah glared at the defense lawyer across the room, his animosity brimming to a boiling point at the smug look on Ledbetter's face. Ledbetter had been wearing it all morning, and that had the hairs on Noah's neck bristling. Normally by now the defense was a quivering mess.

Not Randall Ledbetter.

His unprecedented cockiness meant Ledbetter had something up his sleeve. Something that the defense obviously considered to be a bombshell. And that was an experience Noah was not accustomed to.

Yet as much as he dreaded what his opponent was up to, he also welcomed it.

Noah loved a challenge. And the tougher the better. He was born for this.

The judge adjusted the glasses teetering at the end of his bulbous nose and glanced over the top of the rim at Ledbetter. "Please, call your next witness, Mr. Ledbetter."

Ledbetter's eyes flicked to Noah with a blaze of excitement; then he stood, buttoned up his jacket, and cleared his throat. "The defense calls Doctor Adam Bancroft."

When Noah's client released a gasp, he glanced down at her. What he saw confirmed that she'd just committed his least-tolerated error in judgment. Bridget Stoneham had withheld information from him. Whatever it was, judging by the fear piercing her eyes, it was critical.

The double doors at the back of the courtroom opened, and a tall man sporting horn-rimmed glasses and dark hair pulled into a ponytail shuffled into the room. His eyes remained downcast, and it was obvious he was present under duress. Noah had no idea who the doctor was, but Bridget's ashen face was enough to know that he was trouble.

Noah leaned into his client's ear. "I'm very disappointed in you, Bridget."

"I . . . I don't know how they—"

"They always do." He cut her off. "I told you, no secrets."

The doctor slouched into the witness chair and was read his rights.

"Please, state your name and occupation for the record." The judge's voice was cloaked with boredom.

"Doctor Adam Bancroft. I'm the senior OB/GYN for New York OB/GYN and Associates."

Bridget groaned, and Noah glared at her. The stupid bitch's decision to conceal information meant she was going to pay the price. He was too. And that meant he had a record-breaking tsunami on his hands. Ledbetter glanced at Noah, then at Bridget, then turned his gaze to the doctor. "Doctor Bancroft, please, advise the court what your specialty is?"

He cleared his throat. "I'm a board-certified obstetrician with specialized training in abortion."

A couple of the jurors gasped.

"I see. I know you are restricted by doctor-patient confidentiality. However, can you please confirm to the court if you have ever met the plaintiff, Mrs. Bridget Stoneham?"

The doctor looked like he was about loose his lunch as he nodded his head. "Yes, I have."

Ledbetter's stage show was impressive. And while he did a worthy job of avoiding questions that broke the confidentiality rule, it was enough to cement the implication to the jury that Bridget had indeed visited Doctor Bancroft for an abortion.

The major stake in his case had been that Mrs. Stoneham's husband had claimed to be impotent and therefore had not touched her in years.

If she'd had an abortion, as Ledbetter was implying, then that meant either her husband wasn't impotent or Bridget wasn't as pure as she'd claimed.

When the court adjourned for recess, the look on Ledbetter's face was a triumphant one. But there was something else. His look indicated there was more to come. Noah clutched Bridget's upper arm and led her to his private interview room.

He slammed the door as she crumbled into a chair and burst into tears.

"Shut the fuck up."

She gasped, and he relished in the fear blazing across her eyes. "I don't deal with liars."

"I'm sorry. I thought—"

"Well, stop fucking thinking and start talking."

Bridget sucked back a sob. "I got pregnant three years ago."

"Who's the father?"

Remaining silent, she wriggled her head and sucked her lips into her mouth.

"Tell me!"

Again, she shook her head.

He slapped his palm onto the table.

Yelping, she jumped back. "No. I'll never tell."

"The defense knows, and in about twenty minutes the whole world will know."

"That's impossible. Nobody knows. We were careful." Tiny blood capillaries snaked across the whites of her eyes.

God. If Noah had a dollar for every time he'd heard that, he'd be able to update his jet. He chuckled. "You stupid, naïve shit. I'll tell you now, Ledbetter has his name. So, whether you tell me or not, I'm about to find out anyway."

Bridget ran her long pink fingernails dangerously close to her eyeballs, catching the tears before she looked up at him. She swallowed, then sat back with her hands folded across her chest. "I'll take my chances."

A knock on the door indicated the judge was ready for them to return. He made one final plea to his client. But whoever the father of her aborted child was, Bridget was willing to risk everything to keep his name a secret. Noah was both furious and fascinated by the mystery.

He made a show of portraying confidence as he shuffled Bridget along the aisle of the packed courtroom to their seats at the front. The judge required three bangs with his gavel to quiet the courtroom before he looked down at Ledbetter. "Please, call your next witness."

"The defense calls Mr. Timothy Pearce."

Noah's jaw dropped. Bridget gasped. The courtroom erupted into a frenzy of excited voices, and Ledbetter's grin had Noah's gut churning.

Noah's brain was in a fog as he turned to the back of the courtroom and watched the double doors swing open and his very own business partner walk down the central aisle.

Noah could count on one hand the number of times someone he knew and trusted had betrayed him. But when Pearce met his gaze, Noah knew this one was going to be the most costly.

The remainder of the afternoon crawled along like a crippled dachshund, and the realization that he'd lost a case hit him in the final grueling hours of the day. The second the judge hit the gavel for the last time, Noah stormed from the courtroom with Pearce calling after him. But Noah had nothing to say to him. Not yet, anyway.

He quickly sought out two of his girls, who were standing behind the frenzied reporters salivating at the court steps, before he slipped into his waiting car. As the limo pulled away, he saw his client and his partner crawling through the throng of voracious reporters.

As Mansour navigated the limo along the busy New York streets, Noah deflected call after call. Every second one was Pearce. But he wasn't ready yet. The next time he spoke to Pearce, he'd have an arsenal of ammunition to throw at the man he'd considered his only confidant.

At his office, he strode to the liquor cabinet, poured a healthy dash of XO cognac and swallowed the shot in one gulp. He poured another and strolled to his window with the glass in his hand. Closing his eyes, he clenched his teeth until his jaw hurt.

Noah didn't lose.

But that wasn't what infuriated him the most.

It was the humiliation.

He gulped back the cognac and hurled his glass at the floor-to-ceiling window. When it bounced off and landed back at his feet, he kicked it across the carpet, leaving a trail of golden drops in its wake.

His phone continued to hum in his pocket, and he ignored it. Very few people had his number, and those who did were important to him. But he couldn't bring himself to respond to what was likely to be a major blip in his career. He needed his brain to simmer, and he needed a plan of attack.

The door clicked, and he turned to watch Indigo and Tarsha sashay into the room. They strode to him with seductive movements of their hips and an alluring sparkle in their heavily made-up eyes. The girls were young, gorgeous, and handpicked by him at Madam Athena's exclusive service. Madam Athena was paid well for both the abilities of her team and their confidentiality.

Confidentiality.

It was a powerful word. A powerful commitment. One that he'd used many times in the courtroom.

But never had it been used against him. Indigo touched his shoulder, and he slapped her hand away. He wasn't ready yet. With the flick of his hand, the women turned to each other. Their lips met, and as Indigo cupped Tarsha's breast, Tarsha glided the zipper down Indigo's back.

Noah topped up a fresh glass and sipped his cognac while watching the erotic show before him with zero interest. Even when the girls were stripped completely naked, his arousal remained nonexistent. That showed the extent of the damage his partner had caused.

The phone on his desk trilled, and his eyes snapped to it. Only a handful of people had that number, and he knew who it'd be. Pearce. He had no intention of answering it.

But when the answering machine kicked in, the voice on the phone made his already horrific day a thousand times worse.

"Hello, Noah. Remember me? It's Diego, your partner down under. Are you there, Mr. big-shot lawyer?"

"Get out." Noah screamed at the girls.

They froze, their eyes bulging in his direction.

"I said, get the fuck out." He shoved Indigo in the shoulder, and she stumbled sideways but managed to remain on her feet.

They clutched their clothes from the floor and raced for the door. Noah bolted the door behind them and strode to the phone. Diego's voice still dribbled from the machine.

"What the fuck do you want, Diego?"

"Ahh, you are there. Good. I have fascinating story for you."

"I don't have time for this shit, Diego."

"Oh, but you do. Believe me." Diego's laughter slithered down the phone line like a cobra.

Chapter Twenty-One

Charlene's scream had been cut short when her back slammed into a pool of water. It was like smashing through plate glass, and the impact knocked the wind out of her.

Pushing through the pain, she clawed through the murky water, aiming for the light at the surface. Gasping for fresh air, she screamed again as invisible things brushed against her legs. Hurling herself toward the edge, she dragged her sodden body out of the foul water.

Panting, she rolled to a standing position, and it was a couple of thumping heartbeats before she found her voice.

"Get me out of here!" Her voice echoed about the darkened room.

"Hey!" She screamed until her throat hurt. "Don't leave me here."

But there was no response, confirming that they had indeed left her. Her eyes darted about the space. Above was the circular hole that she'd been thrown through, and she could see blue sky and clouds.

A scraggly vine had made the wall up to the hole its home, and while the root dangled into the water, the rest of it spread like gnarly veins over the brickwork. The room was dome-shaped, and her best guess was that it was once some form of bathhouse.

Squeezing the water from her hair, she stepped from the pool to examine the walls. If it was a bathhouse, then there had to be a door. Nearly every inch of the floor and walls was covered in some kind of vegetation, from moss to vines to shrubs. Some were alive, but most were dead. Sunlight streaming in from above cast as much light as it created shadows.

A series of uneven steps curled around the left-hand side, and using the wall for support, she inched up the stairway. At the top, recessed into a nook, was a door. It looked like something from the Dark Ages. The wood was black and chunky, carved without fanfare, and metal rungs studded with round bolts held the door together.

Charlene banged her fists against the solid wood. "Get me out of here!"

"Hey, please. Help!" She screamed until her throat burned, and her fists were red. Beyond exhaustion, she slumped to the floor and looked down upon the room. The pool was green and swamp-like; lily pads floated on the top, along with olive-green scum.

Above the point where the pool touched the wall, there was a rectangular hole; based on the wear on the bricks, she assumed that was where water was once pumped into the pool.

Charlene climbed back down the stairs and crawled along the raised bricks skirting the edge of the pool. At the rectangular hole, she eased onto her hands and knees and peered into the darkness.

"Hello." She screamed into the void, and her voice bounced back to her.

Charlene wriggled onto her stomach and peered into the black hole. But that's exactly what it was. A black hole. No light anywhere. Something tickled her cheek and, screaming, she yanked her head back and wriggled away.

She climbed to the highest point on the stairs and glared up at the circular hole above the pool. "Hey! Let me out of here!"

It seemed like an eternity before she gave up and returned to the edge of the well. Only now did she realize that she'd lost a sandal in the water. That's where it was going to stay.

The enormity of her situation hit her like a paralysis drug, and she sat staring at her bare foot. Her previous image of being washed up on a shore as a Jane Doe flashed into her mind again. But this time it wasn't American soil she was on. It was Cuban.

A sob burst from her throat. She'd known what she was doing was risky, but she never envisaged anything like this.

She suddenly realized Peter's cane was gone too. In light of this new development, the cane seemed like a stupid idea anyway.

A mild breeze drifted down to her, and she shivered. Slinking into the shadows, she removed her dress, squeezed the excess water from it, and put it back on. A flash of yellow in the corner caught her eye, and she strode toward it.

Her breath caught as she bent down to pick it up. It was a teddy bear wearing a yellow waistcoat. Her heart quickened as she recalled having exactly the same bear when she was a child.

She searched the room again, looking for something, anything that seemed familiar, and little by little the memories came creeping back.

She'd been down here before. Charlene recalled sitting on her mother's lap, as her mother sat with her back to the wall. They'd both been crying. They were scared and hungry, and her mother had an enormous bruise over her eye.

The images that flashed into her mind were so vivid she couldn't understand why she'd never seen them before. They were real, raw, and frightening. Her mother had been petrified. The room had been less overgrown then, and the water wasn't as foul. But there was no doubt it was the same room.

She'd slept in her mother's lap and could recall crying because she was so hungry. How long had they stayed down there? She frowned at that thought, trying to recall every last detail. At night, they'd huddled together, and it'd become pitch-black and cool. The cold stones and rising damp had made her body ache.

Another memory came tumbling in. It was her mother tearing the hem from her skirt. Charlene remembered her mother's bleeding hand, and then—just like that—she knew exactly what it was. Her mother had written a note in her own blood onto the hem of her dress.

Charlene sat upright. They'd hidden the note in this very room. Behind a brick.

A quick glance around the room didn't help. She stood and scanned the nearest wall, directly behind where she'd found the teddy bear. The bricks were covered in vines and moss.

In the twenty-two years since she'd last been trapped down here, the vegetation had flourished and then died. Something had changed to the detriment of the plants—most likely the water, given its disgusting green color and swampy smell.

Yanking at the vines with her bare hands, she tugged them free, desperate to see the bricks beneath. But every brick looked the same. She pushed them with her fingers, hoping the one her mother had hidden the note behind would still be loose.

At a grinding noise, she snapped around. Someone was coming.

She tossed the teddy bear into the corner and stepped to the side of the room in an attempt to conceal herself in the shadows.

The door at the top of the stairs sprung open and banged against the wall. The sound was like a shotgun blast.

Diego entered the room.

He eased down a step, his hesitation confirming he was searching for her.

Second step.

She waited. The lower he was, the better chance she had. A sliver of light crossed his face, allowing her to see the damage she'd already done with her cane. His nose was swollen and red, and a slice of raw flesh was open across the bridge. His left eye was a hideous shade of purple. He wouldn't get off so lightly this time.

"Where are you, Claudia?"

Claudia? The name was oddly familiar. His voice was too. Especially as it echoed about the damp walls.

Fourth step. He was nearly at the bottom. Two more steps to go. Problem was, he'd see her any second now. Her heart slammed in her throat as she silently launched at him, fist clenched, and aimed right at his already swollen nose.

He reacted faster than she'd anticipated, kicking out with his foot, intent on slamming his boot into her head. But he was a few steps above her. Charlene ducked beneath the blow, grabbed his foot at the same time and twisted it, and with an almighty roar, she dropped her weight. Diego lost his balance and tumbled into the room with her.

She sprang to her feet and timed her attack perfectly to slam the heel of her palm at his nose again. Diego howled, and when he shielded his face with his hands, she dropped her full weight on him, elbow first, aimed directly at his solar plexus. He buckled under her blow, howling again. She pushed off him, ready for her next attack.

Her long ponytail was her downfall. He grabbed her hair and yanked her down.

She screamed and rained punches onto his torso. But her close proximity to him lessened their power.

He pulled harder, forcing her to change attack. She clawed at his face, intent on scratching his eyes out.

But he had her now.

He yanked her hair, and she screamed as much from the pain as fury over her failure. Using his grasp on her hair, he pinned her face to the floor and clambered to a standing position.

"You stupid, fucking bitch." He kicked her in the ribs.

Charlene was thrown toward the raised bricks encircling the well. She scraped at the bricks, desperate to find a loose one to use as a weapon.

The second kick came out of nowhere.

Pain ripped up her back.

Howling against the agony, she tried to stand. But she was too late. Diego's clenched fist hit her just below her left eye.

She screamed as she tumbled sideways into the water.

She clawed for the surface, but her head was above the water for barely a second when Diego grabbed her hair and shoved her under again.

Her mind screamed as she attacked his hand, clawing her nails across his flesh. But he held her there. It was impossible to go down, impossible to up either.

Her lungs screamed for oxygen.

Her head was set to explode.

She needed a breath. Had to take a breath.

She thrashed her hands, and desperate for release, she braced for the pain that would come from her hair being yanked from her scalp and pushed herself down. But it wasn't that easy. The pain was more than she could bear.

Stars danced across her eyes, and in that second, she knew she was drowning.

Her recurring vision of her body being washed up on shore flashed across her mind again. Her lips were blue . . . her flesh deathly pale. Then her body was on a metal slab, just like Peter's had been, but the tag on her toe had her labeled as a Jane Doe.

The murky water got darker, muddied.

The adrenaline that'd fed her limbs evaporated, and her arms floated out to her sides. Her legs began to float to the surface. It was peaceful, with the sun piercing the green-tinged water in a sunburst above her.

Charlene was dying, and her thoughts drifted to Marshall, the only person who knew she was in Cuba. She'd failed him.

That thought broke her heart.

Maybe one day, he'd find her again and take her body back to US soil.

The pain in her lungs was beyond excruciating, and without thinking, she opened her mouth and sucked in the foul water.

Her body jerked against this new affront, shaking her from the despair she'd fallen into.

Surrender . . . that was her last resort. Fighting the urge to do the opposite, she put her hands straight up, showing Diego that she'd given in.

He released her hair with one last shove, and she kicked to the surface. Charlene gasped for air, spluttered water, and the pain in her lungs was agonizing, worse than when she'd inhaled the water. Clutching the moss-covered brickwork, she spewed out the rotten liquid.

"You lucky I need you alive. Stupid bitch." Diego's voice was barely a whisper.

Shoving her hair from her eyes, she looked up at him. Blood had dribbled from both his nostrils in dual rivers that ran over his lips and down his chin. She liked that she'd done that to him.

"Why?" Her voice was a brittle croak.

"Because you worth more alive than dead."

His statement rolled around her murky brain, and it was a couple of moments before she realized what he meant. He was planning to use her for ransom. The idea was ludicrous. Not a single person would pay money to save her.

She burst out laughing, and it hurt both the injury to her face and her burning lungs.

"You think this funny."

"You're an idiot if you think someone will pay ransom money for me."

He squatted down at the edge of the pool. "Who said anything about ransom?"

She frowned. "What are you talking about then?"

"Your real father coming to Cuba. He wants to see you for himself."

"Who're you talking about?"

Diego cocked his head, then a creepy grin split across his blood-stained lips. "Do you not know your daddy?"

Charlene didn't answer, and by the conniving look on Diego's face, she wasn't sure she wanted to know. She swallowed back the foul taste in her mouth and fought the urge to throw up again.

"Your father, he Noah Montgomery. Heard of him?"

The only Noah Montgomery she knew was the lawyer for the Hollywood elite, the man who made a habit of appearing in headline news. It obviously wasn't him, so she shook her head.

Diego huffed. "Well, that funny, 'cause he forgot you existed until thirty minute ago. You will meet him soon." Diego pulled back from the edge of the pool and began to walk away.

"Wait!" Charlene coughed up more water and gasped for breath. "Do you mean the Hollywood lawyer?"

"*Sí*. That him."

"But that's . . . that's not possible."

"Oh, but it is. He your father. He rape your mother, and the happy couple make you."

Charlene's heart lurched.

Diego stepped onto the stairs.

"Stop. Please. It doesn't make sense." She pulled herself higher out of the water. "Why does Noah want to save me?"

Diego burst out laughing. "Oh, he no want to save you. He want to kill you his self this time."

Chapter Twenty-Two

Marshall had spent the entire day searching for the bar supervisor from the dance club. But with just her first name of Kamila and her description matching nearly every other waitress in Havana, he'd have more luck finding an escaped convict. It seemed everyone knew a Kamila, and the number of doors he'd knocked on was heading into the dozens.

Each ticking second put Charlene closer to body-bag material, and the thought of a zipper gliding up over her gorgeous unblinking eyes had his gut churning and his hands squeezing the throttle harder.

The onset of daybreak didn't change a thing, and Marshall turned his attention to the workers setting up their shops. Despite how tired they all looked, smiles still lit up their faces when they thought a potential customer walked through their doors.

During the day, he'd filled up the motorcycle twice and stopped only once for food and a piss. It was late in the day, when his energy was taking a nosedive and his frustrations were doing the opposite, that he hit pay dirt.

By pure chance, he'd found Kamila walking toward the center of town. It helped that she was dressed in her white cowgirl uniform. Marshall didn't usually believe in luck, but he'd take this one.

"What did Charlene do?" He asked Kamila once he'd established that she was indeed the supervisor who'd worked behind the bar.

"She took a picture off the wall?"

"What picture?"

"It was photo of one of our dancers. Pueblo García, but he disappeared many year ago." She told him the mystery behind Pueblo, and Marshall assumed it was the man who'd pretended to be Charlene's father. "What'd Charlene do then? Where'd she go?"

Kamila shifted on her feet, obviously nervous.

"It's okay, you're not in trouble. But Charlene may be. I just need to find her."

Kamila looked to the ground. "She go in taxi to see Diego Álvarez."

"Diego Álvarez!" The name stung like a ten-foot wasp. "Why?"

"Pueblo was boyfriend to Diego's sister. Charlene wanted to talk to him."

"Shit! Where? Where is Diego, Kamila?"

"He at Airshee factory."

Marshall frowned and cocked his head. "Where?"

"Airshee factory. Chocolate."

The answer hit him like a sonic boom. "Hershey! Hershey factory?"

"*Sí. Sí.*"

"Shit! *Gracias.*" He pulled his wallet and handed fifty Cuban pesos to Kamila, and that had her smiling. Marshall adjusted his ass on the rock-hard seat, kick-started the Ural, and shot between a Chevy Bel Air and a Ford Skyliner. Both cars had to be at least fifty years old and were in better condition than his five-year-old Dodge RAM back home.

The motorcycle farted at the ancient cars, lurching Marshall into the cruising traffic, and he raced through the middle of old-town Havana heading toward the setting sun.

On any other day, he'd appreciate the golden glow shimmering off the water. Not today. Not when a young woman's life was in eminent danger.

His brain was a raging torrent of unanswered questions. Is she still alive? Could she be related to Diego? *Why did she go alone?*

That last one was answered easily; she didn't have anyone. But the fact that she went anyway highlighted both her bravery and her desperation. Together the two attributes created the perfect storm.

Charlene had nothing to lose, and that made her dangerous. I
t was the implication of her potential relationship to Diego that was freaking him out.

Marshal had never met Diego Álvarez, but he knew enough about him to know this shit had just gotten real. Diego was the leader of the notorious crime gang Sangre Por la Libertad.

Blood for Freedom.

Although the only freedom that was guaranteed was some poor sucker's death.

Sangre Por la Libertad specialized in prostitution, and a woman like Charlene would be a prize catch. After seeing her determination beneath the bow of *Miss B Hayve*, he could picture her fighting like hell. But this gang fought dirty. She wouldn't stand a chance against the likes of Diego and his band of hired thugs.

His heart invaded his throat as he shot around a gravel corner without tapping the brakes. He only just managed to keep the beast on the road, yet he didn't slow down.

Despite the hellhole Charlene had fallen into, the good news was that Diego would want to keep her alive. With her beauty and stunning physique, she'd start a bidding frenzy. No . . . Diego wouldn't kill her, not yet anyway.

And that glimmer of hope put a rocket up Marshall's ass like he'd never experienced before.

He'd heard of the Hershey factory—not so much about the history of it, but because Mr. Hershey had built the one and only electric train service in Cuba.

Apparently, it was a tourist attraction.

Although why anyone would want to take a jarring, sweaty ride along tracks covered in weeds and grazing cows was beyond him. Fortunately for Marshall, those tracks were going to lead him directly to Diego's hideout and, hopefully, Charlene.

The good news was that Marshall had an easy route to follow. The bad news was it was going to be a damn rough forty miles to get there, as long as the damn motorbike didn't shatter into a million pieces in the meantime.

Marshall headed straight for the rail intersection near Casablanca that he'd driven over a dozen times. From there, he manhandled the motorcycle along the roads that ran parallel to the rail track. When the roads ran out, he shot along the track itself.

Darkness swooped in with a vengeance, and the bike's only head-lamp was about as useful as a candle. Dodging from the potholed road to the decrepit train track was just as dangerous as the track itself. In the end, he opted to stay on the tracks. Most of the sleepers had worn down in the past century, but the shit between the ancient wooden slabs was both dangerous and unpredictable.

Every bone in his body rattled with the shuddering ride, and his arms and fingers ached like hell. He had to clamp his jaw to stop his teeth from jamming together when he hit something he couldn't see.

It'd be a damn miracle if the sidecar was still attached by the time he got there.

The last gasp of Havana's eclectic residences ended abruptly, making the blackness around him as thick as molasses and the endless miles of nothing a new kind of hell.

But Marshall was a man on a mission.

He'd been on bone-jarring treks before. The ones in Iraq were the worst . . . fucking sweltering desert sand, pockmarked with rubble and land mines, all the while being shot at by men who'd had guns shoved into their hands when they were kids. He had to tell himself that this was child's play compared to that.

He hadn't seen a single human for a half hour or so, but that was to be expected. Outside the bustle of Cuba's major cities, people spent their nights indoors with their families. There'd be no trains running either. The last hurricane that'd ripped through the area had messed up a couple of the overhead lines. He only knew that because Tajo, Aleyna's younger brother, used to catch the train to the port of Matanzas occasionally for work.

Every five or so miles, he shot past a train station that was barely a shack beside the tracks. Most had a name dangling from the roof by a couple of chains, but many had no identifying marks at all.

He hoped like hell Hershey station was marked or he'd shoot right on past it. Marshall had to dodge his share of animals along the way too . . . chickens, goats, dogs, and the occasional cow dotted the tracks. One cow wouldn't budge until Marshall got off the Ural and smacked the bovine on its ass.

When the Hershey station finally materialized out of nowhere, Marshall's body just about went into meltdown. He lurched the motorbike off the track and aimed for the twin smoke stacks just visible against the star-studded backdrop.

A few lights speckled the town in the distance, but they were few and far between. It was the faint light emanating from within the Hershey factory's derelict walls that got Marshall's attention. He aimed the motorbike toward the brick wall that marked the entrance to the factory and killed the engine.

Every bone and muscle in his body continued to vibrate, even once he'd dragged his body upright. His knees just about buckled beneath him, and Marshall paused at the arched entrance with his hands on his thighs until the quivering settled.

A flock of birds burst from what was left of the building on the right-hand side, and once they disappeared into the night sky, the ticking of the motorbike engine was the only other sound.

Once he'd decided he was the only human around, Marshall headed in.

Hugging the side wall of a building that looked to have suffered from a severe seismic rattling, Marshall crunched over broken paving stones and brittle weeds, heading toward the structure at the back of the central courtyard. It was the only building with any form of illumination, which came from somewhere within the building's crumbling walls.

Three jeeps that looked to have been stolen from a bad war movie were parked out front. Marshall eased in behind the closest one and peeked inside. Any hope of finding a weapon was short-lived. The jeep barely had seats.

A gas can caught his eye, and an idea of making a firebomb flashed into his mind and out again. While setting the bastards ablaze was appealing, he'd risk endangering Charlene too.

One touch of the hood confirmed the engine was still warm—it hadn't been parked long. Hopefully that meant the gang was still there, and more to the point, that Charlene was too.

He paused at the lead car, listening. At first, he heard nothing. But then his ears picked up the faint beat of music. Stepping toward a set of crippled double doors, he peered into the entrance but was treated to nothing but blackness. A shout from his left had him jumping back and darting for the first jeep.

His heart thumped in his chest as he waited for whoever owned the voice to come barreling out of the doorway. Seconds ticked along, but nothing happened.

A woman's scream reverberated right through him.

It had to be Charlene.

The agony in her cry cut shreds in his flesh. Yet it was a good sign. She was alive.

More shouts came from somewhere inside, but these weren't from Charlene, and they weren't shouts of terror; these were spiked with excitement. And they were growing louder by the second. The light source was intensifying too.

They were on the move. And that meant Marshall had to get the fuck out of there.

He dashed to the corner of the courtyard. But the intersection between the two derelict buildings was a crap hiding spot, so Marshall made a snap decision and raced as fast as his already tortured legs could take him toward the building he'd walked past.

His only hope was that the members of the rowdy mob were too focused on whatever they were planning to notice him sprinting up the courtyard. Three feet from the doorway, the boom of automatic weapons went off behind him. He dove through the entrance, hitting the broken concrete on his knees, and rolled to one side.

The shots continued, as did the shouts, and it was a couple of thumping heartbeats before he realized they weren't shooting at him. He crawled over glass and crap toward what was left of a window and eased up on his knees. What he saw had his heart firing.

Two of the jeeps now had their headlights on, aimed at the double doorway. Three men emerged at once, all in army fatigues, all with ancient-looking Kalashnikovs shooting at the heavens.

Charlene surfaced next, and his heart squeezed at the sight of her. Bruising and blood covered half her face, and she was limping. But that might've been because she only had one shoe.

She was wedged between two men, both of whom were shorter than her, and she was wrestling against them despite her arms being locked up behind her.

"Let go of me!" she screamed and tried to yank herself free.

But they shoved her forward, pushing her toward the car parked between the other two.

When Diego stepped from the building, Marshall's pleasure revved up at the mess that was the Cuban's nose. Marshall had no doubt that Charlene had done it. He smiled at that.

Charlene released a shill cry, doubled over forward, and with a move that surprised the shit out of both Marshall and the two men who had hold of her, she used her bare foot to whack both of them in the head. Free now, she kicked the first man in the nuts and the second in the face, and both men howled in obvious agony.

Charlene took off, hitting a stride that should've been impossible with only one shoe, and Marshall was torn between yelling at her to run and telling her to stop. She wouldn't get away, not when they had the advantage of weapons and vehicles. Especially not with her arms still tied behind her *and* the uneven pavement.

She tumbled forward, landing on her knees and face. Her scream raked shivers over his spine. It must've hurt like hell, yet Charlene rolled to her feet and took off again. But now barefoot, she was slower this time, her gait uneven, and his heart thundered as he watched them narrow in on her.

If Marshall had had a gun, he would've picked them off one by one. But he didn't. All he could do was watch the hell unfold and wait for his opportunity. He was still banking on the fact that they needed to keep her alive. She was worth nothing dead. He hoped.

Just as they were about to launch at her, she turned on them. Some kind of sixth sense had her ducking away and kicking out at the same time. He watched with a mix of pride and apprehension, yet at the same time he wondered where the hell she got her courage.

She managed to get two of them down, and each of them was rewarded with a kick in the nuts. The third guy got lucky. He tackled her to the ground, and Marshall's gut crumbled as he watched the fight fade out of her.

In the space of about three minutes, Charlene had managed to fight four men, three of whom were now walking like their balls were the size of melons. In addition, Diego's right eye looked to be swollen shut.

Picking these guys off was going to be easy. Marshall just needed the right opportunity. Patience was an asset that was hard learned, but it'd saved him more times than he could count.

Two uninjured men dragged Charlene back to the jeeps. Diego waited at the cars, legs apart, fists clenched at his side. He was the only man Marshall would need to be wary of. Unlike his ragtag crew, Diego seemed to have some kind of training behind him.

The second Charlene was within spitting distance of Diego, she did exactly that. She spat in his face. Diego reached up to wipe away her spittle; then he slapped her across the cheek. Her head snapped sideways, and Marshall saw her blood float through the beam of one of the car's headlights.

In that moment, Marshall knew that no matter what happened from here on out, Diego wouldn't see daybreak.

Charlene's arms went limp, followed by the rest of her body. She'd lost her fight. Two men tossed her into the back of a jeep like a sack of potatoes, and Diego shoved in beside her.

The other men climbed into the front, the engine fired, and seconds later, the car raced for the entrance with the remaining men in the two cars behind.

Marshall didn't even wait for them to be out of sight before he dashed for the motorbike. He jumped on and kicked the starter in the same instant.

The second the ignition fired, he rammed the throttle to full and raced after Charlene.

Chapter Twenty-Three

C harlene didn't really think she'd get away. Not with eight men to fight off. But the last time she'd sat back and done nothing, Peter had been killed.

She wasn't going to give up without a fight.

Now, though, as her body throbbed with her injuries, she wondered if it'd been a foolish move. She probably should've waited until her chances were improved.

But that moment might never come.

And if what Diego had said was true, she would soon have another man to contend with. Noah Montgomery.

Her mind snapped to the New York City lawyer who claimed to be her father. Could that even be possible? From the limited footage she'd seen of him, he was an arrogant ass. Besides, he was an American, yet her mother was apparently Cuban.

She had no idea what to believe anymore. She'd gone from being a boring twenty-eight-year-old who'd never stepped out of America to the niece of a honcho in some kind of Cuban mafia.

None of it made sense.

The bloodstained strip of fabric stuffed into her bra might shed some light. *If* she got the opportunity to have someone translate it for her.

She'd had all day to search for that hidden note that she'd recalled her mother hiding behind a brick. But she'd remembered wrong. It was only once she'd conceded defeat and curled up in a ball with the teddy bear that she'd found it. The note was inside the bear, shoved into a hole that was concealed by the miniature waistcoat.

She'd cried when she'd found it. She'd cried even harder when she realized it was written in Spanish. It was a cruel joke . . . *here's a clue to the greatest mystery of your life, little girl, but guess what . . . you'll never know what it says.*

Charlene fought the lump burning in her throat. She'd never give Diego the satisfaction of seeing her cry. It was a cruel twist to have the potential answers to her questions close to her chest at the same moment when she was heading to meet the man who wanted to kill her.

She'd never given thought to how she'd die before, but even if she'd had a thousand years to stew over it, she'd never have contemplated it would be in Cuba, nor at the hands of a complete stranger who claimed to be her father.

She shifted her gaze from her bloodstained dress to her apparent uncle. "Where are you taking me?"

Diego's eyes snapped to her as though he'd thought she was unconscious. Even in the dim light, she could see the extent of the bruising around his eye. She liked what she saw. And she'd give him a hell of a lot more when the opportunity arose.

A sick grin crawled across his mouth, displaying a row of crooked teeth. "To your daddy."

"He's not my fucking father."

"Oh, but he is."

"Bullshit!"

"My sister. . . ," he slowly shook his head as if disappointed. "She stupid to keep that secret from me."

"What secret?"

"About Noah raping her and he your father."

"I don't believe you."

Diego shrugged. "I no care what you believe. Noah believes. That what matters."

Charlene tried to piece things together, but nothing made sense. "Why would he believe you?"

Diego shifted on his seat, easing back from her. "We go back long way, me and Noah. Well before he a hot-shot New York lawyer."

That comment surprised her, she couldn't picture Noah in the company of a man like Diego. "How?"

Diego frowned and looked at her like he was weighing his options.

"You already said he was going to kill me, so what's the harm in giving me answers?"

The side of his mouth twitched. "That is true. He going to kill you."

She clenched and unclenched her jaw at the certainty in his voice. "Did he kill my mother?"

"*Sí.*" He actually looked pleased with himself.

Charlene wrestled against the restraints, growling her fury. "How could you let that happen? She was your sister."

He shrugged. "She was pain in ass."

She'd give anything to knock his lights out, and by the look on his face, he knew exactly how dangerous she was.

"Calm down, little girl."

She glared at him. "Don't tell me to fucking calm down." She wanted him to know that, given the right opportunity, she'd crush his larynx beneath the heel of her foot.

Diego snapped his eyes away, and she liked that he'd seen her fury.

"How did Noah kill my mother?"

"Strangle her."

She sucked the air through her teeth. "Did you see him do it?"

Diego let the question hang, and the only sound was the roar of the engine and the crunch of the tires over the rough gravel. Finally, he huffed out a sigh and turned back to her. "*Sí.*" His voice was way too calm considering what he was admitting to.

"Jesus! Did you report it to the police?"

He captured her gaze with his, and the urge to head-butt him was huge. "He pay me lot of money to keep secret."

She clenched her jaw against her simmering rage. "Asshole!" She kicked out with her foot, but her stupid dress was caught beneath her thighs, restricting her movement, and her toes stubbed the driver's seat instead. She screamed with both pain and fury.

Diego laughed, a quick spontaneous snort. "Soon, I very rich asshole."

"Really?" She said it sarcastically. "How much is he paying you?"

"One million dollars."

A million dollars. For Charlene Bailey, or Claudia Álvarez, or whoever she was. She burst out laughing, and Diego's eyes festered with suspicion.

"What?" He snapped.

"You're a fool if you think he's going to part with that kind of money. He doesn't even know me. Why would he believe I'm his daughter?"

"Because Benita tell him when she begging for her life."

That comment was like a punch to her stomach. It took the wind out of her and weakened her resolve. The timbre of the car's tires slowed, and she turned her gaze outside the vehicle. A jumble of ancient memories came flooding back at the first thing she saw.

It was a set of marble stairs that'd been painted in a potpourri of vibrant contrasting colors. The building surrounding the magnificent feature was long gone. Four people sitting on the stairs played musical instruments and stared into the flames of a fire built in a rusted forty-four-gallon drum.

The scene was exactly the same as twenty-two years ago when Charlene had been driven along this street. She contemplated calling out to them. Yelling for help. But at the same time, she knew it was pointless. Not with Diego beside her.

Although she'd barely had an hour with him, she remembered enough from her childhood to know Diego was a man to be revered and feared. Nobody would go against him. Not his ardent followers and not the strangers on the street.

Charlene was on her own.

Her thoughts tumbled to Marshall again. A little piece of her heart crumbled at the thought that she'd never see him again. It wasn't very often she met a man who captivated her as much as he had.

She blocked out her brutal reality and took her mind back to that moment on *Miss B Hayve* when he'd wrapped his arms around her to chase away the bitter cold with the warmth of his own body. She went over that embrace in her mind, hitting rewind each time their hug ended.

Something about how she felt in his arms had her heart aching. It was impossible to believe that she'd never see him again.

The minutes rushed by, as did the miles. *And* endless fields of nothing. Charlene didn't need to ask where they were going again.

She already knew.

They were going to the same remote airstrip where she'd last seen her mother. She was coming full circle. The hellhole that'd been the venue for her mother's murder was about to witness her end too.

No! She sat upright and clenched her jaw.

Fear of impending death blazed through her body like a firestorm. *No!*

This was not the end. Charlene Bailey was not finished yet. She had so much more life to live.

Her cocoon of despair vanished in a flash, and she turned her attention to surviving this mess. She'd had hundreds of hours of self-defense tutorials. Utilizing those lessons, she studied her surroundings, beginning with the men around her.

The man behind the wheel had a face that'd seen way too much sun and was full of ancient acne craters. He was shorter than her and was so slim his collarbones jutted above his shoulders.

The man in the passenger seat was just as scrawny, and his mouth was permanently open as if he couldn't breathe through his nose. Maybe he couldn't. He must've sensed Charlene staring because his head snapped around to her. His wild hair whipped up in the breeze, covering his eyes for a couple of beats, before he turned his attention back to the road ahead.

No, she decided. These two wouldn't give her too much trouble.

Diego was the problem. And with her hands tied behind her back, her chances with him were slim. But not completely dead. Not yet anyway.

She adjusted her position on her seat so her hands were closer to the side and she was facing more toward Diego. Feeling along the door, her fingers snagged on a splinter of rusty metal jutting out from where the trim used to be. It was her lucky day. Without moving her arms too much, she began rubbing the coarse rope against the metal.

An hour or so into this journey, she'd been begging for the ride to be over. Now, though, as the painstaking job of cutting through the rope proved to be taking forever, she begged for the trek to take longer.

Each time the jeep launched over another pothole, the rusted makeshift blade sliced one of her fingers. It wasn't long before she felt the dribble of her own blood. But she forced through the pain.

No pain, no gain.

God, she'd heard that mantra a thousand times over the years at self-defense lessons. It was never more pertinent than now.

She glanced over her shoulder. Two more vehicles followed them. Three men were in the one just behind, so she assumed the remaining two were in the last jeep. The middle jeep didn't have any headlights, which was probably why it was cruising so close.

If Charlene had a gun, she would've easily been able to shoot them. She'd had a few shooting lessons over the years.

The driver shifted down a gear, and Charlene snapped her eyes forward. Her heart lurched to her throat as she recognized the lone shed. They'd arrived. No longer caring about caution, she tripled her friction on the rope.

But when the jeep lurched to a stop at the side wall, she knew she was too late. Barely three seconds later, she was yanked from the jeep.

The instant her feet hit the ground, she planted her heels, crouched down, and drove upward with all the force she could muster.

The top of her head connected with the chin of the nearest man. He flew backward, hitting the ground as a lump of lifeless meat.

She didn't stop to admire her handiwork; instead, she flung herself at the second man, ramming her knees into his groin.

He buckled forward at the exact moment she raised her knee again. This time she slammed into his nose, and he too was on the ground, passed out with his mate.

Charlene took off at a sprint, but seconds later, she howled in agony at the rivers of pain in her scalp as she was yanked backward on the dirt.

When she opened her eyes, Diego had a clump of her hair wrapped around his fist and his gun aimed at her forehead.

That was the second time her hair had failed her, and she decided there and then that if she made it out of this alive, she was cutting it all off.

Diego screamed something in Spanish, and a cloud of dust was the prelude to the feet of four men reaching her side.

"Get up, you stupid bitch," Diego hissed.

Charlene rolled to her side, allowing herself a close-up view of the man she'd kneed in the face. He was out cold, missing a few teeth, but not dead . . . unfortunately.

Before she was fully standing, the four men had her in a grip that she'd have no hope of escaping. They dragged her to a pole beside the shed, and while three men held her in position, the fourth cut her ropes and promptly tied her hands back up and secured her to the pole.

Once that was done, they stepped back with their weapons raised. The headlights of the two jeeps were aimed right at her, silhouetting the six men. It was easy to spot Diego, not just because he was stockier than the remaining five but also because of the confidence in his stance. He didn't seem at all perturbed that she'd taken out two of his men with her bare hands.

She, on the other hand, was incredibly proud of herself. "Your men could use a little more training." She grinned at the two lifeless forms in the dirt.

"Shut up." Diego yelled, then stomped forward and slapped her across the face.

Charlene bit back the scream in her throat. When the stars dancing across her eyes evaporated, she unclenched her jaw and tried to eyeball Diego. "Why should I? Like you said, I'll be dead soon."

As if on cue, the distant roar of an engine had Diego and his men turning their attention skyward.

Chapter Twenty-Four

Marshall breathed a sigh of relief when the convoy slowed down at the end of a road that'd lasted an eternity. He'd been watching the empty fuel indicator for at least ten miles; certain the Ural was about to offer its last gasp.

While Diego and his band of goons aimed the three jeeps at a distant shed, Marshall drove the motorbike into a thicket of gnarly weeds and cut the engine. He lunged into the bushes and crawled on his hands and knees toward a better vantage point.

They'd positioned the jeeps' headlights to capture the show, and what a show it was. Out of nowhere, Charlene reduced two men to pulp, and Marshall had to resist cheering her on. *And* running in to help her.

Her stamina was incredible. He just hoped she didn't run out of steam before he got to her. She'd need to run like hell once he grabbed her.

Marshall saw Diego's cowardly slap across Charlene's face, and that's when he decided that the asshole wasn't just going to die tonight; he was going to suffer an ugly, painful death.

The sound of an engine had him searching skyward, and his heart slammed into his chest at the site of a lone floodlight descending from the darkness.

The whole time he'd been chasing Charlene, he'd assumed Diego was taking her to some kind of secret meeting point, where rich assholes with fistfuls of money would buy her in a bidding war.

Not once had he considered the possibility of Diego having her flown somewhere.

This new twist threatened to finish what the motorbike had started —to knock him completely off balance.

It also showed just how valuable she was. It had him wondering what the hell he'd gotten himself into. And Charlene, for that matter.

He had no doubt that if she got airborne, she'd vanish. He was kicking himself for agreeing to take her to Cuba. He should've ignored her plight and returned her to the safety of the US of A.

But the debate was pointless. He'd done it now, and that made him responsible for getting her home.

It was a perfect night. Mild temperature. Clear sky. No breeze.

Perfect for killing bad guys.

In his past life, whenever he'd spearheaded covert operations, most of the time he'd had intricate details of the lay of the land. Most of the time he'd had the backup of able-bodied men and top-notch equipment.

Not tonight.

Tonight it was just him, his bare hands, and a kick-ass woman who was a better fighter than some of his old navy crew. But with a jet closing in on that tiny runway, he no longer had the luxury of time to scope out the area or plan an attack.

Whoever was on that jet had both the means and the money to get here quick . . . and that reeked of trouble. It also meant that the second the damn thing landed, the scales tipped in favor of the bad guys.

It was time to notch this shit up to extraction mode.

With the men distracted by the incoming jet, Marshall made a snap decision, and hunching over, he raced hard and fast at the closest jeep.

One hundred yards.

Ten years ago, he'd have covered this distance in the space of fifteen seconds, and that was with an eighty-pound pack on his back. Now, though, it seemed to take an eternity.

Fifty yards.

If one of the men turned now, it was all over.

The jet's roar intensified, and it was impossible to hear anything else. *Twenty yards.*

He didn't dare look up. He just put his head down and aimed for the closest tailpipe.

He covered the last five yards with a dive and rolled right up to the well-worn tire. His heart was in his throat as he clutched onto the back of the jeep and pulled his head up to survey the scene.

The plane looked to be skimming right over the distant treetops. Eight men were still visible. Two were passed out before Charlene, but the rest were more spread out than when he'd last eyeballed them. Two were positioned right alongside the runway.

Damn idiots were so close they'd likely get knocked out by the bird's wings. If only he should be so lucky. Two men were near the far edge of the shed. They had their weapons lowered and were taking a moment to puff on fat cigars.

Two men stood next to Charlene, but they obviously didn't trust her as their weapons, though relatively loose, were trained in her direction. They were his first plan of attack. The engine noise was his greatest ally, and one look at the lowering beacon had him guessing he had all of about one minute till touchdown.

Hunched over, he dashed for the next jeep. Charlene was twenty yards away, but it might as well have been fifty. Marshall sucked in a huge breath, let it out in a steady stream, then ran straight and hard at the nearest man. He crossed the distance in about six seconds and didn't dare look at Charlene. His focus was on the man. The man's focus was on the jet.

Marshall was on him and whipped his head around with a vicious crack before the man even saw him coming and tossed the body aside. The second man, though, was a different story. His weapon snapped from aiming at the ground to aiming at Marshall within a millisecond.

"Marshall!" Charlene screamed.

Marshall shoved her screams from his focus and ran straight at the scrawny asshole. He was banking on both inexperience and surprise to get him through the next three seconds.

As a soldier, he'd been taught how to simultaneously ignore the threat of imminent death and finish the job at hand. Didn't make it any fucking easier. With each step, he expected to be shredded to bits by the rapid fire of the AK-47. By the look on the man's face, he was just as surprised as Marshall when Marshall got there first.

In the same instant, Marshall's left hand slapped the gun away, while his right slammed fist-first into his rival's nose. Despite the heavy rumble of the plane's engines, he heard the crunch that marked the bones breaking beneath his blow.

He heard something else too. Shouts from the other men.

Marshall rolled to his side and grabbed hold of the battered Kalashnikov, and as he prayed there were still thirty rounds in the magazine, he pulled the trigger.

In a tenth of a second, the man running toward him went from upright to flat on his face in a cloud of blood.

Marshall shot the next Cuban before the others had even moved. The remaining two scattered like mice, and Marshall's breath caught in his throat as he picked them off one after the other.

The gun's sights were off, and instead of hitting them dead center, he took out their legs and hips. It was effective enough.

The jet still hadn't touched down before Marshall had reduced the men to bloody messes on the dirt. Marshall wanted to look Diego in the eyes as he took him down. But with no time to spare, he had to settle with the sounds of Diego's agony, as Marshall carved a spray of bullets up the length of his body.

Marshall got to his feet and pumped a few more rounds into each of them.

The squeal of tires striking the tarmac had Marshall forcing back the urge to get up close and personal with Diego and confirming the asshole was dead.

Instead, he turned to Charlene. Her gaze locked on him so intently that he had to remind himself to breathe. As he dashed toward her, he tossed the used weapon aside and paused to gather the first thug's weapon from the ground. He slung it over his shoulder as he approached her. "You okay?"

"Oh, Marshall. Thank you. Thank you." Tears streamed down her bloodstained cheeks.

He stepped in behind her and worked on the ropes. The jeep's headlights provided enough light to see both the knot and her messed-up hands. "Don't thank me yet."

"I can't believe you found me."

"Got lucky. That's all." The knot was proving a bitch to unravel, and it was time they didn't have. "Come on," he hissed under his breath. Finally, he wrestled the knot free, and Charlene stepped from the pole and twisted around to face him.

She curled her arms around his neck. "Thank you." Her embrace made every second of the last twenty-four hours' worth it.

He wrapped his arms around her delicate waist for the briefest of hugs, then he eased back. Despite everything she'd been through, the goddamned woman still looked as sexy as hell. "Come on, we've gotta go."

He grabbed her hand, and after a quick glance to position the downed plane, he dragged her toward the nearest bushes, praying they remained hidden behind the cover of the shed.

Charlene's gait was erratic and, based on her groans, painful too. And it probably wasn't just because she was in bare feet. Considering the beatings he'd witnessed, it was a wonder she could move at all.

The rugged terrain off the gravel wasn't any better, and they weren't anywhere near as far as he'd hoped when the roaring engines were replaced with the whir of the easing turbines.

"Wait! Wait." Charlene released his grasp and crouched down.

"What?" He snapped his eyes to her.

"I have to see."

"What?"

Her eyes were a feisty combination of determination and anger. "I need to see who's on that plane."

Chapter Twenty-Five

The headache that had begun nipping behind Noah's eyes when he'd stormed from the courtroom had hit a whole new level by the time he'd hung up from that wretched call from Diego.

But the downward spiral didn't stop there.

When he'd called his pilot, the narrow-minded asshole had insisted on triple his normal fee to make the urgent illegal flight to Cuba.

His two bodyguards had done the same. The greedy fools had just written themselves off Noah's payroll; they just didn't know it yet. It would be the first topic of discussion when they returned to New York. If they returned. Who knew what they were flying into?

And more to the point, what that conniving crook Diego had planned.

At least Madam Athena hadn't let him down. She'd provided Stella without debate. The Swedish bombshell was usually booked up months in advance, and even then, she was very fussy about whom she was reserved for.

Stella was beyond stunning, with eyes the color of a cerulean pool and lips like cotton candy. She was five foot eight, had a figure that would have any men's magazine editor drooling, and spoke with an accent that oozed sensuality.

It'd been a whirlwind of an afternoon as he deflected calls from badgering reporters and his soon-to-be ex-partner, and also made urgent arrangements to get himself to Cuba. By the time Noah sat in the plush leather seat on the jet, he was mentally drained. Just two hours had elapsed between ending the call with Diego and taking off from JFK.

Once the pilot extinguished the FASTEN SEAT BELT sign, Stella poured Noah a glass of cognac over ice and gave bottled water to the others. Then she led him to his private office at the rear of the jet, stripped down naked, and attempted to take Noah to a whole new set of heights.

Normally, his time with Stella was mind-blowing, and he'd savor every single second with the kinky minx. Not tonight, though. When he'd decided to book her, he had hoped the exquisite blonde would take his mind off the unpredictable mess he'd slipped into. He'd also hoped her magical touch would release the tension jamming up his body. She hadn't done either.

His climax was disappointing, more whimper than mind-blowing release, and the entire time, he was trying not to focus on the exorbitant fee Madam Athena had charged for her top performer. Stella had outdone herself, though, and Noah commended her for her efforts with a promise of an additional bonus.

He returned to the plush seats in the middle of the jet and glanced at the time. Two more hours to go. And the worst part was that the configuration of the plane meant he had to sit opposite the ugly twins. His identical twin bodyguards no longer looked alike. Colt had broken his nose so many times it faced his left ear, and Steele had a jagged scar across his left eyebrow that stopped just above his eye.

They were both beefed-up chumps, though, all muscle no brains, and were more the Bruce Willis style of bodyguard than the Bond type. He'd used them on and off over the years . . . whenever someone needed to be reminded of who was in charge.

Noah hated that he needed the overpaid thugs at all. But he did.

The twins had also been there twenty-two years ago when things had gotten out of control. And he'd paid them well to keep that unexpected incident confidential. They had. This time their mission, other than to protect Noah, was to finish what they should've done last time . . . to kill Diego.

Noah would handle the girl himself. Just the thought of wrapping his hands around her neck had his heart rate tripping.

Stella stepped from his office dressed in a designer pants suit and topped up his cognac. As he sipped the succulent nectar, Noah dwelled on the last time his life had spiraled out of control so quickly. It was in Cuba . . . twenty-two years ago. The one night that had changed the course of his life forever.

After the incident, he'd berated himself a few times over his stupidity. Only a few, though, because his reckless decision had come with some surprising advantages. He'd been twenty-eight at the time. Young, foolish, with the world at his feet, and driven to make a name for himself.

So when a friend's bachelor party morphed into a stupid illegal midnight run to Cuba, he'd decided to up the ante and, in an effort to impress them, went in search of quality cigars and rum. He could never have envisaged the devastating repercussions that decision would have.

Diego had been young too, and his eventual rise up the criminal ranks was still in its infancy. It was hard to believe the two of them were similar in *any* way. Yet they were when it came to drive and determination.

Stella stepped out of the jet's bathroom, and as she strolled toward him, Noah cast his mind back to the Cuban woman who'd changed his life. Diego's sister. He'd only touched her twice, and yet the impact of each of those times had been life changing.

Her body was that of a temptress . . . luscious olive skin, silky hair, youthful flesh. But it was the fire in her eyes that remained the pillars of his recollection. When he'd first seen her, he'd been sharing a rum with Diego to celebrate a deal that was set to make the pair of them a decent amount of money.

Benita had silently stepped into the room to place another bottle of rum on the table. It was obvious she was under Diego's instructions, as she was in and out of the room in a flash. But it'd been enough to mesmerize Noah. Enough so that he'd asked Diego about her.

When he'd declared Benita as his sister, Noah had thought that would be where any attempts at seeing more of her would end. But he was wrong. It turned out Noah could handle his alcohol much better than his new Cuban partner. So when Diego passed out drunk, Noah had raped Benita.

From the second he'd grabbed her, he'd known it was wrong. But he couldn't stop himself. He'd had plenty of women before Benita, but they'd all been willing sluts who'd practically thrown themselves at him. It was the Cuban woman's rejection that'd driven him wild.

Even while he'd had her pinned down, raping her—his hands around her neck, her fingers clawing at his flesh, hatred burning in her eyes—he still couldn't believe he was doing it. But he had.

It was the most brutal, shocking, unexpected, yet utterly powerful experience in his life at that time. In the space of five minutes, he'd become a different man.

Empowered. Invincible. Dangerous.

What he hadn't envisaged, though, was Diego using that moment to blackmail him.

For five years, he heard nothing, and Noah had thought he'd come away from the incident unscathed. But evidently Benita had kept the rape a secret too.

That all changed when Diego overheard his sister confessing the rape to a friend. Consequently, five years after that fateful night, Diego made his first attempt to blackmail Noah. Today Diego had made his second attempt. Noah would ensure it was his last.

He swirled the amber liquid around his crystal tumbler, then swigged back a large gulp of the top-shelf cognac. It stung his throat and put fire in his belly. A fire that would rage until he'd finished off Diego and his Machiavellian tactics forever.

The twins began snoring at exactly the same moment, as if they'd choreographed it, and Noah was torn between pegging his tumbler at one of them and being grateful that he didn't have to endure their blank stares anymore. Opting for the latter, he picked up his phone and opened it to the photo Diego had sent him.

When he'd killed Benita twenty-two years ago, Noah had thought he'd eliminated that blackmail threat. But before she'd died, she'd mentioned the daughter who was apparently his. At the time, Noah had cast aside her comment as a desperate plea for mercy, especially given that he was strangling her.

Now it appeared that Benita's deathbed confession was true. Noah hadn't believed Diego until he'd sent the picture. He stared at the photo, expanding it to look directly into her eyes. Claudia looked exactly like her mother.

Noah's missing finger twitched as though the damn bitch was haunting him again.

He shook his hand and rubbed his stub with his other fingers. He was going to enjoy killing Claudia. The fact that she was potentially his daughter made it even more thrilling. But he'd take his time with her. He needed answers first.

He had to know why she'd turned up now, after twenty-two years in hiding.

When the pilot announced they were coming in for a landing, Noah cast all his tumbling thoughts aside, clicked off his phone, and finished his drink in one gulp.

Speculation was over. It was time for answers.

Stella buckled into the seat beside Noah.

He wished he was as calm as the Swedish beauty appeared to be.

The approach to the runway looked exactly the same as it had two decades ago. Unwelcoming. There was nothing but darkness below. And above, for that matter. Except for the scattering of stars, there were no lights anywhere.

The damn backward country hadn't advanced at all.

Noah leaned into the curve of the jet's window, hoping to get a glimpse of the landing strip. At first, he saw nothing. It was like they were landing in the middle of the ocean. I

t was a good minute or two before a light appeared. He squinted at the scene, trying to establish the layout. A rumble beneath his feet confirmed that the landing gear had been lowered, and the roar of the wind increased as it buffeted against the tires.

At a clicking sound, his gaze shifted from out the window to the twins. Both had their weapons out, checking the magazines and clicking them back into place. It was obviously something they'd done many times over as they were almost synchronized to perfection.

Stella was checking her phone, and if she was at all worried about the display of weapons, she didn't show it.

The squeal of tires announced the jet's touchdown, and Noah glanced out the window in time to see a pair of car headlights shining onto a rusty old shed.

He also thought he saw a few bodies lying on the dirt.

But it all whizzed by too fast.

He squinted again, trying to confirm his vision, and what he saw had his heart invading his throat. Two people were running toward the bushes. One was a woman in a red dress.

Fury shot through him like a raging inferno.

He was not going to let her slip away this time.

But the image was so fleeting he couldn't be certain. He snapped his eyes to his bodyguards. "Get those guns ready."

"Yes, boss," they answered simultaneously.

The pilot slowed the plane to a crawl and turned it around at the end of the runway, ready to take off. Noah glanced out the window again, but the view was nothing but darkness.

Noah and the twins stood up before the FASTEN SEAT BELT sign was extinguished, and he allowed them to lead the charge off the plane. After all, he'd hired them to protect him.

Colt opened the door that doubled as the stairs and lowered it to the tarmac. Steele climbed down first, followed by his twin, and Noah was the last to step on Cuban soil.

The threesome strode around the front of the plane and entered what looked like a war zone. Colt and Steele raised their weapons, angled their bodies into what Noah could only assume was a defensive move, and ran toward the side of the shed.

"Jesus!" Noah's heart was in his throat as he crouched down and raced after them.

At the edge of the shed, he had a close-up view of one of the bodies. What was left of the bloody mess looked more like roadkill than a human being. And it was lit up in the jeep's headlights as though it'd been arranged for maximum effect.

The acrid smell of gunfire and bodily fluids invaded his nostrils, and Noah had to fight the urge to flee back to the plane.

He'd never seen a dead body before, except for the woman he'd killed himself. But that had involved zero blood.

Now there were eight of them covered in blood. And none of them were female.

Colt and Steele stepped out from cover and played their weapons over the area. It was as silent as a mass suicide. When the twins lowered their weapons, Noah assumed it was safe and stepped out from behind the shed. "What the hell happened?" He cast his eyes from one body to the next.

"Looks like an ambush," Colt volunteered.

"More like a bloodbath," Steele said.

"Same thing, dickhead." Noah strolled to the nearest body and kicked what was left of the man's foot. He jumped back when the body groaned. "Hey, this one's alive." It was impossible to see the man's face. "Anyone got a flashlight?"

"Nah, boss."

Colt strode over, picked up the hand of the groaning man, and dragged him into the beam of the jeep's headlights. The wounded man howled the whole way, but Colt's ability to care was nonexistent. Yet another reason Noah had hired him.

The ugly brute tossed the bloody man down, and Noah leaned over him. "Huh, it's Diego. Go check the others; see if anyone else is alive. And find that damn woman."

The twins strode away, and Noah turned his attention back to what was left of his Cuban nemesis. "Hey, Diego, you still alive?" Noah nudged his foot into Diego's ribs.

The bloody body groaned.

"There you are." Noah squatted down to get a better look at the mess. "What the hell happened?"

Diego spat out blood, and it landed on his chin in a thick globule. "*Por favor. Ayuadame. Por favor.*"

"English, Diego."

"Please." Diego spluttered more blood. "Help me."

"Yes. Yes, I will. Tell me what happened."

"I . . . I not know. Man, he just started shooting. Help me. Please!"

"Where's the girl?"

A small gasp released from Diego's throat, and Noah wondered if he'd succumbed to his injuries.

Colt approached Noah's side. "They're all dead, boss."

A scream burst through the silence, and Noah jumped up and spun to the shrieks. It was Stella. Her hands were in her hair, her eyes wild as she stood over the body of the nearest man. "Shut the fuck up," Noah yelled at her.

She didn't.

"Jesus, woman, get back on the fucking plane."

But Stella just stood there, screaming like a banshee. "Ahh, for God's sake." She was a problem, and Noah realized, too late for her, that it was stupid to have brought her along.

"Give me that!" Noah snatched Colt's Ruger from his oversized hand, aimed at the wailing woman, and put a bullet in her belly.

Shrieking, she flew backward with a burst of crimson across her tailored suit and slammed onto the dirt.

It wasn't his best shot, but given the tension blazing through his brains, it was a wonder he'd hit her at all.

That was Noah's second murder. But it wasn't anywhere near as satisfying as his first.

Killing someone at a distance paled in comparison to watching the life drain out of their eyes and feeling their body dwindle beneath his fingers.

Next time Noah murdered someone, he'd do it properly.

And if things went according to plan, his daughter would own that designation.

When Stella moaned, he extracted her murder from his repertoire and handed the weapon back to Colt. "Go finish her off. Then drag her body into the bushes and make sure she's well hidden."

Colt swaggered over to Stella, who was clutching her stomach and groaning. He raised his gun, and Noah glanced away before the blast of the gunshot shattered the silence.

"Such a shame." He mumbled to himself. It occurred to him that he'd have Madam Athena to contend with next. But she was the least of his worries.

He turned toward a new disturbing noise to witness Colt and Steele dragging Stella through the dirt by her wrists. "Pick her up!" Noah barked at them. "Goddamn apes. And make sure she has no jewelry or identification on her."

If her body was ever found, she'd be just another Jane Doe on the coroner's table. Noah glanced around the surroundings. *If she was found.*

The first time he'd been here, Diego had told him the remote runway hadn't been used in decades. It was once a key asset in a drug cartel's distribution center. But all that changed with a major drug bust here at the end of Batista's reign.

Anyone under the age of forty probably didn't even know it existed. Noah never did ask Diego how he came to know of it. It was one of the things about the Cuban that'd impressed Noah.

Diego had been a man who got things done.

Had been . . .

One glance at Diego was enough to know he was a dead man. Noah jabbed his leather shoe into a part of Diego's hip that wasn't covered in blood. "Hey, you still alive?"

Diego's lips moved, and Noah squatted down to hear if he was speaking. "You say something?"

"Help me." His voice was a strange, wheezy gurgle.

"Yes, I will. Where's the girl Diego, Claudia? Where's my daughter?"

A bloody bubble formed on Diego's lips, followed by an exaggerated sigh that could only mean the end.

"Shit." Noah stood up, stepped away from the body, and glanced around. His eyes fell on the rusted pole the jeep headlights were aimed at.

Two decades ago, Benita had been tied to that pole. At that time, he'd flown from New York to Cuba without any concept of what would greet him. His sole purpose had been to eliminate Benita. This time he'd had prior knowledge of the setting, yet the mounting bodies and missing target confirmed that his plan had tipped irreversibly off course.

Noah was not accustomed to losing. Losing twice in one day was unprecedented. Losing the same target twice was incomprehensible.

To top that off, he couldn't fathom a way to cut his losses.

Noah eased up to the pole and placed his hand on the cold metal. It was hard to believe this bleak spot was the site of his life-changing moment. He had hoped to replicate that delicious experience with Benita's daughter.

His daughter, if Benita was to be believed.

His gaze drifted to the area where he'd thought he seen the woman running into the bushes. It had to be her. But who was the mystery man with her? The last time he was here, Claudia had been whisked away by Pueblo.

Diego had told him Pueblo was dead. Looks like he was wrong, or maybe he'd lied on purpose.

The crunch of gravel had him turning toward the twins. They'd both managed to get themselves covered in Stella's blood, and Noah had a good mind to kill them both here too. Ignoring the stupid fools, he glared back at the bushes again. "I thought I saw the woman running into those bushes." He pointed ahead. "Go check it out."

Without a word, Colt and Steele strode, side by side, in that direction.

A gunshot cracked through the silence, and a millisecond later an explosion of blood burst from Steele's neck and shoulder. The brute flew backward in a howl of agony.

"Shit!" Noah dove for cover behind the nearest jeep. "Shit. Shit. Shit."

Steele was on the dirt, clutching his neck and writhing in apparent agony. Colt ran to his brother and fell to his knees at his side. "Steele, Steele, no!"

Steele curled into a fetal position, wailing as his blood squirted through his fingers.

Another round of bullets pinged off the jeep, taking out the headlights. Bullets continued and whizzed barely inches from Noah's head. "Fuck!"

If the twins noticed the barrage, they didn't show it. Colt was leaning over his brother, smothering him with his body as if for protection. He seemed to be crying.

Noah stared in disbelief. The mission had careened dramatically off the rails. It was time to get the hell out of there.

Colt flung backward with a spray of blood bursting from the back of his head. His body hit the dirt in a sickening crunch, and it took Noah only one look to know the fool was dead.

"Fuck!"

The next sound Noah heard shot a blaze of panic through his veins. The pilot had fired the engines. Noah snapped his eyes to the plane and could just see the pilot in the glow of the cockpit lights.

"No!" He screamed and waggled his finger at the pilot.

There wasn't a chance in hell the pilot heard him, but when he finally looked over, he gazed right at Noah.

"No!" Noah screamed, shaking his head.

The pilot's response was to set the plane into motion, inching forward.

"Fuck!" Noah didn't think. He didn't even breathe. He just jumped up and, casting caution aside, sprinted at the moving jet.

One hundred yards.

He felt the crosshairs on his back. Felt the fierce concentration of the shooter. Felt the tingle in his spine where he imagined the bullet would hit.

Felt the intensity of imminent death.

He dodged left, right, careful not to enter into the remaining jeep's headlights. *Eighty yards.*

He forced power into his limbs. His arms pumped, his legs pounded the dirt, and he clenched his jaw, determined to make it.

Sixty yards.

Even with the whir of the engines, he heard another round of bullets whiz past. One slammed into the tail of the jet, taking out a small chunk in the tip.

Time seemed to move at two speeds, fucking fast and painfully slow.

Thirty yards.

Noah had to get around to the other side in order to get onto the steps. If the asshole hadn't pulled them up that is. He prayed for that miracle as he aimed for the back of the plane. If he went for the front, the pilot would probably run him over.

Surging pain filled his lungs.

Ten yards.

He ducked beneath the undercarriage and gasped at the miracle. The stairs were still there. "Wait for me."

Adrenaline spiked his veins. He was going to make it.

He couldn't breathe. His legs burned like acid.

Two yards.

Noah dove at the steps and clutched the railing.

The engine noise became louder. The speed increased. Noah strangled the rail, desperate to hang on.

His energy vaporized in a flash.

His legs wouldn't move.

Instead they whipped around, pulled by the drag of the g-force.

To his horror, the plane left the ground.

Noah screamed. The engine roared. And the plane barely skimmed over the tops of the trees.

"Pull me in, you bastard," Noah shouted at the pilot.

"Fucking pull yourself in. I'm trying to get us outta here."

Noah forced his brain to think. Forced his body to move.

Inch by inch, he dragged himself into the cabin.

"Shut the fucking door," the pilot yelled.

Noah hauled himself onto his hands and knees, crawled into the cabin, and, clutching the rail, used the last of his strength to drag the door up. The wind slammed into him . . . blinding his eyes, screeching in his ears, clawing him from the plane.

"Pull it in!" The pilot screamed.

"I am!"

"Fucking faster! Or we're both dead!"

The plane shuddered, rattling every bone in his body. Releasing an almighty growl, Noah fought the door upright and latched it closed.

He crumbled to a heap on the floor, and the plane surged higher. It was an eternity before Noah rolled to a standing position and flopped into his seat.

When the pilot turned to him and smirked, Noah didn't know whether to thank him or kill him.

Chapter Twenty-Six

Charlene couldn't believe what she'd witnessed. In the space of about five minutes, eight Cubans and three Americans were dead. One of whom looked like an innocent woman.

And then there was Noah Montgomery.

If she hadn't seen him shoot that woman without any hesitation, she would never have believed it. The Noah Montgomery she'd seen on television was poised, distinguished, and respected.

The Noah Montgomery she just saw was a cold-blooded murderer.

When Diego told her that Noah had strangled her mother, she couldn't imagine the New York lawyer doing that. After all, he fought for the innocent.

She now knew it had to be true. It was impossible to believe that monster was her father. Charlene had never wanted someone dead before, but when Noah had begun running for the plane, she'd screamed at Marshall to shoot the bastard.

Marshall had tried, and he'd cursed at the ancient weapon throughout the attempt.

But, once again, Noah had gotten away with murder.

It wasn't until the plane was airborne that Marshall stood up. He offered his hand to help her up too. She groaned at the pain searing through her body. It seemed that every bone and muscle was screaming for attention.

Marshall clutched her hand in his. "Come on. We need to keep moving."

Charlene winced at every footfall, and her bare feet were no match for the scrappy weeds and sharp rocks. The clearing was only slightly better, and she tried to ignore the stabs to her insteps as they made their way toward the massacre.

The scene was unbelievable. Brutal and shocking. She wanted to look away, but at the same time, she couldn't. Five ghoulish bodies lay in the beams of the jeep's headlights.

All deathly still.

The metallic stench of blood and death invaded her nostrils, and silence, as haunting as a graveyard, hung in the air.

Charlene made a direct line for the gory mess that was Diego. She had thought witnessing Peter's bloody death would be the worst thing she'd ever see. But the wound on Diego's face was much worse.

Still, she had to confirm he was dead.

What he'd done to her mother was inhuman, and it only seemed fitting that he should die an agonizing death. Blood and gaping holes covered his corpse. His eyes were open, staring into the headlights.

He was dead.

She snapped her head away, fighting a wave of nausea that was stinging her stomach.

A muffled groan broke the silence, and she turned to the sound. It was a couple of creepy seconds before she realized who'd made it. It was one of the American men.

"Marshall, he's still alive."

Marshall strode to the muscle-bound brute and nudged him with his foot. "Hey, man, what's your name?"

The man gurgled a response.

Marshall shook his head. "He's not going to make it."

"Good. After what they did to that woman, they don't deserve any mercy." It was impossible to comprehend why the woman had been on the plane. They might never know. But it was obvious she'd been as shocked about the killings as Charlene had been.

Marshall turned to her, and the look on his face was a curious mix of horror and justice. "Come on." Marshall turned from the dying man and strode toward her to clutch her hand again. "Let's go."

He marched to the jeep she'd traveled in, reached into the back, and removed a gasoline can. When it emitted a sloshing sound, Charlene wondered how he'd known the can was even there. "Hey, is this yours?" He held up her bag.

"Huh, I didn't think I'd see that again." Resisting a look inside, she wrapped it across her chest. The chance of her money still being in there was minuscule, but the fact that Diego had kept it meant there must be something inside.

Marshall clutched her hand and led her toward the bush.

"We're not taking a jeep?"

"No. Got something better."

The playful lilt in his voice had her doubting his statement. A dozen questions raced through her brain at once, but she couldn't voice even one of them. It was like she was swimming through that murky well again. That already seemed like weeks ago.

"Stay here." Marshall stopped at the edge of the clearing, let go of her hand, and took a step away. Then he turned back. It was too dark to see him properly, but she felt his presence, felt the warmth of his body. His hand touched her cheek, and she leaned into his palm. "Are you okay?"

His concern and careful embrace had all the knots in her mind unraveling. She barely knew this wonderful, brave man, yet she felt like she'd known him forever. "Yes and no," she finally said.

"I know what you mean. We're nearly out of this, so I need you to stay strong for a little longer."

She nodded. "Okay."

"I'll be back in a sec." He released his hand and trotted away with the gasoline can.

In the last twenty or so hours, Charlene had thought she was going to die several times. But when Marshall had appeared out of nowhere and her breath had caught at the intensity in his eyes, she knew he'd save her.

It was six men against one.

The odds were against him, yet she never doubted it. Never doubted him.

It was strange to be so certain about a man she barely knew.

When she'd started her stupid quest for answers, she'd never stopped to consider the dangers. But the fact that she'd also put Marshall in that danger horrified her.

He could have died trying to save her.

No matter how many words she said, they'd never be enough to thank him for that. But as soon as they had a quiet moment together, she'd try.

She traced his footfalls through the bushes and then frowned as he grunted and cursed for a few minutes before a motor roared to life and a dim light pierced the vegetation. The light was like an alien beam as it wove a path toward her.

When she finally saw what it was, she burst out laughing. "Really?"

He shrugged and climbed off. "Your trusty steed."

"You want me to get into there?" She pointed at the metal capsule that was about the size of a baby crib.

"Well, unless you can drive this thing, then yes. Come on." He nudged her toward the sidecar.

Charlene placed her hand on the side for support, and her aching legs seemed foreign as she lifted them up and folded them into the car.

The instant she sat her bottom on the bare metal, she knew this was going to be hell. Her legs were too long to lie flat, and she couldn't cross them either as the space wasn't wide enough, so she bent them up beneath the metal cocoon at an awkward angle. She was still wriggling around when Marshall climbed back onto the bike.

"Ready?"

"I feel like a sardine."

"You don't look like one."

"I smell like one."

Marshall chuckled. The engine roared to life again, and with a jolt, he kicked the machine into gear. She glanced one last time at the bloody scene in the headlights as they pulled away. Eleven people had been killed right before her eyes, and she felt sorry for only one of them. Did that make her a monster too?

It was just another unanswered question flooding her brain.

The sidecar bounced over the uneven ground, and Charlene felt every single bump. In an attempt to take her mind off the new barrage, she watched Marshall's battle with the steering. His arms bulged and flexed with each movement. His jaw was clenched, symbolizing his fight to keep the clunky bike on the road.

Even though she couldn't see his eyes, she could easily picture his emerald-green pools, flecked with copper.

When he looked at her, he truly looked at her. Other than Peter, no man had done that.

When the plane had landed, Charlene had thought she'd never see Marshall again. Now, though, as he whisked her away, she never wanted to leave his side.

He'd touched something in her soul that hadn't experienced so much as a flicker before.

Yet it was impossible to believe he felt the same way. Marshall was a navy man driven to complete his mission. Saving her was his duty. Nothing more.

It both surprised her and saddened her that she wanted more. On one hand, she told herself that it was her desperate loneliness that was driving her attraction to him. But on the other, she knew it was much more than that.

It didn't bother her one bit that Marshall had killed people. She would have killed them herself if she'd had the opportunity. It was a case of kill or be killed. Every one of those men deserved to die. She was just lucky she had Marshall on her side.

Or she'd be one of those bodies left to rot in the middle of nowhere.

She had no doubt about that.

It was an eternity before the engine slowed, lurching her from the abyss her brain had slipped into. After a series of serpentine bends, the scenery changed from fields of nothing to streets lined with a mixture of housing. Most were still shrouded in the blackness of night.

Marshall angled the motorbike off the road onto a dirt track, and when she saw Aleyna's house, Charlene just about cried with relief. The bike shuddered to a stop, and it took all her effort to peel her fingers off the rim of the sidecar.

Despite the engine being shut off, her body continued to quiver. Groaning at the agony in her limbs, she tried to lift herself out, but her legs refused to move.

Marshall raced around to her side. "Okay, here we go." His voice was a wonderful melody after hours of the roaring engine. He helped her from the sidecar, and just when she thought her legs would buckle beneath her, he hooked his arm around her waist for support.

Aleyna and her siblings appeared from nowhere, and although she was aware of them, Charlene felt like she was in a fog. Between them and Marshall, they spoke a thousand miles an hour in Spanish, and she was helpless to comprehend. Marshall barked orders at them, and they raced back and forth from the house carrying out his urgent instructions.

Within a couple of minutes of arriving, they were on the move again. This time it was back into the bushes and down to the creek where Marshall's runabout was secured.

Charlene's trembling legs only just managed to deliver her safely into the boat, and she sat on the middle seat with her suitcase beside her. Marshall accepted a couple of other bags from Aleyna and put them at Charlene's feet. Next second, he pulled the rip cord and they roared away.

She tried to stay awake, but the lull of the rocking boat had her dozing in and out of consciousness. At one point, she glanced at the horizon and noticed the sun kissing the ocean. It was only now that she realized she'd been awake for over twenty-four hours.

"Okay, Charlene, wake up." Marshall gently rubbed her shoulder.

Groaning, she opened her eyes and was surprised to see them pulled up alongside Marshall's boat. "Okay." She croaked her response, and shoving sleep from her brain, she worked with Marshall to climb aboard and secure the runabout to the back.

He helped her downstairs, and deciding a shower could wait, she poured herself into the bed.

She vaguely heard the rumble of the engines before sleep overwhelmed her.

Chapter Twenty-Seven

Charlene snapped her eyes open, and it was a couple of thumping heartbeats before she realized where she was. The sound of the engines had her assuming that *Miss B Hayve* was still motoring toward America.

She dragged herself upright and fought a wave of dizziness by clutching onto the wall. Her entire body ached, yet it was her hunger pains that were commanding attention now.

Sunlight streamed in the windows, and she squinted against the glare as she crawled toward the kitchen. At the galley, she pressed the intercom button. "Would the captain like a toasted sandwich?"

"Hey, there." He chuckled. "I thought you'd sleep for a week." The boat lurched to a slower speed, and then the ensuing silence indicated he'd turned the engines off altogether. Charlene helped herself to a bottle of water from the fridge, and before she'd even opened it, Marshall had slid down the stairs.

"I can't believe you're up." Marshall had obviously cleaned up while she'd been sleeping. His beard was nicely trimmed, and his manly scent was enchanting.

"My rumbling stomach woke me."

He placed his hand on her arm, and his warm, tender touch had little butterflies dancing across her stomach. "Here, let me make you something while you have a shower."

She looked up into his stunning eyes. "I smell that bad, huh?"

"It'll make you feel better."

"Just being with you makes me feel better." The words slipped from her mouth before she could stop them, and a blaze of embarrassment raced up her neck. She stepped back and cleared her throat. "I'll, ahh, I'll go freshen up."

The copper flecks in his eyes twinkled in the sunlight. "Take your time. There's a towel in the cupboard."

Charlene took her toiletries bag from her suitcase, stepped into the tiny bathroom, and cringed at her reflection in the mirror. Her hair looked like she'd wrestled with a wildcat.

A hideous bruise surrounded her left eye, and a dribble of dried blood trailed from a jagged cut on her cheek. Reaching up, she winced as she touched the wound. She had no recollection of how she'd gotten it.

Dragging her eyes away from the mirror, she turned the taps to full, stripped off, and stepped into the shower. The hot needles stung her scalp, and in contrast to the wound on her cheek, she could vividly recall Diego yanking her hair out.

Just washing her hair hurt, and the rest of her body was just as painful. Bruises were dotted all over her body.

By the time she stepped from the shower, she felt remotely human again. She dried herself with the towel and then wrapped it around her body.

When she went to pick up her clothes, she spied the rolled-up strip of fabric that she'd hidden in her bra. Charlene wrapped her hand around the ragged scroll, clutched it to her chest, and said a silent prayer that this tiny inscription would finally give her answers to the questions that'd plagued her since Peter's death.

She stepped from the shower, and Marshall's eyes raced up her body. Her heart danced a jig at the pleasure in his eyes. Never before had a man looked at her with such desire. It took all her resolve not to step up to him and wrap her arms around his body.

He cleared his throat. "Feel better?"

She nodded. "Somewhat. I'll just get changed."

"Sure." He rubbed his hand over his beard stubble and gave her one last glance before he turned back to the kitchen.

Hiding behind the open cupboard door, she tugged on a button-up shirt and a pair of shorts, and placed her filthy clothes inside her case with the rolled-up note. With the towel wrapped around her hair, she stepped back into the kitchen. "Smells good."

He turned to her, and the corners of his eyes crinkled when he smiled. "Bacon always smells good. But before we eat, let's treat that cut on your cheek." He placed his hand on the small of her back to guide her toward the bed, and his delicate touch shot unprecedented pulses through her.

"Sit." His deep voice oozed authority.

She sat on the end of the bed, and he placed a tube of lotion and a few other first-aid items at her side. Then he knelt down in front of her, meeting her eye to eye. When he placed his hand on her knee and she inhaled his glorious scent, her whole body seemed to shimmer.

She watched his eyes as he cupped her uninjured cheek and angled her face to examine the wound. His full, kissable lips were fascinating, and as if he knew she was watching, he ran his tongue over them.

She cleared her throat. "How bad is it?"

"It's only a flesh wound. No stitches required."

"That's good."

"You're lucky. You took one hell of a beating out there." He reached for the tube of cream. "Where'd you learn to fight like that anyway?"

"Self-defense classes."

"Right." His eyes flared. "Mental note not to wrestle with Charlene."

She chuckled. "It's the first time I've ever fought anyone outside of the classroom."

Using a tissue, he dabbed the cream onto her face, and she flinched despite his delicate touch. The look of concern on his face was really sweet, and she had an overwhelming desire to lean forward and kiss him.

But she fought the craziness. They barely knew each other, and in light of what he'd just gone through to save her, he probably couldn't wait to get rid of her.

"You were amazing." His words caught her off guard.

"Really?" She thought he'd be furious.

"I couldn't believe it when you took those guys on at the Hershey factory." His tone was a soothing melody. "You still had your hands tied behind your back."

"You were there? How did you find me?"

"It wasn't easy, that's for damn sure. What the hell were you thinking going off on your own?"

She clenched and unclenched her jaw. "I am on my own. I told you that."

His eyes softened, and when he tilted his head and captured her gaze, her heart fluttered. It wasn't pity in Marshall's eyes; it was understanding.

He leaned forward a fraction, and his tongue glossed his lips. When his gaze flicked from her eyes to her mouth, anticipation sizzled between them like a bolt of electricity.

Reaching up, she removed the wet towel from her head, allowing her hair to tumble down her shoulders, and when his eyes blazed, Charlene couldn't hold back a moment more. Hoping she was reading his signals right, she did the craziest thing. She closed her eyes, leaned toward him, and silently begged him to kiss her.

Within a heartbeat, his lips touched hers, and she melted at the sensation. It was delicate at first, his kiss soft, innocent, barely a tease. But when his hand curled around her neck, their kiss deepened.

He smelled divine, a heady scent of fresh soap and hot-blooded man. His hands brought shivers across her flesh as he glided them up and down her neck. Fire and passion mingled together, and she opened her mouth, allowing his tongue to explore.

Her hands cruised across his shoulders and delved into his thick hair, pulling him to her. Somewhere in the back of her mind, she urged herself to stop, deeming it to be too soon, yet she couldn't. She wanted him, and if his kiss was any way to judge, Marshall wanted her too. Her body pulsed, and her heart danced, and she lost herself to the moment.

The injuries and hunger pains that had dominated her thoughts when she woke up faded into oblivion, replaced instead with delicious throbs that had her battered body coming alive.

It'd been an eternity since she'd experienced such heavenly sensations, but they'd never been this special, nor this intense. She traced her hands down his back, feeling the heat of his flesh beneath her fingers, and a moan tumbled from her throat.

Marshall pulled back, concern clouding his eyes. "You okay?"

His eyes and his words told her everything she needed to know; the two of them had slipped from casual acquaintances to become so much more.

That thought alone was a wonderful aphrodisiac that had her mind racing and her body aching. "I'm better than okay." She slid her hands beneath his shirt and raised it up over his head to reveal his superb body. Marshall had muscles in all the right places, and his chiseled chest glistened in the filtered sunlight.

The passionate restraint that'd held them captive evaporated in a flash, and while Marshall fumbled with the buttons on her shirt, Charlene explored the planes of his chest. She ran her fingers through his coarse chest hair and circled his hardening nipples with her fingers.

A delicious shudder tickled her flesh as he peeled the shirt from her shoulders. Marshall eased back to take in her nakedness. Her nipples peaked and hardened beneath his heady gaze. He reached up and sucked in a sharp breath as he touched his finger to a bruise above her right breast. "Oh, Charlene."

"It doesn't hurt."

He leaned forward and kissed the bruise, barely touching his lips to the purple mark. His hand curled beneath her breast, and she placed her hands on the bed covers and arched her back toward him, offering him more.

Marshall didn't miss a beat. He leaned forward and trailed his tongue from one breast to the other, drawing out her nipples until they were hardened pebbles.

Her mind became a vacuum. Her senses became heightened. The touch of his lips . . . the caress of his hands . . . the deep moans tumbling from his throat . . . the smell of his body. Months of torment were whittled away.

Nothing in the world mattered but the two of them. Right here. Right now.

He ran his tongue around her nipple, creating a thrilling tingle that started at the tip of her breast, and cruised all the way down to the throbbing pulse between her legs. She drove her fingers through his unruly curls, dragged her nails across his scalp.

He moved his hands up and down her thighs, each time edging higher. She parted her legs, letting him know she liked it. The sensations shuddering through her were like nothing she'd ever experienced before. And she wanted more.

She wanted it all.

Charlene flopped back on the covers and wriggled out of her shorts. Marshall reacted by standing up at the end of the bed, and it was impossible to miss the bulge in his pants. His eyes cruised up her body, drinking in every curve of her flesh. It was the most erotic moment of her life, and her body pulsed with a need to have him with her. In her.

He whipped his shorts off, and his manhood bounced toward her, large and proud.

She licked her lips at the glorious sight. Never before had she wanted a man so much. He paused there, and as much as she enjoyed the tantalizing moment, he seemed to as well.

His chest rose and fell with rapid breaths. He licked his lips, leaned forward, placed one knee on the bed, then the other, and crawled up her body, taking his time to kiss every one of her bruises.

Her hands roamed over his flesh, greedy to explore every defined muscle. He paused at her breasts, licking, caressing, sucking, and Charlene writhed beneath the delicious onslaught.

When he drew himself up to gaze into her eyes, she imagined he was looking right into her soul. His lips lowered to her, and she opened her legs, letting him know she wanted him.

He entered her gently, taking his time to ease into her in one slow glorious movement. It was exquisite. Utterly perfect.

They moved together as one, slowly at first, each displaying measured control. She opened her eyes to see Marshall's eyes flicker beneath his eyelids, lost in their own blissful world. She lifted her hips, and his thrusts grew deeper. Faster. As did his breathing.

She let herself go and rode a climax that had her calling out with pleasure.

Marshall's eyes shot open, but he didn't seem to be seeing. When he squeezed them shut again, he released a primal growl and thrust into her again and again until finally he collapsed to her side, panting.

Charlene nuzzled into the crook of his arm and resisted wincing as she rolled to face him. As she trailed her fingers up and down his chest, she wondered if meeting Marshall had been her fate—so many puzzle pieces had had to slot into place to put them in this bed together.

When he leaned forward and kissed her forehead, she decided it had been.

Chapter Twenty-Eight

Marshall admired Charlene's gorgeous physique as she crawled off the bed and strolled to the bathroom. His body hummed with after-sex contentment, something he hadn't felt in a very long time.

Too damn long.

He'd been shocked when Charlene had let him kiss her. No, shocked was a fucking understatement. He'd been blown away. She was young and stunning, and didn't need a has-been like him in her life.

Yet she'd been the one who'd initiated the sex. Not that he was complaining.

But he did wonder if it was some kind of crazy notion of hers, just to thank him.

He hoped like hell it was more than that.

Marshall crawled off the bed, tugged on his clothes, and returned to the kitchen to finish the bacon and cheese toasted sandwiches. He still had so many questions that needed to be answered, and before they anchored on American soil, he was determined to get them.

When Charlene stepped from the bathroom a short time later, her face was delicately flushed, and she smelled incredible. But it was her cheeky smile that caught his attention. He turned to her. "What?"

She curled a hand around her wet hair and shrugged her shoulder. "I wasn't expecting that."

"Nope. Damn surprise to me too." It took all his might not to pull her to his body again.

She stepped closer. "Are you complaining?"

"Hell, no. That . . ." For the first time ever, Marshall was lost for words. "That just doesn't happen to me."

"Hmm, shame." She glided her fingers up his arm, and he clutched her hand.

"Charlene . . . look, there's no doubt we have some chemistry or something going on here. But—"

"But what?" she stepped back, frowning.

He turned to the sizzling toasted sandwich maker and lifted the lid. "But you've been through a very traumatic experience."

"And?"

"And people do all sorts of weird shit after trauma."

"Weird shit? Is that what you call it?"

"You know what I mean." He plucked the sandwiches out and placed them onto two plates.

"No, I don't actually. I certainly don't make a habit of flopping into bed with every man I meet."

Marshall wanted to punch himself. Charlene was affecting him in so many ways, both physically and emotionally, but he had to tread lightly.

He'd fallen off the rails before.

And fallen so bloody hard it'd taken him years to find the tracks again. He had no idea where this—whatever *this* was—was going, but he'd rather cut it short now than risk crashing and burning big-time.

He turned to her with the plates in his hands. She had her arms folded and her butt against the counter. Despite the incensed look on her face, she was as sexy as hell.

"Come on, let's eat, and chat, and see where the conversation takes us."

Her shoulders softened, and she grabbed the plate and bottle of water, and he led the way up to the flybridge.

The day was glorious. Blazing sun high in the sky. Handful of clouds on the horizon. Stunning brunette to share it all with. It didn't get much better than that. He told himself to simmer down as he took his seat behind the wheel.

Charlene wriggled in at his side and placed her plate between them. "Where are we?"

"About forty miles out from Key West."

"Hmm. Is that good?"

"Better than being on Cuban soil." He took a bite of his sandwich.

She raised her water. "I'll drink to that."

Marshall shifted in his seat to look at her. The bruising over her eye looked to be getting worse by the second. Seeing it infuriated him all over again. Crazy woman nearly got herself damn-well killed.

"What?" She must have seen his fury.

He huffed. "You nearly died out there, Charlene. What the hell drove you to go off on your own like that?"

Her eyes flared. "I told you. I am alone."

"It's more than that. I know it, and you know it."

She nodded, and when she inhaled a deep sigh, he had a feeling she knew her ruse was up. After another bite of her sandwich, she slipped off her chair. "I'll be back in a sec."

He'd finished his meal by the time she returned.

Charlene slipped back onto her seat and turned to face him. "At the dance club, I found a clue to Peter's real identity, and that led me to Diego. I had no idea who Diego was. All I knew was that he might help me find answers."

"Was it worth it?"

"I don't know. Maybe you can tell me." She held forward a roll of cloth.

"What's this?"

"At the chocolate factory, Diego held me captive in a room; actually, it was more like an old well or something. Anyway, I found a teddy bear with that note inside."

Frowning, Marshall unrolled the fabric. "Is that blood?"

"Yes. I remember my mother writing it."

"Whoa. Back up the bus. What do you mean?"

"When I found the teddy bear, I recalled having it as a child. And . . . well, it was some kind of trigger that brought back a heap of memories

I'd somehow forgotten. Diego had locked my mother and me in that hellhole once before. I think I was six at the time. Maybe my mother knew she was going to die."

She sighed and shrugged her shoulders. "Anyway, she tore off some of her skirt and used her own blood to write that note. I need to know what it says." She leaned forward and placed her hand on Marshall's knee. "Can you read it for me?"

He shifted his gaze from her to the bloody note and back again. "You may not like what it says."

"I know." Her caramel eyes were simultaneously fearful and pleading.

He huffed out a sigh and flattened the note on his thigh.

"I am Benita Álvarez, mother of Claudia . . ."

He frowned at her. "Claudia?"

"Yes. I didn't remember being called by that name until Diego said it yesterday."

Marshall's confusion deepened as he returned his gaze to the note.

"I am Benita Álvarez, mother of Claudia, sister of Diego. 6 year ago, Noah Montgomery raped me. He is very dangerous American man. My daughter is his child."

Marshall cocked his eyebrow at Charlene, and she simply shrugged.

"Diego is blackmailing Noah, and he is coming to Cuba. If you find this, I am dead. I pray he saves Claudia."

He flipped the note over. "That's it." He turned his attention to Charlene.

Tears pooled in her eyes, and she was sucking on her bottom lip. Marshall slipped over on the chair and pulled her to him. "Hey, don't cry."

But she did cry. Her shoulders heaved, and he rode out her wave of sadness with a brick in his heart. An overwhelming desire to help her nearly crushed him. The smart thing to do would be to tell her to walk away and let it all go. But he didn't always choose the smart thing. There wasn't any fun in that.

He waited until the tears stopped; then he pulled her back from him and looked into her red-rimmed eyes. "You believe this Noah dude killed your mother?"

"Diego told me he watched Noah strangle my mother to death." Her chin dimpled, but she managed to hold it together.

His mind flipped to Noah shooting that woman. He'd done it without hesitation. Just point and shoot. Noah was a cold-hearted killer, and that clearly wasn't his first time. Noah thinks he's invincible. A nd Marshall looked forward to the day he lobbed a grenade into the cocky bastard's ivory tower and dragged him to the gutter, where he belonged. He just had to prove it first. "I promise you he won't get away with this."

A frown rippled across her forehead.

"Montgomery. That asshole is going to pay."

"How?"

"Let's start with you telling me everything that happened with Diego."

As *Miss B Hayve* took the repetitive three-foot swells in her stride, Charlene replayed everything she'd gone through with Diego. By the time she'd finished, it was getting dark, and Charlene had elevated herself to one hell of a woman.

Not too many people would've survived what she'd been through. But she hadn't just survived, she'd kicked ass. With each blow she'd recounted from Diego, Marshall grew more and more pissed off that he hadn't taken his time when he'd shredded the bastard's body to bits.

Diego got off way too lightly.

He was going to make damn sure Noah didn't.

He eyeballed the time—it was nearing seven o'clock. Time to head back to home country. Charlene remained silent as he fired up the engine again and set a course for Key West.

As the stars began dotting the blackness above them, Charlene continued her silent brooding. It wasn't until they saw lights in the distance that she let out a big huff. "I guess this is the end of the line, huh?"

"What?"

She curled her shoulders up in a shrug. "Well . . . I paid you to take me to Cuba, and you have. So, I guess this is the end."

"Hell, no."

Her face shifted into a look of confusion. "No?"

"No. This is only the beginning. Noah's going to pay."

A smile lit up her face, and when she tugged her lip into her mouth, it was the cutest thing he'd ever seen. *Miss B Hayve* charged into a wave that curved over the front windshield, and once the water cleared, Charlene leaned over and kissed Marshall's cheek. "But how? We have no proof."

"Not yet. I have a few navy buddies who may help me out."

"Really?"

"What? You don't think I have buddies?"

"Of course, I do." She slapped his shoulder. "But why would they help?"

Marshall winked at her. "Let's just say I keep them stocked up with quality Cuban cigars and rum."

Charlene burst out laughing, and her unexpected reaction was adorable. She eased sideways on the chair and kissed his cheek again. "Thank you."

His stomach flipped at her incredible scent. "Don't thank me yet."

"I am thanking you. No matter what happens, I'm already happy."

"I won't be happy until that smug bastard drowns in his own vomit."

"Actually, you're right. Me neither."

He guided *Miss B Hayve* into the marina and eyeballed Warren's boat. He'd hate to think what would've happened had Charlene committed to the illegal trip with Warren and his dipshit brothers. He doubted she'd have made it home. It occurred to him that she didn't have a home to go to.

He'd been like that once, some six or so years ago. It hadn't bothered him at the time; he'd have slept on a park bench if he needed to. Not that he ever did. Someone always took him in. But Charlene didn't have that someone. It blazed across his brain that he'd like to change that.

He turned to her. "I assume you have nowhere to sleep, so you're coming with me."

She managed to suck her bottom lip into her mouth and smile at the same time. The smile quickly broadened, and he just about burst with pride when she nodded. "I'd love to."

Charlene helped him tie *Miss B Hayve* up to the wharf; then they grabbed their things and locked her up. Marshall led the way and helped Charlene down onto the marina pontoon. Within five minutes of turning off *Miss B Hayve*'s engines, they were in Marshall's Dodge and on their way to his shack on the beach.

He could easily remember the last time he'd had a female in his bed; it was a good three years ago when he'd picked up a woman at Pirate Cove. Actually, truth be told, she'd picked him up. She'd been nice enough, though, and he'd wanted nothing more than a quick roll beneath the sheets. Thankfully, she'd wanted the same.

Charlene was more than that. So much more.

He pulled into his driveway, which hugged the cliff face, and offered no hint at what lay at the end of the road. The handful of people who'd visited his home had liked what they'd seen, yet for some obscure reason, Marshall's gut twisted at the prospect of showing Charlene.

"Don't expect much," he blurted out as the truck bounced over a pothole he'd been meaning to fix for months.

"I'm sure it's lovely."

He huffed. "I dunno about that."

"As long as I have a roof over my head, I'm happy."

Considering her back history, he believed her. The headlights lit up the corrugated iron roof first, followed by the roughly cut planks he'd put into place himself. When he'd bought the place, it'd barely been standing.

But he'd committed himself to fixing it up, and he didn't believe in doing things in halves. He'd replaced nearly everything—the walls, the floors, the verandas, even the roof. Only the stumps and the plumbing were original.

It might not have been much, but it was practical, *and* he owned it. Building it had been good therapy too—so good, in fact, it was a wonder the place wasn't three times its size.

He pulled the truck to a stop next to the back landing and jumped out. Charlene was out by the time he reached her side. "So, this is it."

"It's fantastic."

"Not very big, but it's got everything I need, and wait till you see the view."

"It doesn't need to be big to be grand."

He chuckled. That was a saying he'd never heard before . . . he liked it. Before he'd climbed the three short steps to the back veranda, the damn stray came bounding around the corner with a strained bark that always sounded like the dog was being strangled. Marshall groaned at the three-legged mutt. "You still here?"

Charlene flopped to her knees at the top step and gave Hoppa probably the biggest hug the mutt had ever had.

"Don't encourage him," Marshall muttered as he unlocked the front door.

"He's adorable. What's his name?"

"Dunno, he's a stray. I call him Hoppa."

"Oh, you're mean."

"Mean? Why?"

"He's only got three legs."

"Exactly! That's why Hoppa suits. He's lucky I don't call animal control." He pushed through the door. "You coming."

"Can Hoppa come in?"

"Nope."

"Aww." Charlene whispered a few sounds to the dog and roughed up his fur before she stepped through the front door.

"So, this's the kitchen."

"It's nice."

He led her though his tiny cabin. It was just three rooms—a combined kitchen and dining and living room, a bedroom, and a joint bathroom and laundry.

"It's really nice, Marshall." She slotted her fingers into his hand and squeezed.

A blaze of desire rocketed through him. The damn woman was lighting fires all over the place, and if she wasn't careful, he'd have to douse those infernos. "Come, I'll show you the bedroom."

He strode away with more speed than was required, as the room was barely ten feet away, and paused at the bedroom door. "You can stay in here tonight."

"Oh, no. I can't do that. I'll sleep . . ."

"Charlene, don't argue. You sleep here."

She stepped up to him. The flames in her eyes licked his libido, and this time he didn't step back. He couldn't stand it a moment longer. He wanted her. *Now.*

Reaching around her waist, he tugged her toward him and planted his lips on hers. Charlene didn't resist. Instead, she did the opposite. She melted her body into him, pushing her breasts into his chest, grinding her hips against his. Her lips parted, allowing his tongue to explore, and deep moans tumbled from her throat.

Somehow, Marshall had become the luckiest man in the world.

And he didn't believe in luck.

He yanked at her shirt buttons, eager to see the rest of her stunning body again.

She, in turn, tugged his shirt up, and when he lifted his arms, she managed to both lift it over his head and suck his nipple into her mouth. Her hot breath and slick tongue had his manhood begging for attention.

With their lips locked together, he picked her up, and she straddled his waist, resting her hot zone on his belly. He just about ignited at the gloriousness of it. A couple of strides later, he lowered her down and took a moment to study the exquisite woman on his bed.

His bed.

It was a bloody miracle.

He kicked off his shoes, stripped out of his shorts, and stood naked before her. Her eyes were flames, licking at his flesh as they cruised up his body. After she'd reduced him to a quivering mess, she reciprocated by wriggling out of her shorts too. The way she did it had her perfect breasts wobbling delightfully, and Marshall would be happy to watch them do that all day long.

Charlene giggled, and he snapped his eyes to hers. "What?"

"Nothing." Her glorious smile confirmed it wasn't nothing. "Come here." She patted the bed at her side.

But Marshall had other ideas. Her nipples were pink buds, as raised as pebbles on the beach, and they were begging him to suck them. He leaned forward, rested his hands on the bed, and wrapped his lips around her nipple. She moaned, raising her hips beneath him, and Marshall sucked harder. She tilted her head back, showing off the length of her neck, and he released her nipple to crawl up her body.

He ran his tongue from the base of her neck up to her ear, and she clawed her nails up his back. Her eyes were closed, her lips parted. Everything about her was sexy as hell. Maybe she sensed him watching because her eyes fluttered open, and when she looked at him, she really, truly looked at him.

An unprecedented notion of completeness embraced him. Charlene was the woman of his fantasies; someone he'd thought would only ever be in a dream.

In that moment, Marshall knew he was falling in love.

Charlene winced a little as she curled her body to wrap her leg over his hip, and with a move he'd never experienced before, she flipped him onto his back and straddled him.

Her face was the picture of seduction as she lowered her breasts to his lips. He didn't need any further prompting to suck her boobs, so he did. First one, then the other. Rolling his tongue around her nipples, then sucking them until perfect buds peaked and firmed.

Her moans of pleasure had his full-blown erection rock hard. And maybe Charlene sensed he was set to burst because she eased back and, using her hand, guided him to her hot zone.

With their eyes locked, she lowered herself onto him. Marshall wanted to watch the show, to take in every exquisite moment of this gorgeous woman riding him, but his eyes closed of their own accord. He clenched his jaw and concentrated on the heat of her sex, which wrapped around him like a velvet glove.

When an orgasm shivered through her body and a surging heat wave smothered his manhood, Marshall hit the tipping point. In one swift move, he rolled her over and plunged into her again and again. In a moment of release, Charlene cried out his name, and they climaxed together in a mind-blowing orgasm that had her tearing at the sheets.

He flopped onto her chest, she wrapped her arms and legs around him, and they remained as one until their breathing returned to normal. Marshall rolled onto his back and opened his arm for her to sidle up next to him.

She wriggled up, placing one arm and one leg across his body. It was like they'd been together for years, and he felt the most relaxed he'd ever felt with a woman.

She turned to look up at him. Her lip curled into her mouth and popped out again as if she was debating about voicing whatever was on her mind. He waited out the pause.

"Marshall," she finally said.

"Yeah?"

"I feel like we were destined to meet."

He kissed her forehead and squeezed her tighter. "I agree."

A sigh released from her throat, and she wriggled into his body.

For the first time in years, he was happy. No, it was more than happy.

It was utter contentment. Never before had Marshall wanted someone as much as he wanted Charlene. It scared the crap out of him too. Now that he had her in his arms, he wasn't sure if he'd cope if she didn't hang around.

Shoving the wretched thought aside, he decided that no matter what happened, he wanted to be on this ride. They were good together. Every moment with Charlene was a moment worth spending, no matter what the ultimate outcome was.

He glanced at the bedside clock. It was just shy of nine. Time to make the call he'd been stewing over since Charlene had finished retelling her events with Diego. His friend had always been a night owl; hopefully that hadn't changed.

He placed a hand on her shoulder. "Hey, let's get up. I gotta make a call."

"Really?" Her brows drilled together.

"Yeah. It's an old friend of mine who I worked with at the navy base in Guantánamo Bay."

"In Cuba?"

"Yeah, I'm hoping he can help us."

"Oh. That would be nice." Charlene slipped off the bed, and he couldn't drag his eyes away from her ass as she padded to the bathroom.

"Damn." He muttered under his breath as he pulled on his shorts. Shit like this just didn't happen to him. Not good shit anyway.

In the kitchen, he opened the fridge and pulled out a couple of waters. For the first time in years, he wished he had a wine to offer. Hopefully, Charlene wouldn't ask for one. He plucked his phone off the table and scrolled through his contact list. Then, without a moment's hesitation, he jabbed the number to dial a friend he hadn't spoken to in years.

"Crow? Is that you?"

Marshall grinned as he tugged out a chair to sit. "Hey, Harry, long time between chats."

"Sure is. Got me wonderin' why you'd be calling me now."

That's what he liked about Harry; he was a straight shooter who got down to business ASAP. "It's a long story. You got time?"

"Got nothin' goin' on at the minute. Hit me with it."

Charlene stepped from the bathroom, and he pointed at the water. She collected the bottle, twisted off the cap, and plonked herself down in the seat opposite him.

"I met this crazy woman who needed to get to Cuba." He wriggled his eyebrows at her, and Charlene rolled her eyes and took a swig of her drink.

Harry laughed. "I think I'm gonna enjoy this story."

Marshall took his time telling his old navy roommate everything that had happened. Harry had connections in Cuba. More than Marshall did, and more importantly, they were people in authority.

"How do you think I can help?" Harry asked.

"I'm hoping you can point me to someone who can do the right thing for that woman they dragged into the bushes."

"Hmm. Hang on a sec."

Marshall glanced at Charlene, and for the first time, he noticed the cute constellation of freckles across her nose. A series of clicks on the phone had him turning his attention back to the call.

"You there?" Harry's gruff voice had the hallmarks of a lifetime smoker.

"Yeah."

"Got the very man for you." Harry relayed the contact details for a guy who was a senior police officer for Policía Nacional Revolucionaria. Harry went on to say that Alejandro Castillo knew when turning a blind eye was necessary for progress, and Marshall knew exactly what he meant by that.

Harry had given him the right man.

They said their good-byes, and Marshall hung up the phone and swigged his water.

"He seemed like a nice guy." Charlene tilted her head at him.

"Yeah, he's a good man. We served together for many years."

Marshall liked that she didn't ask a dozen questions. It was another aspect of Charlene that drew him in. Hell, everything about her appealed.

"So, what now?" she asked.

"Gotta make another call. But you're not going to able to follow this one.'

"Why not?"

"He probably doesn't speak English."

"Oh." A frown rippled across her forehead, then she pushed back on her chair. "I'll go play with Hoppa then."

"Hey, don't go pampering him too much . . . silly dog will want to stay," he joked, and she giggled as she carried her water out to the front porch.

Marshall turned his attention to the next call. It was going to be a tricky one. He needed to give enough information to get the job done, without implicating Charlene. Or himself, for that matter.

With a plan rehearsed in his head, he made the call. Alejandro answered after the second ring. Marshall told him how he got his number, but he didn't give his name, and thankfully Alejandro didn't ask.

Marshall explained the site of the massacre, how many bodies would be there, where he could find that poor woman. But it wasn't until he mentioned Diego's name that Alejandro's voice hit a whole new level. The impression he'd been portraying of being annoyed by the call quickly transitioned to interested.

Very interested.

"Where did you say it was?" Alejandro questioned in Spanish.

Marshall explained the derelict runway and everything he knew about it from his trip there and back.

Alejandro burst out laughing. Then he dropped a bombshell that ricocheted around Marshall's brain like a stray bullet.

Chapter Twenty-Nine

Noah had spent the last two days fighting both the expectation that the police would come barreling through his door at any moment and the wretched nausea that came with that fear.

But as the minutes ticked on and his brain leveled out from the perilous overload, he managed to put the entire debacle into perspective.

First and foremost, the onus of proof was the critical element that would save him.

There was no proof that he'd been to Cuba. He'd blackmailed his pilot with the legitimate threat that, should something happen to him, then Noah would drag the pilot down with him. He'd also paid the greedy bastard more than enough to ensure that vital evidence was never revealed.

There was also no proof that he'd shot Stella. Fortunately for Noah, Colt had wrapped his hand around the gun's handle to finish the job. A chuckle rumbled from his throat and soon became a full-blown belly laugh as it dawned on him that once again, he'd gotten away with murder. After all, he'd been the one who'd ordered the hit.

In addition, the isolation of that wretched Cuban runway made it highly unlikely the bodies would ever be found. Yet even if they were, identifying them and connecting them to him was negligible.

Noah analyzed his situation like it was one of his own cases, and the more he replayed each facet of the fiasco, the more the acid churning in his stomach dissipated. His ultimate conclusion—that he had indeed come away unscathed, yet again—deserved a toast.

He strolled to his liquor cabinet and poured a glass of his most expensive cognac. The fact that it was only eight in the morning was irrelevant. With the glass in his hand, he moved to the window to sip the liquid gold and admire his multimillion-dollar view.

Noah had earned his place at the top of the world, and not a single person could ever take that from him. Not his imbecile partner who'd just ruined his own career. And now that Diego was dead, that chapter of his life was forever buried too.

The spicy cognac put the fire back in his belly that'd been yanked out when his pilot had intended to leave him in Cuba. That was the first time he'd feared for his life.

Yet as much as it had reduced him to nausea, it had ultimately been invigorating.

Noah was invincible. Untouchable. The king of his world.

He raised his glass. "To the king of the world."

His desk phone rang, and he clenched his jaw at the intrusion. He'd instructed his secretary to decline all calls, and yet, following suit with all his hired help at the moment, she'd ignored his instructions. The second it stopped, it started again, and he strode to his desk to jab the intercom button. "What?"

"I'm so sorry, sir, but this man has called every five minutes for the past hour. He won't go away and, well sir, he wants you to know that Claudia is still alive. So I thought it might be important."

An icy chill shot down Noah's spine pinning him to the floor like a pair of ice picks.

"Sir . . . Mr. Montgomery, are you there?"

He couldn't breathe. He couldn't think.

"Sir . . . would you like me to put the call through?"

It was happening again. How could that be? His mind was trapped in a time warp that bounced from twenty-two years ago to forty-eight hours ago. Twice he'd tried to eradicate that bitch from his life. Twice he'd failed.

He would not fail again.

With his jaws clamped together, he sat down, grabbed his notepad and pen, and forced his brain to focus. After a calming breath, he said, "Put him through, Annabel."

"Yes, sir. Thank you, sir."

She clicked off, and Noah listened to the empty line for a good ten seconds before he could convince his tongue to move. "What do you want?"

"Ahh, there you are."

It was a man's voice on the other end. American. Noah decided it had to be the man who'd helped her at the Cuban runway. "Who are you?"

"I'm the man who's going to ruin you."

"Is that a threat, Mr. . . ." He waited for a name. Noah couldn't work without names.

"Oh, no, not a threat. It's a promise."

"Cut the bullshit. What do you want?" Noah admonished himself for losing his cool. It showed weakness. He curled his fingers into a fist and squeezed until his nails dug into his flesh.

"Claudia wants to meet you."

"That's not going to happen."

"That's where you're wrong, Noah Montgomery. Here's what's going to happen. You're going to jump on that Gulfstream G650 and get your ass to New Orleans."

"I don't take—"

"Shut the fuck up," the man barked down the phone.

Noah bit his tongue, and the sting brought with it the tang of his own blood. This was a whole new territory for him. Nobody gave him orders. Nobody!

"You will meet us at the parking lot at the abandoned theme park Six Flags New Orleans. Repeat it!"

Noah clenched and unclenched his jaw. "Six Flags New Orleans."

"You will be there at four o'clock today."

"I can't get—"

"Bullshit. You flew to Cuba in a day; you can get to New Orleans in four hours. I'm giving you seven."

"What if I refuse?"

"The footage of you shooting that beautiful blonde woman on the runway in Cuba will be plastered all over the front-page news come six o'clock tonight."

Noah's bowels loosened, and a cold sweat flooded his forehead.

"You still there?"

Noah wanted to reach down the phone and strangle the cocky bastard. Just like he'd done to Benita. Squeezed and squeezed until her eyes popped.

"I know you're still there. So here's the final instructions. You're going to drive to the theme park alone, and you'll have a million dollars with you."

A jolt raced through Noah at that final comment. If this was about money, then it was an easy solve. Not that he had any intention of handing over a cent.

"Repeat it!"

Noah repeated the instructions, and when the man abruptly hung up, Noah hurled his crystal tumbler at the windows, and it smashed it into dozens of shards, spraying the golden liquid onto his white carpet.

He stood and paced the floor. Once again, he'd been caught off guard. It was like a switch had been flicked to trigger any and all attempts to crucify him. But he was a fighter. He'd crawled out of tough situations before. He was going to stride out of this one.

He placed a call to his pilot, and they went through the infuriatingly repetitive haggle to agree on a price. Once that was done, he strode to his safe, punched in the combination, and removed his Ruger LCP II and two magazines. He didn't need his holster this time. One of the most appealing aspects about this weapon was that he could conceal it in his coat pocket.

Neither Claudia nor her conspiratorial accomplice will see what's coming at them.

Noah rarely traveled in rush-hour traffic, and he hated that he'd been forced to do it today. He settled into the back seat of his limo on the way to JFK and used the solitude to clear his mind and focus solely on the situation at hand.

The entire journey was consumed with an inner debate over

whether or not the new blackmailer had been bluffing about video footage of him shooting Stella. He mentally listed the facts.

The remote Cuban airstrip had been dark.

If the supposed footage was taken by the couple he'd seen running into the bushes, then they were positioned at a significant distance from where the plane landed. Footage, if there was any, would be of poor quality.

For them to have captured him actually shooting Stella, they would have needed to be positioned at the perfect angle to cover the entire scene.

Halfway to JFK, his brain stammered to a conclusion. It was highly likely they were bluffing.

That led to his next question.

Was money their ultimate intention?

The blackmailer said Claudia wanted to meet him. Why on earth she'd want to do that was beyond Noah.

Maybe she wanted to admire her bloodline.

Maybe she wanted to get a confession from him.

He huffed. If they did secretly record the conversation, it would be deemed inadmissible in a court of law anyway. So that was the least of his worries.

He squeezed his hand around the butt of his weapon. The stupid fools were leading him to an abandoned amusement park, and that would make it all too easy for him to kill them both.

He hoped they were recording the meeting. It would provide him with interesting viewing afterward.

But he had to be careful. Whoever these two were, they'd taken down eight Cubans and his guards to get away last time.

All it took was one bullet. Noah wouldn't miss this time.

The pilot greeted Noah with a million-dollar smile that Noah wanted to slap right off his face. To top that off, the greedy bastard had insisted Noah show him proof of the electronic transfer before he could board the plan. Noah decided there and then that this would be the pilot's last job for him.

Noah buckled into his seat, and before the plane was even airborne, a headache was beginning to burn at the back of his eyes. After swallowing two painkillers, he squeezed his eyes closed and forced his mind to recuperate for the duration of the flight.

A high-pitched squeal cut through the silence, and Noah jolted upright. To his surprise, he'd actually fallen asleep, and the sound that had woken him was the jet's tires touching down at Louis Armstrong New Orleans International Airport. He shook himself awake and strode to the bathroom.

When he glanced in the mirror, he was appalled at his reflection. Noah always prided himself on his appearance. Now, though, his face had a hideous pallid hue, and dark smudges surrounded his eyes.

He hated that he'd let the stress get to him. He was good at stress. Thrived on it.

But this mess was hitting depths he'd never considered possible. For the first time in his life, he was nervous, and he hated that the caller had produced that emotion in him.

Fighting the urge to punch the mirror, he splashed water on his face, straightened his shoulders, and planted the confident expression on his face that he'd projected over a thousand times in the courtroom.

By the time he stepped from the bathroom, he was riding a new high at the prospect that he was about to experience another life-changing event that was destined to eclipse the previous two.

He returned to his seat, glanced at his watch, and was pleased he still had two hours and twenty minutes until the dictated meeting time. According to his research, the drive from the airport to Six Flags New Orleans would take just thirty-two minutes. That gave him enough time to set a trap for Claudia and her accomplice.

In the leather seat beside him was his briefcase containing two hundred thousand dollars. It was everything he'd had in his safe, but if the blackmailer had given him more time, Noah could have fulfilled the requested demand.

Not that it was relevant.

He had no intention of giving them anything . . . other than early funerals.

Chapter Thirty

Charlene didn't think she'd ever return to New Orleans. Not after the horror she'd experienced there. But after Marshall had talked her through his plan, it made perfect sense to return to where it all started for her and, in particular, to involve Detective Chapel again.

Especially after what Alejandro, the Cuban police officer, had told Marshall on the phone.

Her heart had simultaneously skipped a beat and cried at that news.

The implications of it were shocking, and yet it was also exactly what they needed.

Despite falling asleep in Marshall's arms, she'd barely slept that night. It was impossible to shut her mind down from the possibility that within twenty-four hours, she'd be standing face-to-face with the monster who killed her mother.

But she needed to do it.

She'd seen Noah on television many times, touting his case for innocent victims. He seemed intelligent and dignified, yet something had happened twenty-odd years ago that made him a murderer.

Her mind replayed that moment when Peter had whisked her away from her mother. Her screams for her mom had been drowned out by the roar of the plane.

The last image she had of her mother was of a beautiful, distraught woman with tears streaming down her cheeks and fear blazing across her eyes.

Charlene had to know if her escape was the reason Noah had strangled her mother.

After Marshall had made the call to Noah, he'd moved to a safe that was concealed beneath the floorboards and removed a shoebox-sized case. When he'd opened it, he'd glanced at Charlene. Inside was the biggest handgun she'd ever seen.

"Want to change your mind?" he'd said.

She'd dragged her gaze from the weapon and glared into Marshall's pleading eyes. "No."

Nothing was going to change her mind.

Marshall spent the remainder of the evening trying to talk her out of it. But she wouldn't back down. Couldn't. If she didn't get that closure, she would be forever wondering why.

Marshall had pointed out that Noah might have killed her mother simply because he was a madman. And given how easily he'd shot that woman in Cuba, that was potentially true.

However, Charlene didn't buy it.

Their morning had been consumed with packing an overnight bag and Marshall's nonstop attempts to talk her out of meeting with Noah.

On the way to the airport, Marshall dropped into a store, and they purchased some fancy-looking surveillance equipment, which, unlike the gun case, they'd packed into their hand luggage.

During the flight from Key West to New Orleans, they'd unpacked and examined the camera and microphone. Marshall had explained to her that the footage would be inadmissible in court.

However, it was their backup plan. Should Noah get away for some reason, the footage would find its way to all the tabloids in the country.

However, Charlene had already decided that even if he was arrested and convicted, she'd still make sure the footage was released. Everybody needed to know what kind of monster he was. And from what she'd seen of Noah, that would be his worst nightmare.

Everything seemed to be moving at breakneck speed. One minute they were planning the phone calls to Noah, then they were on the plane, and next they were driving the rental car through New Orleans.

Ten minutes into the drive, Marshall pulled the car over at the first phone booth they found and placed his hand on her arm. "You okay?"

The sincerity in his expression had her marveling once again at how lucky she was to have met Marshall. When Peter was torn from her life, she'd plummeted to the depths of what it meant to be truly alone.

Now, though, with Marshall at her side, she felt like she was part of a team. Yet it was more than that . . . they were destined to be together. Her heart squeezed at that wonderful thought, and she placed her hand over his and met his gaze. "I just want this to work."

"It will." Determination simmered in his stunning eyes.

She climbed from the car, stepped into the phone booth, and dialed one of the few phone numbers she'd ever memorized. It rang only once.

"Detective Chapel." His voice was gruff.

"Hello, Detective, it's Charlene Bailey."

"Charlene. Where the hell have you been? We've been looking for you."

"I'm sorry. I had some things to attend to."

"God, girl, you could've let me know. I've been going out of my mind."

Her guilt elevated a few notches. "I'm so sorry about that. Anyway, I was wondering if you could help me."

"You know I will."

"Thank you. Can you please meet me at Six Flags New Orleans at three o'clock today?"

Her request was met with a silent beat.

"Charlene, what are you up to?"

"It's . . . it's involved. I'll tell you once you get there. Can you do that?"

"Why don't you come into the station. We can—"

"No!" She didn't mean to sound so forceful. "I . . . I can't. Please! Just meet us there at three."

"Us?"

"Can you do that, please?" She ignored his implied question.

"You know that theme park is derelict, right?"

"I'm aware of that."

"Charlene . . ."

The way he said it, with a pleading lilt, had the vein in her neck pulsing. "I'll see you there, Detective." She hung up the phone and returned to the rental car.

"All good?" Marshall raised his eyebrows.

She nodded. "He tried to talk me out of it. Wanted me to go to the station instead."

"He sounds like a good man." Marshall put the car into gear and nudged them back into the bustling New Orleans traffic.

Forty-five minutes later, they drove through the dilapidated parking lot that once had been filled with hundreds of cars. The six flags were long gone, and just the bare flagpoles marked the entrance.

Marshall aimed for the poles, which were positioned atop the building that contained the ticket booths. He skirted that building, drove through a couple of gates that were barely hanging on by a hinge, and entered the main street of the abandoned theme park.

Marshall dodged debris as he slowly drove the car to the end of the street and parked out of sight between the crumbling Ferris wheel and what was left of the merry-go-round.

They climbed out, and the wind whistling through the rusted rides had her looking up at the giant wheel. A healthy ivy plant had made the struts its home, covering the once colorfully decorated seats in a living macramé.

The trunk popped up, and she moved to the back of the car to help Marshall with their equipment. He slammed the trunk shut, and they walked through the ramshackle central street, back toward the entrance.

They strode past a giant clown's head that had toppled sideways to rest on its cheek. The clown's nose was now a gaping hole, and only one eye was open. Charlene shuddered at the sight.

She'd been in some pretty creepy places in her life. But this one quickly hit the top of that list. "Why'd you choose this place?"

"It's deserted."

"But how did you even know about it?"

"I took a couple of guys out on a fishing charter who used to work here. They told me about it. They lost their jobs here when Hurricane

Katrina flooded the park beneath seven feet of water for a month, and it never reopened."

"It's a wonder nobody attempted to restore it."

He kicked a rusted can aside. "Too far gone, I'd say."

The colorful buildings lining the street must've been quite pretty prior to the flood, but the colors had dulled over the years, and plants and graffiti now covered the walls instead.

The structures emitted creaks and groans as if sounding a warning. But they weren't the only sounds. The wind howled through the shattered windows and doors like ghostly whispers, and Charlene's mind jumped to the number of murders she'd witnessed in just a few months.

Twelve people killed, right before her eyes. The first one being Peter. It suddenly occurred to her that maybe Noah had caused his murder too. It would be another question she'd ask the bastard.

With each step she took toward the front entrance, her mind screamed at her to take Marshall's hand and march away from all this stupidity.

But at the same time, she couldn't do that. She needed to follow through with this quest to get justice for her mother's senseless murder and the world needed to know what a monster Noah Montgomery was. It suddenly occurred to her that Noah might not even turn up, and she glanced over at Marshall. "Do you think he'll come?"

"I know he'll come."

"How can you be so sure?"

Marshall eased into the shade of the ticketing building and seemed to scrutinize its structure. "He flew all the way to Cuba to kill you. Flying to New Orleans is nothing in comparison."

Her stomach clenched. "Thanks for reminding me." She said it with the horror it deserved.

He cocked his head. "Did you expect me to ignore it?"

Her shoulders sagged. "No. I guess not." It was impossible to comprehend that her own father wanted her dead. And she had no idea why. It was another question she'd ask him. She clenched her jaw and tried to push aside her uncertainty about what they were doing. This had to be done.

Marshall reached for her hand. "He will never get his hands on you, Charlene. I promise."

Every ounce of her breath was taken with his concern, and she leaned into him. When Marshall wrapped his arms around her and squeezed, she knew that although their connection was still so young, it was very, very true.

Marshall was the only sanity in a world that was filled with madness, and she hugged herself to him. The pounding of his heart instilled a strength within her that had been waning.

No matter what happened, they would get through this. Together.

He eased back a fraction and kissed her forehead. "I don't suppose I can talk you out of this?"

"Nope."

"Hmm. Thought you'd say that. So help me get the gear sorted."

Marshall peeked into one ticket booth after the other and finally chose the fifth one. "This'll do the job." The door was secured by just one hinge, and Marshall grabbed it and yanked it free like it'd been held in place with Scotch Tape.

Charlene peered into the booth while Marshall tossed the door aside. It was a tiny room, about twice the size of a standard shower. But unlike every other window she'd seen so far, the one in this booth was intact. A chair, missing all but one of its castors, was toppled on the floor, and assuming Marshall didn't want it, she dragged it outside.

Marshall stepped into the booth and ran his hand over the tiny counter, clearing it of debris and peeling paint. Then he peered out the window and scanned the parking lot ahead. "This is perfect."

"Want me to clean the window?"

"No, the less he can see of us, the better." Marshall put the bag containing the surveillance equipment on the floor, unzipped it, and placed the bits and pieces on the tiny bench positioned in the gap beneath the window. He went to work setting it up.

"What can I do?"

"Pray."

"Very funny."

He turned to her, deadpan. "I wasn't joking." Marshall turned back to the equipment and cursed under his breath.

She stepped from the room, and as she strolled down the street, studying the ghostly remnants of a once thriving theme park, her empty stomach twitched out a chilling warning. Yet she forced her brain to ignore it. For years, she'd wanted answers to what happened to her when she was a child. Now she had the *what*, hopefully she'd soon have the *why*.

Her whole life was a lie. It was time for the truth.

"Shit!" Marshall's voice boomed from the booth.

She spun to his voice. "What?"

"Someone's coming."

Charlene ran to the booth and stepped inside. "Who?"

"We're about to find out. But I hope like hell it's the cop, or we're in deep shit."

Charlene peered through the dirty glass and watched a dust storm rise up from behind the approaching SUV like a demon.

Marshall clenched his jaw as he unclipped his gun from the secure case and pushed the magazine in until it clipped.

The car skidded on the gravel and pulled to a stop.

The moment had arrived.

Ever since she'd been informed that Peter wasn't her father, she'd wondered who the man could be. Now, though, as she tried to see through the SUV's black windows, she wasn't sure she wanted to know anymore.

Marshall spun to her, fierce determination blazing across his eyes. "No matter what happens, you stay behind me."

"Okay."

He clutched her wrist. "Say it, Charlene."

"I stay behind you."

"Right behind."

"Okay. Yes."

He spun back to looking out the window, and she glanced from Marshall to the car and to the weapon. Each second was simultaneously too fast and too slow. If it was Noah in that car, he was early.

Marshall had planned for everything except that.

Chapter Thirty-One

Noah cursed at the sight of the woman jumping into one of the small booths at the entrance to the crumbling theme park. It meant they'd thwarted his plan to beat them to the site and set a trap.

He needed a plan B, and he needed it fast. Slowing the car to a crawl, he bounced through dozens of potholes as he drove toward the middle booth.

For two decades, the wretched Cuban disaster had been a cloud over his life. It was time to put an end to it and to put an end to all those involved in it—Claudia, and whoever the man was that she'd shacked up with.

He scanned the area. The empty parking lot surrounding him was worthless as cover. He'd have to use his car. Lucky for him, he'd chosen one with nearly pitch-black windows that'd make it difficult for them to see him inside.

Now all he had to do was lure them from their cover.

He eased the car to within ten yards of the booth and parked sideways, so they couldn't see through the front windshield. He didn't shut off the engine, nor did he get out.

Instead, he unbuckled and climbed into the passenger seat. If they assumed he was in the driver's seat, they'd be wrong. Once he was in position, he pressed the button to open the sunroof and was immediately blasted with both the oppressive heat and the blazing sun.

Then he waited.

As did his quarry.

Adrenaline coursed through his veins, and he felt the now-familiar rush that preceded each of these life-changing moments. His senses were heightened. He heard the rustling of leaves as they tumbled over the barren concrete. He smelled the mangy scent of the surrounding swamp. He felt the unbearable heat and cranked up the air-conditioning.

A commanding feeling of calm washed over him, and every second passed in slow motion.

He used the time to analyze the situation.

They wanted something from him. Which meant he had the upper hand. It would only be a matter of time before they spoke. Barely three seconds later, they did.

"Get out of the car, Noah." A man's voice boomed from within the booth.

"You take me for a fool, Mr. . . ." Noah hated not knowing his name.

"You are a fool." A woman's voice this time, and he knew it would be Claudia.

"Why don't you come out, Claudia? We can talk."

"So you can shoot me like that woman in Cuba?"

"I didn't kill her."

"You killed my mother." Her voice was shrill, unhinged.

He paused long enough to infuriate her. "Your mother?"

"Benita Álvarez." Claudia's voice rose to a strangled scream.

Noah knew they'd be recording this conversation. But it was futile, as it would be inadmissible in court. Not that it would ever get that far. Once he eliminated the pair of them, he'd save the footage for himself. He was going to enjoy watching his performance later. His lips curled into a grin. "You have me mistaken for someone else."

"No, I haven't. You strangled her to death twenty-two years ago."

"Ahh, but you have no proof." He was pleased to note that his voice retained the air of authority that he'd practiced to perfection.

"You're wrong." This time it was Claudia who paused, and the infuriating wait had him clenching his fist around the butt of his gun.

"My mother bit off your finger."

He didn't respond.

Instead, he analyzed the feasibility of shooting either of them through the murky glass of the booth. The wind howled as it tumbled leaves and debris over the wasteland between them. He'd need to take that breeze into consideration when he pulled the trigger.

"Just before you strangled her." Claudia screamed at him.

Noah's heart thumped at how much Claudia knew. He adjusted his position on his seat so he could aim the gun out the sunroof.

"Do you know what she did with your finger?"

He raised his left hand up and stared at his missing finger. His mind shot to the moment when it was bitten it off. The pain had blinded him to everything but the blood pouring from his finger and the shock of what she'd done. After that, it was pure rage that had dominated everything.

"My mother swallowed your finger!"

Excruciating pain shot through his missing finger as though the rotten bitch was biting it off again. His heart erupted in a blaze of fury, and he squeezed his fist around the gun and eased up onto his knees.

"That's right . . . you stupid bastard." Claudia burst out laughing. "The Cuban coroner was so fascinated by it that he still has your puny little stub in a jar of formaldehyde in his office."

In that single, bracing instant, he knew he was in trouble.

They had irrefutable proof.

The holy grail of condemnation.

A parade of images flashed across his mind. Him standing in the courtroom . . . on the wrong side of the lawyers. His wife and father-in-law glaring at him with hate in their eyes. His hands cuffed behind his back and a hundred reporters jostling to photograph his demise.

Then he pictured himself siting in a putrid concrete cell and the metal bars slamming shut.

His brain jolted into focus. He was not going to jail.

When Claudia's accomplice joined in with her laughter, Noah wrapped his hand around his weapon, stood up through the sunroof, and pulled the trigger.

Chapter Thirty-Two

The glass exploded, and Marshall tumbled backward with a spray of blood that burst from his shoulder. Charlene screamed, and icy fear ripped through her as she realized he'd been shot. "No!" She raced to his side. "Marshall!"

"I'm okay." His eyes were wide. His expression morphed to one of excruciating pain, and his hand clutched his shoulder, where thick blood oozed through his fingers. He was not okay.

A bullet slammed into the wood, inches from her head, and Charlene ducked.

"Run, Charlene!" Marshall spoke through clenched teeth.

"No!"

Marshall hurled backward with a howl of agony, and the gun flew from his hand. Screaming, she crawled to him.

"Marshall!"

"Fuck! Fuck, fuck." Marshall's eyes bulged at his forearm.

Fresh blood oozed from a second bullet wound.

"Oh, Jesus! Marshall." Her world titled out of control as she reached for him.

"Charlene, run! Get out now!"

"I'm not leaving you."

Another explosion rained glass over them, and she was thrown sideways. A heartbeat later, searing pain shot up her left arm, equally sharp and blunt. It took her a couple of seconds to realize she'd been shot, and an ear-splitting scream tore from her throat.

"Charlene!" Marshall crawled toward her, spilling blood onto the dirty floor between them.

Every movement was in slow motion, as if she'd fallen into a pool of jelly. A line of blood spewed from her left forearm. Marshall's mouth opened in a cry of desperation. Wood and glass exploded around her as bullet after bullet slammed into the surrounding walls.

Marshall gulped mouthfuls of air, obviously fighting pain as he reached for her. "Run, Charlene. Run!"

She'd brought Marshall here. She'd put him in danger.

Another bullet slammed into the wall near her ear.

An inch closer, and Noah would have finally succeeded in killing her.

An odd feeling zapped through her, like a blast of frigid air, and in that very second, she knew what she had to do. Years of training took over. Her movements became robotic, as though she were watching somebody else take action.

Marshall's gun was just outside the door. She scrambled to it, clutched her fingers around the weapon, stood up, and fired a few shots out the window.

With Marshall screaming at her to run, she raced to the next booth along and dove inside.

Her knees hit the concrete, and rocks and glass tore her skin to shreds, but she didn't falter. Ducking beneath the cover of the front wall, she raised the weapon and peered just high enough to see and pulled the trigger.

The car's side window exploded in a million pieces, and a nanosecond later, Noah howled. She fired twice more, then, hoping he was distracted enough, she dashed from that shelter to the next booth.

Ducking for cover inside, she again peered over the countertop.

But Noah was impossible to see. S

he raised the weapon and fired another couple of shots, punching holes in the windshield and the passenger door.

"Jesus Christ!" Noah bellowed.

Charlene raced out the door again, but this time, rather than run for cover, she held the gun directly ahead with her uninjured arm and ran straight at the car.

She'd never felt so exposed in her whole life. R

age filled every vein in her body, and as it built to the bursting point, she used Marshall's agonizing groans to drive her determination. Her fingers squeezed the trigger over and over as she ran faster than she'd ever run in her life.

Two more bullets slammed into the windshield, and the rear passenger window shattered. One of the headlights exploded, as did a front tire.

The car was closer than she'd anticipated, and within seconds of leaving the booth, she dove for cover at the front fender and rolled to a crouching position with the gun aimed and ready to shoot.

Her heart slammed into her throat as she tried to calm her ragged breathing and listen for signs of Noah.

Her forearm screamed in agony, blood pouring from the burning bullet wound. She sucked in a huge breath, and using that pain, she moved again.

Crouching down, she inched along the passenger side beneath the window, and with her hand on the gun and her finger on the trigger, she stood.

Noah was right there, head between his knees, a bloodied hand pressed against his temple.

She aimed the barrel at the back of her father's head. "Don't move."

"Don't shoot." He held his hands out, and she spied his trembling fingers. The rank odor of his sweat dominated his sickly cologne.

"Give me the gun. By the handle. Do it steady, or I'll shoot you again."

He reached between his legs, and when his right elbow drew back, a gun was between two fingers. "Toss it out."

The gun clattered to the asphalt, and she kicked it across the parking lot.

Charlene stepped aside and yanked the door open. "Get out."

"Don't shoot." Half his ear was missing, and a bloody gash carved a gruesome line through his silver hair.

"Get out!"

He turned in the seat, placed his feet on the ground, and held his hands above his head as he stood.

Her heart froze at the evil standing before her.

Charlene had been waiting for this moment for a very long time.

She clenched her jaw and fought the urge to put a bullet into his belly as she studied his icy-blue eyes . . . searching for something recognizable. Something to link him to her as her father.

But there was nothing.

Nothing but evil behind those eyes. It didn't matter if she had the same DNA as this monster, she refused to admit she was related. "Get on the ground."

Noah groaned as he lowered to the asphalt. He sat with his legs out before him and glared up at her. "What do you want?"

Charlene squeezed her fingers around the gun and took a step closer. She intended to look right into the bastard's eyes when she asked her next question. "Why did you kill my mother?"

An evil grin formed on his lips. "Because I could." He said it with a cocky, you-can't-touch-me attitude, and a sick cackle rumbled from Noah's lips as he began laughing.

It was all true. Noah was a monster.

Charlene aimed the weapon and pulled the trigger.

A shrill scream burst from his throat as he tumbled sideways, clutching his knee. Blood squirted through his fingers, his face flushed red, the veins on his temple bulged blue. He howled in agony before he turned to her, his eyes glaring with hate. "You fucking bitch."

Charlene stepped forward and placed the barrel of the gun against his temple. Every ounce of her being wanted to kill him. Her hands trembled. Every muscle in her body was on a knife edge.

"Steady, Charlene. Give me the gun." She glanced sideways to see Marshall standing at her side. He glided his fingers down her arm and pried the weapon from her hand. It came away easier than she thought it would.

Noah groaned as he sat up and tilted his head at Marshall. "Thank you."

Charlene took a step forward and kneed him in the head. Noah tumbled over in a whimpering mess.

Satisfied he wouldn't get up again, she turned back to Marshall, and the look of pride on his face had her heart swelling.

The sound of a car had them both turning to look at the approaching police cruiser.

Marshall huffed. "Now he arrives."

Charlene glared down at Noah with triumph coursing through her veins. "Looks like you're finally out of luck. Asshole."

Chapter Thirty-Three

Charlene watched the news from the hospital chair for the third time that night. It was amazing how much information they added to the story with each broadcast.

When they interviewed the Cuban coroner, she chuckled at the man's proud grin. After he'd found that severed finger in Benita's throat, he'd kept it in the jar for over twenty-years.

Apparently, he'd always known the owner of that finger would one day be found. After that scene, the news flicked to a photo of Noah: the hand with the missing finger was circled.

The footage of Noah's pained face as he was lifted onto the ambulance stretcher was her favorite part of the segment. According to the reporter, Noah was now out of surgery and being kept under police guard. Thankfully, he was in a different hospital from where she and Marshall had been taken.

Once the segment shifted to something less sensational, Charlene stood to turn down the volume. When she turned back to the bed, Marshall had his eyes open. She stepped to his side and placed her hand on his arm. "Hey, you're awake."

"Hey."

"How are you feeling?"

"I'm good." He swallowed, and smacked his lips together.

Charlene held a cup of water with a straw toward him, and after he drank a few gulps, she leaned forward to kiss his forehead. "You're missing all the action."

"Hmm, what did I miss?"

She wove her fingers into his and kissed the back of his hand. "I've missed you."

A smile curled on his lips. "How long have I been out?"

"Most of the day. They tell me the operation went well, and you should have the full use of your arm again once you recover."

"What about you?" His eyes fell on her bandaged arm.

"It was just a graze. I'll be fine." Compared to Marshall's wounds, she'd gotten lucky. All she needed was a dozen or so stitches, Marshall had required surgery to both his shoulder and his bicep.

He huffed. "It wasn't just a graze. I saw it." A frown corrugated his brow, and he shook his head. "Can't believe he got me."

"Yeah, well, I got him back."

Marshall grinned. "You were amazing. I'm glad you didn't kill him, though."

She nodded. "I thought about it."

"I could tell. What stopped you?"

She thought about that moment when Noah's life was in her hands. If she'd pulled the trigger, she would have become a monster too, just like him. She wanted to be nothing like him. Ever. "He needs to suffer. Death would be too easy."

"I bet he's wishing you did kill him."

"Possibly."

"Have you spoken to Detective Chapel?"

"Yes. He's viewed our video, and he spoke to Alejandro Castillo. The news has been featuring the Cuban coroner holding his jar with Noah's finger floating inside. He looks like one happy man."

"I bet he is." Marshall chuckled and then groaned in pain.

"You okay?"

"Yeah. So, what about Montgomery?"

"Noah's facing a series of charges, including rape, attempted murder, and first-degree murder. He's all over the news. Do you want to watch?"

He shook his head. "Nah, I've seen enough of that asshole."

Charlene chuckled. "Are you hungry?"

"Famished."

Despite the trauma he'd been through, his masculinity shone through. Marshall was all man, and it broke her heart that Noah had brought him to his knees.

She leaned forward and touched her lips to his. It was just a brief kiss, but a lovely tingling heat permeated her body as she marveled at how perfect it felt. "Stay here."

He rolled his eyes. "Alrighty."

"You missed dinner. But I'll see what I can find."

"Thanks, babe."

Babe. Charlene was riding a wave of delight as she drifted out the door. At the nurses' station, she informed them that Marshall was awake, and they promised to look in on him. But they couldn't help her with food and suggested she try the vending machine on the lower level.

She made her way down the stairs and found not just one, but seven vending machines lining the length of one wall. She moved from one to the next, studying the options.

"Hello, Claudia."

Charlene spun to the voice and froze. The woman in front of her was Peter's murderer. She gasped and started to run, but the woman clutched her arm. "Please, wait. I want to tell you everything. Please, I won't harm you."

Charlene contemplated screaming. She also contemplated ramming her fist into the woman's throat. But the look in the woman's eyes stopped her. It wasn't the tears that pooled in her eyes. Nor her look of utter despair. It was that her eyes looked exactly like her own.

"I am so sorry for what happened to Pueblo. I never meant to hurt him."

"Who are you?" Charlene snapped her arm back.

"My name is Juaneta Álvarez. I am your mother's sister."

Charlene raised her eyebrows. So far, meeting her family had proved deadly.

"Please, can we sit?" Juaneta stepped back, her arms wide in a peace offering.

Charlene indicated a pair of chairs in the corner. Juaneta sat first, and Charlene eased into the seat at her side.

The woman was clearly distraught. Her bloodshot eyes were so red they looked to be bleeding, and her top lip quivered, along with her hands.

Charlene didn't fear her, not now. Not when the woman looked ready to crumble into a heap. She waited out the silence, and it was a few heartbeats before Juaneta cleared her throat and heaved out a sigh. "I am sorry. Pueblo was a good man and did not deserve what I do to him."

"Why did you do it?"

She lowered her eyes, and her chin dimpled. "I . . . I . . . I thought he killed my sister."

Charlene shook her head. "He didn't. It was Noah Montgomery."

"I know. I saw it on news. All these years I blame Pueblo, but I was wrong." Juaneta shook her head, and a sob burst from her throat. "I didn't mean to stab him. It just happen. I try to find him for many, many years. And one day he just there." She looked up. "With you." Her shoulders heaved back and forward. "I sorry. I sorry"

Charlene adjusted on her seat to be closer and touched the woman's shoulder. "It's okay. You didn't know."

Tears slipped down her cheeks as she gazed into Charlene's eyes. "No, but I should have known. Pueblo loved Benita. He loved you. He thought you were his daughter."

And with those beautiful words, a sense of understanding washed over Charlene. Peter *was* a good man. She *knew* he was. Despite everything she now knew, she would forever think of Peter as her father. She reached over and placed her hand on Juaneta's trembling knee. "Thank you."

Juaneta's eyebrows drilled together, and she blinked at Charlene. "What for?"

"For coming here to tell me. I know it wasn't easy."

She shook her head. "I don't know what to do."

Charlene frowned. "What do you mean?"

"I should tell police."

"No. Please, don't do that. You didn't mean it. I want you to pretend it never happened."

"But I scared police will find me."

"Pfft. Trust me, the police have no clues about who you are." Charlene was now truly grateful that Chapel didn't have any video footage of Peter's death.

Juaneta stared at her, her chin quivering, tears pooling in her eyes. "Thank you." She burst into a sob, and Charlene wrapped her aunt in her arms. They squeezed each other, crying twenty-two years' worth of tears.

Juaneta had suffered years of torment over her sister's death. And her extreme guilt over her murder of Peter was enough punishment.

Charlene leaned back and took Juaneta's hands within her own. "Trust me, Juaneta, you will not be arrested. And if you are, I will deny that you are the woman who stabbed him."

She blinked a few times. "Really? You would do that . . . for me?"

"Yes. Yes, I would."

Juaneta opened her arms and pulled Charlene into another hug. For the first time in decades, Charlene felt the loving embrace of a true relative. Tears tumbled down her cheeks as she squeezed the tiny woman to her chest.

Chapter Thirty-Four

Charlene woke in Marshall's arms. She was still on her side, curled into the crook of his arm, and it seemed she'd barely moved all night. The steady beat of his heart was as wonderful as the warmth of his flesh on her cheek.

Her mind danced around the delightful notion that she'd found her home, and she didn't mean the walls around her. She meant the man at her side.

Every time he looked at her, he took her breath away with his intense gaze and the desire in his eyes. When he kissed her, he seized every wrong in her world and made it right. And when he wrapped his arms around her, she knew that no matter what happened, it would still be okay.

Her heart fluttered with love for this incredible man.

He stirred, and she used the opportunity to slip out of bed to go to the bathroom. When she returned, he was up, and she followed the scent of coffee coming from the kitchen. "Morning."

He turned and smiled. "Hey, did you sleep okay?"

She returned the grin and nodded. "I think it was the best sleep I've had in years. Maybe ever."

He pulled her to his chest and wrapped his arms around her. "Me too."

She trailed her finger over the bandage covering the bullet wound in his shoulder. "How is it?"

He shrugged. "My pride hurts worse."

"Oh, stop it." She slapped his chest. "You're just jealous I got to shoot him."

"Damn straight I am. He deserved worse." He poured boiling coffee into two mugs.

"He'll get much worse in jail. They say he'll get twenty years."

"If he lasts that long."

"Hmm. Anyway, enough talk about him. Let's talk about us." She wriggled her eyebrows.

"Us?"

"Yes. You, me, and Hoppa."

Marshall growled. "The mutt doesn't form part of us."

With a cheeky grin, Charlene grabbed the two steaming coffee cups and headed toward the front door.

"You're impossible, woman." He lightly slapped her bottom before opening the front door.

Hoppa came bounding to her side, and despite missing a back leg, he still managed to waggle his butt like crazy.

"In a minute." She smiled at the dog and inhaled the delightful ocean breeze as she slipped into the bench seat on the veranda.

Marshall sat beside her, and she handed him a mug.

Clutching her cup to her chest, she leaned forward and tried to give Hoppa a scratch behind the ears, but the dog was so excited, he spun around and flipped his body from side to side.

"Settle down, boy." As if he knew what she'd said, Hoppa spun around twice and then curled up at her feet.

The sun pierced a few clouds on the horizon, coloring them gold and orange, and the ocean was only just beginning to turn from black to blue. "I could look at this view all day."

Marshall groaned. "Are you sure?"

She turned to him, frowning. "What does that mean?"

He cocked his head. "From what you've told me, you don't like to stay too long in one place."

She tugged her lips into her mouth, trying to hold back a smile that wanted to burst from her lips. "Would you like me to stay?"

He swept his hand toward the view and grinned. "If you could handle the pressure."

She took his mug from him, placed both cups on the floor, then climbed up to straddle his lap. Gently curling her hands over his shoulders, she drove her fingers through his hair. A lovely sigh of contentment whispered off her tongue. "I would love to stay."

He guided his hands around her back and touched his lips to hers, and she melted into his embrace. His kiss was gentle on her lips but brutal on her heart, and as their tongues met in a delicious dance, Charlene knew she'd found the man of her dreams.

When he pulled back, she fell into his vast, emerald-green eyes. "I love you."

He reached up to cup her cheek, and she leaned into his palm. "I love you too."

THE END

Turn the page for more books by Kendall Talbot

Dear Fabulous Reader

Thank you for following Charlene and Marshall's incredible quest for the truth. I hope you enjoyed Zero Escape.

If you're looking for more action-packed romance set in exotic locations you may be interested in the other two books in this Maximum Exposure series - EXTREME LIMIT and DEADLY TWIST.

These are also stand-alone books, so you can read them in any order.

Or if you have already read them, you'll find more thrilling romantic suspense books by Kendall Talbot on the following pages.

Would you like to know when I release a new book? Or when one of my books go on sale? Send me an email at kendall@universe.com.au and I'll send you a quick message when either of these events happen.

Cheers to you,
Kendall Talbot

Escape Mission

A feisty parolee and jilted ex-army hero must work together to escape a deadly corporation. . . if they don't kill each other first.

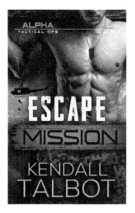

When hot-headed Zena's parole conditions lead her to the local turtle breeding ground to investigate the decline in hatchlings, she and her sister make an unexpected and horrific discovery. Now they're dodging bullets and running for their lives, and there's only one person who can help: her sister's ex-boyfriend.

A failed mission robbed ex-army hero, Blade, of both his best friend and his military career. Desperate for a distraction from his shattered life, he agrees to rescue the sisters. But saving them has Blade fighting on two fronts. One is his unwanted attraction to Zena. The other is escaping a merciless corporation that pushes Blade and his team past their limit.

Will they complete their mission? Or will Zena and Blade die trying to save each other?

ESCAPE MISSION is a **standalone, action-packed romantic suspense full of action, danger, and passion, featuring a broken woman and a jilted ex-army hero who has forgotten how to love.**

Lost In Kakadu

WINNER: Romantic book of the year.

Together, they survived the plane crash. Now the real danger begins.

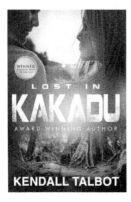

Socialite, Abigail Mulholland, has spent a lifetime surrounded in luxury... until her scenic flight plummets into the remote Australian wilderness. When rescue doesn't come, she finds herself thrust into a world of deadly snakes and primitive conditions in a landscape that is both brutal and beautiful. But trekking the wilds of Kakadu means fighting two wars—one against the elements, and the other against the magnetic pull she feels toward fellow survivor Mackenzie, a much younger man.

Mackenzie Steel had finally achieved his dreams of becoming a five-star chef when his much-anticipated joy flight turned each day into a waking nightmare. But years of pain and grief have left Mackenzie no stranger to a harsh life. As he battles his demons in the wild, he finds he has a new struggle on his hands: his growing feelings for Abigail, a woman who is as frustratingly naïve as she is funny.

Fate brought them together. Nature may tear them apart. But one thing is certain—love is as unpredictable as Kakadu, and survival is just the beginning...

Lost in Kakadu is a gripping action-adventure romance set deep in Australia's rugged Kakadu National Park. Winner of the Romantic Book of the Year, this full-length, stand-alone novel is about a woman who needs to find herself, and the unlikely hero who captures her heart. Lost in Kakadu is an extraordinary story of endurance, grief, survival and undying love.

Jagged Edge

A grieving detective with nothing to lose.
A dying town with everything to hide.

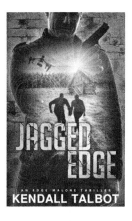

After the shocking death of his daughter, suspended detective Edge Malone who seeks oblivion in a bottle and plans to photograph a rare blood moon in isolated Whispering Hills, California. But his night takes a deadly turn when a high-tech drone is shot from the sky—and a ruthless gunman murders an innocent bystander who dares to visit the crash site. Driven by instinct, Edge seizes the drone and escapes into the woods.

Now being hunted, Edge unwittingly thrusts Nina Hamilton into the chase—a street-smart beauty who is no stranger to men with dangerous motives. But when the drone data leads them to a shocking discovery, they quickly learn that no one in Whispering Hills can be trusted. The truth of the small town is anything but quiet, and the price of secrets runs six-feet deep...

Get ready for the adventure of a lifetime with Jagged Edge, a full-length, stand-alone thriller featuring a kick-ass woman and a jilted man who needs to find himself again.

Deadly Twist

FINALIST in the Wilbur Smith Adventure Writing Prize 2021.
An ancient Mayan Temple. A dark family secret. A desperate
fight for survival.

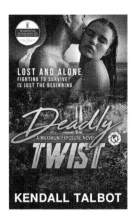

When a mysterious ancient Mayan temple is discovered by a team of explorers deep in the Yucatan jungle, the world is entranced. But Liliana Bennett is shocked by the images sweeping the headlines. She's seen the temple before, drawn in great detail, in her late father's secret journal.

Refusing to believe she's out of her depth, and despite objections from her family and friends, Lily heads to Mexico, determined to see the temple for herself.

To reach the heart of the jungle, she must join forces with Carter Logan, a nature photographer who hasn't called a place home in over a decade. His work gives him the excuse to roam wherever his restless feet take him, ensuring his secrets are buried deep.

Lily, Carter, their overweight guide and his crazy pet rooster traipse into the brutal wilderness. But lost and alone, Lily and Carter stumble upon something they should never have seen and her quest for answers becomes a desperate race for their lives.

Deadly Twist is a gripping action-adventure romance set deep in Mexico's Yucatan Jungle. This full-length, standalone novel is full of danger, suspense and passion. It features a strong-willed

heroine and the rugged-yet-mischievous Australian who steals her heart.

Extreme Limit

Two lovers frozen in ice. One dangerous expedition.

Holly Parmenter doesn't remember the helicopter crash that claimed the life of her fiancé and left her in a coma. The only details she does remember from that fateful day haunt her—two mysterious bodies sealed within the ice, dressed for dinner rather than a dangerous hike up the Canadian Rockies.

No one believes Holly's story about the couple encased deep in the icy crevasse. Instead, she's wrongly accused of murdering her fiancé for his million-dollar estate. Desperate to uncover the truth about the bodies and to prove her innocence, Holly resolves to climb the treacherous mountain and return to the crash site. But to do that she'll need the help of Oliver, a handsome rock-climbing specialist who has his own questions about Holly's motives.

When a documentary about an unsolved kidnapping offers clues as to the identity of the frozen bodies, it's no longer just Oliver and Holly heading to the dangerous mountaintop . . . there's also a killer, who'll stop at nothing to keep the case cold.

Will a harrowing trip to the icy crevasse bring Holly and Oliver the answers they seek? Or will disaster strike twice, claiming all Holly has left?

Extreme Limit is action-packed romantic suspense full of drama, danger, and passion, featuring a fiesty heroine and the rugged-yet-mischievous hero who steals her heart. Head to the Canadian

Rockies and get ready for the adventure of a lifetime, with a happily ever after guaranteed

Treasured Secrets

Sunken treasures. Dangerous enemies. Action-packed romantic suspense.

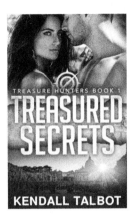

When Italian chef Rosalina Calucci finds a clue to an ancient treasure, she makes the mistake of bringing it to rogue treasure hunter Archer Mahoney, a dangerously sexy, frustratingly irresponsible, Australian millionaire. Something she knows all too well since he's also her ex-fiancé, a man who would rather keep his secrets to himself.

Archer Mahoney, will do anything to drown out his painful past; breaking up with the irresistible, smokey-eyed, woman of his dreams is proof of that. But his talent for finding lost treasure is almost as good as his talent for finding trouble and his feisty ex is just the beginning.

Rosalina's clue could be the key to locating an ancient treasure that's haunted Archer for years. But some treasures are buried in blood, and a deadly nemesis will stop at nothing to keep a sinful secret contained. Can they mend the ocean between them, or will Rosalina's quest for answers be just the beginning to Archer's nightmare?

Treasured secrets is book one in the steamy romantic suspense Treasure Hunters series, full of drama, danger, and passion. It features a strong heroine and the rugged-yet-mischievous millionaire who steals her heart.

First Fate

Prepare for a cruise like no other.

When an electromagnetic pulse (EMP) strikes Rose of the Sea, the pleasure cruise becomes a drifting nightmare. Powerless and desperate, the eleven hundred passengers and crew must face their new reality: No one is coming to save them.

The First Mate. The EMP destroys the captain's pacemaker and when he dies, Gunner McCrae is thrust into the top position. But no amount of training could prepare him for the savagery of desperate humans and an unforgiving ocean.

The Anchor-woman. Gabrielle Kinsella is known for bringing shocking stories to the world. She should be reporting on the headline of the century. Instead she's fighting for her children's lives.

The Acrobat. Held captive by a predator as a child, Madeline Jewel found freedom as the ship's acrobatic dancer. But being trapped in an elevator brings her worst fears back to life.

The Gambler. Zon Woodrow, notorious gator hunter, won his ticket in a poker match. But that isn't the only pot he's looking to score. With the ships security system obliterated, Zon turns his attention to the casino's vault. And this time, the house won't win.

As resources dwindle aboard Rose of the Sea, the body count continues to rise. Will ordinary people survive an extraordinary disaster? Or will human nature drown them in darkness?

Find out in this gripping survival thriller. FIRST FATE is book one in the Waves of Fate series.

Double Take

A crime of love. The chance of a lifetime.

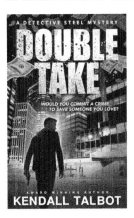

Jackson Rich is at risk of losing the love of his life, and he'll do anything to save her. Even if it means robbing a bank. So it's time to call in a few favors from his old gang because they owe him. Big time.

Gemma's spent her entire life doing the right thing. Now doing the wrong thing could be the best decision she's ever made, if she's brave enough.

When Detective Steel gets a tip-off of a planned heist, he doesn't know where the robbery will be. Only that it's going to take place during the famous horse race that stops a nation—the Melbourne Cup. And when it goes down, he'll be ready.

Except what happens next, only one of them sees coming. And for the others, it's suddenly no longer about the money. It's about retribution.

Get ready for a heist thriller that will have you turning the pages all night long. Double Take is a full-length, stand-alone bank robbery mystery featuring a desperate man, the burley cop hell-bent on bringing him down, and a crazy woman with a mission of her own

What readers are saying about DOUBLE TAKE:

"This story is so well planned and well written, it was as if it had actually happened! I was riveted to my chair while reading the twists and turns. If I could give it 6 stars, I would." ★★★★★ Multi-Mystery fan.

Printed in Great Britain
by Amazon